The Apex Cycle
Book 1

Written By

M.T. Zimny

This is a work of fiction. Names, characters, places, and incidents are either the product of the author's imagination or are used fictitiously. Any resemblance to actual persons, living or dead, events, or locales is entirely coincidental.

Copyright © 2020 by M.T. Zimny

Editing by Melissa Ball

Cover Illustration and Special Characters by Maria Mondloch
Back cover photography by Andrew Rossi
Fonts: Cinzel, Marcellus, Roboto, Merriweather

ISBN: 978-1-7356571-0-3 (Paperback)

For Connor.

You told me not to write a cutesy dedication, so I won't.

(But I caribou)

TABLE OF CONTENTS

1

The Statue in the Bay

I didn't like having my face so close to a public toilet. The ferry boat lurched beneath me, and my stomach moved in tandem with it. It was all I could do to hold my hair back and hope that the galley bathrooms were cleaned nightly.

A gentle knock sounded on the other side of the door.

"Everything okay, Sammy?" Mom asked. She must have followed me in.

"Going great," I managed to choke back between heaves. So much for breakfast.

I'd been sick the last few days, but I thought I'd been feeling better. The dizzy spells had mostly stopped, and even though I still got winded going up a single flight of stairs, I figured the sickness must have run its course. It totally figured that whatever stomach bug I had contracted would redouble its efforts the day we were supposed to move. A new city, new school, new home, and a new day with my head in a toilet.

I wiped off my face the best I could and stepped out of the stall. I would've preferred to puke in private, but I was grateful for the bottle of water Mom handed me at the sink. I did my best to rinse my mouth out, but I couldn't get rid of the bitter taste of stomach acid.

"Still sick, then?" Mom asked, leading the way back to the passenger deck.

"Just nerves," I lied.

A man stepped in front of us as we walked out of the bathroom. He pressed a flyer into Mom's hand.

"Excuse me, ma'am, are you aware of the Apex epidemic in the city?"

"Sorry, we're not interested." She pulled me past him as another passenger exited the bathroom behind us. He turned his attention to her instead.

"Excuse me, did you know the city is being held hostage by genetically altered super humans?"

I followed Mom back to the window booth where Dad and Avery were sitting. Avery pressed his hands against the window while Dad carefully surveyed the passenger deck. His shoulders relaxed when he saw us, but he still looked tense.

Dad was usually a careful man. He was naturally suspicious and spent most of his time glaring at strangers from behind his tawny beard, from which I'd inherited my hair color. I always thought anyone would be an idiot to mess with him. He towered over most people at six and a half feet, and his muscular arms were covered in tattoos.

Despite always being a little on edge, the way Dad was acting, you'd think we were all moments away from catastrophic disaster. Maybe it was the stress of moving his family to the island city, although it was also possible he was just trying to cope with sending his very favorite daughter off to boarding school— even if I'd be less than a mile away from his new job at the university.

Or, maybe, and this might sound crazy, it was the woman who had been staring at us from across the ferry galley that was getting to him. She'd been there before I'd left for the bathroom and she was still there, carefully watching us, as I returned with Mom.

"Stop that." Mom swatted at Dad's hands as she sat down across from him. He hadn't seemed to notice he had completely balled up the morning paper in his fists. He exhaled heavily and compulsively stretched his fingers, letting the paper fall to the linoleum. He leaned back in the booth seat, trying to look more relaxed, but his foot bounced nervously as I took the seat next to him.

Mom waved the flyer the man had handed her in front of Dad.

"Can you believe this tripe? The Apex ruining the city? The Apex *made* that city."

The flyer was a simple dark blue sheet of paper. The words "No More Apex- No More Problems" ran across the top and bottom. In the center was an illustration of a dark gray helmet with a visor. It was crossed out under a big, red X.

Dad shrugged.

"They have a point." He'd never spoken highly of the vigilantes that ran rampant in the Floating City. Yet, here he was, moving his whole family to the city he grew up in. The world's most hero-ridden neighborhood. He glanced back at the woman.

To be fair, she was hard to ignore. She looked young but had waist-length, snow-white hair. I could see her in my periphery, carefully observing our family from behind her steaming cup of ferry boat coffee. She made no attempt to hide that she was watching us.

"What's wrong with Dad?" Avery pried himself away from the window, where he'd been watching the ocean froth up around the boat. Mom smiled and pulled my brother close to her.

"He's just a bit stressed. It's not easy moving to a new place," she said, brushing a long clump of hair out of his eyes. He needed a haircut.

"I don't think so." Avery shrugged with the kind of contempt only twelve-year-olds are capable of. "All the kids at my old school were stupid."

"Those aren't nice words, Avery," Mom warned. Avery rolled his eyes and pushed away from her.

"Yeah, well, they were." He went back to his window seat to watch the water. There wasn't much to see, though, as the whole bay was shrouded in a heavy morning fog.

I looked straight ahead towards the bow of the boat, but focused on the corner of my vision, where the white-haired woman took another long swig of coffee without looking away from our booth.

"Samantha?"

I jumped when Mom said my name, and she scowled.

"Calm down! You're just as wound up as your father!"

"I'm not wound up," Dad grunted while he continued to silently assess every other passenger on the boat. He was careful not to look directly at our observer.

Now it was Mom's turn to roll her eyes as she turned back towards me from across the booth.

"Are you feeling any better?"

Dad stopped scanning the room and looked at me, too. I shrugged.

"A bit, I guess."

"Faker," Avery muttered without turning away from the window. I suppressed a smile.

Truth be told, I still didn't feel great, but maybe it really was just nerves. Dad tried to press the back of his hand against my forehead, but I ducked away.

"I'm fine," I insisted. "I promise. I haven't even fainted today!"

"Is that the bar now? 'Not fainting'?" he scoffed.

I turned forward just enough to look for the white-haired woman in the corner of my vision, but didn't see her. I risked looking over at her seat, but, sure enough, she'd left. Her paper coffee cup was still sitting in the cup holder. My stomach fluttered. I'd rather have her staring than not know where she had gone.

There was a sudden stirring of skirts next to me, and I flinched away. Dad grabbed my wrist. The white-haired woman had come back and passed next to me. She was at least six feet tall and had to stoop to pick up her coffee cup where she had left it. She turned back towards us and mouthed "Oops" as she threw it in the trash before walking away, her yellow maxi-dress swirling around her ankles.

"Vic," Mom said, using her trademark Mom Voice. "You need to calm down. She's just a lonely lady who forgot her trash. You're freaking out the kids."

"I feel like I've seen her somewhere," Dad murmured, squinting after the woman. "Does she look familiar to you?"

Mom didn't dignify him with a response. He grumbled something more under his breath, then looked at me and forced a grin.

"Sorry, Sammy. This city is full of creeps. Can't be too careful."

"It's fine," I mumbled, not wanting to admit I hadn't liked her any more than he did. The thing was, I really wanted to believe she'd been watching all of us as a family. Maybe she was just a lonely weirdo who liked people watching. But the way the hairs had stood on the back of my neck, and the way she sat motionless, except to drink her coffee...I just couldn't shake the feeling she'd been watching me.

The fog horn split the low hanging fog as the ferry drifted through the mist. A great bronze smile materialized through the haze. I watched as the form of a colossal man took shape.

His metal hair and cape could have been frozen in time. They looked wind-ruffled, but neither moved. He was standing proudly on a barnacle-studded platform in the middle of the bay. "New Delos's Finest Hero" was engraved into the metal at his feet.

"Mom, look!" Avery twisted away from the window to pull Mom over to him. "Look! It's Paragon! Mom, do you see him?"

My younger brother wasn't the only passenger gawking at the great statue. Several other tourists were struggling to get a good picture through the foggy windows.

"You should've seen the real thing." Mom leaned over Avery and set her chin on the top of his head. "He was much more impressive than some statue before he passed."

Dad snorted. He was the only one on the boat that wasn't pressing against the windows.

"He wasn't that great, dear."

Mom turned back towards him so that he could see her scowl.

"You don't like any of the masked heroes."

The statue passed back into the morning mist. The city began to take shape, as if rising out of the water. The outlines of the skyscrapers formed slowly, pushing the glinting buildings forward.

Avery lost interest in the view out of the window now that we had passed the Paragon statue. He turned towards Dad, looking expectant. He held out a single, open palm.

Dad glanced up at him and sighed.

"Fine." He wriggled a ten dollar bill from his pocket. "Get me a coffee, too."

Avery's eyes lit up as Dad extended the money towards him, but Mom plucked it out from between them. She reached over Dad to hand it off to me instead.

"Go with your brother," she said. Dad opened his mouth in protest, but she shushed him. "I don't know how you expect her to be on her own at school if you won't even let her go get coffee."

"Yeah, well," he said begrudgingly, "there's security at the school, not to mention she can't go ten minutes without passing out lately."

"Dad!" I groaned. "I told you, I'm fine now!"

"Here." Mom added a few more dollars from her own pocket to my hand. "You get yourself a snack, too. If you do get kidnapped, remind them your brother can't have peanuts."

Avery ran ahead, but my head spun as I stood up. Dad grabbed my arm to steady me.

"Sammy?"

I waved Dad away and hurried to catch up with Avery. Mom called out, "Avery! Wait for your sister!"

"Don't talk to anyone you don't know!" Dad said gruffly.

"I told you. I'm fine!" I gave him a double thumbs up, crumpling the money in my hand.

"Come on," Avery whined behind me.

I led him towards the ferry's galley. Other passengers were yawning into their coffees and muffins.

"What's up with Dad?" Avery asked as we walked.

"You'd have to ask him." I shrugged.

"He was crying last night, you know."

I looked at Avery in surprise. Not to say that large, bearded men with tattoos didn't cry, but it was hard to imagine him even tearing up.

Avery quickly moved on from the topic when we entered the tiny cafeteria, and he beelined towards the chips display.

"Dad'll kill me if I let you get chips at eight in the morning," I said. "Don't you want hot chocolate instead?"

"That makes zero sense," Avery pouted. "Chips are just salty potatoes, and Dad makes potatoes for breakfast all the time."

"You know it isn't the same," I smiled, pouring myself a hot chocolate at the nearby coffee station.

"Yes, it is!" Avery pulled a bag off the rack. "Look, they're basically crispy hash browns. And what about you? You're having liquid chocolate for breakfast. Is that really better than potatoes?"

"That," I said, grabbing a lid from the dispenser, "is a very solid argument."

I handed Avery some of the money. He thought about it for a second, grabbed a second bag of chips and rushed over to the cashier. I pressed the lid down onto my cup. An advertisement was set up over the coffee station. An intense looking couple in suits stared down at me under the words "Have you or someone you love been negatively affected by under-regulated Apex activity? Call Ratcliffe and Ratcliffe, Attorneys at Law."

So far, New Delos didn't seem like the Apex haven Mom had always made it out to be. Between the ads and the Anti-Apex campaigner stationed outside the bathroom, it was starting to seem like the last place I'd want to be if I was harboring secret super abilities. As if on cue, a hand grabbed my shoulder.

"Excuse me, miss, are you a student at New Delos prep?"

The man from outside the bathroom held his stack of flyers close as he glared down at me. Before I could say anything, he continued.

"Are you aware that New Delos Prep and New Delos University support unregulated Apex activity that puts the citizens of the island at risk?" His pitch sounded well-rehearsed.

"I-I'm sorry," I stammered, stepping away. "I don't—"

"Did you know they both take money from Adrian Schrader, a known Apex sympathizer?"

The boat lurched under us, and a sudden dizziness washed over me, flipping my stomach and spinning the galley.

"I'm sorry." I tried to step away again, but tripped. I grabbed onto the counter to keep from falling. I hadn't fainted all day and refused to now.

"Did you know that by choosing to attend either school, you are inadvertently contributing to a system that protects The Apex from the justice they deserve?"

The boat shifted again. I slipped onto the floor. My hot chocolate splashed across the tiles beside me.

"Hey! Did you just push her?"

"No, she just fell, I swear—"

"I'm so sick of you people thinking you own the place!"

"We think *we* own the place?"

A fight broke out above me, but I was too busy trying to steady myself. I pushed myself onto my knees and grabbed my head in both hands as if that might make the room stop spinning.

Just breathe, I told myself. I'd done this a half dozen times in the last few days.

Someone touched my shoulder. A face swam into my vision, inches from mine. A lock of white hair had fallen in her face. I stumbled backwards.

"Are you alright?" The white-haired woman asked. She was grinning. There was a crash overhead. The man with the flyers had been pushed into a postcard display. Photos of the city drifted down into the hot chocolate puddle.

"She's fine." I winced at the sound of Dad's booming voice. The white-haired woman shied away as Dad helped me to my feet. Avery stood behind him, wide-eyed and clutching his potato chips to his chest.

Dad ushered us away just as a security guard showed up.

"Aren't you going to pay for that?" A sullen cashier pointed at the spilt hot-chocolate. Dad scowled and slammed a five dollar bill onto the counter and kept walking. The Anti-Apex man continued to shout about inequality and abuses of power as he was cornered by the security guard.

Mom was waiting by the stairs that led down to the car deck.

"I'm sorry," I said. Dad didn't look at me.

"It's okay." Mom reassured me. "That man was weird. It wasn't your fault."

She opened the stairway door as Dad led the way back down to the family car. The ferry was almost to the island, but I still felt like it was my fault we were already headed to the car. Mom handed me an orange juice.

"I stopped by a vending machine for you." She patted my shoulder. "Might help with the lightheadedness."

We clambered into the car. Most of our things had already been moved to the new townhouse earlier this week. There were only a few suitcases in the back along with my bags for school since I'd be living there. I wasn't too sure about the thought of boarding school, but Mom had gone to New Delos Prep as a teenager. It couldn't be bad if she was willing to send her daughter there.

We sat in an uncomfortable silence that was only broken by Avery crunching his chips. It was a relief when the boat finally bumped up against the dock, signaling our arrival. Butterflies churned my stomach. Again, new city, new school.

Dad looked at us in the backseat as he started the engine. He was smiling now, even if it did look a little forced. Hopefully it meant he was starting to relax.

"Everyone ready?"

The cars ahead of us started creeping forward.

"Gonna have to be at this point," I said, but I smiled back. Sure it was a brand new place for us, but what was there to really be nervous about?

2

The Roommate

The city of New Delos had looked intimidating from the ferry as it had slowly taken form out of the dense marine fog, but up close it didn't seem nearly as ominous. From where I sat behind the car window, it felt like any other urban area, with congested streets and angry cabbies. "No More Apex-No More Problems" flyers hung off of poles and building sides. Some had been up for a while and were faded or covered in graffiti. One restaurant had a big sign in the window that read, "APEX NOT SERVED HERE". I saw benches covered in the same advertisements for "Ratcliffe and Ratcliffe, Attorneys at Law" that had been posted in the ferry galley.

"It's changed a bit since we were last here," Mom laughed nervously.

I craned my neck to try to see the top of the skyscrapers above us, but it wasn't long before my stomach was turning with car sickness. The nerves didn't help.

"Mom, look at all the pigeons!" Avery said with his nose pressed against the window. "Do you think there will be this many at the house?"

Mom laughed, but it sounded forced.

"I hope not!"

"Look, Mom, I think that one's hurt." Avery pressed a finger against the car window, pointing at a pigeon lying motionless on the pavement. I thought it must be dead, but then its wings fluttered feebly.

"It'll be alright," Mom said. She reached back and patted Avery's knee. She looked at me. "Are you getting excited yet?"

"I've been excited!" I said defensively. Dad grunted.

New Delos Prep was on the east side of the island city, not far from New Delos University down the street. The buildings weren't as tall here, and shop windows displayed flags donning the school colors; red and white- as if to match Paragon's famous costume.

Instead of anti-Apex flyers, Paragon looked down on the sidewalks proudly from white and red posters. A top-to-bottom mural decorated the side of a sandwich shop, displaying Paragon alongside other famous vigilantes from the city. A gray-clad figure in a helmet like the one on the anti-Apex flyers stood near the edge. Across the top of the mural, the painter had written in large letters, "WITHOUT THEM, THE CITY SINKS".

We passed the University first. Shops gave way to old brick buildings and well-kept lawns. The titan mascot greeted students as they moved into their new dorms.

The prep school was next to the university. This campus was much smaller, but still had quite a few buildings. The main school building, Schrader Hall, was made of stone and brick and faced the main road. A much smaller version of the Paragon statue that stood in the bay stood in the middle of a water fountain in front of the building. Beyond the school hall, there were a couple of dorms and a separate building that I remembered Mom saying had the cafeteria and gymnasium. I could see athletic fields peeking from between the buildings.

The university had more students, but this campus seemed just as busy. Parents pulled up to the curb to quickly unload their kids' belongings before going to find parking. Dad let the car idle outside the girls' dorm while Mom and I pulled my bags out of the trunk. Looking around, I could see I had less stuff than many of the students unloading their cars around me. One girl's parents had driven up onto the well-maintained lawn and were pulling bag after bag out of their car. She stood nearby, typing on her phone, letting the move-in volunteers from the university carry her many duffle bags into the building.

"I wanna go with Sammy!" Avery burst out of the car and ran to help pick up my pillows.

"You guys all good?" Dad leaned out the driver window as he looked at Mom.

"We're good." She kissed him. "Room 403, when you come find us."

I hoisted my duffle over my shoulder. Avery gawked up at the dorm building looming over us.

"I can't wait until I get to come here!"

"You've got a couple years to go," Mom laughed, leading us towards a fold-out table where two teachers were handing out room keys.

One of them looked up at us from behind thick glasses balanced on the tip of his long nose.

"Of all the people I thought I'd never see again!" he exclaimed. "That can't be Alison Taylor, back after all these years?"

"It's been Alison Havardson for a while now, you know that." Mom gave the man a hug as he stood up and came around the table to greet us.

"Would I know that? I don't recall receiving the wedding invite." His tone was joking, but there was something strained in his face. He was tall with unkempt hair and appeared about Mom's age. There were bags under his eyes, which he must've been trying to battle with the extra-large coffee sitting on his table.

"We eloped." Mom blushed and cleared her throat. "Maybe you'll have my daughter in one of your history classes this year."

The man looked at me in shock.

"I had no idea you had a daughter!" He extended a hand to give a firmer-than-expected handshake. "Mr. Fleming."

Before I had the chance to introduce myself, he was back on the other side of the table flipping through the box of folders.

"Havardson, you say?" He pulled a paper from the middle of the box and inspected it. "Samantha?"

"That's me."

He grinned at my mom as he handed me the paper and the attached envelope.

"Your room key is in the envelope. And looks like I'll be seeing you in World History on Monday. Excellent," he said, glancing at the class schedule. "Let's hope you're less of a nuisance than your mother was."

"Please, Alex," Mom clipped as she led me away to make room for the next student and her parents, "we both know it was always you getting me in trouble."

"That was awkward," Avery chortled and Mom glared at him from the corner of her eye as she held the dormitory door open.

"Mr. Fleming is an old friend." She patted my shoulder. "If you ever need anything, Samantha, find Mr. Fleming. He'll help you."

Inside the dormitory, a girl stood in the elevator, a few bags at her feet. I recognized her as the girl whose parents had driven up onto the grass to unload her things. Her steel-blonde hair was perfectly curled and her make-up flawlessly contoured over her round cheeks and angular chin.

"I really can't wait until I get to come here," Avery whispered. I shoved him jokingly.

"Don't be weird."

"Sorry, no room," the girl said, her eyes barely flicking upwards from her phone. I looked at Mom, shrugged, and moved towards the stairwell.

"I'm sure we will squeeze in somehow," Mom said. We fit in with room to spare, but the girl huffed as she moved her bags to the side.

The fourth floor was full of daughters and parents hurrying down the hall as if it was a race to see who could set their room up the fastest. The girl in the elevator hoisted her bags over her shoulder and joined the fray without a word to us.

"This way, I think." Mom led the way down the opposite hall, side stepping bags and boxes that littered the walkway. A familiar, stubbled face peeked out from one of the rooms and grinned at us.

"The Havardsons!" Mr. Hendricks rushed to meet us and pulled the duffle-bag I was carrying away from me. "I was wondering when you'd get here!"

"Roy," my mom smiled and gave Mr. Hendricks an awkward hug around the bags they were each now carrying. "How's Winnie? She settled yet?"

Mr. Hendricks led the way to Room 403.

"Oh, Winnie is Winnie." He shrugged. "You know teenagers. They like to pretend they aren't excited, but I think she's happy to be back at school."

I hadn't seen Winnie in over seven years, and I almost didn't recognize the girl setting up her side of the room with her mother. The chubby third grader I remembered was now lithe and toned. Her once mousy hair had been dyed strawberry blonde, though remnants of her natural hair color showed in her perfectly plucked eyebrows. She flashed an awkward smile.

"Been a while," Winnie said. "I hope you don't mind, I took the left side."

She gestured at her side of the room. Her bed had already been done up, and the wardrobe on her side was half-full of her clothes.

Avery climbed up onto the bare mattress on the right side of the room. He frowned.

"This isn't very comfortable," he said, bouncing up and down.

Mom shooed him off the bed and pulled sheets out of one of my bags.

"It's a good school," Mrs. Hendricks assured her as she made my bed. "You'll remember that from your time here. Safest place in New Delos."

"It's Vic who's more on edge about leaving her here," Mom sighed. "But he'll be close by during school hours, and I'm sure she'll be fine."

She smiled at me, and I gave her an over-enthusiastic double thumbs up as I started unpacking. Mr. Hendricks laughed.

"That's the spirit!" He clapped me on the back, nearly knocking me into my opened closet. "Speaking of Vic, where'd he disappear to?"

"Right here." Dad appeared in the doorway. He smiled and seemed more at ease, probably feeling better now that he was in the company of old friends. "I saw Harry in the parking lot. He was hoping to get a last minute meeting in before the weekend was up."

"Harry needs to learn how to send emails in advance if he wants to spring meetings on us."

"That's alright if we need to head over to the college," Mrs. Hendricks said. "It'd give me a chance to check on Amanda, anyway."

Winnie rolled her eyes at the mention of her older sister, and Mr. Hendricks scoffed.

"Amanda's made it clear she doesn't want any of our help."

"What's up with Amanda?" Dad asked. Mr. Hendricks's face turned stormy.

"She quit swimming. And everything else."

"What?" Winnie spun away from her wardrobe to stare at her parents. "Did she really?"

She sounded gleefully surprised. Mr. Hendricks glowered.

"She quit everything?" Mom repeated. Her brow furrowed.

"Everything except class." Mr. Hendricks threw his hands in the air helplessly. "Best swimmer in the state, years of private lessons, all for nothing! So much for her scholarship!"

Amanda had been a top athlete at both the high school and then again during her freshman year of college. Looking at the wide smile on Winnie's face, it was easy to see that she must have resented her sister's prestige.

"Oh, but it's alright," Mrs. Hendricks gushed. "She gets free tuition as long as Roy works there, anyway. And if she didn't really like swimming or her other clubs, I don't see why she had to keep doing them."

Mr. Hendricks harrumphed. It was clearly still a sore spot for him. He glanced at his watch to change the subject.

"Might as well head over to the university and see what Harry wants."

Mrs. Hendricks pulled Winnie away from her pile of clothes and into a hug.

"Do you want us to come get you for dinner?" she asked her daughter. Winnie tried to push away, but Mrs. Hendricks managed to land a single kiss on Winnie's forehead.

"I'm fine." Winnie returned to her bag of clothes. Mr. Hendricks shrugged.

"If you want cafeteria food, that's less money out of my wallet." He patted Dad on the shoulder. "I'll see you later today."

Mrs. Hendricks gave me a hug, too, as they exited.

"Don't let Winnie's attitude fool you, she's very excited to have you here," she said.

My family didn't hang out for too long after Winnie's parents left. I didn't have as much to unpack as some of the other girls I'd seen on the floor. Once my clothes were all hanging in the closet and my desk set up, I was pretty much set.

I hugged them each goodbye, ending with Dad. He wrapped his large arms around me and held me close.

"If you need anything," he mumbled through my hair.

"I know," I interjected.

Mom gently pried him away. He gave me one last sad smile, ruffled my hair, and let Mom lead him out the door. Winnie closed it behind him.

"God, about time," she scoffed. "I swear, parents would go to class with us if they could."

I laughed uncomfortably. Winnie sat down at her freshly organized desk and opened her laptop.

"First things first," she said, spinning her chair to look at me. "My computer. Don't touch it. Ever."

"I wasn't going to..." my voice trailed off. Winnie was already talking again.

"Second, I've made some changes since third grade, and I mean more than my hair color." She snorted at her own joke before continuing. "I'm a small business owner of sorts. My work keeps me very busy, and I will not let anything get in the way."

"What kind of small business?" I asked, since that's what it seemed like she wanted me to do.

"Freelance photography." She pointed at the camera resting on her pillow. I knew nothing about cameras but could tell that this one was very nice and probably very expensive. She glanced at the door and then back at me. She had on a mischievous smirk. "I sell Apex photos to papers and bloggers and whatever."

She slid aside so that she was no longer obscuring her computer screen from me. The photo she had pulled up was dark and difficult to make out, but there was a discernible figure, crouched atop a parked bus. It looked like it was wearing some kind of helmet, but its dark uniform blended too much into the background to tell what else they were wearing.

"That's an Apex?" I asked. I gravitated towards the picture. "I thought they'd look more like Paragon."

"That version of heroes died when Paragon did." Winnie shrugged, closing her computer. "The Apex heroes these days are uniform and covert. A lot of people think they work out of the high school and college."

"And what do you think?"

"I don't think, I know. I just have to prove it. In the meantime, a good photo can get me a couple hundred bucks. My last roommate couldn't handle my work, I'll admit it can be a lot. Just thought I'd give you a heads up before the year starts."

Winnie had never been this intense growing up. I wondered if her new edge was from living in New Delos for so long. I wondered if it would happen to me.

I hoped it didn't.

We had our first floor meeting around lunchtime. All the girls on the floor crowded into the common room by the elevators as our Resident Assistant, a college student named Renee, passed around a plate of sandwich wraps along with paper packets. I sat with Winnie along the perimeter. None of our classmates came to say hi or ask her how her summer had been. Rather, they all seemed to give Winnie a wide berth, and, after our conversation about her passion project earlier, I couldn't blame them.

Renee started introductions, and as I scanned the group, several girls darted their eyes away from me. They'd been staring. The girl from the elevator smirked from a far couch, and her friend tapped her knee as if trying to get her to cut it out.

Faces glazed over as Renee read rules and expectations from the paper packet. One girl took a bow out of her long, dark hair and began playing with it while another stared out the window towards Schrader Hall. I wondered if Winnie had accused any of them of secretly being an Apex. If she had, it made sense they would keep their distance.

"Last thing, I promise!" Renee clapped her hands excitedly. She'd finally reached the end of her packet. "Tomorrow the Welcome Back carnival will be held at the East Pier from eleven until nine for both the prep school and the college. The last page in your packet has the information on how to get there."

She dismissed us, and Winnie was the first one out of the common room, leaving me cross-legged on the floor. I scrambled to follow her, but my head spun as I got to my feet. I grabbed onto a couch back for support and closed my eyes to block out the spinning carpet.

"Hey, neat scar."

I opened my eyes at the sound of the cool voice. The room had stopped spinning, but my stomach lurched. I swallowed hard.

The rude girl from the elevator was standing there flanked on either side by girls just as impeccably dressed as she was. I raised a hand to the scar that ran down the left side of my neck, across my shoulder, and to my collarbone.

"Thanks," I said, unsure how else to respond. People were normally polite enough not to mention the jagged, gray remnant of a long past bike accident.

"How'd you get it?" The girl pressed. She and her friends had me cornered against the wall and the couch.

"It was a bike crash a few years ago." I looked over their shoulders and down the hall, searching for the bathroom.

"Cute," the girl on the left snickered. She had long, shiny hair that was an unnatural shade of red.

"Too bad," the girl in the middle tutted. Her round cheeks and sharp chin made her look like a cat. "If it had been an Apex, my parents could've helped you out."

"Jamie's a Ratcliffe," the red-haired girl explained. "Her parents are lawyers."

"Yeah, I saw their ad." The room grew warmer, and my throat tightened. Hot, painful bile rose up from my stomach. "Sorry, I need—"

I tried to push past the girls, but Jamie held an arm out.

"You're Winnie's new roommate, right?" she crooned. "What's your name?"

"Samantha." I tried to look casual as I leaned back against the wall. The room was starting to spin again. Why did this have to happen now?

"I'm Jamie, and this is Madison and Naomi," she said. Naomi glowered at me from under a wide halo of black curls. "You know there's a floor-wide bet on how long you last."

Jamie's perfect skin swam in my vision. My stomach reeled, and I knew I needed to leave immediately.

"That's nice," I tried to push past them. Jamie was rude, but I didn't have time to be irritated with her. I needed a trash can or a toilet or even a window.

"That's it? 'That's nice'?" Jamie kept her arm stuck out. "It has to bother you at least a little."

"Fine, it bothers me. Please, I—"

"Rumor has it you two know each other from when you were kids," Jamie mused as she continued to block the way. I could feel impending disaster rising from my stomach to my esophagus, to the back of my throat...

"Jamie, let her go," the third girl, Naomi, said.

"God, Naomi, you're no fun anymore."

"I mean it, Jamie!"

But it was too late. I caught myself on the floor with one hand, grabbing at my hair with the other to keep it out of my face as I ruined

Jamie's tennis shoes with my half-digested sandwich wrap. She shrieked and leaped back, falling into Madison.

Naomi knelt down behind me, gingerly holding my hair back.

"Go get Renee."

Madison hurried away to find the resident assistant as I continued to retch onto the floor. A timid hand patted my back. Jamie continued to wail in disgust.

"Are you kidding me!?" A crowd gathered as curious students popped their heads out of their rooms at the sound of Jamie screaming. "God, you and that freak in 403 are perfect for each other!"

"Where is she?" Renee appeared at my side. "Samantha, right?"

"Please don't call my parents," I choked.

"She owes me new shoes!"

Renee helped me up, and someone forced a paper towel into my hand. Chagrined, I wiped my face off.

"I'm just getting over a bug, I'm fine."

"I can take you to the nurse's office."

"No, I'm okay, I promise."

"Don't worry, I'll help her!" Winnie was at my side, having been drawn out by the noise like the rest of the floor. She wrapped an uncharacteristically nurturing arm around my shoulders.

"What about my shoes?" Jamie had wriggled out of her tennis shoes, which, to be fair, had missed the bulk of the spew. The carpet had been less lucky.

The crowd split to let Winnie lead me through.

"Not how I would've chosen to introduce myself to a new school," she laughed when we got back to our bunks. "Of course, what do I know about first impressions?"

"I didn't mean to." My entire being burned with embarrassment. Every sophomore girl at the school had just seen me vomit on my new classmate.

"Doesn't matter, it was still amazing!"

Winnie hadn't paid me much attention since we'd moved in that morning, but now her eyes glittered with admiration.

"Somehow I don't feel like Jamie thought it was all that amazing."

Winnie helped me onto my bed. The dizziness and nausea had passed for the most part, but I settled back on my pillow and closed my eyes, thankful to be lying still.

"I'm going to the Welcome Back carnival at the East Pier tomorrow. You think you'd want to go with me?"

I opened my eyes to look at Winnie. She was smiling for what I was pretty sure was the first time that day.

"Yeah," I said. "That sounds like fun."

The first night in the dorm didn't improve. We kept the door open, but no one stopped by to say hi, though I caught a few of our neighbors peeking in, probably hoping to glimpse the girl that Jamie was still loudly complaining about down the hall. Girls shrieked happily as they ran room to room, excited to be reunited after a summer apart, but Winnie sat at her desk, hunched over her laptop. She either didn't notice that our room was being largely ignored by the others or she didn't care.

Winnie and I both jumped when there was a knock on the door frame. Renee smiled sheepishly at us as a looming man in lavender scrubs appeared behind her. The fluorescent lights gleamed off his dark, bald brow.

"How are we feeling, Samantha?" Renee asked. I pushed myself into a sitting position on my bed, blushing furiously.

"I'm fine," I insisted as Winnie snickered from her side of the room. "I don't need a nurse."

The man in the lavender scrubs stepped forward and extended a hand.

"Jacobi Everly. Nurse Practitioner." His voice was low and smooth. His hand dwarfed mine as I took it. "So, you got sick earlier?"

I scowled at the ceiling. Why did no one believe me when I told them I was fine?

"I got sick about a week ago, but I'm okay now."

"You're okay now?" Everly chuckled, setting a bag on my bed and pulling out a blood pressure cuff. "Then the carpet stain by the elevator wasn't you?"

Winnie snorted at her desk. I glared at her as Everly wrapped the cuff around my bicep and applied the disc of his stethoscope to my inner elbow. He frowned at the dial on the cuff.

"Blood pressure's a little low," he said.

He pulled more tools from his bag and checked my temperature and pulse. I begrudgingly let him look in my mouth and ears and listen to my breathing.

"Have you ever had an IV?" he asked. I wrinkled my nose.

"I did when I had surgery to fix my collarbone."

His eyes darted over the scar that Jamie had called neat. Winnie turned her seat around to watch Everly poke my arm with the IV needle.

"Sit tight, and I'll be back in a little bit to check on you," he said, hooking the fluid bag on a shelf above my bed. "Renee, you mind showing me Heather Hisakawa's room? I need to check on her, too."

Renee led the nurse away, and I glared at the needle in my arm. If Dad could see me with an IV sticking out of me on my first night in the dorm, he'd have a fit.

Winnie got up from her desk and closed the door. She gave me a sly smile.

"He's on my list, you know," she grinned and patted her laptop. "I'm almost certain of it. Who better to have as a school nurse than an Apex?"

"He seemed perfectly normal to me." I grumbled. I didn't care if the school nurse was an Apex or not. I was busy worrying over how quickly the news that Winnie Hendricks's new roommate already had a visit from the nurse would spread.

Winnie threw her head back and laughed.

"If anyone seems perfectly normal, it's because you aren't looking hard enough."

I exhaled and stared up at the ceiling. If what Winnie said was true, I hoped no one looked too hard at me. It was only day one, and I already stuck out much more than I'd wanted.

3

The Carnival

No one had been eager to meet me when I was just Winnie's roommate. Now that I was also the girl who puked on Jamie's shoes, no one wanted to so much as come near me. For better or for worse, I still had Winnie, whose newfound respect for me I couldn't help but feel was a little misplaced.

The school nurse had come back to unhook the IV as he'd promised and left me with a box of granola bars. I did my best to look for any hints that he might be an Apex like Winnie believed him to be, but Jacobi Everly seemed like any other ordinary nurse.

Winnie sat with me at breakfast the next morning, which, despite her haughty behavior, I was thankful for since no one else seemed willing to eat with me. She outlined the plan she'd come up with for the day between bites of her pancakes. I hardly listened. I was too busy tearing into my own breakfast. Whatever had been in that IV had worked. My appetite was back and making up for the meals I'd missed while sick.

The East Pier was a two mile walk from campus and even though the school was offering a free shuttle to all students, Winnie insisted on walking. I wasn't sure I could walk that far without getting dizzy, but Winnie was dead-set on her decision so I'd have to soldier on.

We set out just after noon, walking along a boardwalk trail that connected the high school and the college campuses to the East Pier. Across the glittering water, the mainland rose from the ocean in rounded shadows of distant greens and grays. Winnie's camera bounced against her chest where it hung from a neck strap.

"I can't carry it in a bag," she explained when she saw me eying it. "I need it ready at a moment's notice! You never know when an Apex might show up."

Winnie leaned over the wooden railing, peering into the water. Her camera dangled dangerously from her neck, but she didn't seem bothered.

"The water is five hundred feet deep, you know, and it's a straight drop to the ocean floor," she said. "It's like that all around the city, which sucks because why live on an island if there are no beaches? Just docks and boardwalks."

Even though it was a warm, late summer day, the sea breeze was cool. I was glad to have brought my jacket. It would only get colder the later we stayed out.

"The island is man-made, isn't it?" I asked.

"One hundred percent!" She was on tip-toe now, leaning out precariously. "You'd think they'd think to put in a beach since the whole thing is by design. No tides, either. The island rises and lowers with the water. New Delos was supposedly created to give Apex a place to live, but I don't know. The guy who started the project wasn't one himself, so I don't know what he'd want to help them for."

"It doesn't seem like the city likes them too much."

"Not lately, no." She pointed towards the part of the city where the buildings rose up the highest. "See the one with the glass dome on top? That's the Schrader Enterprise Building. Adrian Schrader's great grandpa was the guy who paid for the island to be built. Now the family business pretty much runs the city."

"Is that good or bad?"

Winnie shrugged.

"Both, I guess. Mr. Schrader donates a lot of money to a lot of places, including the school. The whole island would be bankrupt without him."

"But?"

"I've heard he's a jerk, and I don't think jerks should get to run anything, even if they do have money. He's basically bought all his influence."

Live music drifted over the boardwalk from the pier, growing louder as we got closer to the carnival. A ferris wheel peeked out over the top of vendor stalls. Winnie quickened her step, and I hastened to keep pace with her.

We showed our student IDs, and the carnival gate worker gave us each a handful of tickets. A large banner stretched across the entry walk reading, "WELCOME BACK TITANS!" Students from both the high school and the college lined up at booths, carrying carnival food and large plush prizes. The younger high schoolers ran between the stands, unable to contain their excitement.

We made our way to the food trucks first for lunch. I left Winnie in the line for cheesesteaks. The next truck over was selling fried calamari, and I couldn't resist the smell.

"Calamari?" Winnie wrinkled her nose at me. "You know that's squid, right?"

"Doesn't matter what it is if it tastes good," I called back from the calamari line.

"As long as it makes Jamie scream again when you puke it up on her shoes!" Winnie threw her head back and cackled at her own joke.

The boy in front of me turned back to look at us. His large ears stuck out of the dark, shaggy hair that framed his summer-tanned face.

"You're the girl that puked on Jamie Ratcliffe?"

"She sure is!" Winnie confirmed.

"You heard about it?" My stomach dipped. It was bad enough that every girl on our floor knew, but I wasn't ready for the one thing everyone at school knew about me was that I herfed all over the prettiest girl in our grade.

"Everyone has. Andersen told us all after it happened."

"Who's Andersen?"

The boy pointed across the pier. Jamie was at a game booth carrying a massive pink giraffe. A brown-haired boy with a pointed nose and bushy eyebrows had his arm around her waist.

"Andersen Lewis. He's Jamie's boyfriend. He's pretty angry at you for the shoe thing." The boy beamed and stuck out his hand. "I'm Anthony, by the way. My roommate is somewhere around here, too."

"Samantha."

"Yeah, I know," he grinned. "Everybody knows."

Winnie and I got our food, but I wasn't very hungry anymore.

"Told you the squid would be gross," Winnie said, looking at my untouched food as she devoured her sandwich.

"I've been here a day, and I'm already the vomity weirdo."

"Yeah, and I'm the obsessive conspiracy freak." Winnie shrugged. "Everybody's something, and everybody's a jerk about it. At least you figured out your thing early."

Winnie was, if anything at all, candid. She knew her place at the school and had no shame about it. I didn't know if it was refreshing or jarring. Her pep talk wasn't exactly what I wanted or needed to hear at the moment, but I at least felt good enough to eat. I wriggled a bit of calamari at her.

"It's good, by the way. This squid."

"Great, you can be the vomity weirdo who eats cephalopods. Now hurry up, I heard there was a virtual reality simulator at this thing."

We spent the afternoon spending tickets on carnival games and snacks. I recognized some of the girls from the dorm, but none of them said hi. Jamie, Madison, and Naomi walked with a huge group that seemed to be led by the brunette boy that Anthony had called Andersen. Our eyes locked from across the pier. He glared and turned away.

We were standing in line for a ring toss game when Winnie groaned.

"What?" I asked. For the first time, she looked embarrassed. She bowed her head and let a curtain of strawberry blonde hair fall in front of her face.

"Are you trying to hide from me?"

I turned around. Winnie and her sister Amanda didn't look much alike. Amanda's brown hair was at the awkward length somewhere between a pixie cut and bob, as if she was trying to grow it out. Whatever height Winnie was missing, Amanda made up for. She was even taller than me, and I considered myself tall for a girl.

"No," Winnie grumbled. She flipped her hair back over her shoulders. "What are you doing here anyway?"

"I'm a student, too."

"Whatever. I heard Dad was mad at you." Winnie faked an apologetic smile.

"Dad can deal. If he's so mad about it, why doesn't he join the swim team?"

"You remember, Samantha, right?" Winnie gestured at me. "She's my roommate now."

Amanda glowered at me as she scanned me from top to bottom as if sizing me up.

"Yeah, I heard."

"It's been a while," I said. I didn't know why Amanda was being so cold to me. We hadn't seen each other in years. "How's being back on campus so far?"

"It's fine," she spat.

"God, Amanda," Winnie groaned. "Don't be so freaking weird."

"I'm far from being the weirdo here."

"Yeah? What's that supposed to mean?"

"It means exactly what it sounds like." She glared at me as she said it. I racked my brain, trying to think of something I might have done to offend Amanda. Had Winnie said something to her about me? But even if that was the case, I couldn't think of anything I'd said or done that Winnie might've told her. Besides, Winnie hated talking to her sister.

The line moved forward, and Winnie stepped up to the ring toss. Amanda grabbed my wrist. Her grip was aggressive and surprisingly hot against my skin.

"Listen," she hissed. "I know you've got everyone playing this game of yours, but you keep me out of it, alright?"

"Game?" I repeated dumbly. I looked back at Winnie for help, but she was already engrossed in the ring toss.

"And leave Winnie out of it." Her face was inches from mine. "I don't know what this whole thing is, but we don't want any part, understand?"

"I don't—"

"I asked if you understand."

"Yeah, sure," I said, completely nonplussed. She let go and turned to Winnie, who was jumping up and down having just landed a ring.

"Don't stay out too late."

Winnie scowled at Amanda as the booth worker handed her a green teddy bear.

I had no idea what game she was talking about, or how she thought I was involved, but as confused as I was, I'd received her message loud and clear. Stay away from her, or else.

We spent the rest of the afternoon feasting on shaved iced and funnel cakes. I wasn't sure it was Everly's care from the night before or the surplus of greasy foods, but I was feeling better with each passing hour. I didn't get dizzy at all, and even though Winnie was still the only person who'd hang out with me, I was having more fun than I thought I would.

As the sun began to disappear behind the city, Winnie suggested we get in line for the ferris wheel before we had to head back in time for dinner. We were out of food tickets and would have to make it to the cafeteria if we wanted to eat.

The ferris wheel carriage swayed when we sat down in it. We began to rise up over the water, stopping in intervals as other students got into the carriages behind us. Winnie's camera was still around her neck.

"Guess you didn't need that," I said, pointing at it. She lifted the camera to her face and peered through, checking the lens.

"You also don't need health insurance, but it makes me feel good to have with me, just in case." She lowered the camera. "Remind me to take a look at your schedule when we get back. Hopefully we have some classes together."

We neared the top of the ferris wheel. I looked out over the city. Golden sunbeams peeked out from between the silhouettes of skyscrapers, but something caught my eye down on the street. A dark mass was moving towards the pier.

"What's that?" I pointed. Winnie twisted in her seat and pressed against the glass, causing the whole compartment to rock.

"It looks like people," she murmured. "Do you hear that?"

"What?"

She shushed me, and in the silence, I heard it, too. The distant chanting rising from the crowd became louder. Winnie watched through her camera lens.

I slid to her side of the carriage. We were at the top of the wheel now, so I had the perfect view of the angry crowd of people forcing their way through the street. They were getting closer, and a short, disheveled man in all black led the way with a bullhorn.

"No more Apex, no more fear!" he screamed. The crowd took up the chant, waving their signs furiously. Police were stationed near the perimeter of the mob, but stayed back. There was no need for them to intervene.

"It's a protest!" I said, amazed. "Are they the ones posting the flyers around the city?"

Many of the picket signs were identical to the flyer the man had tried to give me on the ferry yesterday.

"They have to be," Winnie said, clicking away at her camera. "This is perfect, an Apex is bound to show."

"Now what's happening?"

A fight had broken out near the front of the group. The police had finally stepped in and blocked the path of the mob.

"It looks like they're trying to get into the carnival!"

Sure enough, the crowd had begun to press against the front gate of the pier. Police tried to form a barrier, but there were simply too many protesters. The man with the bullhorn led the charge.

"The schools worship the Apex!" he shrieked. "They idolize and harbor their heroes while the rest of us are burdened by a city plagued by unchecked and unregulated violence and non-Apex discrimination!"

"Is that true?" I asked Winnie.

"Not really." Her camera clicked multiple times in succession. "But it sounds better than the truth."

"Which is?"

"They don't like Apex because they don't like that they're able to do things others can't."

"We are done being forced to feel inferior just because we don't have the Epsilon gene!" The man yelled. "We are done letting employers pass us up for jobs because they'd rather hire a super-human!"

The crowd roared in agreement.

"What's the Epsilon gene?" I asked Winnie as our carriage finally came to the bottom of the ferris Wheel.

"It's what the Apex have that gives them their abilities."

The workers ushered us out of the carriage but didn't tell us where to go next. They seemed just as frazzled as the students. The entire mob had forced its way onto the pier. The front gates had been toppled, and students rushed out into the street.

The protesters on the perimeter of the herd harassed students trying to get out of the way of the mass of people. I'd been uncomfortable when just one of them had cornered me on the ferry. Now there seemed to be hundreds of them. Breathing suddenly became more difficult.

"Done are the days when an Apex gets a pass just because they are different from us!" The man on the bullhorn had a raspy voice.

The crowd cheered louder.

"No more will we stand by and let them ruin our city!"

Winnie ran to get closer to the growing mass of people.

"What are you doing?" I pulled her back by her shirt. "We need to get out of here!"

The police focused on ushering students away rather than controlling the crowd. Sirens screamed in the distance. It was only a matter of time before it escalated further.

"I'm not passing this up, Samantha! Go back without me if you have to!"

She tore herself away and disappeared between bodies. The swarm of people pushed me back, further separating us as panic swelled inside me. Students and protesters alike pressed against me, and I was subject to the will of the crowd.

"You an Apex Idolizer?" Someone pushed me hard from behind. I spun around. An angry stranger loomed over me. His shirt read in big letters, "Ban the Epsilon Gene".

I stumbled away. Someone grabbed me under the arms to steady me. Anthony from the calamari food truck stared at me with wide eyes.

"Are you okay?"

"Yeah, thanks." I pointed towards the flashing lights on the opposite side of the crowd. "I think I saw an exit that way."

"Makes sense," Anthony said over the roar of the crowd. "The other way would land us in the bay."

We tried to stay along the edge of the mob, but the farther we went, the harder it was to get through the throng of people. Someone pushed me, but I couldn't tell if it was on purpose or not. I focused on the back of Anthony's head, trying to keep calm.

My foot caught on a discarded bag, and I fell into someone else. They pushed me off of them and away from Anthony. I struggled to catch up to him, but by the time he looked back and scanned the crowd, almost ten yards had been put between us. I saw his mouth form my name, but I could barely hear him over the chanting.

"Anthony!" I shouted back. He couldn't see me. His brow furrowed, and he resolved to move forward. The panic that I'd been keeping at bay threatened to overwhelm me. "Anthony, wait!"

I tried to push through the crowd, but they pushed back, spitting insults about New Delos Prep and the university. First Winnie, now Anthony...

"Hey, it's you!" I recognized the man from the ferry as he got in my face. "You have any idea how much trouble I got in for that stunt you pulled yesterday, huh? Bet that's what you wanted, right?"

I backed into a booth, grabbing the table behind me for support. I shook my head at the man.

"N-no, I—"

"You what? Freaking Apex lover, we'll show you when the Apex are finally run out of the city! And then what'll you do with no one to protect you?"

"Leave me alone!" I shouted and shoved him hard in the chest. As he stumbled backwards, I crouched down and disappeared under the table cloth. I bumped into something solid.

"Hey! Watch it!"

The voice sounded strange, as if its owner was speaking through a voice modulator. I looked up and found myself staring straight into one of the helmets depicted on all the flyers that had been scattered around the city.

I was face to face with an Apex.

4

The Apex Under the Table

Fear clashed with relief as I stared numbly at the Apex in front of me. I knew Apex were supposed to be protectors, but something about stumbling into one turned my insides to lead.

Despite the lack of light under the table, I could tell he was a guy, probably no older than I was. He had a slim frame that was bolstered by some kind of armored padding. His helmet hid most of his face, but his mouth and chin remained uncovered. It was hard to make much more of him, as he was on his hands and knees like me.

"What are you doing?" he asked in his robotic voice.

"Me? What are you doing? Shouldn't you be out there?" I jerked my thumb over my shoulder. "You know, restoring peace or whatever?"

The Apex pulled me the rest of the way under the table so that my shoes didn't stick out from under the table cloth.

"Yeah, that's what I should be doing! But I didn't realize how quickly they were moving, and if I went out now..."

"They'd tear you apart," I finished for him, thinking about the man who'd gotten in my face just for being a student. My surprise at finding the Apex was subsiding, especially as it became more clear that he was a kid like me. "But you're an Apex, aren't you? You can't take them?"

The Apex scoffed.

"And give them more reasons to hate us? Besides, the paperwork alone would be a nightmare."

I smirked at him. I'd thought the island was supposed to be safer because of the Apex. I didn't think the first one I found would be hiding under a table, not that I could blame him. The crowd was swelling outside and could probably handle a high schooler, even if he did have super powers.

I lifted the fabric an inch off the ground and pressed my cheek against the wooden planks to try and see what was happening. All I saw were shoes. The crowd's chant of "We want Epsilon Epsi-*gone!*" seemed to be getting louder.

"It looks like we might be stuck here for a while." I dropped the fabric back down. "There's no way we're getting past that crowd."

The Apex shook his head.

"They've started tearing apart booths farther down the pier. It's only a matter of time before they flatten this one."

The table overhead shuddered as it was jostled by the crowd, and I froze, half-expecting it to collapse on us right then. The shaking passed, and I sighed in relief. I pressed the heels of my hands into my eyes, trying to think of a way out, trying not to imagine how mad Dad was going to be once he found out I'd gotten myself into this mess.

"Why don't you just take off your uniform?" I asked. "I can't get through all those people, but maybe you can? Without your uniform, no one will know you're an Apex, and maybe you could help clear us a path to the exit?"

"That's a no-go. I, uh, I don't have anything on under this, and if I took off my helmet, you'd see my face, and that'd be paperwork for both of us, maybe even a memory alteration—"

"Fine, I get it." I was glad it was dark. I didn't want him to see me blushing.

The crowd outside was getting louder. The table shook harder. We were running out of time.

"I could probably punch a hole in the pier, and then we could drop and swim away?"

I stared blankly at him in the dark.

"I'm sorry. Punch a hole in the pier?"

"It might take a couple goes, but—"

I threw my jacket at him.

"Hey!" he exclaimed. "It's a good idea!"

"It's ridiculous. Put that on over your uniform, and we'll do my plan."

He wriggled into the zip-up in the cramped space. Judging by how difficult he was making it look, super-flexibility wasn't in his wheelhouse. When he finally managed to zip it up he looked back at me.

"And what about my helmet?"

"Try the hood?"

He flipped the hood up over his head. While it did fit over his helmet, it was still very obvious.

"Can't you carry it?" I asked. "Look, it's dark under here, and I promise not to look at your face. Just keep the hood up, and no one will look twice at you."

He was silent for a moment. There was a loud bang outside the booth.

"Now or never," I prompted.

"Fine," he growled. "Look away. And don't tell anyone I did this."

I lowered my gaze and held a hand up to my eyes. When he gave me the go-ahead to look again, his back was to me and the hood up. His helmet was under his arm. He lifted the side of the table skirt that led into the empty booth.

"Stay close. If you lose me, I might not be able to help you." He spoke low, trying to disguise his voice without the help of the voice modulator in his helmet. I wriggled the handle to the back door of the booth, but the vendor had locked up when the protestors had descended on the carnival.

"Over the table, then," I said. He extended a hand to me, his head bowed so that I couldn't see his face under the hood.

"Keep up, and hold on."

As soon as my hand was firmly in his, he slid across the table into the crowd. I clambered behind him awkwardly, using one arm to hoist myself up and over while holding on tight to him with the other hand.

The crowd was chanting "Schrader is a Traitor!" The people standing closest to the booth yelled out in shock and anger as the Apex bowled us into them. He passed his helmet back to me before using his free arm to push protesters out of the way.

He made clearing a path look easy. Full grown men and women fell back as he shoved past them. I stayed as close as I could, accidentally stepping on the heels of the Apex's boots more than once.

"Sorry!" I panted.

"It's fine! We're almost through!"

But just then someone grabbed my elbow. I shouted in pain as the Apex continued forging forward, pulling at my arm.

"Hey!" The man who'd grabbed me yowled. "This girl's got one of those helmets!"

I twisted away, but the crowd grew thicker around us. The Apex's hand slipped out of mine. I struck out at the man, smacking him in the nose.

"You filthy, little Apex!" he cried. He lunged at me, but the real Apex jumped between us. He used one hand to shove the man back, toppling him as well as the three people behind him.

The crowd grabbed at us, but the Apex put one arm around me and broke through the swarm of bodies. Luckily, most of the crowd remained oblivious to the Apex in their midst because of the chaos and sheer mass of the mob. As we reached the gate, another stranger tried to stop us, but a police officer stepped in, ushering us into the street.

We didn't stop running for another two blocks. We finally turned a corner in a small alley between two shop fronts. I leaned against the brick wall, wheezing.

"Helmet?" The Apex asked.

I tossed him the helmet. He turned his back to me to put it back on, but I caught a glimpse of a mess of brown hair. I quickly looked at my feet before he could turn back and catch me staring.

"Thanks," he said, back to his robotic voice. He handed me my jacket. In the light, I could barely see a black number "7" painted on both of his shoulders. "I probably would've been stuck under that table without your jacket."

I shrugged.

"Unless you, what was it? Punched a hole in the pier and swam away?"

"Property damage is paperwork." He smiled under his visor.

"Right. And you hate paperwork."

He fired finger guns at me.

"Exactly."

I peeked out into the street. No one had followed us.

"So why does half the city hate you guys?" I asked. The Apex frowned under his helmet. "My roommate said people are just bitter, but there's got to be more to it than that."

"There was an incident a while ago. People got hurt, and even though no one actually knows who caused it, The Apex became a popular theory. It's been a downhill slide for our popularity since then."

"I'm sorry." I wondered if that was why Dad didn't like Apex.

"It's not your fault," the Apex laughed. "It's not so bad, anyways. We just have to be a bit more covert now."

"Is that why there's no cape?"

"Nah, Paragon just made them look too good. The rest of us can't seem to pull it off after that." He tilted his head to the side and then pointed up through the alley. "I can hear the campus shuttle a few blocks that way. It's still picking up stragglers if you want to grab it."

"What about you?"

"What about me?"

"How are you getting back to campus?"

His lips tightened, and he paused a moment too long.

"I don't know what you mean."

"You're a student, aren't you? You can't be that much older than me."

He shrugged and turned away.

"Still don't know what you mean." He crouched down and leaped upwards, much higher than any normal person should be able to. He grabbed onto a fire escape railing and pulled himself over. "Besides, I've got my own way home."

As he ran up the steps towards the roof he waved back down at me.

"Thanks again! Now hurry! The shuttle won't wait forever!"

And he disappeared over the lip of the roof.

Wide-eyed and harried students had already filled every seat on the shuttle, but the teachers present continued to shove as many kids into it as they could. I found standing room up near the front, silently marveling that I hadn't passed out or puked yet.

"Samantha?"

Winnie squeezed herself into the shuttle just as the doors closed. Her hair was disheveled, and there was dirt on her face. Her camera was back around her neck, and she was grinning.

"How'd you get so dirty?"

"There was a protest, didn't you notice?" She rolled her eyes at me. "And speak for yourself. Did someone scratch you?"

I twisted around to look at my elbow where the protester had grabbed me. Bright red marks raked across my skin.

"Didn't even notice," I murmured. Something buzzed in my pocket. "Oh, no."

I pulled my phone out. Sure enough, I was receiving a call from Dad.

"Hey, Dad!" I forced myself to sound casual.

"Sammy? Are you okay? You weren't at the carnival, were you?"

Winnie giggled next to me. I raised a finger to my lips to shut her up.

"No, I'm fine, nowhere near it!"

"Where are you, then? It sounds loud on your end."

"Oh, it's, uh, just the cafeteria. Dinner rush, you know."

Winnie rolled her eyes at me and mouthed, "Nice." I waved her away.

"Alright, well," Dad grunted. "Stay on campus, okay? I don't want you getting too close to those nutjobs."

"Do you mean the protesters or the Apex?"

"Both! Is Winnie with you? Is she safe?"

"Yes, Dad! She's right here," I hissed. Other students were starting to stare at me. "She actually just found us a table, so I gotta go."

"Okay. Love you, kid. Stay safe."

"Yeah, love you, Dad."

That night, no one in the dorms felt much like sleeping. Even with class starting the next morning, everyone stayed up late, swapping stories from the pier. The TV in the common room blasted the nightly news report, showing footage of trampled booths and broken gates.

"Honestly, I don't blame them," Jamie said loudly, her voice drifting down the hall for everyone to hear. "Those Apex are menaces, and at least someone is finally holding them accountable."

"How could you say that?" Madison gasped. "What about Paragon?"

Winnie shut our door, blocking out the sounds of the ensuing argument.

"I can cross Jamie off my list." She shook her head. "This whole thing might just make it easier for me to figure out who is and isn't an Apex."

I sat at my desk, staring at my jacket in my lap as I replayed the day's events in my head. It had only been a matter of time before I saw my first Apex in the city. I hadn't thought it would be so soon, and definitely not so close.

"Samantha? You sleeping over there?"

"Hmm?" I looked up at Winnie. "Yeah, sorry, I'm just tired."

"How? I'm pretty sure you are the only person not talking about the carnival right now."

I threw my jacket in the hamper as I stood up.

"Not much to talk about, I guess. We were all there, we all know what happened." It was probably best not to tell Winnie about the Apex. I didn't need or want to give her any excuses to involve me in her project.

Winnie flung herself onto her bed.

"Ugh, no need to be so boring about it, though."

"Nothing wrong with boring," I yawned. "You might consider trying it sometime."

A knock at the door interrupted us. Winnie made a face but opened it anyway. A girl I didn't recognize wrung her hands on the other side. Her eyes were red, and make-up streaked down her cheeks.

"Have you guys seen Lannie?" she asked.

"Who?" Winnie looked at me, but I shrugged. If Winnie didn't know her, I definitely didn't.

"Lannie Bryce," the girl hiccuped. "She's my roommate on the third floor. I lost her at the carnival, and no one's seen her."

Winnie perked up.

"You're saying she's missing?"

The girl sniffled, and her whole body shuddered.

"I've already been to all the rooms on the third and second floor, but so far, nothing."

Winnie glanced at me.

"We'll keep an eye out. Hope you find her."

The girl sniffed again and tried to smile before moving onto the next door.

"I hope Lannie's okay," I said. Winnie flicked off the lights and crawled under her covers.

"I'm sure she's fine." She sounded distracted. I got into my own bed and looked over at Winnie before turning over. The light of her digital clock reflected off her open eyes as she stared at the ceiling, deep in thought.

I pulled my covers up over my head, blocking out thoughts of Lannie, the carnival, and Apex under tables.

5

In the Hall of Heroes

W hen we woke up for the first day of school the next morning, the whole floor was talking about Lannie Bryce. By the sounds of the gossip at the bathroom sinks, she still hadn't been seen since yesterday.

Winnie couldn't be bothered, however. She was much more concerned with getting to the cafeteria before the breakfast rush. Apparently, they served waffles on the first day of class, and if we waited too long, the cafeteria would run out. The cafeteria was still relatively empty by the time we got there, so we grabbed our waffles and sat at one of the highly coveted window booth tables.

"I'm so glad I had my camera last night," Winnie sighed.

"Did you want pictures of the protests?"

Winnie laughed.

"No, of course not, but that kind of event draws attention." She leaned over her plate to get close. "Apex were there, if you knew where to look."

A piece of waffle lodged itself in my throat. I coughed and threw back my glass of water.

Was Winnie about to tell me that she'd seen me in the alley? I hoped my coughing fit kept her from noticing the panic I was sure was plastered across my face.

"I got some good pictures of them, too. You'd already disappeared, otherwise I would've pointed them out to you."

I tried not to look too relieved. So she hadn't seen me, after all. Good.

"Do you think maybe you got a picture of that missing girl?" I asked. "It might help them find her."

Winnie screwed her face up at me.

"I'm a photographer, not a detective."

I wanted to point out that trying to figure out who was an Apex and who wasn't sounded like detective work to me, but I thought better of it. It wasn't hard to notice that Winnie wasn't generally well-liked among the other students. Not only had they avoided our room all weekend, but even now, as the cafeteria filled, I could see a radius of empty tables around us. Other kids didn't even want to come close to her, and I had a feeling it was because of her open obsession with The Apex.

"You have Fleming for First Period, right?" she asked as we finished our breakfast. "Me, too. I'll show you the way."

She led me out of the cafeteria and across the lawn to the main school building, Schrader Hall. We went up the back stone steps into the well-lit corridor lined with classrooms. The walls were covered with "Welcome Back, Titans!", as well as plaques and pictures from past classes.

Fleming's classroom was on the second floor, and we were among the first to arrive in class. Winnie took a seat in the third row and patted the spot next to her.

"Here you go," she said. I slung my backpack over the chair back and sat down.

The teacher who had been posted outside the dorm on move-in day was up front organizing a stack of papers. His glasses perched on the end of his long nose, and his tie had a crease that cut across the middle of it.

"My mom knew him. I think they went here together," I said.

"That'd make sense. My dad knows him, too."

As if he knew we were talking about him, Fleming looked up at us over the heads of students as they meandered into class. He smiled, and I quickly looked down.

"That's my seat," someone said behind me. I turned around to see the brown-haired boy that Jamie had been with at the pier glaring down at me. Jamie was holding his hand next to him.

"I didn't—"

"It's definitely not your seat, Andersen," Winnie said, cutting me off. Andersen scowled.

"I sat there all last year," he said. "Now move it."

I grabbed the strap of my backpack and made to stand up, but Winnie held out her hand.

"You don't own the place," she snapped. "You should've gotten here sooner."

The bell chimed overhead.

"Come on, Andy," Jamie said. She retreated to an empty seat, but Andersen didn't move. Fleming glanced over the rim of his glasses.

"Andersen, take a seat, please," he said. He was handing the papers out to the front row.

"I would, but she's in my spot!"

It was only the first class period of the first day of the school year, but Mr. Fleming already looked exhausted.

"That's funny, I don't recall having a seating chart for this class."

Winnie winked at me in triumph and folded her arms smugly in front of her. Andersen hesitated above us but must have realized that Fleming didn't seem like he was going to warn him again. Grumbling, he made his way to the empty seat directly in front of us.

"Welcome to World History, I recognize almost all of you from last year's US Social Studies class, but I'm happy to see some new faces." He clicked a small remote. The class syllabus popped up on a screen at the front of the room. "Those who have had me will remember, if you aren't seated by the time the bell rings, you'll be counted as late."

Andersen grunted.

"I'll give those of you who weren't a pass for today."

The papers had made their way to our row. Winnie handed me one and passed on the rest. It was a copy of the syllabus that was on the screen but with a permission form stapled to the back.

"While our main focus in World History will, in fact, be world history, Schrader Industries is hosting an academic fair, giving all sophomore students enrolled in a social studies class on the island the opportunity to win a small scholarship to New Delos University. I recommend you all take this opportunity seriously. You'll be working in pairs."

The class perked up, and the other kids started throwing hopeful glances at their friends across the room, but their hopes were quickly dashed.

"I'll be assigning partners for this project," Fleming said, and the class responded with a collective groan. "I'm sure you've all survived much worse."

"Don't worry," Winnie hissed next to me. "He'll have to put us together since you're new."

"Each class has an assigned time this week to visit the New Delos Museum in the Schrader Industries Building to work on their assigned topic." He clicked his remote, and a blown up version of the permission form took over the screen. "And that brings us to the back page of your packets. We will be leaving the school Wednesday at two o'clock. Your other teachers have been informed, all I need from you is a parent's signature. There's an electronic version of the form on my website if you need to email it to get it signed."

Fleming spent the rest of the class going over rules, what to expect, and major test dates. I looked over my class schedule as he talked and wondered if all my classes would be this boring today.

I tuned Fleming out, looking around the classroom. I recognized most of the girls from the hall meeting we'd had on move-in day. Anthony was sitting up front with another boy. Naomi sat near Jamie next to a girl with a large bow fastened to the back of her head.

When the bell finally released us, Winnie glanced at my schedule, too.

"I'm in French next, what about you?" She snatched up the paper before I could respond. "Chemistry? Gross, I don't have that until Fifth Period."

Our classes were in the same direction so Winnie volunteered to show me where my next period was. We made our way up to the third floor, and as we walked down the hall, we passed a glass case. Winnie faltered and stopped to stare at it.

"So much for all this, right?"

Plaques and medals listing the names of past State Champions for various sports lined the shelves. "Amanda Hendricks" was engraved into several different plaques along with the year and the swim event she'd won.

There was a picture of her standing on top of a podium with a medal resting on her chest. She looked as sordid as she had at the carnival, despite having won first place. I wondered if she'd ever enjoyed swimming. I couldn't blame her for quitting.

"I was on the phone with my dad last night." Winnie sounded beside herself with giddiness. "He's so mad at her, but I always knew she wasn't as perfect as she acted. I think he might still be angry by Christmas time!"

"Did I do something to make Amanda mad?" I blurted. Winnie screwed her face up at me.

"Not that I've heard. Why?"

"She was acting really weird yesterday at the carnival and said some things when you weren't listening." I stared at the picture of her. She looked more than unhappy. She looked miserable. "She was angry at me and told me she wasn't going to play my game? But I don't know what she was talking about."

Winnie snorted and turned away from the display case.

"She's such a freak," she said. "It probably meant nothing. She's just rude is all."

I decided that it didn't really matter whatever beef Amanda had with me. It was easy to forget about her as I sat through my new classes, even if they were all just reviews of the syllabus.

I didn't have any more classes with Winnie until after lunch but found that the other students were more likely to talk to me when she wasn't around. In chemistry, I met Heather, who had the big bow in her hair. In English Literature, a girl named Bethany sat by me. I recognized her from the dorm room across the hall. Then, when I walked into the cafeteria alone, Anthony waved me over.

"Hey, shoe-barf!"

I cringed at the nickname, but he seemed to mean it in a nice way. He was sitting with the same boy he'd sat with in Fleming's class.

"Are you sitting with anyone yet?" Anthony asked, already scooting over to make room. "This is my roommate, by the way."

The other boy waved and pushed his glasses back up to the bridge of his nose.

"Wesley," he introduced himself. "You're the girl Andersen was mad at this morning, right?"

"She's also the girl who puked on Jamie," Anthony added. Wesley laughed, choking on his sandwich.

"I didn't do it on purpose," I said.

"We wouldn't hold it against you if you did," Wesley smiled. His brown hair was messy, and he had a pencil smudge on his cheek.

"What are you doing?"

I spun around in my seat. Winnie towered over me, holding a tray of food.

"You wanna sit?" I gestured to the empty seat next to Wesley, but she remained standing.

"I thought you were going to meet me for lunch."

"Yeah, I am. Look, there's room."

Anthony and Wesley had become very interested in their lunches, not looking up at us. Winnie looked around and rolled her eyes before sitting down with a sigh.

"This isn't what I had in mind," she mumbled.

"How was your summer, Winnie?" Wesley asked. She sneered at him, but he didn't waver.

"It was fine. I guess. So you've met my roommate, then."

"I'm Samantha, by the way," I said, realizing I hadn't actually introduced myself to Wesley.

"Oh, Samantha!" Anthony suddenly yelped. "I'm so sorry! Did you get out of the carnival okay yesterday? I lost you and had to keep going!"

"No, it's fine!" I insisted. "I found my way out. I'm glad you kept going."

"Man, I'm really sorry." Anthony turned bright red. "What about you, Winnie? Were you okay?"

"Okay?" she scoffed. "I was great. That was the coolest thing to happen since we've been here. Real history happening right in front of us!"

"What do you mean history?" Wesley asked.

"Isn't it obvious?" Winnie rolled her eyes again. "That crowd was huge. Public favor with The Apex is at an all-time low. We are watching the world's most Apex friendly place become one of the most dangerous places for them to be."

"Don't sound so excited," Anthony grumbled.

"If they didn't have a point, there wouldn't be that many people that support a less Apex-friendly city," Winnie sang.

"So, how did you get out of the carnival?" Anthony asked me, ignoring Winnie. "It was almost impossible to get through that crowd."

"Oh," I faltered. "I found another student, and we kept pushing until we'd made it out. It was scary, though."

It wasn't really a lie. I was certain the Apex had been a student from the school, but I couldn't imagine the interrogation Winnie would give me if she found out about him. Luckily, neither Anthony or Wesley asked any more questions.

"Do you think the protesters will come to campus?" Anthony furrowed his brow.

"That'd be something!" Winnie sighed wistfully. Wesley shook his head at her.

Winnie was masochistic in her need to be at the center of the action. As far as most awkward lunches went, that one definitely ranked up there, but I was grateful that Anthony and Wesley had invited me to sit with them. If Winnie remained my only friend, I wasn't sure how I'd survive the school year.

Anthony and I had gym together after lunch, which was luckily in the same building as the cafeteria. Winnie and Wesley went to their classes while we went to sit in bleachers while a middle-aged man in shorts handed out PE uniforms.

Bethany from English class joined us, along with another boy named Charlie. We spent the hour dribbling basketballs and half-heartedly shooting hoops, but I was happy to be meeting more people who weren't Winnie.

I ended the day in math. Andersen was already sitting at a desk when I showed up. He glared at me, and I made a point to sit as far from him as possible. Winnie met up with me and scrunched her nose at the seats I'd chosen.

"You really want to be in the back corner?"

I shrugged.

We only had to endure one more class of talking about syllabi, and then a half hour Study Period. Luckily, the teacher, Mrs. Young, knew we wouldn't have much schoolwork on our first day and let us pass the Study Period doing whatever we wanted.

Winnie pulled her camera out of her backpack and began flipping through pictures, deleting one out of every few photos.

"Are those from yesterday?" I asked. She nodded.

"I got some good ones here. Look!" She turned the camera screen, and I leaned in to see a picture of a seagull lying on the pavement.

"A dead bird?"

"No," she sighed. "A *paralyzed* bird. I've been seeing them around lately. They said in the news that there is some kind of virus affecting small animals on the island, but they recover after a few hours, so I'm not sure it's a virus at all."

I remembered Avery pointing out the window at all the pigeons after we'd gotten off the ferry the other day. There had been one lying on its side with its wings twitching. I recoiled from Winnie's camera. Even if she said it was paralyzed, it still looked dead to me.

"Too bad you're a photographer, not a detective," I smiled. "Otherwise you might be able to figure out what's happening to them."

Winnie scowled at me for turning her own words against her and returned to her photos. When the final bell finally released us from our first day of school, she hurried off to the computer lab to edit them, and I was relieved to have a break from her.

There were no more protests and no more angry sisters for the next two days, and I was finally able to start establishing my routine. On the second day of school, Winnie rushed us from breakfast to First Period. She sat in the same spot as she had the first day and patted the seat next to her. I suspected she was doing this just to irritate Andersen, but I obliged and sat down. He glared at us when he showed up but didn't say anything.

I liked my classes, especially the fact that I only had two of them with Winnie. No one brought up Jamie's vomity shoes anymore unless to give me a high five. Anthony and Wesley let me sit with them whenever Winnie skipped dinner to work on her pictures. Bethany even started to say hi to me outside of English and PE. By the time two o'clock rolled around on Wednesday afternoon and it was time for the field trip to the museum, I was finally feeling settled at my new school.

Fleming waited for us in the rotunda out front of Schrader Hall. He perused his clipboard as we gathered around him.

"Angela! Is Angela here?" He scanned our faces until he found Angela. "Perfect! Everest? Where's Everest?"

Once he was sure he had the whole class there, he stepped aside to let us onto the school bus.

As we maneuvered through downtown traffic, I pressed against the window to try to see up to the tops of the buildings. The museum took up the bottom four floors of the Schrader Industries Building, the tallest skyscraper on the island, so I searched for the domed top where Winnie said Adrian Schrader lived.

"I'm going to be so mad if Fleming splits us up for partner assignments," Winnie said in the seat next to me.

"Yeah me too," I lied.

Fleming stood up in the seat at the front of the bus and faced us, waving a clipboard with one hand and holding onto a seat back for balance with the other.

"Attention here, please!" he said. "Listen for your name for your assigned partners! Naomi Bradford and Winnie Hendricks! Your report will be on the ferry system!"

Winnie groaned next to me.

"Just my luck. One of Jamie's clones."

Naomi sat next to Jamie with her curly black hair pulled into a perfect bun, showing off her long neck. She was gorgeous, like I was sure any friend of Jamie's was required to be. She gave Winnie a small nod as we looked back at her. Winnie sank in her seat, still grumbling.

"Madison Thomas and Heather Hisakawa!" Fleming continued reading off his list of pairings. "Andersen Lewis and Olivia Orwell!"

Finally, I heard my name.

"Samantha Havardson and Wesley Isaacs, you'll be presenting on the city's hydraulic lift system," Mr. Fleming called out. I found Wesley sitting next to Anthony near the middle of the bus. He grinned behind his thick-framed glasses and gave me a thumbs up.

Fleming finished dividing the class into pairs as the bus pulled up to the curb in front of the massive stone steps that led up to the main doors of the Schrader Industries Building. The front windows stretched four stories high, decorated with long banners advertising the Island Industry Fair in October.

A park sprawled out for several blocks on the opposite side of the street. Behind the white gazebo at the park perimeter, trees rose up to cast the park in gentle shadows.

Fleming ushered us off the bus and up the great stone steps to the museum entrance, where a middle aged man in a tailored suit surveyed us from under his neatly combed salt-and-pepper hair. A kind smile crinkled the skin around his blue eyes and pulled the edges of his dark beard upwards.

"Everyone, this is Dr. Cunningham, the head curator at the museum. He'll be available to help you find anything you might need."

Dr. Cunningham stepped forward, his blue eyes scanning the crowd. Maybe I was paranoid after the last few days, but I thought his gaze lingered on me for a half-second. I resisted the urge to hide behind Wesley. I was tired of being stared at.

"Welcome, New Delos Prep!" he said, opening his arms. Despite his smaller than average stature, his voice carried down the stone steps. "Mr. Schrader is happy to welcome you to his collection. There's a directory inside to help you find your way, and please stop by the cafe if you've got the time."

The front foyer of the museum took up the first three floors of the building. Wide doors to our left and right led to different exhibits. A raised pool of water sat in the middle of the foyer, shooting streams dancing through the air. Behind that, a grand stone staircase led up to a landing that then branched out two different directions.

"Third floor for New Delos's industrial history exhibit," Wesley said, squinting at the directory. The other students fanned out around us. Winnie and Naomi were already climbing the steps ahead of us. I didn't know which one of them I felt worse for.

We hurried up the main stairs, following the signs to the left and up another flight. The exhibit entrance was a long, dark hallway. Both walls were adorned with backlit timelines and information boxes. It wasn't as crowded as other exhibits we'd passed and took our time jotting notes down in our notebooks.

The hall led to a darkened room. Glass cases lined the curved walls, showcasing blueprints, sketches, and photographs of a city under construction. A model of the city glittered bronze under display lights at the center of the room.

"Hey, there's the school!" Wesley stood at the easternmost point of the model. He crouched down to eye level with the miniaturized school.

I stood over the island's north end, above the ferry terminal. The sculptor had made sure to include a tiny Paragon statue in the bay. A toy ferry boat was floating past him.

"Where are we?"

Wesley squinted at the city for a moment and pushed his glasses back up, pointing into the middle of where the towers were the tallest.

"That one there. See Schrader's penthouse?"

Sure enough, I recognized the domed top.

I wandered over to the display cases.

"Hey, there's lots of stuff we can use here."

Wesley looked at the blueprints under the glass from over my shoulder.

"Is that the hydraulic ballast system?"

"Yup!" I already had my notebook on the glass, taking notes on the mechanisms that used tidal forces to raise and lower the city with the ocean's tide. "If we trace over the blueprints, we can add that to our poster."

We divided the room between us, working from either side to meet in the middle with whatever notes and drawings we'd gathered. Wesley took out his phone to snap a few pictures of the city model. He frowned at his screen.

"Not the best quality photo, but it'll be okay." He shoved his phone back into his pocket and glanced around. "That's everything we need, right?"

I glanced around the room and scanned over the notes I'd compiled to double check. A framed newspaper article on the far wall caught my eye. It had been on the side of the room Wesley had been in charge of so I hadn't seen it on my first sweep.

I recognized Paragon immediately, grinning from the black-and-white print. His cape was wet and clung to his form, his hair dripping onto his forehead. Even with a mask covering half his face, I could tell he couldn't have been that much older than us.

"'Sinking city plot foiled by Paragon'," I read from the headline. I frowned, suddenly uneasy. "The city sank?"

Wesley laughed and joined me in front of the article.

"Only a couple feet," he admitted with a half-cocked smile. "It would've gone completely under if not for Paragon. It's what made him the city's favorite hero until he died. You don't have to worry about any surprise swims, though. It's been a couple decades, and no one's tried sinking the city since."

I pulled away from the article. The Apex I'd met had been thwarted by an angry crowd and fold-out table. I couldn't see him saving New Delos from city-wide destruction like Paragon had.

"Do we have time to look around the rest of the museum?" I asked.

"Yeah! Snack break, first, though." He had a pencil smudge on his face after taking notes, just like he had the first day I'd met him.

"Sure," I smiled. "Snack break, first."

We found a small cafe on the fourth floor and ate our snacks out on the viewing deck that overlooked the park across the street. We made quick work of our cafe pastries and hurried back to the first floor to explore the exhibits there. It seemed most of the other students had finished working on their projects, too, and were also making their way through the artifact-lined halls.

After Wesley and I meandered through old Egyptian jewels, we stopped to stare at a sword glittering in a case at the center of a room. The pummeled hilt supported a heavy blade that was engraved in old text.

"It's a Viking sword!" I said, recognizing the style. "It looks so clean compared to the ones on the wall."

The wall behind the case housed rusted sword pieces mounted against a dark velvet backdrop. Wesley pointed at the display plaque.

"It says this one's a replica of a tenth century Viking sword. The others must be the real deal."

"Oh," I blushed. Something about the replica sword made me want to reach through the glass and grab it. "It just looked so real."

There was a derisive laugh behind us.

"It's still a real sword," Andersen smirked. He and his partner Olivia were looking at a case of helmet shards. A blond boy with an angular chin was with them. I remembered his name was Skyler. "Just not a real Viking sword."

"I know that." I turned away and pretended to be interested in a small box carved out of whale bones. Wesley followed.

"I know what you meant," he said. I grunted back. "Andersen is a jerk to everyone who isn't his girlfriend."

"It's fine," I sighed as Andersen, Olivia, and Skyler laughed behind us. Winnie, along with my own inability to keep food down on my first day here, seemed to have solidified my place in the social food chain.

The museum was much larger than I had realized and seemed to have everything and anything. There were collections of old fossils that had been harvested from the seabed where the city's foundation had been laid.

There was modern art alongside centuries-old portraits. Adrian Schrader's personal Monet collection was on full display.

We'd only explored the first floor and half of the second when we stumbled upon a brightly lit exhibit. The ceiling arched up into the third floor above it, and the museum linoleum gave way to opulent marble tiles that matched the marble statues lining either side of the hall. Greek symbols were carved into the arch over the words, "The Hall of Heroes".

"Woah," Wesley whistled, stepping into the hall. He craned his neck to look at the larger-than-life statues where they stood on their pedestals. Each one was carved out of white marble, as if they were made to adorn the Parthenon itself. Glass displays hung behind each statue, printed with text.

I recognized the statue closest to the door. Paragon's pupil-less eyes stared ahead at some unseen foe, his stone cape billowing around him. The plaque on his pedestal read, "Paragon: New Delos's Greatest Hero." Another Apex Hero that I recognized from pictures stood on the pedestal next to him.

"'Zephyress: Lady of the Wind'," I read out loud. "Are these all Apex?"

"I think they might be." Wesley pointed at a statue farther down the line. "But I don't remember hearing about George Washington being one."

I snorted in disbelief and led the way to the marbled George Washington. "George Washington: A Force for Freedom" glinted across his plaque.

"He can't have been," I said. "I thought the Apex only came about a few decades ago."

"You might be surprised to learn that The Apex have been hiding in plain sight for quite a while now," a voice said behind us. Wesley and I both flinched, neither of us having heard Dr. Cunningham join us. Up close, I could see his strong jawline under his gray-flecked beard. He looked up at the Founding Father statue with admiration etched in every line on his face. "Every statue in this hall has been sculpted in honor of history's greatest Apex."

He beckoned around the room.

"Even George Washington?" Wesley asked. Cunningham laughed.

"Oh, yes, definitely George. He was the man no one seemed to be able to hit in battle." He gestured towards a glass display case on the wall behind George Washington. Old parchment was pressed between glass panels, covered in nearly illegible cursive script. "We have a multitude of letters detailing Washington's forcefield-like abilities. No one was as strong as Paragon, though. Super strength, flight, he had everything. Truly the greatest hero."

I stared down the line of statues at a stony Ghengis Khan. At least thirty statues lined the hall and Dr. Cunningham stared up at them with the sort of pride a parent might regard their children with.

"It wasn't until this city was built as a safe-haven for The Apex that they felt comfortable coming forward. Since then, historians have recovered hundreds of documents outlining the abilities of many historical figures, many of which are featured here."

I walked down the line towards the back wall. I recognized many of the names. Marilyn Monroe, Harriet Tubman, Sir Francis Drake, William Shakespeare, and so on. I was too embarrassed to admit when I saw a name I didn't recognize. My history knowledge couldn't keep up with the Apex that filled the hall.

The final statue was slightly larger than the rest, and he surveyed the hall from under a Spartan-style helmet. His plaque read, "Adrestus the Unkillable, Father of The Apex."

Wesley snorted.

"This guy is hardly historical," he whispered, possibly so Dr. Cunningham wouldn't be offended. However, the curator was too busy telling an older woman off for using flash photography for him to notice. Wesley continued. "It's just a legend."

"I've never heard of him."

"It's well-known on the island. It's the story of how The Apex came around. An Ancient Greek warrior was granted immortality, and after living hundreds of years, he discovered the secret to creating humans with superpowers."

"Oh," I looked up at the statue, noting whoever had carved out his thighs had been very generous. "And what happened to Adrestus the Unkillable?"

"He got killed." Wesley pointed to a nearby empty pedestal. "By her."

It lacked a statue, but the pedestal still housed a plaque identical to all the others.

"'The Scourge Queen Eydis: Destroyer of The Apex'," I read. The name alone was enough to cause goosebumps to crawl across my skin. "Well, she sounds like she's a good time at parties."

"Unfortunately, the Scourge is away for routine cleaning."

Wesley and I both jumped again as Cunningham snuck up behind us once more.

"Why would you have a villain in the Hall of Heroes, though?" Wesley asked.

Cunningham nodded thoughtfully, his pale, blue eyes locking with mine as he did.

"Without adversity, we wouldn't have heroes, and as long as we have something to stand for, there will inevitably be someone who stands against us. She's an important reminder of that."

"We'll have to come back once she's out of cleaning," Wesley said politely and looked at his watch. "Hey, Samantha, it's getting late. We should head back to the bus."

I was still looking up at Adrestus, decked out in his Ancient Greek armor, swinging his sword triumphantly. He looked more threatening than heroic. Maybe the Scourge of the Apex had been onto something when she'd killed him.

"Samantha?" Wesley said my name again.

"Sorry!" I looked away from the statue and smiled apologetically. "Just a cool statue, you know?"

"You're always welcome back," Cunningham purred as he escorted us out. "Students get in free, and, really, you should see the Scourge Queen once she's done with her cleaning. She's quite something."

6

A Big Favor

Winnie caught up with me as we boarded the bus and pulled me into the seat next to her before I had the chance to consider sitting with someone else. Wesley looked back at me as I fell into the seat and kept walking to find somewhere closer to the back of the bus to sit.

"Excuse you," I mumbled, rubbing my arm where Winnie had grabbed me.

"You're fine. Listen, I've got a favor to ask." She bit her lip. I wasn't sure I wanted to know what the favor was.

"Your face is scaring me a bit. How big of a favor are we talking?"

The last of the students took their seats. Winnie glanced around at them nervously and lowered her voice.

"You know my, um, my hobby?"

"You mean the pictures?" My stomach was already twisting into a wadded mess. This was exactly what I wanted to avoid. She blushed.

"Yeah, the pictures. I've got a tip that something might be going down on the loading docks tonight, and I need someone to watch my back."

She smiled at me hopefully.

"You want me to go with you. How do you even know if an Apex will show?" I held back a laugh. Two days ago, I would've thought she was joking, but I knew better now.

The bus shuddered to life, and we pulled away from the museum.

"All it takes is one anonymous tip, and they'll be there. Listen, I get it if you don't want to go. It'll be dangerous, and if we get caught breaking curfew—"

"Whoa, back up." I cut her off. "Break curfew?"

"Oops?" Winnie grimaced bashfully. "I mean, heavy duty crime deals don't typically go down in broad daylight, you know? They happen late at night, when they can pay off security guards to let them into empty places."

"I don't know," I said. I was annoyed Winnie would put me in this position in the first place, but I was careful to let her down easy. "It doesn't really sound like my thing. Don't you have anyone else that would go with you? What did you do last year?"

"I went alone," she admitted.

I sighed.

"What kind of crime is supposed to be happening?" Just saying the words out loud made it obvious how much of a bad idea this was.

"In this kind of setting, probably just a weapons deal."

"Oh, yeah," I exclaimed. "*Just* a weapons deal. And how do you know this is going to happen?"

"I told you, I've got a source."

I raised an eyebrow at her.

"Fine, it's one of the dock security guards. He gets a cut of whatever I make off the pictures I get, and I'm willing to give you a cut, too, if you come."

"Do you even know how sketchy this all sounds?" I hissed.

"I was scared the first time, too," she insisted. "But it'll be so easy. You won't even have to do anything, probably. I have an emergency key to Amanda's car, so we just sneak over to the campus, take her car, park a few blocks away from the docks, and the guard will leave a gate unlocked for us."

"And then we wait for weapons dealers and super-humans to show up?"

"Exactly! See, you get it."

"No." I shook my head. "I don't."

Winnie huffed and slumped back in her seat.

"Think about it, okay? I'm not gonna force you to do anything, but I'd really like it if you came with me."

"I'll think about it, but I'm not promising anything else right now," I said, knowing full well I had no intention of joining her.

When we got back to the school, Winnie headed to the computer lab. She said she'd gotten some good photos the other night at the pier, and apparently someone with an Apex blog wanted to buy them.

I had resigned myself to a lonely evening in the dorms when Anthony tapped my shoulder.

"We're heading across the street to get froyo," he said. Wesley stood with him, smiling. "You wanna come?"

"Yeah!" I said, and then cleared my throat to hide my obvious excitement at being invited anywhere that wasn't a weapons deal. "I mean, sure, that'd be fun."

The frozen yogurt shop was only a block from campus. A few other students had the same idea and were making a mass pilgrimage across the street. No one was avoiding me. No one was yelling "Shoe-barf" at me. Winnie wasn't there to stress me out with thoughts of dangerous escapades across the city. The growing pains of starting at a new school were subsiding.

A line had already formed at the shop, but I didn't mind. I'd never had froyo before, and I watched in fascination as the kids in front of us pulled levers to dispense the creamy treat into bowls.

"We got almost nothing done on our project," Anthony said as we waited. "It took us forever to get to the right exhibit. We got distracted in that Apex hall."

"I heard Fleming say there'd be another chance to go back," Wesley said. Anthony sighed in relief.

"Good. We have maybe one page of notes total."

I followed Wesley in line, scooping generous amounts of fruity candy onto my frozen yogurt. He looked at my bowl.

"So, you like gummy worms?"

"Maybe." I grinned, drowning the gummy worms in a river of chocolate syrup. Wesley pulled a face.

We sat down near a table of other kids from our First Period. Even though they spoke in low voices, it was easy to overhear them.

"The island is only so big. How many places could she be?" A boy said.

"You can leave the island, Dylan. Don't be an idiot." The girl next to him snorted. "Maybe she ran away."

"Or she was kidnapped," another boy at the table suggested. "I heard a middle schooler at the secondary school is missing, too."

Anthony twisted around in his seat.

"Are you guys talking about that missing Junior?" he asked. "What was her name? Lannie?"

I remembered the girl crying in our doorway after the carnival as she looked for her roommate.

"She's still missing?" I asked.

"Yeah, maybe she fell in the bay? There were so many people, she might've been pushed over the railing."

"Don't say that," Wesley frowned. He stabbed his yogurt with his spoon. He looked miserable, and I wondered if maybe the girl was a friend of his. "She's gotta be fine. They'll find her."

The shop door jingled as another girl arrived at the shop. I recognized her from my floor. She was small, and a smattering of freckles highlighted her cheeks. Anthony shrank back into his chair.

"Speaking of disappearances," he muttered to Wesley, "it might be time for you to make one. Look who just showed up."

Wesley groaned as the girl locked eyes with us. She wrung her hands and tip-toed over.

"Hey, Wes," she said quietly, making a point not to look at Anthony or me. "Do you think we could talk?"

Wesley had turned the color of Paragon's cape.

"Do you think maybe I could finish my ice cream?"

"It's yogurt, not ice cream," Anthony said. Both the girl and Wesley glared at him.

"Hi, Anthony," she said flatly. He waved his spoon at her.

"Remi."

Remi turned back to Wesley.

"I've just been thinking, and I saw you guys walking here."

"So you followed me?"

She blushed but tapped her foot impatiently, refusing to be put off.

"Please, Wes?"

Wesley gave his froyo a forlorn look before sighing.

"Yeah, fine. But I'm bringing my ice cream."

"Yogurt," Anthony corrected again.

Wesley's chair squeaked against the linoleum as he stood up. He looked back at us apologetically.

"I'll see you guys later."

Remi led him back out onto the street. Anthony grumbled and rolled his eyes.

"Who was she?"

"Wesley's ex," Anthony said as he shoveled whip cream into his mouth. "They dated on and off a bit last year, and when it finally ended, it wasn't pretty. I swear, if they get back together again, I'm transferring."

While I enjoyed my dessert down to the last gummy worm, Anthony didn't finish his. He grumbled about how it wasn't even real ice cream and let Freddie from First Period have the rest. He invited me to dinner, but after eating at the museum cafe and having frozen yogurt, I wasn't very hungry.

I walked back to the girls' dorm, wondering what sort of awkward conversation Wesley was trapped in. It at least kept thoughts of missing students and crazy roommates at bay.

However, my crazy roommate was waiting for me in the room, ready to reclaim her position at the forefront of my attention. Winnie had changed into all black clothes. Her strawberry blonde hair was pulled into a low ponytail.

"There you are! We need to go over the plan for tonight."

I dropped my backpack on my desk and kept my back turned to Winnie. However, she forged forward.

"Try to dress in dark clothes. As soon as night falls, we'll head over to the college for Amanda's car."

I sighed.

"Winnie," I started. Her face fell at the tone of my voice.

"Come on, Sammy! You have to come!"

I had told her I would think about it, but that had just been a way of putting off telling her no. Winnie was bossy. That was something I remembered from elementary school, so she hadn't changed completely in our years apart. If I had outright told her I wasn't going to help, she would have spent every moment between the bus ride and nightfall harassing me until I changed my mind.

"Listen, I really wish I could help, but it doesn't sound safe. I heard some kids talking, and apparently they still haven't found Lannie Bryce!"

"Oh, please, I do this sort of thing all the time! You'll be perfectly safe as long as you do what I say."

"Even if nothing happens, we could still get caught breaking curfew," I pointed out. Winnie laughed.

"That's what you're worried about? That's too cute."

I bristled but instead of responding, I sat down at my desk. I pulled out my chemistry textbook and flipped furiously to the page with the assigned homework questions. If Winnie wasn't going to take me seriously, I definitely wasn't going to take her seriously, either.

"How about I cut you a deal?" she sang. "If you go tonight and don't like it, I won't ask for your help ever again."

It didn't seem like much of a deal. I didn't need to go sit on a cold dock in the middle of the night to know I wouldn't like it. The fact that I didn't want to should have been enough for Winnie, but she was stubborn and liked to get her way. Was she stubborn enough to pester me for the rest of the year until I finally gave in?

"I already know I won't enjoy it."

"No, you don't! It's actually really fun work."

She wasn't going to budge until I gave her a chance. I stared at my chemistry homework. Classwork, not crazy friends, should be the most difficult part of school.

"You really won't ask me to do this ever again?" I asked.

"I swear," she breathed. "So you'll do it?"

I sighed. I hated myself for what I was about to do. Dad would kill me if he ever found out.

"Only if you really mean you'll leave me alone."

"Yes!" She helped herself into my closet and pulled out all of my black clothes. "Samantha, this is great! I really think you're going to love it!"

I looked back at my chemistry homework. There was no way I was going to get any of it done tonight. I'd only been in class three days, and I was already making a mess for myself.

"Whatever," I said. "Just know, if I get murdered out there, or expelled for breaking the rules, I'll kill you."

Winnie only laughed.

The midnight breeze cut through my hoodie like it was nothing, and the body heat I had left seeped into the metal container beneath me. I hugged my knees close to my chest.

Winnie seemed unbothered by the cold. She stretched out on her stomach across the top of the cargo holder, a pair of what looked like military-grade binoculars pressed against her eyes. Her camera dangled from her neck over the edge of the container.

"Could you hold still?" she hissed. "You're shaking the whole thing."

I tried to stifle my shivering and pulled the neck of my jacket up over my mouth and nose, so just my eyes peeked out from under my hood. I hadn't worn it on purpose, but it was the same jacket I'd lent the Apex at the pier.

Stealing Amanda's car had been easy. Winnie knew which building her sister lived in, and we only had to prowl the parking lot for a few minutes before finding her sedan. Driving across the city to get to the docks, however, had been nothing less than a harrowing experience. Winnie was not a great driver.

"How much longer?" I asked through clenched teeth.

"My source told me they'd be here by now. There's always a chance the rendezvous got changed, but I'll hate myself if I miss an Apex."

"So we're going to be here all night if we have to?"

"Not all night," Winnie giggled. "Just until daybreak."

I rolled my eyes. No, not all night. Of course not. Just until, you know, day starts.

"You do know it's a school night, right?"

Winnie stiffened and pushed herself into a sitting position, squinting into the darkness. She held up a hand to silence me.

"Did you hear that?" she whispered.

"Hear what?" My heart jumped into my throat. I didn't want to wait out here all night, but I realized that was a much better option than possibly getting caught by criminals.

Winnie pressed a hand against my mouth. We sat motionless for several moments, but the docks were silent.

"I think you're just—"

This time, it wasn't Winnie that hushed me, but the sound of a car door slamming in the dark some distance to our left, towards the water. Winnie's eyes shone wide in what little light was available.

"We need to get closer," Winnie hissed.

"No, we do not!" I protested, and she glowered back at me.

"You promised you'd come along, you can't back out now."

She was already swinging her legs over the edge of the cargo container.

"Yeah, and here I am! But if you think I'm going to go risk being murdered by mobsters—"

"Mobsters?" she scoffed. "Please, Sam, this isn't the 1920s. But if you want to miss out on the good stuff, feel free to stay put. I'll be back after I've gotten my pictures."

"Forget your pictures, you're gonna end up dead in the bay! You don't even know if an Apex is gonna show!"

Winnie ignored me. She swung her camera and binoculars over her shoulder to keep them from bashing against the metal wall of the container as she lowered herself carefully over the side. She dropped the last few feet to the ground and landed silently.

She looked up at me, beaming with defiance. She didn't say anything else, but readjusted her camera strap and slunk into the shadows between two shipping containers.

I didn't dare even breathe. My fingers cramped where I gripped the edge of the metal. Winnie had disappeared so quickly. She might already be several rows of containers away from me.

A beam of thin light silhouetted the tops of shipping containers about five rows away. It was shining from the same direction we'd heard the car door. The same direction Winnie had gone.

The light disappeared. The only sounds came from the city behind me, but they were distant. In the darkness, there was no sign of Winnie, or mobsters, or Apex.

I was cold and alone and afraid and only here because Winnie had insisted. But I couldn't leave without her. I had come because she'd begged. Maybe she'd leave if I did the same.

I was careful as I scooted towards the edge of the container. My eyes had adjusted as much as they could to the dark, but the ground still seemed far and hard to see. I did the best I could to mimic how Winnie had dropped her feet over the side and slowly turned and lowered herself.

It was not as easy as she had made it look. The top of the shipping container was at least nine feet high, and with my arms outstretched above me, I knew I was still a few feet from the ground. I squeezed my eyes shut and dropped.

My landing would've been as graceful as Winnie's had my elbow not swung back and hit the hollow metal. My stomach turned cold, and I froze in panic. A moment passed, but I didn't hear anything.

"Winnie?" I hissed. My voice was barely louder than a breath, but in the silence, I felt like I might as well have yelled her name.

I snuck around the edge of the metal crate to where she had disappeared into the shadows of the next row.

"Winnie?" I chanced whispering into the dark a second time, cringing at how desperate I sounded.

Again, no response.

I could leave her, of course. And I wanted to. I could probably find my way back to the car and stay there hoping Winnie would know to look there for me. It's not like she'd be able to find me any easier if I decided to stay where I was. The containers all looked the same in the dark. She'd forget where she'd left me for sure.

But just as I'd made the decision to go back to the car, there was a violent clang up ahead, as if someone was beating against the side of one of the metal boxes. Half of me screamed to run, the other half screamed I was safer to stay where I was. I pressed myself against the metal, my brain numb with indecision and panic.

I steeled my nerves. I didn't dare say her name again, but I had to find Winnie so I could get us both out of here.

As I crept forward through the rows of shipping containers, I could hear what sounded like muted voices. They were too low and too far to hear clearly.

Something scurried across a metal surface overhead. As I froze, whatever it was above me followed suit. My heart thundered, and I knew someone was watching me. I raised my gaze to scan the tops of the nearest shipping containers, but saw no one.

"What the hell are you doing?"

The sound of Winnie's angry hiss scared me so bad that I jumped and let loose a terrified squeak. I clapped my hands over my mouth as if that could undo any sound I'd already made.

Winnie stood at the end of the aisle. I tried not to think about how that meant she could not have been the person running across the shipping containers overhead. The lens of her camera glinted in the dull light, of which there was just enough for me to see her face go from irritated to horrified.

A large hand clamped over my mouth, easily covering half my face. Hot breath warmed my ear as my captor leaned in.

"Another sound and you die, little bird."

7

Trouble and Trunks

Winnie was gone before the reality of the situation hit me. Everything had gone numb, like it had when I first heard the sounds in the dark. I couldn't think. I couldn't move.

Not that I would've been able to if I'd wanted. The man had one hand over my mouth and the other gripped my arm. His breath reeked of vinegar.

"You're a bit far from the dorms tonight, aren't you?"

Bits of wiry hair brushed my cheek as he straightened up behind me and led me forward. I didn't even consider trying to escape. Instead, I hoped beyond hope that Winnie was running away and calling for help.

But it was Winnie, and she definitely wasn't the shy, sensible third grader I used to know.

The man whistled a listless tune. He had taken his hand off my face to better steer me forward, but I knew if I tried to yell, I probably wouldn't last long enough to see help come.

The voices I'd heard earlier were getting closer. Dim light peeked from behind a shipping container. Shadows shifted across its plane. We rounded the corner.

"Look what I've found!"

The man paraded me into a lit aisle. Two cars were on either side of the clearing. One lit the space with its headlights while the other had backed in with its open trunk towards the people who waited for us.

A willowy woman leaned against the hood of the first car. The long skirt of her dress unsettled the dirt. She brushed a long lock of snow-white hair behind her ear as she grinned. It was the woman who'd been watching my family on the ferry.

"Great work, Hackjob," the woman purred. "Adrestus will be very pleased."

The name Adrestus set off alarm bells in my head. Who was bold enough to take the name of the immortal warrior of Apex legend?

She pushed herself off the hood and lilted forward. She cocked her head to one side as she took me in, very much looking at me the same way she'd stared at me on the boat.

"Esther," she said without looking away, "how many others are out there?"

A ginger woman stretched a palm out in front of her before replying.

"Just one."

Just one. She must've been an Apex, otherwise how else could she know Winnie was still hiding among the containers? And why, why, was Winnie still here?

The white-haired woman squinted.

"That'll be fine," she murmured. "Hackjob, throw this one in the trunk."

Everything turned cold, and I couldn't feel my hands. The scraggly man named Hackjob pushed me forward, towards the car with the open trunk.

"No!" I resisted. Hackjob's grip tightened on the back of my neck. I acted instinctively. My foot rose back, and I raked the heel of my boot down Hackjob's shin. He growled in pain, and I took my chance to twist away from him. I hit him with a hard left hook that I didn't know I was capable of delivering.

He roared and lunged at me, but the white-haired woman stepped between us. She wrapped one hand around my wrist and stretched out the other towards Hackjob. As soon as her hand made contact with my skin, my whole body tensed. It was as if an electrical current had rushed through me, causing every muscle to suddenly contract. I couldn't move. I could barely breathe.

"You can fight?" She sounded surprised. Honestly, I was, too. "Never would've known the way you collapsed on the ferry."

"Give her to me!" Hackjob roared. He shook his left foot out, and I knew his leg must still be smarting from my heel-attack.

It was difficult to even move my eyes, but I strained against my locked facial muscles to look at the woman. She glared at Hackjob.

"You've done well tonight, Hackjob." Her voice purred but hinted at venom. "I can promise a generous bounty from Adrestus, possibly enough to gain his Blessing, but that reward will be even greater if she makes it to him without any significant trauma."

Hackjob backed off, though he seemed reluctant. He bared his teeth at me, but my attention was still on the white-haired woman. She considered me thoughtfully.

"I hope you appreciate that I've just saved you from a great deal of pain," she said. "Please be sure to remember that, and be a good Beta for us."

I didn't know what a Beta was but didn't have the time to worry about it. A second current of electricity sprung from her hand, still enclosed on my wrist. My legs hobbled forward without permission. I fought against the movement, but my feet wouldn't listen as they dragged me towards the car.

The white-haired woman had to be an Apex, too, and she had complete control over my every muscle.

"The other one is getting closer," the woman named Esther warned.

The car trunk popped open. I started to climb in against my will.

"Hackjob, go find them," the white-haired woman commanded. I tried to open my mouth to scream at Winnie to run away, wherever she was. She could still get away. She could still get help. Her stupid pictures couldn't be this important.

I was laying flat on my back in the trunk, with my knees bent to the side. My arm was raised straight up above me, the woman still clutching my wrist. She lifted her hand towards the trunk door and let go of me as she closed it.

My whole body relaxed as her hold over me disappeared, and I was enveloped in darkness.

"WINNIE!" I screamed. "WINNIE, RUN!!"

She had to be able to hear me still. I thrashed against the confines of the trunk. I was afraid of a lot of things, but luckily small spaces were not among them. Being kidnapped, however...

I let out one long, continuous scream that ripped at the back of my throat. I twisted violently, feeling the car bounce from the force of my efforts. They all seemed to have powers, but I would not be taken easily.

Someone hit the outside of the trunk. I froze. There was shouting, but it was indistinct. The car bounced, as if a heavy weight had been lifted off it. More shouting.

I screamed and pounded on the side of the trunk. Winnie must've found help, but what if they didn't know I was in here? Dad had told me something about being locked in a trunk a long time ago and what to do if it happened to me. I fumbled in the dark for the corner and braced my foot against it when I found it.

The first kick wasn't nearly as hard as it needed to be. I steeled myself and kicked harder. The material splintered and after several more attempts, my boot punched through. Dusky, orange light filtered in through the hole I'd made in the taillight. I pressed my face against it to scream for help.

The shout caught in my throat. Through the jagged frame of broken plastic, I could see Esther lying on the ground. She wasn't moving. The white-haired woman stood behind her, watching Hackjob try to fight hand-to-hand against an opponent half his size, but at least twice his strength.

I recognized the dark gray, armored suit contoured to his body. His helmet glinted in the headlights of the other car. The number "7" splashed across his shoulder pad. It was the Apex from the pier.

A single round kick knocked Hackjob to his knees. He struggled to get up, but was unable to before a foot square in his chest sent him tripping backward over Esther and into the white-haired woman.

The Apex disappeared from my sightline, and I strained to see where he'd gone. The metal overhead crunched and caved in as something heavy landed on top. The car wobbled as the roof of the trunk bent backward. There was a metallic pop, and the trunk bounced open an inch.

I pushed it open. The Apex was back on the ground, running at the white-haired woman.

"Stop! She—"

My warning was too late. He lunged, but she side-stepped him easily. She swung an open palm and latched onto a bare patch of throat just below his helmet line. The Apex's armored body went rigid. The woman smiled.

"Adrestus is going to love meeting you." She cocked her head to one side as she spoke. "You'll have to ride with me, though."

Even though he was unable to move, I could tell he was struggling against her control. His whole body shook with the strain of it.

"Hey!" I shouted, half-standing, half-kneeling in the busted trunk. The woman turned, and I lunged. The same instincts that had taken over to get me out of Hackjob's grip took over again. I whipped off my zip-up jacket and wielded it ahead of me. The woman raised her free hand, but I twisted it in my coat and pinned it to her side as I tackled her to the ground.

Someone grabbed the back of my shirt and pulled me to my feet. The Apex had gotten free thanks to my impromptu linebacking skills.

"Run."

He didn't have to tell me twice. I ran towards the city lights that rose up above the surrounding shipping containers. I didn't look back at the white-haired woman and Hackjob still struggling to their feet. I didn't look back at the broken car trunk. I didn't even look back to see if the Apex was following me. I just ran straight and tried not to think about where Winnie might be.

I didn't stop until I made it past the gate Winnie and I had come in through several hours earlier. I doubled over and retched. The frigid air burned my throat, which was already sore from screaming.

A hand patted my back. I cried out and stumbled away, expecting to see Hackjob or the white-haired woman. It was just the Apex who'd now helped me out twice in one week. He was holding my jacket.

"Are you crazy?" he panted, striding towards me. I backed away from him. "Are you actually crazy? What are you doing out here?"

"I–my friend, she—" I couldn't answer his question because for all the times I'd asked myself the same thing in the last hour, I still hadn't come up with a good answer. Why did I let Winnie drag me out of the dorms for this?

"Your friend?" His snarl sounded funny coming through his voice modulator. "The same friend that took off twenty minutes ago? That friend?"

My stomach twisted.

"She what?" I gaped at him. He had to be lying, Winnie wouldn't abandon me. "No, she can't have, she drove me—"

"And she drove away." He glanced over his shoulder. "Keep moving. The big one is following us."

But I stared motionless at the pavement, barely hearing him, still reeling from Winnie's betrayal.

He grabbed my hand, wrapping his gloved fingers around my palm as he pulled me towards the city. He had seemed okay when we fought through the protesters on the pier last weekend, and Winnie had said these uniformed Apex were the good guys. However, Winnie had also just left me to be kidnapped by a bunch of goons, and despite working with the Apex previously, I wasn't in a very trusting mood.

But when it came down to it, my choices were to go with the super-strong Apex who'd just busted me out of a car trunk or risk being caught by the jerk who'd put me there to begin with. I pulled my hand away from his, but continued to follow him. We walked carefully, making sure to stay in the shadows.

"I was out here because my friend was looking for you. She wanted to prove some stupid theory about Apex at the school." She acted tough, I thought bitterly, but when it mattered most, Winnie had been a coward.

He stopped and spun to face me. The helmet didn't cover his chin, and I could see his lips pressed together in a tight line.

"Winnie's an idiot," he said. "You shouldn't listen to anything she says."

"You know her?" I said, maybe a little too loud. "You know Winnie! You are a student!"

He held up a hand to shush me.

"No, that's just the name you were shouting in the car," he covered, but I couldn't shake the feeling that he did seem familiar, and not just because I'd already met him earlier that week.

"Fine. But then who were those people at the docks?"

"I was hoping you would know." He shrugged. "We got a tip that something was going down tonight but didn't put much stock in it. Tips are usually a load of crap, but they sent me for surveillance to be safe."

"We? Who's we?" I pressed. "Is there a secret Apex team at school?"

He fell silent again.

"There is! That's why you were at the pier last weekend! You weren't keeping the protesters in check, you were at the carnival!" I exclaimed. Even though most of his face was hidden by his visor, I could tell he was glaring.

"It's easier if you don't ask questions right now."

"No." I stopped walking and crossed my arms. "I think now is the perfect time for questions. I almost got kidnapped because my idiot roommate was looking for you so I think I have a right to know who you are."

"You're the idiot that followed your idiot roommate into a dangerous situation so you don't deserve answers at all!" He stepped towards me. "And I'm the one who is going to spend the next day doing paperwork because of this whole mess you made!"

"Well, fine!" I shot back. "Next time, let them kidnap me since you obviously hate paperwork so much considering you don't shut up about it!"

I pushed past him and continued stalking down the sidewalk. He'd seemed so nice at the pier, but now he was being overbearing and self-important. The buildings rose up around us as we got farther from the water. I could hear his boots tapping the ground as he followed after me.

"That's not— I don't think you—" He struggled to find the words to come at me with. "I didn't mean it like that."

"Sure. Well, I'm sorry I don't care about your paperwork," I sneered, "but maybe you shouldn't have gone into the hero business if that's your biggest concern right now."

He grabbed my shoulder gently and turned me back around.

"You're right. I'm sorry, and I'm very sorry about this, too."

"About what?"

A black car came screeching around the street corner. We stumbled out of the way as its front tire mounted the sidewalk.

"I know you've already been forced into one car tonight, but now you need to get in this one."

8

The Apex in First Period

You know, if you had just told me you were trying to get me back to campus, I wouldn't have hit you."

He still had his helmet on, but I could feel the Apex glaring at me. The skin around his exposed lip was already turning purple. He wiped a drop of blood off his chin with the back of his gloved hand.

"I thought I was pretty clear that I was on your side."

"Just because you sprang me from one car trunk doesn't mean you get to shove me back into any other car of your choosing."

We were in the back of the black sedan. After I refused to get into the car after the Apex told me to, he'd tried to push me in. So I hit him. Now, the dark streets were flying past outside the windows. Street lights lit the car interior in flashes as we drove by. I couldn't see who was driving because of a partition between the front and back seats, like a limo driver would have.

Even though I couldn't see out the front windshield, I recognized the streets we passed. The college loomed to our left, so I knew we were almost to the high school.

"Do you have a name?" I asked.

"Everyone has a name," he replied. I rolled my eyes.

"I meant what's your name. Or at least what should I call you?"

"Don't call me anything. You won't see me again."

"Sure, I've already seen you twice in the last few days alone, but okay."

The car door opened. We had come to a stop outside the girls' dormitory. The Apex stared at me, and his lips pressed together expectantly. I snorted in exasperation.

"Yeah, fine, I'm leaving." I slid out of the car and looked back at him with my hand poised on the door. "Thanks, I guess."

He didn't respond. I glared and slammed the door.

As the car sped away, birds chirped in the trees that lined the walkway. My heart sank. How late- or early- was it? Even though the sun hadn't started to rise yet, class was probably only a few hours from now.

The dorm halls were quiet, and I tiptoed towards my room. I felt as if even breathing too loud might wake the whole floor. I fumbled in my jacket pocket and was happy to find that my keys had managed to stay there throughout the night's ordeals.

Winnie's eyes grew wide when I walked in. She was still wearing her dark clothes but was on her bed. Her laptop and camera sat in front of her.

"You're back!" she sputtered. "I-I wasn't sure what had happened to you so I—"

"You watched a stranger grab me from behind," I spat. Seeing Winnie safe on her bed, going through her pictures as if nothing had happened when I had been locked in a trunk and dragged across downtown...I had been so careful to be quiet in the hall, but now I could feel anger and all the noise that comes with it boiling in my stomach. "You watched them take me, and you left? Did you even call the cops?"

"I didn't think that—" Her eyes grew wider, and her lips parted and closed as they struggled to come up with the words to defend her.

"You didn't think anything!" I marched forward and slammed her laptop shut. "You didn't think about anything other than yourself and your stupid pictures! They shoved me in a trunk, and you did nothing!"

Winnie's face screwed up as I berated her. She burst into tears.

"Sammy, I was so scared!" The words came out between haggard breaths. "I saw him take you, and I don't know, I just ran! Something took over, and the-the police! I couldn't call them! Then they'd know what I'd been doing, and it wouldn't have helped you and—"

She took in a gulp of air that made her whole body shudder. She stared me down with large, watering eyes, her lips quivering.

"How'd you get away? I thought you'd be dead!"

"You were right about the Apex showing up," I decided to tell her, still angry but trying to quash the feeling for now. She was an idiot, sure, but she had to have been just as scared as I was. "Lucky for me, considering they locked me in their car trunk."

Winnie covered her mouth with her hands.

"No way! Which one was it, do you know?"

Her tears were already clearing, and with them, my patience.

"How am I supposed to know, don't they all look the same?"

Now it was Winnie's turn to be irritated.

"They definitely do not! Could you tell what their powers were? Flames? Levitation? Prehensile hair?"

"I don't know, strong?" I snapped. "I was a little busy trying not to be kidnapped or murdered to pay close attention."

Winnie's eyes were positively glittering now.

"That has to be Apex Seven!" she muttered as she reopened her laptop. "I knew it!"

She spun the computer around to show me a photo. Sure enough, the subject of the picture was in the same outfit as the Apex who'd helped me, but it was hard to tell if it really was the same person. She'd taken the picture at night, so, just like the picture she'd shown me last weekend, it was dark and hard to decipher.

"I guess that could be him." I shrugged. "He had a seven painted on his armor, anyway."

Winnie fell back against her pillow and threw her hands in the air.

"Samantha, do you have any idea what this means?" She was elated, which only irritated me more.

"It means you're lucky he showed up because if I'd been murdered out there, I'd've killed you."

She sat back up, grinning.

"Samantha," she whispered. "I've been suspicious of Apex being in our class. I never reported the weapons deal tip. I only had to tell you on the bus and hope one of them overheard. And they did."

"Someone in Fleming's class?" I repeated dumbly, forgetting to be angry at her. She nodded. "Wait, I was there as bait?"

My anger rekindled tenfold, but Winnie tried to douse it.

"No, no, no! Not on purpose! It kind of happened that way, but I promise I didn't bring you to lure in any Apex."

I rubbed my eyes. It had been a very long night, and now Winnie was telling me the Apex that I had now run into twice was actually in our First Period.

"Do you even know how lucky you are? To see him up close like that?"

"Do I know how lucky I am he was there to stop me from being kidnapped? Yeah, I've got a faint idea, actually."

"Sorry," she said. "You must've been so scared. I know I was."

"Forget it," I mumbled, burrowing under my blankets. I could've continued chewing her out, but my exhaustion was catching up with me. "Just don't count on me going anywhere with you ever again."

"Deal," Winnie sighed. "That's not so bad considering you probably want to murder me right now."

"Haven't ruled it out." I rolled onto my side and pulled my comforter up over my face.

Three short hours later, I was sitting in history class. There was a dull, empty ache in my stomach. Whether it was from lack of sleep or the immense stress of everything that had happened in the last twelve hours, I couldn't tell. I had managed to choke back some dry toast before class, but even that wasn't sitting well.

I held my hands in my lap. They were scraped up, as was my knee, and I didn't feel like answering any questions as to what had happened to them. A faint bruise painted my wrist purple where the white-haired woman had grabbed me. I wasn't sure why, considering her grip hadn't been all that tight. I tugged my sweater sleeves farther over my hands.

Winnie danced into class as the bell rang. Fleming gave her a stern look as she took her seat next to me, but she shrugged him off.

"Not technically late, Mr. Fleming," she chirped, pulling out her notebook and pencil. I hated how awake she looked.

"Yes, well, check the class policy," he said as he turned towards the board, "and in the future, try to be in your seat before the bell rings."

Andersen twisted around at the desk in front of me once Fleming's back was to the class.

"You look like crap," he grinned. Jamie turned, too, and gawked at the bags under my eyes. "Hope you weren't breaking curfew last night."

"Stuff it," Winnie said, too loudly. Fleming turned back towards the class.

"Eyes forward, Andersen," he said.

"Sorry, boss." Andersen leaned back in his seat. "Just making sure Samantha doesn't fall asleep at her desk. I'd hate to see her have points *docked* for sleeping in class."

He glanced backwards as he said it. I tried to swallow the lump in my throat.

"Worry about yourself, Andersen," Fleming said, the faintest hint of a warning in his voice. "Everyone, please remember, I expect the rough drafts of your Industry and Infrastructure projects next Monday, so if you need to join us for the extra museum trip tomorrow evening, don't forget to sign up after class."

He launched into the lesson, casting slides about the Bronze Age onto the board. I flipped my notebook open to an empty page and scrawled in the corner: *Andersen knows*!

I casually nudged the notebook towards Winnie. I was still mad at her, but she was the only person I could talk to about this. She glanced first at my note, then at me in confusion.

Last night, I mouthed. I had no doubt about it. Andersen knew I'd been at the docks.

Winnie's eyes widened, and she inhaled softly.

Apex Seven? She wrote back in her own notebook before pretending to be focused on Fleming's presentation.

I shrugged.

Or sketchy dock-dweller, I wrote. Winnie stifled a giggle by passing it off as a cough.

I tried to pay attention to the lesson, but it was hard with Andersen's head right in front of me. Rude, bullying Andersen. He couldn't have been the Apex at the docks. I couldn't imagine Andersen taking the time and effort to rescue anyone, except maybe Jamie, and that was still a big maybe.

But then, how else would he know? And if Winnie was right, then the Apex was in this room. Of all the people here, I'd least expected Andersen to become Suspect Number One.

I pressed the heels of my palms to my eyes. Maybe I was paranoid and Andersen really was just being his usual rude self, but he was about the right height and the right build. Plus, no one who knew him would ever guess his secret identity because no one would think Andersen would ever willingly help someone.

The hour passed slowly. I only jotted down a few notes from the lesson. Maybe Wesley would let me copy his down when we met to work on our project.

The bell finally rang, and Fleming issued one final reminder about museum sign ups.

"Also, Samantha." He waved me down from over the heads of students packing up to leave. "Could I see you a moment before you head out?"

Andersen snickered and looked back at me as he swung his backpack over his shoulder. For a moment, I hoped that it had been Andersen last night. I would've loved for him to be the one I punched.

I made my way to Fleming's desk as students filed out of the room. He was organizing his lesson material on his desk. He looked up as I got closer.

"Ah, yes, Samantha." He straightened up and pulled his glasses off his nose. "How are you adjusting to the new school? Is everything going okay?"

I tugged my sweater over my bruised wrist behind my back and gave him a carefully composed smile.

"It's fine." I pretended my voice didn't just break.

"I'm glad," Fleming said, definitely not convinced. He pulled a green slip from his bag. "So you'll have no issue coming to my office today for Study Period."

He handed me the slip.

"No, really, I'm doing great," I insisted. "I don't want to bother—"

"Give that to your Study Period teacher, and I'll see you in my office on the basement floor."

As I took the paper from him, my sleeve slid back up my arm, and I thought I saw Fleming's gaze flicker over my bruised wrist for a half second.

"I wasn't actually sleeping in class," I protested. "Andersen was just being a jerk because he's still mad about his seat."

Fleming's next class of students was beginning to show up. He gestured towards the door.

"Don't be late to your next class. It would only give Andersen more fuel."

Mrs. Young squinted at me suspiciously over the top of Fleming's green slip.

"Already behind in history class?" she asked. My cheeks warmed, but she waved me away before I could respond. "Fine, go."

Winnie wrinkled her nose at me on my way out.

"What does Fleming want with you?" It sounded like an accusation.

"No idea."

The basement floor of the main school hall was not as well kept as the upper floors. The carpet was peeling, and many of the overhead fluorescents either flickered haphazardly or didn't work at all. I wondered what Fleming could have done to the administration to be given an office here.

His door was at the end of the hall. I hesitated before knocking. What was I supposed to say? "Sorry I didn't pay attention in class. My roommate got me kidnapped last night. Promise it won't happen again"?

"Come in," Fleming said when I knocked. He looked up as I pushed in through the door. "Samantha. Please, take a seat."

He sat at his desk, which was as disorganized as the one in his classroom. A glass case towered behind him, full of old photos and dusty prize ribbons. I took the seat across from him. He folded his hands on his desk. I didn't like how serious he looked.

"How are your classes going?" he asked. I frowned.

"I told you this morning, everything's fine."

"Dr. Cunningham said you and Wesley seemed to be getting along at the museum."

"Yeah, so far he seems nice." I shifted uncomfortably.

"Good," Fleming smiled but furrowed his brow. I could tell he was choosing his words before he said them. "And how's Winnie been? I heard you're rooming with her."

"Yeah, I knew her before coming here."

Fleming nodded as if he'd known that already.

"Right, her father Roy is friends with Alison. I went to school with them, too, you know."

"You mentioned that when I checked into the dorm."

"Right," Fleming nodded. "Of course. Samantha, you know you can trust me, right? If something were to happen, you could come to me."

I wiped my palms on my jeans as they erupted in sweat. Mom had said the same thing.

"I promise everything is going great," I assured him. "Can I go now?"

Fleming leaned back in his seat and stared me down from behind his glasses with a raised eyebrow.

"Not yet," he said. "Maybe after you tell me what happened at the docks last night."

9

Sabotaged

I was going to get kicked out of school, and it was all Winnie's fault.

"I need you to answer the question." Fleming's eyebrow remained hitched, and I doubted he would lower it until I'd answered him.

"I don't think I know what you mean," I lied. My parents would kill me if I got expelled less than a week into the year. If I played dumb, Fleming couldn't prove anything.

"You aren't in trouble." Fleming's tone said otherwise. "We need to know why you were there and what happened."

I could only blink stupidly through the static in my brain as a response.

"Around 2:40 am, you encountered a group of criminals on the docks, who then attempted to kidnap you before being stopped by a member of Apex Team," he said, skimming his computer screen. "Is this all correct so far?"

"It was Winnie's idea," I blurted. There was no use lying, and I didn't feel bad throwing Winnie under the bus when she'd left me in the hands of creeps. "She wanted to get pictures of Apex to sell and—"

"And you went with her?" Fleming asked. I looked at my hands.

"There were three of them," I explained. "Two women and a man."

"Were they all Apex?"

"I don't think so. The women, yes. The man was scary, but there wasn't anything special about him. They called him Hackjob. I thought it was a stupid name."

Fleming typed all this into the computer, not looking away from the screen. When he finished, he looked back at me, waiting. I grimaced.

"What else?" he prompted.

"Are all the teachers in on the secret Apex team?" I asked. "Or is it just you?"

He glared at me over the top of his glasses, and I gulped.

"The women, what were their powers?"

"I don't know, one of them could control me when she grabbed my wrist."

I rolled my sleeve to show off the hand-shaped bruise.

He nodded.

"Our team member reported this as well."

"So there is a team of Apex at the school?"

He ignored me again.

"Did they say anything about why they were there?"

"No." I shook my head. "Winnie said it would be a weapons deal, but it was almost like they were there waiting for..."

I trailed off. It didn't make sense. Because then how would they know?

"Like they were waiting for you?"

"I don't know." I shrugged. "It was weird. Winnie must have been set up because as soon as they had me, they were ready to go. But then the Apex showed up."

"There isn't anything else you heard them say?"

"They said someone's name," I said, suddenly remembering. "One of the women mentioned someone named Adrestus."

Fleming scoffed and took his glasses off to scrutinize my face.

"Adrestus? Like Adrestus the Unkillable?"

"I could have misheard it," I said quickly. "But it sounded like she said Adrestus."

The name felt funny on my tongue. When I said it, I got the distinct feeling that there was something very important that I was supposed to remember, but couldn't quite grasp what it was. It was like walking into a room and suddenly forgetting what it was that I needed there. Was it something about the statue?

"I'm sure it is some made up moniker. Some Apex found a name he liked in a history book and adopted it." He typed more, frowning slightly. "It's not a name we've had on our radar, so thank you for that."

"So the Apex in the suit," I said, switching gears away from Adrestus, "he's in our First Period, isn't he?"

Fleming looked away from his computer to stare at me. He could probably teach classes in deadpanning as well as history.

"How many questions are you going to ask before you figure out I'm not answering them?"

I crossed my arms.

"It's not fair that everyone treats Winnie like a freak for thinking there's a secret Apex team working out of the school when there obviously is."

"If there was a secret team, and I really mean *if*, don't you think those classmates involved might resent Winnie for making every effort to expose them?" Fleming asked. "This island was built for Apex to live safely in the open, and yet most of them prefer anonymity. Winnie has made it her mission to destroy that privacy."

I felt my face go red with shame. I hadn't thought of it like that, and now I was complicit in Winnie's harassment of any classmate that might be an Apex.

"You didn't see any of the other missing persons?" Fleming forged on with his questions.

"No, but I guess they wouldn't have had room in the trunk for me if there'd been others."

Fleming bit his lip, and I wondered if he was trying not to chuckle.

"Still worth asking." He pushed his keyboard away and folded his hands in front of him with sudden conviction. His brow furrowed as he leaned forward on the edge of his seat. I shrank back into my own chair under his sudden scrutiny. "Samantha."

"Yes?" I cleared my throat. "I mean, yes, sir?"

"Has Alison, I mean, has your mother..." He trailed off as he searched for the right words. "What has she told you about, well, about the city, I suppose?"

I wasn't expecting the question.

"The city?" I half-laughed, confused. "Not much. I know she went to school here and met Dad at the college and that he doesn't like New Delos much."

"That's it?"

"Is there more she should have said?"

He shook his head and pursed his lips.

"No, that about covers it." He stood up and walked around his desk to his door. He was about to pull it open to whisk me out, but I stopped him.

"Wait!"

He looked down at me apprehensively.

"That was everything I needed," he said brusquely. "Try not to break curfew next time."

"But you didn't answer any of my questions."

"You didn't ask any questions." He pulled the door open and gestured towards the hall. "But I've asked all mine, so you're free to leave."

"Study Period isn't over yet," I pointed out, "and I asked you several questions about Apex."

Fleming scowled and let the door swing closed.

"The city is infamous for Apex activity, and there have always been rumors of an organized team based in the school, but," he raised his voice and held up a hand as I opened my mouth to interrupt, "as a rule, I refuse to acknowledge these rumors as they are unfounded, and quite frankly, ludicrous."

"But they aren't unfounded." I did my best to not smirk. "For one, my history teacher just grilled me on my run in with Apex, and then said history teacher referred to one as his 'team member'."

Fleming flushed red, his hand still frozen on the door. After a moment he returned back to his side of the desk, sat down, and buried his head in his hands. Finally, he raised his head to look me square in the eyes.

"Listen to me," he said slowly. "There is no Apex Team at this school."

"Is that what they're called? Apex Team? It's a bit on the nose, but it makes sense, I guess."

"Samantha."

"Are you an Apex, too?"

"Samantha!"

I shrank back into my chair. Fleming rubbed his temples.

"Please," he said. "I just need you to say that there is no Apex Team."

"But—"

"Please. I would hate to have to order a memory alteration."

I couldn't tell if he looked more frustrated or desperate. Either way, I had found the end of his patience. I still had so many questions, but it was clear he had no intention of answering anything, despite having all but confirmed the existence of a group of super-teens on the campus.

"Yeah, fine." I looked away. "There's no Apex Team, okay?"

Fleming's shoulders relaxed, and he leaned back, slowly exhaling.

"Thank you," he breathed. "And, please, no more late night adventures off campus. We won't be so forgiving next time."

Fleming let me spend the last few minutes of Study Period working on homework despite having just tried to rush me out of his office. It was a relief when the final bell rang, and I was freed from the awkward silence that had settled between us.

As I fought through the throngs of students eager to start their Thursday afternoon, I could see Winnie's tight ponytail a few yards ahead of me. She appeared to be headed towards the dorm, and I was thankful I had arranged to work on the New Delos Industry project with Wesley in the library.

The library was on the fourth floor of the school hall, and normally I'd force myself to take the stairs. Today, however, I probably could've fallen asleep standing up if I tried, and my legs still felt leaden after sprinting through the docks. Besides, I'd only just gotten over my weird dizziness and nausea.

I leaned into the elevator call button, and the doors slid open just as Winnie turned to look back. I ducked out of sight. Winnie would be wondering what Fleming had wanted, and I didn't feel like being interrogated again.

I snagged a table in the back of the library, next to a window that overlooked the athletic fields. Beyond them, the college stood resolute in the glittering city light, and I wondered if Dad was teaching today. I hit send on a text to Wesley, letting him know where the table was, before pulling out my notes from the museum.

A sudden weight pulled on the back of my chair, and I flinched away as Andersen's face appeared inches from mine as he leaned over my shoulder.

"Heard you got called to Fleming's office," he crooned.

"Go away."

Andersen did not go away. He released his grip on my chair and flopped into the seat across from me. In the short time I'd known him, he seemed to always travel with his pack of friends, or at the very least Jamie, so it was odd to see him alone. He leaned across the table, grinning.

"What did he want?"

"Nothing." I pulled my papers closer. Andersen was leaning over them, and they were starting to wrinkle.

"I bet I could guess." His grin widened. He looked like a shark. I'd spent the day convincing myself that Apex Seven hadn't been Andersen, but here he was again, taunting me as if he knew about last night.

"He just wanted to see how I was doing with my classes, okay?" I snapped. "Now can you please leave?"

"Jamie says she saw you coming back into the dorm at four this morning." Andersen continued. "Is that why you look like crap today?"

"If you don't leave, I will," I said flatly.

"I mean, geez, you're not that bad looking normally, but today?" Andersen chuckled. "I'm just saying, you look like you slept in the trunk of a car."

I gripped the edge of the table to keep my hands from shaking. It was Andersen last night, it had to be. Here he was to hold it over my head that if it weren't for him, I might still be in a car trunk. I hated him. I hated his smug grin, and I especially hated that now it felt like I owed him something.

"You're in my seat."

Neither of us had noticed Wesley come up to the table. Andersen rolled his eyes and made a show of getting up and offering Wesley the chair.

"Yeah, whatever," he said. "I was just telling Samantha here that she looks like crap."

"And you don't?" Wesley quipped. Andersen scowled.

"Oh, come on!" He gestured at me with an open palm. "I was being nice! I even said she normally looks okay!"

"Somehow I don't think 'Normally Looks Okay' is going to win any awards for Best Compliment," I said.

"Fine, if you want to be stuck up about it," Andersen sniffed. "I guess that's what I get for being nice."

He sauntered away, and Wesley waited a moment before speaking.

"He's right, you know."

"Excuse me?" I flushed.

"I mean about how you look," he said quickly. "No, not like that! I mean, you look tired."

I slumped back in my chair and crossed my arms at him.

"That's just a nice way of saying I look like crap."

"You don't look like crap," Wesley said empathetically. "It's just, you don't look very awake."

"Yeah, well," I pushed away a couple stray hairs that had fallen from my ponytail and glared at him, "didn't sleep great."

"Winnie keep you up?"

I snorted.

"Actually, yeah, she did," I said, spreading my notes back out on the table. "How'd you guess?"

"Her last roommate only lasted a week. She mentioned Winnie never slept, and by that first Friday, she kinda looked like you do now."

I looked up from my notes to glare at him again.

"Tired!" He swallowed. "She looked *really* tired. And then she suddenly transferred. She didn't say it was because of Winnie, but we all figured."

If Winnie had put her roommate last year through the same things she'd done to me, I couldn't blame her for leaving. I was still surprised at myself for not murdering Winnie last night.

"Winnie can be...She can be a lot."

"No kidding, I think you might be her only friend here."

My stomach clenched uncomfortably. Being Winnie's only friend sounded like too much responsibility.

"I knew her growing up," I admitted. "It's been a while since I've seen her, but she wasn't that bad back in the third grade."

Wesley laughed, pulling out his own notebook. He looked over the papers already on the table and wrinkled his forehead.

"Hey, did you have the sketches we did of the lift system and the turbines?"

"Yeah, they should be here." I reached for where I'd set them on the table, but they weren't there. I stood up and rustled through the papers. "They should definitely be here, I just saw them."

Wesley flipped through his own notes, but I knew the sketches had been with mine. He looked up at me gravely.

"You don't think..." He turned to look towards the library doors, where Andersen had just left.

"No." I shook my head. "I would have noticed if he'd stolen my homework."

But I wasn't sure. If he really was an Apex, he might have all sorts of tricks that'd allow him to take things right in front of me without noticing.

"What is it?" Wesley waved a hand at me. I shook my head, realizing I had just completely glazed over.

"Is there something weird about Andersen?" I asked, staring at the library exit.

"You mean other than the obvious?" Wesley raised an eyebrow.

"No," I sighed and sat back down. I deliberated for a moment and then leaned in. "Can you promise not to think I'm crazy?"

"Sure, but that sounds like something only a crazy person would ask."

"I think Andersen might be a secret Apex." I said it quickly, as if saying it faster would make it sound less insane. Wesley's eyes widened.

"Okay, now you're starting to sound like Winnie."

"It was Winnie's fault this whole thing happened to begin with!" I whispered. "She dragged me out to the docks last night after curfew and basically left me for dead when these, I don't know, creeps showed up."

A ghost-like pallor seeped across Wesley's face.

"She what?" He shook his head. "Hold on, why—"

"Because she's Winnie," I said, exasperated. "What other reason does there need to be? Yeah, I shouldn't have gone with her, obviously I figured that much out after I was shoved in a car trunk!"

"You were what!?"

"Quiet!" I hissed. "That part doesn't matter! What does matter is how I got out."

I glanced around the library again, but our back corner was still empty. I leaned in even closer.

"An Apex showed up and got me out. I've got this gut feeling that it was Andersen."

Wesley's face fell. He shook his head.

"I take back what I said. I definitely think you're crazy."

My heart dropped.

"I'm serious!" I hissed.

"Me, too! First off, think about who you are talking about here. Andersen? Help someone?" Wesley smirked. "Not to mention we aren't allowed out of the dorms after eight on school nights."

"Didn't stop me and Winnie."

"Doesn't matter! Andersen might not care about rules or people, but he definitely isn't about to go break rules for other people."

"Unless he wasn't breaking any rules."

"Now you really do sound like Winnie. Is this the secret school squad theory she has?"

I hadn't expected him to sound so condescending. My cheeks warmed.

"No. Kind of. Fleming was acting real weird about it today, though! He even said the words 'Apex Team'! He's gotta be in on it. And if teachers are in on it, then maybe the students involved have special privileges!"

Wesley pushed his chair away from the desk, shaking his head.

"You need to stop listening to your roommate."

"I'm telling you, it was Andersen!" It was taking all of my self control not to yell. "And trust me, I wish it wasn't because now he gets to hold it over me for however long he likes."

Wesley laughed. A girl across the room looked up from her homework to glare at us.

"You wouldn't be laughing if you'd been there." I lowered my voice back down to a whisper. Wesley rolled his eyes at me. "He was insane. He ripped the trunk door off of the car!"

Wesley's smile dissipated.

"I really doubt Andersen is able to—"

"And he beat the crap out of a guy twice his size. I hate that it was him, but it was incredible."

"Okay, I get it!" Wesley looked downright stormy now. "Andersen's amazing and powerful and can do anything. Whatever. You know, I really thought you were smarter than to fall for Winnie's nonsense."

"It's not nonsense," I said, trying to ignore the sting in Wesley's words. "Do you not hear what I'm saying? I saw it, it was him."

Wesley stood up and picked up his backpack.

"Where are you going? We haven't even started working yet!"

He slung his backpack over his shoulder.

"How are we supposed to work without those sketches?" he demanded. "Besides, you aren't making any sense so maybe we should just reschedule. It isn't even due until next week."

I stared at the loose papers still strewn across the desk.

"Fine, you can go. I'll work on it on my own."

"What you should do is go take a nap."

The room froze and I could tell by Wesley's face that he knew he'd said the wrong thing.

"And maybe you should mind your own business."

"Yeah, maybe I should."

Wesley stalked away from the table, leaving me dumbfounded as to what had just happened. We'd been laughing minutes ago. Now, my hands were shaking with barely contained anger.

"Super job," I whispered to myself. That's what I got for trusting someone. By morning, I could count on being the New Winnie after Wesley starts telling everyone I thought Andersen was an Apex.

But he is! I screamed in my head. *I'm not the crazy one here!*

I began stuffing my papers back into my bag. Moments ago, I had worried about them getting wrinkled. Now, I could see them conglomerating in my bag as one giant, crumpled mess, squished between a binder and a notebook.

I kept my head down the entire way back to the dorm. Even if Winnie was there, at least she didn't think I was crazy. The dorm lounge was full of students hanging out and working on school assignments. Jamie was in the corner with Naomi and Madison. I could see her looking at me from the corner of my eye, but I ignored her.

As I expected, Winnie was in the room. She looked up from her desk as I came in, and her face lit up.

"There you are! I wanted to ask about your meeting with Fleming. You never came back to Study Period."

There it was. The interrogation I'd been expecting from her.

"He wanted to see how school was going," I lied. "My mom probably put him up to it."

Winnie's expression fell.

"That's it? I thought maybe he knew you'd broken curfew."

"Nope." I crawled onto my bed with my shoes still on to lie face down on my pillow, trying to shut out Winnie.

"What about Andersen?" She continued to press on. "This morning you thought he might be Apex Seven."

"Mhmm." I kept my face pressed against my pillowcase.

"Do you still think so?"

"Yup."

Winnie was the only person who was going to be straight with me about The Apex, and she was the only person who was going to openly believe me about what happened at the docks, so why did it still sting to think about Wesley telling me I sounded like her? She was the only person being nice to me, but I couldn't stand that she was the only friend I had.

Leaving you to be kidnapped by the bad guys isn't nice, I reminded myself.

"That's it? Come on, you've got to give me more!"

I flipped onto my back and fished my phone out from underneath me.

"There's not any more to give," I sighed, pulling up my text messages. I tapped on Dad's icon. "It doesn't matter, does it?"

"How could you say that?" Winnie got up from her desk and sat down on her bed across from me. "Of course it matters!"

"He's either an Apex or he isn't. Either way, it doesn't really affect us." I propped myself up on my elbow to look at Winnie. "You keep investigating, and sell your pictures or whatever it is you plan on doing, but I'm done."

I flopped back down against my pillow and held my phone over my face as I typed out a message to Dad.

Miss you. Dinner tonight, please?

I hit send and set my phone back down. It buzzed immediately.

No.

Before I had the chance to be offended, the phone buzzed again, and a second message appeared under the first.

JK. I'm hilarious. Pick you up at 6.

Winnie had pulled her laptop out and was scrolling, squinting at the screen. When she found what she was looking for, she spun the computer around to face me. I continued to look at my phone.

"I already told you, I can't really tell if it was the same guy. Your picture is too dark."

"Oh, this is a different picture." I didn't like the edge in her voice. It was incensed and a little accusatory. I turned to look at the new picture, and everything inside me turned to ice.

I was on her screen with my back to the camera, my zip-up jacket held loosely at my side. My head craned back to look at the Apex as he waved down at me from the fire escape in the alley.

"You spied on me?" I hissed through gritted teeth.

"Yeah, well, you lied to me!" she said indignantly. "Good news for you, I'm willing to look past it."

I covered my head with my pillow. It wouldn't do any good to yell at her, but, wow, was Winnie aggravating.

"I didn't want to be involved," I said slowly, still under my pillow. "I knew you'd do something like this if I told you."

"Like what?"

I threw the pillow across the room and leaped off my bed to get in her face.

"Like this! Like last night! That's why you brought me! I *was* bait!"

"You know how frustrating it is that I have spent the last several years tracking these guys and you meet one face-to-face your first full day here?" Her face was beet red. She slammed her laptop shut. "Of course I needed you there, you already have rapport with one! And it's freaking Apex Seven!"

"I don't want to have rapport with anyone!" I shouted back. "I didn't want you dragging me into this mess! It's no wonder no one here wants to even talk to you!"

There was a knock at the door. We both froze.

"Everything okay?" Renee asked in a sing-song voice.

"Yes!" we both shouted.

"Okay, but if you need anything, I'm trained in conflict resolution. You are too good of friends to fight!"

We stood silently, listening to Renee's footsteps retreat. I closed my eyes and rubbed my forehead.

"I'm sorry, I shouldn't have said that last part."

Winnie shrugged.

"It's true, though. I'm a liability, and they all know it."

"I want to have a normal year," I pleaded. "No Apex, no late night kidnappings, and no more car trunks."

Winnie smiled but still looked sad.

"I get it. Tell you what, you just tell me one last thing, and I'll drop it forever."

"Forever?"

"This is the last thing, I promise."

I raised an eyebrow at her.

"I mean it," she insisted.

I sighed heavily as she opened her laptop back up. She gestured towards the picture.

"That was the same Apex you saw last night?"

"Yeah."

"And you really think that maybe he could possibly be Andersen? Look closely."

I leaned into the picture. It was hard to say. I had caught a glimpse of his brown hair, which Andersen also had.

"Sure, if you put Andersen in a suit and mask, he might look like that."

"Is that really the most definitive answer you can give me?" Winnie huffed.

I shrugged.

"Until you get a picture of him pulling his helmet off, yeah. It is."

"Fine." She turned the screen back towards herself and slumped back against the wall. "But if you feel like it, I'll happily welcome you back into the investigation."

"You won't have to worry about that." I kicked my shoes off onto the floor and rolled onto my side, away from Winnie. My mind was made up. I was done with Apex.

I couldn't help but smile when I saw Dad's car idling out front. He hadn't seen me yet, but I could see him bobbing his head to his music and tapping out a beat on the steering wheel. When he finally glanced out the window and saw me getting closer, his beard stretched into a grin. The car door flew open, and suddenly my neck was in the crook of his elbow as he pulled me close.

"Hey, kid," he chuckled and kissed the top of my head. I pulled the sleeves of my cardigan down over my hands to hide my scrapes and bruise. "How's sushi sound?"

"I'm pretty sure my cafeteria credits work at the college," I said, climbing into the passenger seat.

"You want me to pass up an excuse to get sushi?"

"I'm not sure if I like sushi," I admitted. "Actually, I'm not sure I've ever even had it."

It was common knowledge that Mom hated seafood, which was probably why Dad wanted to take this chance to get it. Whenever we'd gone out as a family, it was always burgers or Italian and never seafood, despite it being Dad's favorite.

"Oh, you're gonna like sushi," Dad assured me, turning down a street opposite the college campus. We were driving deeper into the city now.

He found street parking downtown. We were only a few blocks away from where the Apex that had saved me had shoved me into the back of the black car.

Where Andersen shoved you into the back of the car, I reminded myself. I did my best to squash all thoughts of Apex, docks, and Andersen. Dinner was for me and my dad.

The restaurant was on the boardwalk, overlooking the ocean. Being a Thursday night, it wasn't too crowded inside, and a waiter was able to seat us next to a window.

"What's up?" Dad asked. "Why the sudden dinner invite?"

I shrugged.

"I told you, I just miss you."

He plucked an edamame up from the bowl the waiter had just brought us and sucked on the end.

"Yeah, I'd miss me, too. How's school going, then?"

I stared out the window at the water. The sun hung over the ocean, turning the horizon orange. It'd start getting dark in another hour or two. Would those creeps be out again, looking for someone else to take?

"It's okay. The classes are fun, I guess. We already went on a field trip to the museum."

"Field trip?" he said quickly. "I didn't sign any field trip forms."

"Mom did."

"Huh," Dad grunted, discarding his empty edamame shell before going for another. He glanced at the order card and checked off several boxes before handing it off to a waiter. "Don't worry, I only ordered good things. How's Winnie?"

Somehow, it felt like being associated with Winnie had become the most interesting thing about me.

"She's fine," I admitted, "but she can be really intense."

"She was intense as a little kid, too. She gets it from her dad, I think."

I stared at the backs of my hands. I was being careful to keep my palms facing the table top so that Dad couldn't see the scraped skin.

"What's wrong?" Dad prodded. I shrugged, still looking at my knuckles.

"I feel bad for Winnie, I guess. No one really likes her, and since she's my only friend, no one seems to like me much either."

Dad frowned and leaned forward.

"I like you," he assured me.

"Yeah, but that's your job."

"It still counts." His expression softened. "I'm sorry Winnie is giving you trouble. Is that why you wanted to go to dinner with me?"

I shrugged.

"It was either go to the cafeteria with Winnie or go alone, and I didn't feel like doing either one."

"I see how it is," Dad said, putting on an air of fake indignation. "You don't really miss your poor old dad, you just wanted to use me for food."

"No, I did miss you!" I laughed. "It just also happened to solve my dinner problem."

"I'm happy to help," he said seriously. "Just know that I can't take you to dinner every night. You're a cool kid, you'll make friends, and Winnie will calm down."

"Sounds like everyone has been waiting for her to calm down since the beginning of last year," I snorted. "She's obsessed with Apex. And I mean really obsessed."

"That's not all that surprising," Dad frowned. "A lot of people in the city are fascinated by them, don't ask me why."

A waiter swung by the table, dropping off the first plate of rolls. Dad's face lit up. He deftly scooped a few onto his plate before noticing me struggling with the chopsticks.

"You're as hopeless as Alison." He reached over and positioned them in my hand. "Try not to embarrass me, I want to be able to come back."

I maneuvered a roll onto my plate and beamed back at him. He chuckled and gestured at the plate, his mouth already full.

"This one is a salmon roll," he mumbled. "Try and eat it in one bite."

I balanced it carefully between the chopsticks and tried not to visibly grimace as I pulled the raw fish closer to my face.

"It's good, I promise." He was already working on his next piece.

I dropped the sushi in my mouth.

"Woah," I said, between chews. "You said Mom doesn't like this stuff?"

Dad laughed. He'd been right. Sushi was amazing.

By the time we left, we'd cleaned four plates of rolls and a fifth plate of sashimi just between the two of us. I was amazed at how full I felt walking out.

"Thanks for dinner, Dad," I said as we walked back to the car. The sun was dipping under the ocean's horizon now.

"Anytime, kid." He patted my shoulder. "You can call us whenever. We like hearing from you."

I smiled.

"And, Samantha?"

I looked up at him.

"You be careful in this city. Winnie isn't the only one obsessed with Apex on the island. Just try to be safe, alright?"

I tugged on my cardigan sleeves and grabbed my bruised wrist with my other hand behind my back. He didn't need to know about the Apex I'd seen twice now. Besides, moving forward, I had no intention of seeing him again.

10

Return to the Museum

With a belly full of sushi, I had the best night of sleep I'd had in a week, and the next morning in the cafeteria, I was happy to be feeling awake and healthy. I didn't even mind that Winnie was the only person willing to sit with me. Wesley avoided me in the line for hash browns, but I shrugged it off. I was determined to have a good day.

"I think Naomi and I are going to go on the extra museum trip tonight," Winnie said between sips of orange juice, watching Naomi across the room. She was sitting with her usual crowd, Jamie and Andersen sitting in the center, demanding everyone's attention.

"Yeah?"

"We worked on it a bit last night," she said, "but there are a couple things we're missing for our poster board."

I stared over Winnie's shoulder at Wesley. He was eating with a couple of his friends, but he sat back in his seat and didn't seem to be taking part in their conversation.

"We might have to go, too." I left out the part about Andersen stealing our homework. I wasn't about to sour what was going to be a good day by reopening the subject into whether or not Andersen was a super-human. Luckily, Winnie didn't care enough to ask questions.

"At least we'll be able to go together." She smiled at me, but it quickly slid into a frown. "Hey, I wanted to say sorry. I shouldn't have made you go to the docks, and I definitely shouldn't have left you behind."

I stared at her in surprise. Winnie was more likely to sprout wings than she was to apologize.

"I'm over it," I said honestly. She smiled in relief. "It's behind us. Just don't ask me to come with you ever again."

"I already told you that I won't!" She blushed and looked away. "But thanks."

As we finished eating, I told Winnie to go ahead without me. She gave me a curious look but obliged, bouncing out of the cafeteria to First Period. Andersen and his crew were still sitting at their table.

Maybe it was because I was feeling better than I had in a long time or maybe it was because I didn't want to spend my Friday night back at the museum doing school work, but I stalked up to their table, my rage and sudden confidence manifesting on my face as a wide, expectant grin.

"You need something?" Andersen sneered.

"Yeah, actually," I said. "Those papers you took from me yesterday. You know, in the library?"

Andersen smiled and cocked his head to one side.

"I didn't take your stupid papers." Several of his friends giggled.

"Yes, you did. They were on the table, and you took them."

"Geez, calm down," the blond boy named Skyler said. My face flushed. Andersen sighed and leaned back, his hands behind his head.

"Listen, if this is all some ruse to just be able to talk to me, I get it—"

"You think I owe you, but I don't!" I slammed my hands on the table and leaned across to get in Andersen's face. "I didn't need or want your help, and you don't get to do whatever you want because that's not how this works!"

Jamie turned to Andersen, confused.

"What is she talking about?"

Andersen glowered at me in response.

"Come on, Andersen," Naomi grunted. "Just give her papers back, and she'll go away."

"I'd love to give you back your stupid drawings," he snapped, "but I dumped them in a garbage can somewhere between the library and the dorms. Consider it a favor, because they really were trash."

Someone touched my shoulder. I spun around to see Wesley glaring.

"It's fine," he insisted.

"He just admitted that he threw away our work!"

"We can redo it."

"We shouldn't have to!"

"Come on." Wesley led me away from the table. Andersen's friends jeered as we walked away. "You'll just add fuel to his fire."

"He's never going to stop if no one stands up to him. He doesn't get to think he is better than everyone else, not for any reason."

Wesley raised an eyebrow at me.

"Any reason? Like being a secret Apex?"

"Yeah, like being a secret Apex," I snapped.

Wesley shook his head.

"Our project will be fine. We can sign up to go back to the museum tonight to finish it. Nothing is ever going to stop Andersen from being a creepy jerk, so just leave it."

Wesley turned his back and marched away before I could argue further. I watched the back of his backpack until he rounded the corner towards the main school hall. Andersen's friends were still laughing behind me.

When I finally trudged into First Period and fell into my seat next to Winnie, she looked at me with a raised eyebrow.

"Why's Wesley glaring at you like you filled his cereal with sour milk?"

"He's just mad that we have to go back to the museum," I lied. It didn't make sense that Wesley was so worked up with me. Anthony gave me an awkward wave as I sat down, but he glanced at Wesley and then down at his desk.

Andersen walked in with Jamie hanging off of him. He glared at me from the doorway, and I felt a surge of satisfaction knowing I had gotten under his skin. I wondered if Jamie knew he was an Apex, or if she'd even care. Andersen probably wasn't willing to risk her finding out if she didn't know already.

"Geez, he looks mad at you, too!" Winnie whispered. The bell rang overhead and Andersen begrudgingly took his seat in front of us. "Maybe I should've hung back in the cafeteria a little longer this morning."

I only grunted in response.

I'd been so determined to have a good day, but after I confronted Andersen, and Wesley then confronting me, any hope of that seemed to have been lost. Luckily, Andersen avoided me for the rest of the day, but Wesley did, too, which in turn meant Anthony was also keeping his distance. I saw Anthony in the lunch line, but he avoided eye contact. He even stayed away in gym, despite the fact that Wesley wasn't in that class with us.

I was stuck hanging out with Winnie for lunch and dinner, scrambling to find a bright side to having to go back to the museum. I'd be stuck dealing with Wesley's broody attitude, but if we finished fast enough, I could explore more exhibits. Maybe the statue of the Scourge Queen was done being cleaned.

After dinner, I walked with Winnie to the rotunda out front of the main hall. Only three groups needed to go back to finish off their projects, so Fleming loaded us into a school van rather than a bus. Wesley still wasn't looking at me so I sat in the back row of seats between Winnie and Naomi.

Naomi spent the short ride staring out the window. I had thought she might take up Jamie's crusade of making everyone around her feel like crap, but she didn't seem bothered enough. Winnie was scanning her notes on my other side. I stared at the back of Wesley's head, stuck between Anthony and his project partner, Charlie, in front of us.

Fleming pulled the van up to the curb outside Schrader Tower, and we filed out onto the sidewalk. Dr. Cunningham waited at the museum entrance.

"You've got two hours," Fleming said through the open passenger door. "Dr. Cunningham is in charge while you are visiting his museum, and he will tell me if anyone misbehaves."

"Sure thing, Mr. F," Anthony said, slamming the door. Dr. Cunningham waved Fleming away, reassuring him he had it under control.

"Remember," he told us as he shepherded us up the stone steps, "the museum technically closes in a half hour, but Mr. Schrader has granted you access until Mr. Fleming returns." He handed us each a badge as we walked into the foyer."The doors to each exhibit lock automatically at eight, but these keycards will get you into wherever you need."

I looped the lanyard around my neck and turned to Wesley, who forced himself to be busy with his notes.

"We lost the sketches of the ballast system, so I'm going to redraw those ones first, and since we're here for two hours, we could probably find more stuff to add if you like."

"Hmm? Oh, yeah, sure," Wesley mumbled. He flipped his notebook shut. "I was thinking about maybe adding something about the storm-safety mechanism since we are going to be up there anyway."

The others were already dispersing to various rooms. There were only a few other visitors despite it being a Friday night, and most were on their way out. The City Hydraulics exhibit was empty, save a single patron lingering over a set of backlit city schematics in the corner.

"Over here." I led Wesley to the charts I'd wanted to add to the report. "If you copy down the notes on the tidal lift system, I'll do the ones on the internal energy turbines. And if there's time, it'd be cool to try to sketch out the city model to put behind our poster title."

"Sure, yeah, that'd be cool," Wesley echoed. He was determined to look anywhere that wasn't at me.

"Thank you for visiting The Schrader Industries Museum," a cool voice said over the intercom. "The exhibits will close in five minutes."

We were the only ones in the exhibit now. I braced my notebook against the wall next to the glass case and jotted down all the important notes on the city's underwater turbines that fueled almost all the electricity on the island. It was hard to focus, though, with Wesley doing his best to pretend I wasn't there.

"Should I include this bit here about the filters?" I pointed to a sketch under the glass cover. "I don't know if it really applies, but it might be good."

"Yeah, looks good," Wesley said without looking over.

I threw my notebook down on the glass and crossed my arms. Wesley froze, but stayed hunched over his work. I could tell he was watching me carefully in his peripheral vision.

"Is there a problem?" I demanded. "Like, did I do something? Say something? Is this about what I said in the library? Because it's not fair for you to call me crazy and then go on to act super weird."

"I think you're imagining things." He pretended to keep working.

"You're doing it right now!" I pointed at his paper. "Look! You're rewriting the same sentence over and over just to avoid looking at me!"

Wesley dropped his pencil and straightened up. For someone who claimed to be fine, he looked incredibly resentful.

"Is this better?" he snapped.

"See? You're being weird! What did I do?" I pleaded.

"You didn't do anything," he said. "It's fine. I'm fine."

"Obviously you're angry at me."

"I'm not angry."

"Then why are you upset?"

"I'm not."

"Then stop ignoring me!"

Wesley glared at me and picked his notebook back up.

"I'm going to go trace the schematics." He pivoted to cross the room. I followed.

"Please, just tell me what's wrong."

"How about you drop it?" He tore a paper from his book and laid it over the glass with the schematic drawings. He penciled over the lines, aided by the case's backlighting.

"How about you help me understand and maybe I can fix it."

He whirled to face me.

"If help is what you need, why don't you ask Andersen?"

He flushed red and turned back to his work.

Andersen? What did Andersen have to do with anything?

"I don't–I can't stand Andersen!" I blurted. "Why would I ask him for anything ever?"

Wesley kept his back turned resolutely towards me, furiously shading in part of his tracing.

"I don't know what Andersen has to do with anything, alright?" I said gently, forcing myself to sound calmer than I felt. "If it makes you feel better, you're way cooler than him. Or at least I thought you were."

Wesley looked back at me. His face was still bright pink.

"I'm sorry. I shouldn't have said anything. I promise to be less of a jerk."

A small cut stood out against the flushed skin of Wesley's lip. The wound looked a couple days old and like it was almost healed. He'd avoided looking at me all day, so it was the first time I'd gotten a clear look of his face since the library. Even then I'd been so preoccupied with Andersen, I wouldn't have noticed. My jaw went slack. All the pieces of the bigger picture were coming together, but I couldn't quite get them to fit in my mind.

"Oh," I whispered, raising my own hand to my lips as if I'd feel Wesley's cut there. "OH!"

Wesley was angry because I thought it had been Andersen at the docks. But it hadn't been Andersen.

"Forget it," Wesley said, too quickly. "It doesn't mean anything, I'm sorry."

I stared back at him blankly, still trying to make it make sense.

"Samantha," he pleaded. "I'll get in so much trouble."

There was a sudden thud. We both turned to see a security guard outside the exhibit doors slumped on the ground.

"Hey!" I yelled and ran towards him.

"Don't!" Wesley shouted. The exhibit doors slammed shut before I could make it out of the room.

11

Swords and Statues

The main lights flickered off, and we were left in darkness for the few moments it took the emergency floor lights to come on.

I tried the doors, but they were locked.

"Sam, get back." Wesley pulled me away from the doors.

"He's hurt!" I held the badge Dr. Cunningham had given us up to a pass-scanner. It beeped, but the doors didn't budge. "It's not working. You try yours."

Wesley shook his head.

"Something isn't right," he said. "We need to stay put. At least the doors are locked so no one can get in."

We both froze as screams rang out down the cordoned hallway.

"Never mind, you're right," I whispered. "We can stay here."

Wesley pressed his ear up against the door. He strained for a moment, and then his eyes went wide.

"We're leaving," he said. "Stand back."

"No, it's fine! We can stay!" I'd had enough close calls in the last week. I wasn't eager for another.

He backed up as far as he could before charging at the doors. He dropped one shoulder like I'd seen football players do on TV. The doors splintered and metal bent as Wesley charged. It clattered violently to the floor under him.

"We need to move!" He beckoned for me to follow. I looked around for the security guard, but he was gone. "They'll have heard that!"

"Who's they?" I asked, running down the hall beside Wesley, passing other darkened halls and exhibits. "And you! You're the Apex! You're—"

A roar bellowed at our backs. I turned and saw Hackjob bearing down on us. Wesley skidded to a stop and threw me behind him. I stumbled to the floor.

Wesley stood between me and Hackjob with his shoulders squared and ready to fight. Hackjob came to a halt, peering at Wesley from behind a filthy curtain of wiry blonde hair.

"I'm just here for the girl," he snarled. "No reason for you to get hurt, too."

Wesley's back tensed as he whipped his glasses off and raised his fists.

"Sam, find the others and get to the exit."

But I was still reeling. Wesley was Apex Seven. It had been Wesley the whole time. And here we were, in peril together again for the third time this week.

"I said move, boy!" Hackjob's small amount of patience had already run out. He raised an arm to backhand Wesley out of his way, but Wesley caught him by the wrist and swung him into the wall. Hackjob's eyes narrowed in recognition.

"You wouldn't be the Helmet from the other night, would you?" Hackjob grinned, showing off a set of teeth that was surprisingly white given the dirty state of the rest of him.

"Sam, I'm serious!" Wesley warned. I scrambled to my feet. If Wesley really was the Apex from the docks, and judging by the way he demolished the exhibit doors, he had to be, he'd already beaten Hackjob once. I'd only get in the way if I stayed.

I spun around and ran back down the corridor, my sneakers echoing on the tiled floor. There was a shout, and something smashed behind me.

"Wesley!" I stumbled to a stop at the top of a flight of stairs to look back, but I had turned a corner and couldn't see them anymore.

"Keep going!" Wesley's shout was strained. My feet were glued to the floor. He needed help. I had managed to land a left hook on Hackjob before. Maybe the two of us together would stand a better chance.

But then, more screams rang out from the lower floors. I recognized Winnie's shrill shriek. As tough as Winnie was, she couldn't hold her own like Wesley could. I raced down the steps two at a time, skipping the last few steps to the main floor.

The fountain bubbled in the middle of the otherwise silent foyer. Night had fallen outside, and street lights cast long, glowing rectangles across the marble floor. Maybe Winnie had made it outside. Maybe if I reached the street, I could find help.

I bolted for the entrance doors, but as I reached my hands forward to push my way through to the stone steps outside, I slammed into an invisible wall. I fell back onto the ground, rubbing my smarting forehead.

I reached a tentative hand towards the glass, but a full foot before I could touch it, I pressed against something solid.

"It's a forcefield." The raspy voice bounced off the empty floor of the foyer. I staggered to my feet to face the man who'd come up behind me. He wore all black and sneered at me from where he sat on the edge of the fountain. His hair was gelled back, and despite his haughty demeanor, he looked bored. "My forcefield, actually. Do you like it?"

The man looked familiar, but I couldn't place his face. He hadn't been at the docks with Hackjob, so where had I seen him before?

"Miles, quit messing around," a spine-tingling voice crooned from one of the side exhibits. The white-haired woman stepped out of the exhibit to my left, hand-in-hand with a petrified Anthony. My breath caught in my throat as his terror-stricken eyes locked with mine.

The white-hair woman led him towards a dark hall near the back of the foyer, and Anthony followed with jerky, robotic movements. He had no choice but to let the woman lead him away.

"Leave him alone!" I shouted. I charged across the foyer, and the woman looked back at me to watch as I crashed head-first into another forcefield. I sprawled across the floor to the echoing sound of Miles's laughter.

"Don't take too long," the woman warned. "She put up a fight against Hackjob the other day. Best keep it clean and simple."

She turned back and led Anthony into the shadows of the back hall.

"Anthony!" I screamed, slamming my fists against the forcefield. Miles continued to laugh after Anthony had disappeared down the hall, and I spun to face him. "Where is she taking him?"

He shrugged, getting up from his perch on the fountain. A lopsided grin spread across his face. He pulled a small, white patch from his pocket and held it gingerly between two fingertips.

"Just be a good kid, alright?" He held up his free hand, as if to show he wasn't armed, despite the mystery patch in his other hand. I eyed it warily and stepped back so that I pressed against the forcefield.

Where was Wesley? He couldn't still be fighting Hackjob, could he? If I yelled for him, would he be able to escape or would he end up fighting both of them?

Miles sauntered forward, grinning as he savored cornering his prey. The closer he got, the more I felt I recognized him. He was only a few feet away when I figured it out.

"You were leading the protest!"

The protest at the pier had been overwhelming and crowded, but I had still managed to get a good look at the man with the megaphone, whipping the crowd into an Anti-Apex fury. He was the same man lumbering towards me now.

"You were there?" He grinned, looking pleased at having been recognized. "Tell me, did I come off as too forced? Esther said I sounded forced."

"But you're an Apex," I said, half out of curiosity and half out of the need to keep him talking while I looked for an escape. "What were you doing leading an Anti-Apex protest?"

He snickered as he closed the distance between us, and his fingers played with the rectangular patch.

"Just hold still, alright?" he murmured. "The easier you make this for me, the easier you make it for you."

He raised the patch towards my exposed neck. I could feel him watching my face as I watched it draw closer.

"That's it," he whispered. "Nothing to be afraid of."

I didn't know what the patch would do to me and decided I wouldn't hang around to find out. His gaze narrowed in the split second before I grabbed his wrist and twisted his arm behind him. He shouted as I threw him to the floor with strength I didn't know I had.

I sprinted at the nearest exhibit. Unsurprisingly, I smashed into yet another forcefield, but at least managed to stay standing this time. Miles's laugh was cold and humorless.

"That's three times you've done that now."

I rubbed my forehead, blinking rapidly to clear my vision. Miles scowled at me and smoothed the wrinkles in his jacket. I couldn't keep this up. Any attempt at escape would be thwarted by another forcefield to my face, and despite my sudden burst of prowess just moments before, I wasn't sure I could fight a grown man.

"Samantha, run!"

I expected to see Wesley, but the voice was too high pitched and too feminine. Instead, Naomi charged out of a hall on the opposite side of the foyer. I felt the forcefield dissipate into nothingness behind me.

"Watch out!" I tried to warn, but Naomi had already skidded to halt, glaring at Miles. She stuck out an apprehensive hand, and I watched as it flattened against what I was sure was a new forcefield.

"Go find the others!" she called. Miles glanced between us, clearly unhappy to suddenly be on the defensive. Perhaps he could only make one barrier at a time. I reached behind me, my fingers scrambling for something solid, but his forcefield was definitely gone.

"Naomi, he's a—"

"An Apex?" Her jaw was set, and her hands curled into fists. "Yeah, I know. You need to go!"

"But Wesley—"

"He'll be fine!"

I didn't know Naomi. I hadn't made any effort to. Why would I? She was always at Jamie's side so she had to be just as cruel and vapid as her friend. But here she was, in the plot twist of the century, squaring up against an Apex so I could make a break for it.

Miles saw me try to slip away, and I bumped into another barrier. Naomi lunged as he left himself unprotected. He cowered under her flurry of fists and kicks and narrowly dodged a leg-sweep that would've landed him flat on his back.

When Miles finally managed to push her away, the barrier blocking the exhibit dissolved as he threw up a new forcefield between him and Naomi. I'd seen enough to know she'd be fine on her own.

I slipped down the exhibit hall, cautious at first since I didn't want to run headlong into one of Miles's forcefields. After I turned the first corner into a room lined with tapestries, I sped up. I wanted to call out for Winnie as I ran, make sure she was safe, but there might've been more Apex lurking in the dark, waiting to take me to wherever they'd taken Anthony.

I paused to catch my breath, looking over my shoulder to make sure no one was following me. What if I should've been going after Anthony instead? But the thought of the woman with the long white hair made my knees shake.

"Oh my god!" Someone gasped in my ear.

Arms wrapped around my shoulders and pulled me back. I yelped in surprise and stumbled away, but relaxed when I saw it was Winnie.

"You're okay!"

She shrugged and knit her brow.

"What happened to Wesley? Have you seen Naomi?" She led me deeper into the maze of exhibits. "Charlie's back here watching Dr. Cunningham. He doesn't look so good."

I barely recognized the Viking Exhibit Wesley and I had explored just a few days earlier. Glass littered the floor, and several artifact cases had been knocked on their side. The replica sword's case was completely shattered, leaving the blade on its stand, free for the taking.

"What's going on out there?" Charlie hissed from the corner of the room. He hunched over Dr. Cunningham's limp, unconscious body. The curator's glasses were missing, and his mouth hung open.

"Wesley and I were attacked." I looked at Winnie. "It was the same guy from the docks a few nights ago."

Winnie covered her mouth and shook her head.

"We were attacked, too." Her voice broke. "Two women."

"One of them took Anthony," Charlie finished for her. "A woman with white hair."

My insides constricted. I didn't have it in me to admit I'd seen her leading Anthony away. I should've tried harder to help him.

"Is he alright?" I pointed at Dr. Cunningham. A small stream of blood was pooling on the marble tile beneath his head.

"We don't know," Charlie admitted. "We found him this way. We were lucky we had Naomi with us. She's incredible, I had no idea. Watching her fight those ladies like that..."

He trailed off, shaking his head.

"Who are these people?" I asked Winnie. Her eyes widened as I put her on the spot.

"How would I know?"

"You're running around every night spying on Apex so you've got to know something!"

"My guess is as good as yours. Promise." She held up a single hand as if swearing an oath.

We all looked up at the sound of shoes smacking against the tiled floor down the hall. Winnie scurried over to hide with Charlie in the corner, but I hesitated in the center of the room. I gulped and grabbed the hilt of the replica sword, pulling it from its stand.

"What are you doing?" Winnie hissed.

The sword was heavier than I expected, and as soon as I lifted it, the point dropped, hitting the floor with a metallic *ting!* I maneuvered it back into an upright position, holding the blade in front of me. I was no swordsman, but the weapon somehow made me feel more confident.

"That's an artifact!" Charlie hissed. "You can't just take it!"

"It's a replica," I corrected him. "I'll give it back after we get out."

The footsteps grew closer, and we retreated farther back into the corner. The back of my heels bumped up against Dr. Cunningham's side. Winnie placed a hand on my back to steady me, and I brandished my sword.

A curly-haired silhouette ran into the room, and we collectively sighed in relief.

"It's just me," Naomi whispered. We spilled out of the corner. "Oh, good. Everyone's here."

She winced and put a hand up to her head.

"You okay?" Winnie asked.

"I'm fine. I think Wesley might be hurt, though."

Winnie and I exchanged a look. Was Naomi another Apex? At this point, nothing would surprise me. I half-expected Winnie to start shooting fireballs from her fingertips since everyone else was turning out to be super powered.

"We need to go," Naomi said. "I'm pretty sure I'm being followed, and we need to find an exit."

"What about Wesley?" I asked. "And Anthony?"

"They'll be okay." She helped Charlie hoist Dr. Cunningham up, pulling one of the curator's arms over her shoulder. Cunningham's head lolled forward.

"You guys lead the way," Winnie said. "Sammy and I will take up the rear."

Naomi eyed my sword.

"You know what you're doing with that thing?"

"Just slash and hope you hit something, right?" I tried to smile. The sword was heavy in my hands, but it felt good to have something, anything, to protect myself with.

As we followed Naomi and Charlie down the corridors, I couldn't help but to feel like I'd rather have Naomi in the back with me rather than Winnie. Naomi was a proven fighter. I'd only ever seen Winnie run.

The green glow of the exit sign over a heavy metal door down the hall shone like a beacon in the dark. Naomi slipped out from under Cunningham to push against the door. Charlie cursed under his breath when it didn't budge.

"Now what?" Winnie's voice quaked.

"We keep going."

Naomi pulled Cunningham's free arm back over her shoulder and nodded at Winnie to lead the way. I tightened my grip on the sword to keep my hands from shaking.

"What about the police?" Charlie asked. "Where are they?"

"I can't get a signal on my phone," Winnie sighed. "Anyone else?"

I dug my phone out of my back pocket and frowned at the "No Service" warning in the screen corner.

"Hey!" Charlie shouted. I spun around to see him, Naomi, and Cunningham lagging several feet behind us. Charlie looked bewildered, but Naomi raised a shaking hand. I watched in horror as she pressed her palm against an invisible wall.

"No!" I rushed to meet them but was met by the invisible barrier. "Stand back!"

I backed up a few feet and raised the sword over my head. Naomi and Charlie scrambled away on the other side as I brought the sword down. It bounced off the wall, the metal ringing from the force of the hit.

"Sammy!" Winnie squeaked in terror. I turned back and faltered. Miles stood at the far end of the corridor.

"Get out of here!" Naomi shouted. I was frozen in place, but Winnie grabbed the crook of my elbow and dragged me down an adjoining hall.

Naomi could take Miles, but if he decided to follow us instead, she'd be trapped.

Running with a heavy sword was awkward, and I struggled to keep up with Winnie. I hazarded a glance backwards, but couldn't see Miles.

"In here!" Winnie hissed, holding the door of a bathroom open. She disappeared inside, and I hesitated. We'd be trapped in the bathroom if Miles found us, but my heart was pounding and my legs quaking. I couldn't run forever.

I dipped inside just before the door closed. The bathroom was pitch black. There were no emergency lights or exit signs to light the room.

"Winnie?" I whispered.

"I'm in a stall!"

I stumbled forward blindly until my fingertips made contact with a plastic stall door. I felt my way inside, and the tip of my sword clinked against a toilet bowl.

"You good?" Winnie asked from one stall over. "Stand on the toilet. That way if he comes in, he won't see your feet."

I tip-toed up onto the toilet seat, bracing myself against the stall with my free hand. I tried to control my breathing, afraid my haggard breaths would betray our hiding spot.

I stopped breathing entirely when the bathroom door creaked open. The tiniest sliver of light spilled through the cracks of the stall before being snuffed out as the door closed. Shoes clipped deliberately against the restroom tiles. I screwed my eyes shut against the dark. It wasn't like I could see anything anyways.

A crash and a yelp in the next stall over made every muscle in my body locked up. Something heavy slapped against the floor, and a man grunted.

"Gotcha," Miles rasped.

The sword shook in my hands, and I thought for sure Miles would be able to hear my heart thundering in my chest. But the bathroom door opened again and closed.

"Winnie?" I whispered. A hot tear traced the curve of my face.

I stepped down from the toilet. What was I going to do? Attack a man with a sword? Cut him open? My stomach churned. I couldn't move. I couldn't think.

"Winnie!" I barreled out of the stall, still unable to see. I felt for the door and threw it open, jumping when I saw my own harried reflection gaping back at me in the bathroom mirror.

There was no sign of Winnie in the bathroom. There was no sign of Winnie in the corridor. Miles was gone, too. He'd taken her. It was my fault. I should have done something instead of freezing.

I ran down the hall, wanting to scream Winnie's name but afraid there might be more Apex lurking nearby. What if Miles had taken her the other way? There were so many offshoots from the main hall. They could be anywhere.

Hands grabbed at the back of my arms. I spun around and instinctively raised the sword, but Naomi caught my wrist before I could bring the blade down. We stared at each other, wide-eyed in the soft glow of the emergency lights.

"Where's Winnie?"

I gulped and shook my head. First Anthony. Now Winnie. I'd helped neither.

"That's okay." A muscle in her jaw twitched. "Come on, we've got a hiding place."

I followed Naomi up a staircase to the second floor. I'd lost Winnie. If I hadn't hesitated before following her into the bathroom, maybe Miles wouldn't have seen me. If I hadn't been too scared when he'd come in, maybe I could've fought him off. Winnie was my only friend, and I'd failed her.

Naomi led the way through an arched entry into an exhibit with high ceilings and statues lining either side of the long walls. We were in the Hall of Heroes.

We scurried past Paragon, George Washington, and the others all the way to the end of the room towards the Adrestus statue.

The Scourge Queen was out of cleaning and had joined Adrestus at the head of the room. Her stone hair was pulled back into wild braids, and her mouth was open in a permanent war cry. She held a sword, not unlike the one in my own hands. She was thrilling and frightening, and something about her inspired rage, but I didn't know what or why.

When Dr. Cunningham had told me to come back and see her, I was sure this wasn't what he had in mind.

Naomi led me past the Scourge Queen and Adrestus. The emergency lights weren't as bright in the shadow of their pedestals, but I could see Charlie sitting with Dr. Cunningham. The only sign of life the curator showed was the slight rise and fall of his chest.

I sat down with my back against the Scourge Queen's pedestal and drew my knees up to my face. I'd left Wesley. I'd let Anthony be taken away. I'd done nothing to stop Winnie being captured. A timid hand patted my shoulder. Naomi had sidled up next to me against the pedestal.

"It's not your fault."

"I don't know what you mean," I lied. As helpful as she'd been, I didn't need one of Jamie's cronies to make me feel better.

"You feel guilty, but it's not your fault."

I was quiet for a moment, staring at the sword where it lay at my feet.

"You're an Apex. You feel things, don't you? That's how you know Wesley's hurt."

Naomi glanced back at Charlie, but he was too busy hiding in his own knees behind the Adrestus statue to pay us any attention.

"Please don't tell anyone."

I wondered if Jamie knew. I doubted it. Her lawyer parents had made it clear in the various ads across the city that they were Anti-Apex.

"Wesley is, too," I said.

Naomi looked down.

"You really can't tell anyone. Please."

"That's the least I owe you both."

Naomi smiled and glanced at her watch.

"We're going to be okay. Fleming will be returning soon."

I wondered if Fleming would burst in here, powers blazing. After interrogating me about the incident at the docks, I knew he had to be an Apex, too, possibly in charge of all the secret Apex hiding in the student body.

"They're in here," a woman's voice echoed from the opposite end of the exhibit. Charlie's head whipped up, and he looked over at us desperately.

"You sure?" I recognized Hackjob's gravelly voice. Naomi held a single finger to her lips.

"All the way at the end," the woman replied. I grabbed the sword but remained sitting. The woman sounded familiar, too. If she'd been the other woman at the docks, her powers could sense people, which meant we were screwed. There was no point in hiding.

Naomi tried to grab me as I stood up, but I shook her off and stepped out from behind the Scourge Queen, brandishing the sword. I probably looked like an idiot, but I wasn't going to hide like I had when Winnie had been taken. If I was to be captured, too, it wouldn't be because I was cowering behind a statue.

Hackjob cackled. Wesley was slung over his mountainous shoulder. He wasn't moving. A woman stood next to him, looking bored. She was definitely the woman from the docks named Esther. I hoped Naomi was right about Fleming arriving soon.

"Back off," Naomi warned, joining me in front of the statues. I knew she could fight, but it was still the three of us and one unconscious curator against two adults.

"If you all play nicely, there's no need for anyone to come to harm," Esther said. "Adrestus does not want to hurt you."

There was that name again: Adrestus. How fitting that his namesake's statue towered over the scene.

"He has a funny way of showing it," I snorted.

"Please," Naomi said, "don't quip with the bad guys."

"Let's put the sword on the floor, alright?" Esther crooned.

When I hesitated, Hackjob grunted and dropped Wesley to the floor with a thud. He was alive and conscious, his eyes wide open and watching, but didn't move. Naomi grabbed at her stomach as if she might be sick.

"What did you do to him?" I demanded.

"Nothing permanent," Hackjob laughed. "Just needed to make him more manageable is all. If you cooperate, it won't happen to you, too."

"Where's Anthony and Winnie?" Naomi asked.

"Safe," Esther said. "Don't worry, you'll see for yourself. Or..."

She trailed off and looked at me, tilting her head to one side so that her ginger hair cascaded over one shoulder.

"You could leave," she mused, "if this one stays."

"No," Naomi said vehemently.

"In fact, we'll let you all leave, including the two who are hiding, in exchange for Miss Havardson," she grinned.

I didn't like that she knew my name, and I didn't like that I was being singled out. No way did I want to stay behind, but I knew that no matter how good Naomi was at fighting, we didn't stand a chance.

"Fine." I lowered the sword. "But they have to get out of the building before I agree to go."

"Of course!" Esther stepped aside and gestured down the hall. "The emergency exit in the Incan display on the first floor is open."

"Samantha, no," Naomi hissed.

"I'll be okay," I said. "Charlie, get out of here. Cunningham needs help. "

Charlie didn't need any longer to weigh the decision. He moved as quickly as he could, half carrying, half dragging Dr. Cunningham out from behind the Adrestus statue. He gave Hackjob and Esther a wide berth as he passed them.

"Please," I said to Naomi. "Go with them. Take Wesley."

"I'm not letting them take you."

She stepped forward so that she was between us.

"I'll be fine!" I insisted.

An alarm went off, blaring overhead. Lights flashed around the room. Had Charlie triggered an alarm? Or had Fleming finally arrived with help?

"Offer's expired, then," Hackjob growled as Esther swore loudly. "I'll take the girl. You get out of here."

Esther looked around wildly before sprinting back down the hall. Hackjob lumbered forward. The curls that rested on Naomi's shoulders heaved as she took a deep breath before she flung herself at Hackjob. He grabbed her and spun her into a statue.

"Naomi!" I shrieked, but she staggered to her feet.

"When you get the chance, you run," she grunted.

Hackjob stepped closer, and Naomi scrambled to stay between us. He flashed his teeth at me, and my stomach lurched. With a single swing of his arm, Naomi was thrown into the wall. A glass display board shattered as she crashed into it, showering her in glass as she slid to the floor.

Hackjob was stronger than he had been at the docks. There, even I had managed to get a hit on him, but he'd thrown Naomi like she weighed nothing.

"You need to run!" Naomi's words slurred. She tried to get up, but was dazed.

"I'm not leaving you guys," I told Naomi. My fingers tightened around the sword hilt. I'd felt awkward with it all night, but with Hackjob sauntering towards me, it suddenly felt natural in my hands. Hackjob wavered.

"Put that down," he growled, eyeing the blade warily. "You'll only hurt yourself."

But he reached up and ripped the arm off of George Washington and wielded it in front him. A bit of rebar stuck out from the stone shoulder, making a lethal-looking metal end. His strength was monstrous.

"You don't stand a chance, little bird," he sneered. "I've been Blessed since you last saw me."

Wesley's leg stuck out from his body at a weird angle where he lay behind Hackjob, and though he didn't move, he stared across the room at me with wide, panicked eyes. Glass crunched to my right as Naomi struggled to find her footing. They didn't have to protect me, but they both had tried and now both were hurt.

I didn't have to beat Hackjob, though. I just had to stay standing until Fleming brought help. Hackjob swung George Washington's arm, and I braced myself. Stone met metal, and the shock of the hit sent vibrations from my fingers to my toes. Something switched inside me, like someone else taking over, and after stumbling back several feet from the force of Hackjob's attack, I lunged.

I came at him over and over, pushing him farther back. I had to stay on the offensive. I didn't stand a chance defending myself if he gained the upper hand. He parried blow after blow until I finally disarmed him and swept his leg with the flat of the blade. He fell against Paragon's statue, breathing heavily, eyes wild.

"How—" he asked. I cut him off, balancing the blade's tip a fraction of an inch between his eyes.

The alarm overhead cut, and Hackjob's face drained of color. Running footsteps thundered down the hall. Hackjob scowled and batted the blade away from his face with the back of his arm. He leaped to his feet, but instead of attacking, he fled the room, disappearing down the hall.

The room began to twist around me. For a moment I was afraid my dizzy spells had come back but realized instead it was a post-adrenaline rush fatigue. I dropped the sword and steadied myself against Paragon's pedestal as a team of black-clad figures flooded the room. Their helmeted outfits were similar to the one I'd seen Wesley in twice now, but were a shade darker.

"Samantha." Fleming appeared at my side, placing a hand on my shoulder to steady me. "Are you alright? What happened?"

"I'm fine."

But I couldn't look away from the sword, discarded in a pile of broken glass, glittering benignly in the dim emergency lights of the exhibit. I hadn't known I could sword fight, and I still wasn't convinced I could. That couldn't have been me holding off Hackjob. My arms had not been my own. While still in my hands, the blade had made me feel powerful, invincible, unyielding.

Now that I stared at it in the glass, I only felt terror.

12

Underneath Schrader Hall

Wesley probably should've been in the back of an ambulance but instead sat with Naomi and me in the back of a police van on our way back to campus. Fleming held his head in his hands in the front seat while a young police officer drove. Wesley winced in pain with every bump in the road, and Naomi silently held his hand from the middle seat. Even after the night we'd just had, it felt weird to see pretty and popular Naomi holding the hand of goofy and awkward Wesley.

Wesley's autonomy had been restored after an adhesive patch was found on the back of his neck and peeled off. They told us it was probably filled with a neurotoxin, but bagged it for lab analysis to be sure. It looked just like the one Miles had brandished at me in the foyer.

The cuts along Naomi's arms were, luckily, mostly superficial. She was doing better than Dr. Cunningham anyway, who was immediately transferred to the New Delos Hospital after being found in Charlie's care in the foyer. Charlie was taken soon after, but Fleming had ushered

Naomi, Wesley, and me into the back of the police van before we could be offered medical attention.

Rather than driving us to the front of the main hall, the officer drove into the large parking complex next to campus. He turned into the "Authorized Vehicles Only" section, which led to the underground levels. There were only a few cars parked down here.

The officer pulled up next to a heavy metal door. He honked the horn twice, and the door burst open. I recognized Nurse Everly in his lavender scrubs, pushing a gurney into the garage.

"No," Wesley moaned. "I don't need that."

But as Fleming came around the side of the car to aid Wesley, I could see Wesley's leg dangling uselessly from his hip. Everly helped hoist him onto the cart. Wesley groaned in protest but was in no condition to fight. The nurse placed a careful hand on Wesley's leg. He shook his head.

"How bad is it this time, Jacobi?" Fleming asked.

"Tibia broken in two places. Fibula broken in one." He pulled his hand away. "And a dislocated hip. A few fractured ribs and a broken right ulna."

"Do what you need to," Fleming said, waving them away. Wesley scowled through the pain as Everly pushed him through the doors. I watched them go, wondering what a school nurse could do for injuries as extensive as Wesley's. Fleming turned towards Naomi. "Any of those cuts deep?"

"They aren't too bad," she said. "Nurse Everly might want to look at a few once he's done with Wes."

Fleming sighed, but I couldn't tell if it was in relief or exasperation. He held the door open and gestured down the well-lit hallway beyond it.

I did my best not to meet his eyes but could feel them boring into the back of my head as he marched us down the corridor. Naomi seemed to know the way, which wasn't surprising at this point. I figured we must be in their secret hideout, somewhere under the school.

The hall was long and narrow, flanked by concrete walls on either side. A set of double doors were situated at the end of the corridor, through which Everly was already disappearing with Wesley. Naomi smiled awkwardly at me.

"He'll be okay."She seemed so calm as she led the way. I wondered if Wesley got injured like this often.

Naomi pushed the doors open at the end of the hall, and Fleming steered me through them and to the left. We were in a low-ceilinged atrium. A student looked like she was sleeping at the front desk, face down in a mess of auburn hair, but raised a tired hand to acknowledge us as we passed. A door to her right read, "Sickbay".

"Look alive, Desirae," Fleming barked, and the girl lifted her head to scowl at us.

Naomi led us through a different door, and even though the lights were dim, I realized it was the basement hall of the main school building. Fleming's office was only a few yards ahead of us.

We followed him inside, and he took his seat behind his desk. He bowed his head and burrowed his fingertips into his hair.

"Who was it?" he asked without looking up. Naomi slid into one of the seats across from him. "I want to know everything that happened before I showed up with the university team."

I remembered the suited Apex whose armor had looked darker then that I'd seen Wesley in. Had those been Apex from New Delos University, then?

"It was the Adrestus people," Naomi said. "The ones Wesley ran into at the docks."

My face warmed at the mention of the docks. That incident and the one at the museum were definitely connected, and I had been at both. What if it was all somehow my fault?

"Which ones?" Fleming's head was still bowed.

Naomi struggled to remember them. "There was a big guy. He's the one that took down Wesley. And me."

"Hackjob," I said. Fleming finally looked up. "I told you about him. He's the one with the stupid name."

"Wesley beat him easily the other night," Fleming said. "So why did he lose tonight?"

"He said he'd been 'Blessed'," I snorted. "Whatever that means. It was like he'd gained Apex abilities overnight."

"That's not possible," Fleming said flatly. "You're either an Apex or you're not."

"He was definitely stronger today, so something was different."

Naomi detailed the rest of the evening, letting me cut in to detail Miles taking Winnie. Fleming didn't interrupt until the end, when Naomi told him how I had fended off Hackjob with the replica sword. He raised his eyebrows in surprise.

"I'm sorry, say that again?"

"Samantha picked up the sword and attacked, uh, what did you say his name was?"

"Hackjob," I muttered.

"Oh, you're right, that is a stupid name."

Fleming dropped the pen he'd been clicking absentmindedly and stood up. He walked over to the glass case of photographs in his office corner and stared at it a moment.

"Samantha had a sword fight with Hackjob," he said blankly.

"Yes." Naomi looked at me, and, for the first time, I saw her smile. "She was a natural."

"Where did you learn to do that?" Fleming asked. "Was it Alison?"

I laughed. The thought of my mom sword fighting was even more ridiculous than the thought of me sword fighting.

"My mom doesn't fight."

Fleming sat back down, sighing heavily.

"You said Anthony and Winnie were taken. We know Samantha was also a target, twice now if you count the other day at the docks." He was fiddling with the pen again. "Add that to Lannie Bryce two weeks ago, and I'd be willing to bet if we looked into Brent Todd and Lawrence Garcia..."

"Who?" I asked.

"Other students who've gone missing. We've kept it quiet, but I'm not sure if we will be able to for much longer."

"You see a pattern, then." Naomi folded her hands patiently in front of her. "What is it?"

It was almost midnight, to be fair, but Fleming looked uncommonly tired.

"Yes," he said softly, "there is a pattern. Anthony's father was on the Apex Team just a few years before me. And, Naomi, you'll remember Amanda Hendricks from before she quit."

My stomach flipped. Amanda? Winnie's Amanda? Amanda who hated me for mysterious reasons? Had Winnie's obsession with Apex been fueled by her sister?

"Amanda was on Apex Team?"

Fleming nodded.

"She was in the university program, too, but left it this year."

"I thought she quit the swim team," I interjected.

"She's quit a few different things," Naomi said quietly.

"Her father, Roy, had been a junior on the team when I first joined." Fleming's tight frown indicated Roy Hendricks and he probably hadn't been friends.

I knew Winnie was jealous of her sister, but if her whole family really were all Apex except for her, it was easy to imagine how she became obsessed with the secret team. Her sister, dad, and probably her mom, too, had all been in on the secret, leaving her out.

"So, were Anthony and Winnie and the rest...?" Naomi trailed off.

"No, they're not Apex, if that's what you mean." Fleming shook his head. "Which is what makes each of the kidnappings interesting. Adrestus seems to be targeting the non-Apex children of Apex."

Fleming was staring at me expectantly. His brow was furrowed, and his lips pressed tightly together.

"I had no idea," I said. "I've known the Hendricks for years, and...wait...."

The final piece clicked into place in my head, and if my stomach had felt twisted before, it was absolutely knotted now. My head suddenly felt light.

"Samantha, I'm so sorry for you to find out like this." Fleming's voice quaked. "Quite frankly, I'm not sure why she wouldn't have told you before."

I tried to think back and remember any clue, any hint that my mom had been anything more than the ordinary person I'd thought she was. There was nothing. She'd always been a normal mom.

Naomi curled her hands in her lap and kept her head bowed. She'd pieced it together, too. She cleared her throat.

"If you don't need anything else from me, sir, I'd like to go get my cuts looked at."

Fleming waved her out of the room. The door clicked shut behind me as she left.

"But, she's never..." I couldn't fully formulate what I wanted to say. I had too many questions, and I had no idea which to ask first. "So, then I'm not a...uh...you know."

"You would know by now if you were."

"Oh."

I couldn't think of anything weird or unexplainable that had ever happened to me. There was nothing to hint at any latent powers. But if my mom really was an Apex, maybe there was still a chance I might be? After all, nothing had hinted at her having super abilities. Who's to say it wasn't the same for me?

Besides, the way I'd picked up that sword...even I wasn't sure what had taken over me. Was there an Apex ability specific to super sword fighting?

Fleming walked back to the glass case. He opened it and pulled a frame off one of the dusty shelves. He stared at it a moment before setting it down on the desk and sliding it over to me.

I recognized her immediately. She was sitting in the middle of the stone steps that led up to the front of the main school hall. Her blonde hair was neatly braided over one shoulder, and her mischievous grin was the same one I'd seen on Avery many times.

The boy next to her looked as awkwardly stern as he did today, though the Fleming sitting in front of me looked much more tired and sad than the one in the picture.

"You both look so young." I couldn't think of anything else to say.

There were other students in the picture, too. I recognized Mr. Hendricks sitting between two girls. Another boy pretended to be using Fleming's head as an armrest. His confident grin was familiar, but I couldn't place it.

"Who's that?" I asked, pointing at him. Fleming snorted.

"You know him. Just imagine him several stories taller and made of bronze."

I thought back to the Paragon statue standing in the bay.

"My mom knew Paragon?" I gasped. Fleming laughed, but still sounded a little sad.

"They were good friends, even."

"My dad hates him." I didn't know why I said it. "Hey, what about my dad?"

Fleming took the picture back and hesitated as he placed it in the case. He smiled sadly as he turned back around.

"What about him?"

"Was he on the team?"

"No, your parents met much later, after high school. If he's an Apex, he's not in our records."

Even though I still couldn't imagine Mom being part of Apex Team alongside Paragon, I definitely couldn't believe Dad would ever be involved with that scene. He hated Apex, and it was weird enough that he was married to one. Maybe she had given up her vigilante lifestyle to be with him? The thought made me uncomfortable.

"Alison is particularly gifted," Fleming said carefully. "It's possible whoever this Adrestus person is wants to use you as leverage against her."

"What were her powers then?"

"Nope!" Fleming threw his hands up. "I already let one secret slip tonight. That's something you'll have to talk to her about."

"Ok, fine." I slumped back in my chair but immediately sat up again. "But what about you? You're in that picture, too, next to Paragon, even! You said you guys were all on the team together."

Fleming cleared his throat as he crossed his office to the door.

"I think that's enough for tonight. You've been through a lot, and we should have our nurse look over you as well, and I'd like to check in on Naomi and Wesley."

"I promise it's my last question."

Fleming sighed with his hand on the door handle. It was funny that only a few days ago we had been in the same position, me demanding answers while he tried to avoid my questions.

"It's late, and I need to take you to the Sickbay."

"Fine," I said, crossing my arms. "But I'll just make Wesley tell me later."

Fleming exhaled heavily through his nose and rubbed his temples with one hand.

"You're worse than your mother."

"Thank you."

"But you're just going to have to settle with asking Wesley."

Wesley seemed completely unbothered by his injuries. He was sitting up in a hospital bed, and, despite the IV sticking out of his forearm, he was devouring a large plate of fast food burgers. Discarded fry cups littered his blanket, and two empty soda bottles sat on his bedside table.

Naomi sat on top of the sheets on the bed next to his while Everly wrapped gauze around the cuts on her arm. She slurped from a large milkshake using her free hand.

Everly looked up from his work as we walked in and pointed at the empty bed across from Wesley's.

"I'll be with her in a moment," he said.

The girl who had been at the atrium desk popped her head inside behind us.

"Mr. Fleming? Officer Allen is still here. He says he has an update for you."

Fleming sighed and looked at Wesley as he walked out.

"My office, tomorrow, first thing once you are feeling up to it."

Wesley gave him an enthusiastic thumbs-up since his mouth was full of burger. Fleming cast us all one last look-over and was gone.

I sat down on the edge of my bed and gave Wesley a wan smile.

"Sorry about tonight," I said. "And for punching you in the face the other night, apparently."

"Hey, I'm sorry it wasn't Andersen you punched, too," he said, finishing off his burger. "Guess you know our big secret now, huh?"

"Yeah, who would've thought Winnie wasn't crazy?"

My stomach clenched as I said it. Winnie was gone because of me. Maybe Officer Allen was here to tell Fleming they'd managed to get both her and Anthony back. Maybe he was here to tell him that they hadn't.

"It's not your fault," Naomi said, repeating what she'd said to me at the museum. Everly tied up her gauze and crossed over to my bed.

"We meet again," he said coolly.

He took my hand. His palm emitted a gentle heat, and I felt a sweeping sensation travel from my fingers and throughout my body.

"Uninjured," he concluded. "Just a bit tired."

I remembered how he'd placed his hand on Wesley in the parking garage and had been able to assess his injuries that way.

"You're an Apex, too!" I said. Everly smiled but continued to hold my hand in his.

"Did you break your collarbone as a kid?"

"Yeah." I pulled at my shirt collar to show him the scar that ran from my neck to my shoulder. "Bike accident."

His smile dissolved into a slight frown.

"Must've been a bad injury. There's a lot of scar tissue in there." He let go of my hand and glanced down at his tablet computer. "Looks like Fleming wants you here overnight."

"But I'm fine, you just said so."

"Probably more of a security thing than a health thing. They don't know where the museum attackers went, and they don't know if they'll come back. I'm sure it's just for tonight, though."

"Nice!" Wesley cheered from his side of the room. "Party in the infirmary! We're here tonight, too!"

Everly shot Wesley a warning look.

"There will be no parties." He went over to inspect the IV bag still hooked up to Wesley's arm. "And since you are already feeling so energetic, maybe I've given you too strong a dosage this time."

He began untangling Wesley from the tube. Wesley flexed his fingers once he was free and rubbed his arm where IV had been attached. Everly grabbed Wesley's arm and concentrated for a moment.

"Bone fractures are all healed," he murmured, "but you might have some bruising around your hip and ribs tomorrow."

Wesley fired finger guns at Everly.

"I can always count on you to fix me up!"

"And I can always count on you to need fixing." Everly sighed and looked over his tablet one last time. "Keeps me in a job, I guess. If any of you need anything, I'll be on call in the back. I'm sure we will update you in the morning if there is any news."

As soon as Everly shouldered his way into the adjoining office, Wesley and Naomi rushed to my bedside. I had already made myself comfortable on top of the sheets as Naomi perched herself on the end of the bed while Wesley took up residence on the next bed over. He passed me one of the burgers from his tray.

"You gonna tell us where you learned to fight?" he asked, his green eyes bright with excitement. "If I had known you could do that, I never would have wasted time rescuing you at the docks!"

"Rescuing me?" I repeated, taking the burger. "I had that under control."

Wesley rolled his eyes, and Naomi laughed.

"Okay, sure. Next time I'll just leave you. Good luck sword fighting from the trunk of a car."

I swallowed a bite of burger.

"First of all, I can't sword fight," I admitted. "I have no idea where that came from, but neither of you are ones to talk!"

"Guess our cover's blown then," Naomi smirked. "So much for covert."

"What were we supposed to do? Let the bad guys win?" Wesley said.

"They kinda did win," Naomi reminded him. Wesley's smile faltered, but he shook his head.

"No, Everly said they've already got teams from both us and the University out looking for Winnie and Anthony. They'll be back by the morning."

I leaned back against my pillows and crumpled the burger wrapper in my hand.

"I'm just glad I don't have to feel indebted to Andersen anymore. Can you imagine a jerk like him as an Apex?"

Naomi and Wesley shared a nervous glance.

"Nope," Naomi said, too quickly. "That'd really suck."

"Yeah." Wesley nodded. "He'd be the worst."

They had both become very rigid, and neither would look me in the eye. My stomach churned.

"You're kidding," I said flatly. "Andersen? Really?"

They looked at each other again.

"Yeah," Wesley gave in. "He's the worst. He was on call the night of the dock incident so he knew about the whole thing. You were kind of right. He was messing with you on purpose."

Naomi threw my crumpled wrapper at Wesley, but he dodged it.

"What? You were the one that made it obvious!" Wesley turned back to me. "Technically, we aren't allowed to reveal the identities of other Apex, but Andersen's a jerk, anyway. I still can't believe you confused me with him of all people."

"Right," Naomi snorted. "How could anyone *possibly* mistake one pasty boy with brown hair for a different pasty boy with brown hair?"

"I hope he has a dumb power," I mumbled.

"Don't worry, he does," Wesley assured me, just as Naomi admitted, "No, it's pretty cool."

Wesley glared at her. She shrugged.

"You don't get to say who has cool powers when you are able to bench two thousand pounds."

"Two thousand pounds?!" I stared at Wesley with a new sense of reverence.

"No, not two thousand." He rubbed his forehead in embarrassment. "A lot, yeah, but not that much."

I remembered when he'd freed me from the car trunk and the way the metal had bent backwards.

"I figured you were strong when you pretty much pulled that car apart to get me out, but a thousand pounds?"

"Not a thousand pounds!" he repeated. "And as far as that old car goes, I knew the latch was rusted. Popped right open, no problem."

"How'd you know it was rusted?"

"I could smell it," he said nonchalantly, before blushing harder. Naomi gave me a meaningful look.

"Super senses, too. See? No room to judge other Apex when he's positioned to become the next Paragon."

"Super senses?" I looked at the glasses perched on the bridge of Wesley's nose. "So what's up with the four eyes?"

"They make my eyesight worse. I get migraines if I don't wear them."

"Still better than being an empath," Naomi grumbled.

"You're good at surveillance!"

"Then how'd I missed those creeps at the museum?" She shook her head. "That's just about the only thing it's good for, and what use was it tonight?"

"You were great," Wesley assured her, but she continued to frown.

"And I tried to get Fleming to tell me what his powers are, but he didn't want to for some reason," I mused.

Wesley snickered, and Naomi's frown turned into a reluctant smile.

"Sorry," she giggled. "It shouldn't be funny."

"I didn't realize it was a sore spot with him," Wesley added.

"What? Is it really that bad? He was on the team at the same time as Paragon, so he can't have been that lame."

They both laughed harder.

"Yeah, as the water-boy maybe."

Naomi shook her head, still laughing.

"Shut up, you know he wasn't the water-boy!"

"He might as well have been! Can you imagine him and Paragon fighting together?"

I was getting irritated that they weren't letting me in on the joke.

"So what can he do? What sort of Apex is he?"

"Oh, I don't think he'd want us telling you if he didn't say for himself," Wesley said.

"Come on, he told me you would tell me."

"That's a lie," Naomi said quickly.

"Okay, so he said the only way I'd find out is if you told me, which is kind of the same thing as giving you permission to tell me, so what is it? What's his Apex power?"

Wesley bit his lip in anticipation and looked over at Naomi, as if asking for her blessing. She rolled her eyes.

"Whatever. You're gonna tell her eventually, I'm sure."

Wesley turned to me and held his hands in excitement.

"Okay," he said, clearly savoring the moment. "The deal with Alexander Fleming's Apex power is..."

He looked at Naomi and then back at me for dramatic effect.

"...he doesn't have one!"

I stared back at him. Naomi shifted uncomfortably. The bed creaked under her.

"His power is that he doesn't have one?" I repeated. Wesley's smile was fading as he realized the joke was lost on me. "So he isn't an Apex?"

"Nope," Naomi said. "But he still made it through the trials to get on the team, so that's impressive in itself."

"I didn't realize it was so funny to not be an Apex," I said, trying to sound casual but unable to keep the ice out of my voice.

"It's not funny," Wesley backtracked. "It's just, you know, he's in charge of all the Apex at the school and, come on, it's Fleming."

Naomi scooted herself up the bed and leaned against the pillows with me.

"We shouldn't have laughed," she said gently. "There's nothing wrong with not being an Apex, and the way you fought tonight, it was better than anything we did to help."

Wesley nodded and hung his head.

"You were the one person in that museum who didn't need rescuing," Naomi continued. "Including us."

"I still rescued you at the docks, though," Wesley interjected. Naomi glared at him, but I smiled.

"Fine," I agreed. "You saved me at the docks, and I saved you at the museum. I guess that's fair."

I looked at Wesley's leg, dangling over the side of the bed.

"So, does Everly have healing powers?"

"Not exactly," Naomi said. "He can sense pretty much anything in a living body, though I think he still went through extensive medical training to be able to understand just what it was he was detecting."

I ran my hand over the scar that ran over my collarbone from my neck to my shoulder.

"Must be some ability if he is able to feel an injury from five years ago." I looked over at Wesley, who was absentmindedly kicking his legs out in front of him. "If he doesn't heal, how is your leg not broken?"

"The Serum!" Wesley grinned and stuck out his leg, rolling up his sweat pants so I could see how intact it was. "Some Apex have a self-healing factor. I don't get the science behind it, but they donate plasma, which is used to make the Serum."

"Basically," Naomi interjected, "the Serum can be used by anyone to temporarily gain a healing factor that allows their body to repair itself. So far the only known side effect is insane hunger, since it uses energy that's readily available in the body already."

"It can heal anything?" I asked, incredulous. Wesley's IV bag had looked suspiciously similar to the one Everly had given me on move-in day.

"Just about," Wesley said. "Everly says you have to be careful though, since things can heal funny if they aren't set correctly. His job isn't just to diagnose, but to make sure everything is in the right place to be put back together."

"Like your dislocated hip?"

Wesley winced.

"Yeah, that has to be done manually, and out of all the dislocations, hip is the worst."

Wesley seemed like a happy-go-lucky, well adjusted kid that might be into computer games, but the way he nonchalantly ranked dislocations of body parts made my stomach twist. What all could he have been through and fought to have experience in that department?

"Oh, no." Naomi suddenly looked sick. She bowed her head until it was between her knees and pressed her hands against her forehead.

Something crashed outside, and shouting echoed through the double doors into the infirmary.

"Tell me where she is!"

My insides clenched, and I closed my eyes as if that might make the disruption outside go away. It was easy to recognize my dad's angry demands.

The doors burst open, and a flood of adults poured in, led by my dad. He was still dressed for school, in his long sleeved button-up and corduroys, but Mom trailed behind him in sweats. Mr. and Mrs. Hendricks were with them. Mrs. Hendricks's face was red and blotchy.

Fleming brought up the rear of the pack, trying to corral mine and Winnie's parents without success.

"You told me she was safe here!" My dad bellowed. To my surprise, he turned on Mom and Mr. Hendricks. Fleming stepped between the three of them.

"While what happened at the museum is distressing, I can assure you, Samantha wouldn't be safer anywhere else."

"You call nearly being taken out from under your nose safe?" Dad spat. "And how can you say that, after Winnie—"

Mrs. Hendricks wailed and broke down in tears.

"They were safe!" Mom came to Fleming's defense. "If you want to blame someone, blame me since it sounds like it's my fault she was a target to begin with!"

Mr. Hendricks cleared his throat, clearly not as eager to take the blame as my mom.

"Now, hold on, we don't know for sure it's just Apex's kids they're after."

"Don't be so dense, Roy," Mom hissed.

"They haven't bothered Amanda, have they?"

"They wouldn't if it's non-Apex children they want!" Mom and Mr. Hendricks were nose to nose. Mrs. Hendricks whimpered. Everly emerged from his office at the commotion and rushed to comfort her.

Dad looked down at me, as if noticing for the first time that I was there despite having stormed the room looking for me.

"What happened?"

Naomi and Wesley cleared out to their side of the room as the adults descended around my bed.

"I'm fine," I said, pushing both Mom and Dad away.

"Did you see where they took her?" Mr. Hendricks grabbed at my arm. I pulled away.

"No, I—"

"Who were they? Did they say?" he continued to press.

"Samantha has already given her statement." I was taken aback by the authority in Fleming's voice. Mr. Hendricks glared at him.

"Then why am I not getting any answers?"

His eyes flicked to Naomi and Wesley, who were both doing their best to spontaneously develop powers of invisibility as they shrank back into their pillows.

"You two," Hendricks snarled. "Were you the Apex at the museum?"

Naomi gulped, but Wesley nodded.

"You know," Mr. Hendricks said as he stalked towards them, "back when I was in the program, a performance like that wouldn't have just meant removal from the team, but expulsion from the school as well."

Guilt gnawed at my insides, but I stayed quiet. It hadn't been Naomi or Wesley's fault at all. It had been mine.

"Back off, Roy," Fleming warned. Mr. Hendricks turned on Fleming.

"What kind of show are you running here, Alexander?" he demanded. Fleming blushed but didn't back down. "Your students can't even defend their classmates, and I can't help but to wonder if Amanda would still be in the advanced program if she didn't have someone like you in charge of her high school training."

"My *students* were there for a class assignment, not an Apex Team one!" Fleming poked Mr. Hendricks square in the chest.

"It shouldn't have mattered!" Hendricks bellowed. "Winnie can't defend herself! They should've done something!"

"Roy, please," Mrs. Hendricks sniffled. "This isn't Alex's fault."

"You can be damn sure it's his fault!" Mr. Hendricks gestured around the room. "This, this is what happens when they put a Beta in charge."

A deadly silence suffocated the Sickbay. Fleming stood rigid, facing Mr. Hendricks, whose fists were clenched and shaking. Everyone held their breath, waiting to see what would happen next.

"Excuse me," Everly said, deep and slow, "but this is a place of healing. Any further shouting matches can be handled in the arena."

Mr. Hendricks stood opposite Fleming, still shaking, still sizing him up, until he finally turned towards the door.

"Come on, Valerie, we're leaving."

Mrs. Hendricks gathered her tissues and followed her husband to the door. Mr. Hendricks turned back as he pressed the door open.

"Find my daughter, Alex." His voice quaked. "I'll be talking to the council about your position here, regardless."

Even after the door closed behind them, we could still hear Mrs. Hendricks sniffing miserably in the atrium.

I realized that Mom was stroking my hair, and I wondered how long she'd been doing so. Wesley's eyes were wide behind his glasses, and Naomi was visibly shaking.

"He had a point," Dad growled. Mom and Everly shot him a dirty look.

"I'll kick you out, too," Everly warned. Dad waved him off.

"I was told Samantha would be safe here."

"Your daughter is stronger than you give her credit for," Fleming said. Our eyes locked for a split second before he looked away. "Apparently, she's quite the natural swordsman."

Dad went rigid next to me, but Fleming was looking at Mom.

"I didn't teach her sword fighting," she scoffed. "You know I sucked with weapons."

Fleming pursed his lips, and I knew he didn't believe her.

"She's here so that I don't have to worry about her defending herself," Dad said. "She's here so that you do that part for her."

"I know." Fleming bowed his head. "I'm sorry she was put in danger tonight, but you know Apex and their families are safer here than anywhere else."

Both parents turned to look at me in shock.

"It's okay, I already know," I said quickly. "Mr. Fleming—"

They turned back towards Fleming, glaring.

"I mean that I put it together after everything!" I gushed, trying to keep Fleming out of more trouble than he was already in. "It wasn't exactly hard when everyone was freaking out about Apex's kids being kidnapped, but I don't know why you never told me."

Mom pulled me in and continued to stroke my hair.

"I didn't want you to find out this way." Her arms felt unnaturally stiff around me.

"And you know that I'm fine, right?" I pushed away from her and looked at Dad. "Sure, what happened tonight was scary, but I'm okay, and Winnie will be, too, once they find her."

Dad tried to smile. Behind him, Fleming was looking relieved.

"Why don't I take you both to my office, and I can fill you in with what I'm allowed to share?" Fleming beckoned towards the door. "It's getting late, and my students need to rest."

Mom gave me one last hug on the bed and followed Fleming, but Dad lingered for a moment longer. His brow furrowed, and he looked confused.

"Good job tonight, kid," he said gruffly. "With the sword thing, I mean."

He stood there thinking for another half-second, before nodding to himself and following Mom and Fleming out the door.

13

Dr. Weaver

Falling asleep was easy. It was staying that way that was a problem. I would wake up with my stomach in knots, thinking about Winnie. At one point I woke up because I thought I heard someone whispering my name, but both Naomi and Wesley were sound asleep. I wasn't sure Wesley slept well either, as I heard him get up several times to dig granola bars out of a drawer at the far side of the room. The healing Serum must have still been taking its toll on his stomach.

Since the ward was underground, there were no windows. I couldn't see if the sun had risen yet, but a digital clock on the wall read "7:00" in large, red numbers. Naomi and Wesley were still snoring in their beds. They seemed at home here. It made me wonder how many nights they'd spent in the Apex Team's infirmary.

I carefully swung my legs over the bedside and slipped my feet into my shoes. Where was I supposed to go? The cafeteria would be opening for breakfast, but I wasn't hungry. I could go back to my dorm room, but the thought of going back without Winnie sat heavy in my stomach. Fleming or Everly would've woken us up if they'd found her, right?

I tip-toed out into the atrium. The student at the desk was asleep, and I was careful not to wake her as I crept to the far door.

The basement floor of the school hall was lit only by the dim glow coming from under Fleming's office door. I wondered if he'd been there all night.

I knocked on the door and opened it at the sound of his groggy "Come in". His hair was more disheveled than ever, and his eyes were bloodshot behind his glasses. He frowned when he saw me.

"Samantha? Is everything alright?"

"Oh, yeah," I said quickly. "It's just morning so I was going to leave and thought I should let someone know."

He glanced at his watch, and his face fell when he saw the time. He sighed heavily.

"Yes, that's fine. I'll let you know if there is anything else I need from you."

I hesitated in the doorway.

"So," I said quietly, "no Winnie or Anthony yet?"

Fleming shook his head.

"I'm afraid not. I promise we are doing everything we can."

"And what about me? Are those people going to come back?"

"It's..." Fleming faltered. "It's likely."

I clenched my jaw and nodded assuredly.

"Alright." I was surprised at not only how confident I sounded, but how confident I felt, too. But I had evaded these creeps twice now. If they kept coming, maybe I could keep it up. "I'll see you in class."

I turned to leave. I got the sense that Fleming wanted to say more. He was sitting up straight on the edge of his seat and had taken off his glasses but didn't stop me as the door swung closed.

Even though I didn't have an appetite, I went to the cafeteria. It'd be almost empty this early, and I didn't want to deal with the breakfast crowd later in the morning. I found a small table in the corner and ate my scrambled eggs as quickly as I could. I must've looked ridiculous in my wrinkled clothes from the day before and my tangled mess of hair.

There was a sharp gush of cold morning air as a group of hungry students pushed into the cafeteria. My heart sank when I saw Andersen leading the pack. He glanced over at me, and even at this distance, I could see the dark bags under his eyes.

In fact, the entire group of kids looked exhausted as they staggered through the cereal bar. I recognized some of them from my classes. Andersen sat down at a table with his back turned resolutely towards me, but one of the girls from the group broke off and came over to my table.

"Hey," she smiled. Her hair was falling out of its ponytail, and she wore a big pink bow on the back of her head.

"Hi, Heather."

"I heard about last night. Are you okay?"

I looked back at the group she'd walked in with and realized they must all be on Team Apex. That's why they all looked so tired. They'd been up all night trying to find Winnie and Anthony. They pushed their breakfast around their plates half-heartedly.

"Oh," I said, looking back at Heather. After the night I had just had, it wasn't shocking to discover she was also an Apex, but it was a little jarring that she was being so upfront about it. "Uh, yeah. I'm fine."

"Let us know if you need anything. We've got your back."

With a smile and a wink, she bounced back to her teammates' table. I stared at Andersen's hunched shoulders for a moment. Whatever Heather said, I was willing to bet that Andersen did not have my back.

I finished eating my eggs and hurried past their table. I couldn't ignore the guilt festering inside me. Even though Naomi insisted it wasn't my fault, I knew they'd been up all night because of me.

Yesterday, everything had been relatively normal, disregarding a few run-ins with adventure. But last night, it was as if I'd stumbled into a whole new world, and it felt like the city might fall down around me at any moment. All I could do was wait, hovering in some kind of limbo.

Winnie's bed was still messy from the day before. It looked like she could have just rolled out of it, but the room was cold. I carefully pulled her blankets taut and fluffed her pillow. She would want her bed to be made when she came back to it.

I continued to turn over last night's events in my head as I showered. I closed my eyes under the warm water. Mom's an Apex. Wesley's an Apex. Naomi's an Apex. Andersen, Heather, Amanda, Mr. Hendricks. The school nurse. All Apex.

And me? Definitely not an Apex. I opened my eyes and watched the water stream off my fingertips as I held my hands out in front of me. I wasn't an Apex, but I had beat Hackjob when Wesley and Naomi hadn't been able to. I still wasn't sure how.

I stayed in the shower until my fingers began to prune. As much as I wanted to, I couldn't hide out in the warm steam all day, though I should have at least tried, because when I walked back to my room wrapped in my robe, I was stopped by Jamie.

She stepped out of her room as I was about to pass and stuck her arm out.

"Where were you guys last night?" she demanded. "Naomi was supposed to be back in time for Free Froyo Friday."

She glared at me, as if I were personally responsible for her friend standing her up.

"I don't know, how about you try asking me after I've put real clothes on."

I shoved past her. I'd beaten Hackjob, I told myself again. What was a teenage girl going to do to me?

Something tugged at the towel wrapped around my head. My wet hair fell against my shoulders, and I spun around. Jamie was holding my towel in her perfectly manicured claws.

"Tell me where you were!"

"Jamie," I said slowly. "I swear if you don't leave me alone, I'll puke on you again."

She recoiled as if I might projectile vomit right then and there. I reached over and grabbed my towel. She let me take it but scoffed as I turned my back to her.

"I was just asking a question. You don't need to be so rude about it."

"Who's being rude?" Naomi appeared behind Jamie from around the corner. She was in a new outfit and looked like she'd already showered and gotten ready for the day. There was no trace of the cuts that had covered her arms just the night before.

"There you are! Where'd you go last night? We were waiting for you!"

I smiled wanly at Naomi as I turned away to go back to my dorm, leaving her to deal with Jamie's indignation on her own.

After getting ready for the day, I sat down at my desk, finally faced with what I'd been avoiding all morning. I had run out of things to do. I pulled out a list of math problems Mrs. Young had assigned for the weekend and tried to force my way through them. If I thought about math, I couldn't think about last night.

Unfortunately, the opposite was also true. The more last night crept into my thoughts, the harder the trigonometry on the page became. I only got through the first few problems before setting my head down on the open book.

I was about to give up and try to go back to sleep when there was a knock at the door, and Fleming's voice sounded from the other side.

"Samantha? Are you in there?"

I opened the door, and Fleming wasn't alone. The principal of New Delos prep stood at his side. Her gray hair matched her gray pantsuit and was pulled back in a tight bun. She towered over both of us. I froze, trying to remember her name.

"I hope we aren't bothering you," Fleming apologized, but the woman squinted down at me over the frames of her wire-rimmed glasses.

"We're here to collect some of Winnie's things."

She invited herself into the room, and I stepped aside. Fleming hung back in the doorway while the principal inspected Winnie's desk.

"Dr. Weaver heads the council in charge of school-sanctioned Apex activities," Fleming explained, shuffling inside to avoid any eavesdroppers. He looked embarrassed by his superior's behavior. She emptied Winnie's bag out on the empty bed. Her camera landed among notebooks.

"Is this going to help find Winnie?" I asked. Dr. Weaver didn't pay me any attention as she went through Winnie's desk drawers. She found a couple of flash drives and set them next to the camera before moving on.

"It's no secret that Winnie managed to gather a lot of information on us in the last year. With her disappearance, we just want to make sure that information is secure," Fleming explained.

"Oh," I said flatly. They seemed more worried about Winnie's pictures than Winnie herself. "You know, there's a way to secure Winnie's information without having to raid my dorm room."

Dr. Weaver stopped her snooping to give me an icy stare. I could see the reprimand building inside of her, but I kept talking before she could tell me off for my snark.

"You could just find Winnie." I shrugged.

"Samantha, we are doing everything—"

Dr. Weaver raised a hand to cut off Fleming.

"You're Alison Taylor's daughter, right?"

"It's Havardson now, but yes."

Dr. Weaver surprised me by smiling.

"I didn't even know she had a daughter until a couple weeks ago." Dr. Weaver pulled Winnie's laptop out of another desk drawer. It went in the pile with the flash drives and camera. "You're not an Apex, though?"

"No."

She clicked her tongue.

"That's too bad." She scooped Winnie's electronics off the bed. "It would have been interesting to have you on the team."

She handed the items over to Fleming and followed him into the hallway.

"You'll hear from us if we need anything else from you." Dr. Weaver checked her phone. "Hopefully, we'll get your roommate back soon."

She beckoned for Fleming to follow her.

"Wait!" I said. They stopped to look at me where I was paused in the doorway. I wasn't sure what to say. I swallowed. "If it'd be interesting to have me on the team, then why not, um, why not try it?"

My voice got quieter as I spoke. Fleming looked both ways down the hall, making sure no one had heard me. Dr. Weaver's brow furrowed.

"Why would you want that?" she asked.

"To help?" I pointed at Fleming. "He was on the team, and he's not an Apex."

Fleming's face flushed, and he almost dropped Winnie's laptop.

"Wesley and Naomi told me. Also, Mr. Hendricks kinda yelled it in the Sickbay last night. That's what 'Beta' means, right? Not an Apex?" That's what the white-haired woman had called me at the docks, too. "But I've almost been kidnapped twice now, and you can't say I didn't hold my own last night."

Dr. Weaver was smiling again. My heart quickened. What had I just done? She stepped back into my room. I was pretty tall, but Dr. Weaver was at least a foot taller than me. I shrank back against my desk.

"Every student who tries out for Apex Team faces the same set of trials, the first week of October," she explained. "Apex abilities or not, whoever passes will be allowed on the team. Mr. Fleming is the last non-Apex to try out for the team at all."

She wasn't saying no. Had I thought this through? Absolutely not, but that was a problem for later.

"Is this something you really want to do?" Fleming looked sad, but I didn't know why.

"I can help." I shrugged. "Plus, I don't want to wait around until someone tries to shove me in another car trunk."

I left out the fact that Winnie was only missing because of me, and it wasn't like I had done much to help Anthony, either.

"There's no training on the weekends, but Monday, if you go to Fleming's office after class, he'll get you oriented with the group and outline the next month for you."

"Monday is a holiday," I reminded her.

"Training starts at one," Fleming looked ready to throw-up. "Come find me at noon, and we'll talk."

Dr. Weaver leaned back out of the room and glanced down the hall. She pressed her lips together into a thin smile as she led Fleming back towards the elevators. I watched them go, my hands gripping the doorframe, wondering what I'd just done.

News of Winnie and Anthony's kidnapping spread fast. Winnie already had a degree of notoriety about her, even among the upperclassmen. The gossip surrounding Lannie Bryce's disappearance at the pier the weekend before had finally been dying down, but the events at the museum added new fuel to the fire.

I couldn't so much as walk to the bathroom without girls peering out of their dorms at me. When I went to dinner with Bethany on Sunday night, she spent the entire meal sniffling into her potatoes, asking me what had happened. She'd been friends with Anthony, but I hadn't realized just how close they were. I finished eating early so I could go back to hiding in my room. The guilt festering inside me had killed my appetite.

Monday morning, Remi cornered me outside the showers.

"You were there Friday, right?"

I scowled and hugged my shower robe tighter around myself. Just once, I'd like to make it back to my room after a shower without an interrogation.

"What about it?" Two days had passed since the incident at the museum, and there was still no sign of Winnie or Anthony.

"Wes was there, too, wasn't he?" According to Anthony, Wesley and Remi had dated off and on last year. "He's okay, right?" Remi asked. "I haven't seen him around campus."

"He's fine. It was just Winnie and Anthony who were taken."

"That's not what I meant."

I made a show of readjusting my shower caddy in my arms, hoping Remi would take the hint and realize I wanted to leave.

"It's just," she hesitated before continuing, "he can be hard on himself, and Anthony was his roommate after all."

I shifted my weight from one foot to the other. I hadn't seen Wesley or Naomi all weekend. I'd been so busy hiding in shame, I hadn't given any thought to how they might be feeling.

"I haven't really seen him, actually," I admitted. Remi's face fell, but she forced a sad smile.

"Oh. That's alright. Sorry."

I slunk back to my dorm room and tried not to look at Winnie's bed.

It was a school holiday, but I would've preferred going to class to staying holed up alone in my room dodging anxious texts from Dad. He checked in on me hourly, making sure I hadn't been abducted in the sixty minutes since he'd last heard from me.

My phone lit up on my desk, however, when I picked up my phone to text Dad back, I saw it wasn't a text from him at all. I'd set a reminder in my calendar to meet Fleming at noon.

I had an hour before I was supposed to be in his office. My heart hammered in my chest, and I swallowed a lump that had risen in my throat. Was this what I wanted? I'd been able to fight Hackjob, but I'd locked up at both the museum and the docks. What if instead of helping find Winnie, I just got in the way?

But I couldn't just do nothing. I sat down at my desk and put my head down on my chemistry textbook. I'd been meaning to study for a quiz all weekend, but thoughts of Winnie and Apex had kept me distracted. Using the book as a pillow was probably the closest I'd get to actually studying.

I screwed my eyes shut. I could at least meet with Fleming. I'd be mad at myself if I didn't. I could decide in the moment if I wanted to try joining Apex Team. I wondered how Mom had decided if she should join the team or not.

It wasn't like I could ask her, though. If I so much as hinted I was thinking about trying out, her and Dad would make the choice for me, and it would be a resounding no.

I would talk to Fleming. I had an hour to get ready and think about what I would even say. I opened my eyes. Even if I didn't join the team, I knew I could help. There had to be something I could do.

An hour later, I stood in front of Fleming's office door. He hammered on a computer keyboard on the other side. A door opened behind me and I glanced backwards to make eye contact with an upperclassmen with long, dark hair, a tan face, and ears that stuck out like Anthony's. She disappeared through the door I now knew led to the secret Apex base.

I turned back to Fleming's door and knocked. He called me inside, and I braced myself.

Fleming looked less tired than he had when I'd seen him last, but still had a harried look about him. His button-up was wrinkled and his hair a mess, but he managed a weak smile as he gestured towards the seat opposite his.

"I wasn't sure you'd show." He slid a stack of papers across the desk. "You'll need to fill those out. Liability and confidentiality and all that. You need a parent to sign that one there, so just get it to me as soon as you can."

My heart dropped. There was no way Mom and Dad would let me join. I picked up a pen from a dusty mug, pushing away thoughts of my parents. I didn't need to worry about them yet.

"What'll it look like if I join the team?"

"You'll be a provisional member until you pass the Trials in October, along with the eleven Freshmen who've enrolled." Fleming wrung his hands. "It's mostly fitness tests with a touch of combat. No swords allowed, however."

I forced a laugh and put the pen to the forms. I ignored the line asking for a parent or guardian's signature.

"But you don't think I should join, do you?"

"No," he admitted. I scowled. "Not for the reasons you think, though. For one, Alison will flay me if anything happens to you."

"Does she have to know?"

He raised an eyebrow at me.

"I think she'll figure it out when you ask her to sign that permission form. She might be more understanding than you expect. She was on the team once, too."

"And nothing about Winnie, yet?" I asked, pausing halfway through the top sheet of paper. Fleming shook his head.

Guilt mixed with resolve, and I bent over the forms once more. I wouldn't get in the way. I'd be a provisional team member. I could help from the sidelines. I'd figure out what to do about Mom and Dad later.

"Samantha." I didn't like the way Fleming said my name, like he was about to list all the reasons I should steer clear of Apex Team.

"I'm joining."

"I know, but—"

"I don't want to be frozen anymore!" I snapped. Fleming squinted at me over his glasses. "I mean, I'm done being scared. At the museum and the docks…I don't know. Maybe Winnie and Anthony would still be…"

I scrawled my name across the bottom of the first form in a furious scribble before flipping it over and moving onto the next. I didn't read the text. I signed and added it to the first one.

"It'll be a commitment—"

"Actively trying to not be kidnapped has turned into a commitment, too," I said wryly. Fleming mumbled something unintelligible under his breath but stood up. He ran his hands through his disheveled hair and sighed.

"Right," he said. "I suppose we should go introduce you to the team, then."

14

Less Than Welcome

Fleming paused with his hand on the door. I could hear the clanging of metal weights on the floor in the next room accompanied by heavy music. There was a light sheen of sweat on Fleming's forehead even though it was cool in the atrium.

"Listen. I get that you want to do this, but I've been where you are right now, and sometimes I wish that I didn't go through this door." He raised a hand when I opened my mouth to interject. "I'm not saying this to dissuade you. I promise. And I know you'd make an amazing team member, but it is hard even for those with special abilities. You walk in there with no Apex powers, and every mistake will be pinned on you. Not just your mistakes, either. Every mission that fails, they'll blame you. Every success, they'll say you had help."

"That's fine." I knew there were people behind the door who didn't like me, but I also knew there were people who did. Naomi and Wesley, they'd have to be excited to see me. They might already know I was out here with their super senses.

"Samantha, I'm still having to prove myself over and over." Fleming sounded sad. I remembered Mr. Hendricks yelling at him in the Sickbay after the museum incident. "And you might end up going through all this trouble for nothing."

He meant the trials. I waved him off.

"I have a month. I'm sure it'll be fine."

Fleming took a reassuring breath and tried to smile.

The music volume swelled as Fleming pushed open the door into the gym. There were about forty students inside, engaged in a variety of activities. A group of students practiced kicking and hitting a line of punching bags along the back, mirrored wall. Another wall housed heavy weights. Andersen was at the bench press, and a loaded bar raised and lowered over his chest, but no one was touching it. A long window overlooked a swimming center. It would've looked like any normal gym pool if not for the ropes course suspended over it. The rest of the gym was filled with endurance machines like treadmills and stair climbers.

"Do not slam the weights on the ground!" Fleming barked at a couple of seniors who were using the largest dumbbells I'd ever seen. They waved in apology but faltered when they saw me standing with him. "Everybody, listen up!"

Someone turned down the music, and the treadmills all whirred to a stop. In the far corner, Naomi grabbed Wesley's arm to pull him away from a punching bag, and she pointed at me from across the room. His eyebrows rose in surprise, and I quickly looked away from them.

"What's she doing here?" Andersen stood at his bench with his arms crossed.

"Did they find the missing students?" a girl I didn't recognize asked.

Fleming shook his head.

"No, but I do have an important announcement." He gestured at me, and I felt every pair of eyes lock onto my face. "You're all familiar with

Samantha by now, and I'm sure you'd all agree she more than proved herself the other night at the museum."

Fleming paused, but no one had any interjection to make. He cleared his throat and continued.

"She's requested to try out for Apex Team and—"

Everyone seemed to be holding their breath before, but the bubble burst, and several students objected all at once. No one was louder than Andersen.

"But she's a Beta!" Andersen shouted over the caterwaul. "She's a liability!"

"And," Fleming raised his voice, continuing to speak over the din, "the council has decided to allow her to face the trials!"

The shouting doubled in volume.

"Does she even know how to fight?"

"I'm not scouting with her!"

"She wasn't even able to save her own roommate!"

I locked eyes with Wesley. He and Naomi stood at the back of the group. Neither looked happy at Fleming's announcement, but they weren't shouting at me. Wesley gave me a wavering thumbs-up and a grimacing smile.

"Settle down!" Fleming had to yell to be heard. Finally, Andersen was the only one still talking.

"Mr. F!" He gesticulated wildly. "This is a joke, right? A Beta can't be on Apex Team."

"It might serve you well to remember who is in charge here." Fleming was usually so mild mannered, but now, he glowered at Andersen.

"I mean, that's different, you know?" Andersen covered. "You're not really a Beta."

"And it might serve you even better to remember we don't use that word in *my* facility."

Fleming stared around the room, as if daring any of his students to try defying him again.

"No, Samantha is not an Apex," he finally continued, "but you don't have to be an Apex to try out, and non-Apex have proven they are just as valuable as their teammates. She'll face the entrance trials the first week of October along with the other new recruits. I expect all of you to support her as you would any other team member."

Andersen snorted, but didn't dare speak out again. Wesley looked a little more certain now and gave me two thumbs-up this time. A hand shot up in the middle of the room.

"Will she train with the freshmen or the sophomores?" Heather asked. Even in her training gear, she had a large purple bow fastened to her ponytail.

"She'll stay with her classmates on the sophomore team."

Heather beamed at me, and I smiled. Not everyone was against my being there, just most of them.

Fleming released the students back to their training but motioned for Naomi and Wesley to come over. The clanking and whirring of a busy gym returned. The music blared back to life, but was quickly turned down a few notches. The closest students kept their ears turned towards us, and I knew they were listening in as discreetly as they could.

"Are you sure about this?"

I'd hoped the first words out of Wesley's mouth would have been more encouraging. I recoiled at the brazenness of his question.

"Why does everyone keep asking me that?"

"I think it's great," Naomi smiled. "You've got Andersen's panties in a real twist."

"Since you've already worked with Naomi and Wesley, I figured they could give you a proper orientation," Fleming said. "You've seen a small fraction of the facilities, they can show you the rest, and I'll let them start you on combat training."

Wesley perked up.

"Combat training? So we're being made Team Captains?"

"Maybe. Consider this a test for you both just as much as it is for Samantha."

Wesley grinned at me.

"That's it, I'm paying off whoever you draw for the Final Trial. We'll be Team Captains for sure if we can get a non-Apex on the team."

"As long as you keep her from getting killed, I'll be happy," Fleming said, glancing at his watch. "I've got to go meet with the council, so tell me you've got this."

"Tour and combat training," Naomi recapped. "Yeah, we've got it."

"Alright, then. I'm out," Fleming paused as he moved towards the door. "And Samantha?"

"Yes?"

"Good luck."

The secret Apex base hiding under the main school hall was much bigger than I had anticipated. We didn't linger too long in the main gym. The other students began to openly stare at us once Fleming was gone. Naomi pulled us through the next doors, into the locker rooms.

Wesley blushed furiously, and Naomi laughed at him.

"There aren't any girls in here. Don't be so embarrassed."

"I'm not embarrassed, I just know it's not allowed!"

"Oh," Naomi said, "you are definitely embarrassed."

The locker room had a second door that led into the pool room with the ropes course. The smell of chlorine hit us full force as we walked out onto the tiled floor.

"Thursdays are swim days," Wesley said. "Makes sense to be at least okay at swimming when you live on the island."

"Right." I nodded importantly. "Just in case you have to punch through any piers and swim back to shore."

"What?" Naomi looked confused, but Wesley rolled his eyes.

"It would have worked, okay?"

"Anyway," Naomi interjected, "the first trial is usually water treading. It's the easiest one, and the basic idea is to not drown for ten minutes."

They continued the tour through another door that led out into the main atrium. There were more training rooms, but none as large as the first gym. Most were outfitted for specific exercises, like yoga and Pilates or weapon-based combat. One had a large matted area, surrounded by a waist-high wall. Beyond the wall, there was a small set of bleachers. Two doors on the far side were labeled "Sickbay".

"This is where hand-to-hand combat tests happen." Naomi gestured around the room. "That's what the Final Trial is. You have to last two minutes against someone who is already a team member."

I swallowed hard.

"Oh," I said, my voice cracking. "Yeah, no problem. Do I at least get to pick who I fight?"

Wesley shook his head.

"Nope, it's a random draw. I hope you get Andersen, he sucks at fighting, and he can't use his powers if you wear cotton."

"Andersen's weakness is cotton?"

"Not exactly." Naomi glared at Wesley. "He has telekinetic powers, but they don't work on organic material. He can move rocks and metal, but people and non-synthetic clothes? He can't do a thing."

I walked out onto the matted floor, feeling my sneakers sink into the cushions. I tried to imagine an opponent standing across the ring from me, but the thought of it twisted my insides. Fighting Hackjob had been easy in the moment, but that was different. I'd had a sword, for one, and I still wasn't sure what had taken over me to cause me to stand up to him like that.

But another member of Apex Team?

"So you'll let me win if he picks one of you?" I was only half-joking.

"Since we're training you, it's a conflict of interest," Naomi explained. "Neither of us will be in the draw."

"Besides," Wesley said, "you'll do fine against whoever you end up against. We've seen you fight."

My insides twisted.

"But I have no idea how I did that stuff," I admitted. "It was like someone else was driving."

"I know you can punch," Wesley assured me, tapping his face where I'd hit him after he'd saved me at the docks. He squared up in the center of the ring, facing me. "Come on, try again."

I laughed awkwardly and looked over to Naomi, but she was already finding a seat on the bleachers.

"Very funny," I said to Wesley.

"No, I'm serious!" He held his hands up in front of him like a boxer. "Fleming said to get you started on combat training, didn't he?"

"Feet apart!" Naomi shouted from her seat. "Hands up in front of you at all times."

I felt ridiculous trying to mirror Wesley's stance. I'd never noticed before how intimidating he looked. His arms were loose but poised, ready to spring at a moment's notice. They were toned, definitely not the arms of someone you'd want to get in a fight with.

Meanwhile, my legs felt like stilts underneath me, and as I lifted my fists to guard my face, I suddenly had no idea what to do with my elbows. Wesley lowered his hands to gently grab mine. He repositioned them a little higher and tapped on my elbows to lower them.

"Bend your knees a little." He was standing very close and still holding onto one of my fists. "Good, and try to keep more weight on the balls of your feet. Too much weight in the heels, and you'll be easier to knock over."

He continued to make adjustments to my stance, his face uncomfortably close to mine. I tried to focus on remembering how he'd positioned me as he stepped away into a nearby closet.

"I'm gonna go find Marcus and find out what he's teaching the freshmen. We can steal some of their exercises," Naomi said, standing up.

"Yeah, good idea!" Wesley called from the closet.

Wesley returned with a circular mitt on his hand as Naomi disappeared through the door. He tossed me a pair of gloves.

"It's okay to be nervous." His tone was unexpectedly gentle.

"I'm not—" I stopped myself. There was no use lying. "Thanks. It's just a lot to take in."

"No one is making you join the team. You could always walk away."

"I've almost been kidnapped twice. I'm not about to sit around and wait for the third time. Besides, with Winnie gone, you and Naomi are the closest things I have to friends."

My cheeks warmed, but Wesley nodded.

"I get that. It's been weird with Anthony gone."

"I'm sorry." It was embarrassing that it had taken Remi cornering me in the bathroom that morning to remind me I wasn't the only one with a missing roommate.

"It's okay. We'll find them." He forced a smile and threw his hands up in the air so that the mitt was facing me. "And you'll be there with us when we do! So, come on. Hit me!"

I did my best to assume a stance like the one Wesley had just positioned me into. It felt unnatural, but he nodded in encouragement. I struck out with my right hand, and it hit the mitt with a soft thud.

"Yeah, not a bad start, but I've seen you do better."

I tried again.

"Good! Now try it like this." He jabbed at the air. "See how I used my hip?"

We spent the better part of the next half hour going over the different hits. I jabbed, hooked, and uppercut over and over, figuring out how to pivot on one foot to throw my whole body weight behind the punches. However, even my best hits barely moved Wesley.

By the time Naomi had come back carrying a print out of exercises, I'd worked up a light sweat.

"Just a small warning," she said, "Andersen is definitely scheming something up."

"What's that mean?" I asked, grateful for the break but apprehensive at what Andersen might be up to.

"I'm not sure, but he gives off a very particular type of excitement when he has something up his sleeve, and he reeked of it when I was over there."

"He can try," I said nonchalantly, despite knowing perfectly well Naomi would be able to feel how nervous I suddenly was. I threw my gloved fists up in front of my face and swung a right hook as Wesley braced himself behind the mitt.

There was a satisfying slap of vinyl on vinyl, and Wesley grinned.

"Then we better get you started on kicks."

15

A Late Night Visit

Andersen glared at us from across the cafeteria. I didn't need Naomi's unique ability to know that he was pissed, but as I waited in line for burgers with Naomi and Wesley, I couldn't help but smile. It was exciting to be trying out for Apex Team as the first non-Apex since Fleming. Knowing how much it bothered Andersen only made it that much sweeter.

"We got through a lot today!" Naomi looked over her planner. She'd already outlined a training plan from now until the trials. "You might even be cleared to play in the Night Game!"

"Wait, when is that?" Wesley asked.

"Two weeks." Naomi turned her calendar to show Wesley.

"What's the Night Game?" I asked.

"Are you guys talking about The Night Game?" Heather appeared next to us in line. "Are you gonna play in it, Sam?"

"I need to know what it is first!"

"Just the best night of the semester, that's all," Wesley said, loading his plate with potato salad. "It's different every year, but we get the whole city to run around and play a game in the dark."

"It's not a game," Naomi said. "It's a group training exercise."

"They don't call it The Night Training Exercise, do they?"

Naomi scowled, but Heather laughed.

"Last time, it was Capture The Flag," Heather explained. "It was upperclassmen versus underclassmen, and the entire island was the playing field."

"But the upperclassmen cheated," Wesley grumbled.

We finished piling burgers onto our plates and made our way to a table.

"Naomi, we're over here!"

Jamie waved from a booth seat. Andersen pouted next to her.

"I'm gonna sit with these guys tonight," Naomi said, pointing at us. Jamie's perfectly poised face cracked just a little.

"Yeah, okay. I'll see you at the dorm."

We took our seats around the table we'd claimed, and Naomi shook her head.

"She's really upset."

I looked back at Jamie, but she seemed to have already moved on, greeting Madison to their booth while playing listlessly with Andersen's hair.

"She looks fine to me."

"Yeah," Naomi sighed. "She's good at that."

"Wait, this says six thirty!" Wesley was looking over Naomi's planner. "Are we really meeting at six thirty tomorrow morning?"

She snatched the planner from his hands and shoved it in her bag.

"No one is scheduled to be on the track tomorrow or in the pool." She jerked a thumb in my direction. "Samantha can run through the general fitness trials so we know what to focus on."

"Do I need to be there?"

Naomi and I both shot him looks. He shrugged.

"Sorry, but I'm on call duty tonight. I have to be awake until six anyways."

"Great, so what's another couple hours? Besides, you never sleep," Naomi pointed out. Wesley grumbled into his dinner but seemed to have resigned himself to a sleepless night.

"What's call duty?" I asked.

"We have to have someone manning the front desk in the training center at all times," Heather explained. "We usually have a team out at night, either doing surveillance or advanced training, so it's nice to have someone to call in case of an emergency."

Wesley had said Andersen had been on call the night of the dock incident, and after the museum the other night, a girl had been sleeping at the front desk.

"How often do you have to be on call?" I asked. It didn't sound like a very glamorous part of the job.

"Once a month or so." Naomi shrugged. "It's not a big deal. Most people sleep at the desk."

Wesley had already cleared his plate and was standing up.

"I'm gonna go try and nap before I report," he said, glaring at Naomi. She smirked back.

"You wanna be a captain or not?"

He sauntered away with his dishes, and Heather made to follow him.

"I should head out, too. I haven't done any of the chem homework that's due tomorrow," she said. "I'll see you guys tomorrow!"

As Heather made her exit, my stomach dropped. I'd completely forgotten about the chemistry homework. There was a quiz on ion molecules tomorrow, and I hadn't bothered to study.

"You need to work on the homework, don't you?" Naomi asked.

"Yeah, how did you— oh. Right." It was easy to forget Naomi could sense every emotion around her.

"No need to panic," she laughed. "I made flash cards. If we get out of here fast enough, Jamie won't see where we've gone."

After stopping by the dorms to pick up our backpacks and textbooks, we headed to the library. It was strange to think that just a couple of days ago, I'd considered Naomi one of Jamie's mindless clones. Turned out, she was pretty cool.

The library was full of students who'd put off their homework over the long weekend until the last moment, but we were able to find a couple of arm chairs in a corner. Naomi gave me a chance to review the list of anions before busting out her flashcards.

"This one?" she asked.

"Sulfite?"

"Close. Sulfate. Sulfite only has three oxygens. Sulfate has four."

"Oh, right." I was definitely going to fail the quiz.

Luckily, Naomi didn't give up on me, and after running through her cards a couple times, I was getting most of them. I was in the middle of reciting the formula for acetate when Naomi frowned.

"Was that wrong?"

She shook her head.

"No, you got it. But Jamie just got here."

I glanced over my shoulder, but the library doors weren't visible from where we were sitting.

"How can you tell?"

"If I know someone well enough, it's easy to feel them in a crowd. It's like recognizing someone's voice. You start to learn what their emotions feel like."

Naomi shrank back into her armchair. She pulled her hair out of its bun, and it sprung down around her face, as if she meant to hide from Jamie behind it.

"If you don't like Jamie, why do you hang out with her so much?"

Naomi looked taken aback by the question and took a moment to answer.

"It's not that I don't like her. There are good things about her, too." Naomi smirked. "I know she's a jerk, but she's a good friend. Besides, if I'm with her, I can redirect her attention when she starts to go too far."

"You shouldn't have to feel responsible for who Jamie decides to torment," I pointed out. Naomi sighed.

"It's not like that," she said, but didn't seem to believe herself. "Besides, she's one of the only people here who actually talks to me."

I laughed.

"What are you talking about? You're one of the cool kids!"

The idea of Naomi not being popular was ludicrous to me, but she stared absently at her cards.

"Not really," she admitted. "Most of the kids on Apex Team are scared of me. No one likes having their personal feelings invaded. And everyone who's not on Apex Team is scared of me, too, even if they don't know why. It's like some sort of instinct tells them I'm listening to their feelings so they avoid me anyway. But Jamie likes that about me."

"She likes that you are intimidating?"

"I guess? Is that a bad reason to be someone's friend?"

I closed my textbook.

"I don't know," I admitted. "There are definitely better reasons. It's not fair that you have to run behind Jamie, trying to minimize whatever damage she inflicts on people."

I thought Naomi might be offended, but she smiled.

"Most people aren't that honest with me."

"Yeah, well, you can already tell everything I'm feeling, so why not tell you what I think, too?" We were quiet for a moment before I spoke again. "I don't want to abuse your powers, but do you think you could tell me why everyone is so against me joining Apex Team?"

Naomi fidgeted in her seat.

"Usually, I'd say no, but I guess it's only fair that you know what you're getting yourself into." She looked up at the ceiling, as if gathering all of her thoughts there before continuing. "Truth is, everyone has their own reasons. Some people don't like it because it makes them feel less special."

"Like Andersen?"

"Exactly like Andersen. But others feel like you're intruding. A lot of us don't like being Apex. There's a lot of stigma, I mean, obviously you've seen the protests."

I hadn't thought about how Naomi and Wesley might feel being targeted as dangerous by half the city. I didn't like the guilty feeling that was settling in my gut. Even some of the students made their feelings about Apex obvious.

"It's not like I'm trying to be an Apex," I said. "I just want to help."

Naomi smiled.

"I know that. So do some of the others, but people are weird," she explained. "Thing is, a lot of us wish we could be normal like you. I don't like feeling what everyone else is feeling, and I can't turn it off. I'm glad I'm able to put it to good use, but if I could be just a normal student, I would. And then you walk in and choose this."

I couldn't think of anything to say. I guess I'd probably be pretty bitter about me trying out if I was the rest of the team, too. But it didn't seem fair. I had insight, I could help, so I should. This just seemed like the best way to do so.

"Again, Wesley and I don't think that way about you," Naomi assured me. "I'm thrilled you are trying out. Wesley is, too."

"Andersen's not," I snorted. Naomi shuffled her flashcards.

"No, but he's never thrilled about anything," she smirked and paused a moment. I could tell she was debating if she should tell me something or not. "You know, he's actually a little scared."

"No, he's not! What's he got to be scared of?"

"He doesn't trust you to keep it a secret that he's an Apex. Not to mention he's afraid you'll be better than him at fighting after hearing about the museum."

"Huh."

I had thought Andersen was just a jerk. I liked thinking I had just a little bit of power over him. I made him nervous. Good.

"Now," Naomi held up a card. "What's this one?"

"Three oxygens?" I grinned. "That's got to be Sulfite."

She grinned back and flipped it so I could see "Sulfite" scrawled across the back. If Naomi was able to prepare me for the chemistry quiz, helping me pass the trials in a month shouldn't be a problem for her, either.

I held my hand up above my face. I'd been lying in bed awake for a while but had lost track of how long. It felt like the rest of the hall had fallen asleep hours ago. After getting back to the dorms, Naomi left to hang out with Jamie and Madison, leaving me to finish homework alone in my room.

I stretched my fingers out, barely able to make out their outline against the dark ceiling. My knuckles were sore but had escaped bruising from the day's work. I let my arm fall back down to the mattress. I knew I should sleep. My body was exhausted. I could already feel my muscles tightening up and becoming sore, but my mind was buzzing.

"It was a good day," I mumbled to myself. "You did fine. It was fine."

I rubbed my eyes, willing them to be tired. If I didn't sleep now, how was I supposed to get through school and training tomorrow?

Training tomorrow.

I knew we'd have to pick up the pace if I was supposed to be ready to pass the trials in a month. I'd have to start fighting real people and not just Wesley's boxing mitts. I felt sick thinking about it.

"Shhh," I shushed myself, pushing away thoughts of what I was sure was impending failure. "You beat Hackjob."

With a sword! A tiny voice in my head screamed.

"And you'll beat anyone Fleming pits against you with your hands," I whispered. I held both of them out in front of me this time. I could do it. I would do it. I just needed to get some sleep first.

The knock at the door was so soft that I might not have heard it if I hadn't been awake still. I thought I might have even imagined it at first, but then whoever was on the other side of the door knocked again.

I slipped out of bed and unlocked the door. I only opened it a few inches.

"It's okay, it's just me."

Wesley grinned at me from under his jacket hood.

"You can't be in here!" I hissed, pulling him into the bedroom. I checked down the hall before closing the door to make sure Renee hadn't seen him. "No guys allowed after ten! How did you even get in?"

"It's fine!" he laughed.

"Aren't you supposed to be at the call desk?"

"Got off early, which is lucky, because there's something I wanted to show you. Come on, it's outside."

"It's after midnight," I said, glancing at my desk clock. "Can't it wait?"

Wesley had seemed like a stickler for rules so it was surprising for him to waltz into the girls' dorm well past curfew. What's more, he wanted me to break curfew, too, and follow him outside.

"No, it's about Winnie."

"Winnie?" I gasped. "What about her? Have you told Fleming or any of the others?"

"I will, but I thought you should see it first."

I stuck my head back out into the hall to make sure the coast was clear, but the floor was silent. I motioned for him to follow me into the hall.

We took the steps down to the bottom floor two at a time. In my hurry, I hadn't bothered to put any socks on with my sneakers and could already feel my heels chafing.

"How far are we going?" I asked as we slipped out onto the dewy lawn. My jacket was doing very little to stem the cold, and I wished I'd taken the extra time to throw sweatpants on over my pajama shorts.

"Not far," he assured me. We were walking towards the docks where I'd seen the rowing team practicing. The bay slapped rhythmically against the side of the island. A dense marine fog was already rolling in over the campus. "This way."

We were going towards the boardwalk trail that Winnie and I had taken to get to the festival at the pier.

"Are you sure it's okay that we're out? You aren't officially on duty right now, and I don't want to get kicked off before I've even had the chance to—"

"I already told you, it's fine!" he snapped. I stopped, and he spun around to look at me when he realized I wasn't following him anymore. "What?"

The fog was thick enough that I couldn't see the pier up ahead, and I couldn't see how far we'd come from the campus either. It was just

Wesley, me, and the wooden planks we were walking on. The city lights filtered through the fog, giving it a dull glow.

"What?" he demanded again. "I told you to follow me."

"I don't know," I hesitated. "Something doesn't feel right."

He scoffed and turned back around. If it was anyone else, I wouldn't have kept following him. But this was Wesley. He had to have a good reason to be acting this way so I continued to follow him.

"It doesn't feel right?" he repeated without looking back at me. "So, what, you have Naomi's powers now?"

I bit my lip. It was best not to respond if he was this worked up. Maybe something had happened while he was working the call desk to put him in this mood.

The fog was getting even thicker. Maybe it was just a marine layer, rolling in over the island, but something felt unnatural about it.

"Would you hurry up?" Wesley said when he finally looked back and saw I was lagging behind him. The fog was so dense, I could hardly see more than a few yards ahead.

"Just tell me where we're going," I said. "I don't want to be out here all night."

Wesley's face darkened. He usually looked so happy, and goofy, and as he glowered at me through the fog, he was unrecognizable.

"I don't like how you're acting," I said slowly. *Wesley's nice*, I reminded myself. *He wouldn't hurt me.* But his brow furrowed, and his lips curled into a snarl. "What are we really doing out here?"

He tensed up and looked like he might hit me, but then his shoulders dropped, and he smiled.

"Fine, we'll do it here, then."

Something that felt like a human hand clamped over my mouth from behind me while another arm wrapped itself around my torso. I struggled and tried to shout, but more hands grabbed me, pinning my arms to my sides. I twisted against them, and while I could feel the tangle of arms and hands holding me back, I couldn't see anyone in the fog next to me.

Wesley held up a single finger to his lips, smiling as he shushed me. He stepped closer as he pulled a pair of handcuffs from his jacket pocket.

"What is this?" I demanded, twisting my face free of whatever had clamped over it. "Wesley, what's going on?"

"You haven't figured it out yet?" As he got closer to me, his face contorted. I thought I had to be imagining it, but the longer I stared in horror, the clearer it became that Wesley's face was changing. As he laughed, his nose became shorter and his chin more angular. Strawberry blonde hair sprouted from his scalp and fell around his shoulders. Where Wesley had stood a moment before, Winnie had taken his place.

"Winnie?" I gasped.

"Winnie!" she shrieked, mocking me. Laughter sounded next to my ear. "Seriously, how gullible are you?"

She grabbed my hands, and the handcuffs clicked around my wrists. Her hands were rougher than I'd expect them to be. Her knuckles were larger than I remembered.

"You're not Winnie," I accused her. "And you're not Wesley, either."

Winnie hesitated, and for a split second, she looked to my left, where I had heard the laughter. Even if I couldn't see them, someone was there. With my hands still cuffed in front of me, I swung an elbow back, making contact with someone's rib cage. I heard all the air go out of them, and their grip weakened.

Just like at the docks and just like at the museum, a fighting instinct took over. I kicked out at the fake Winnie, using her abdomen to push myself into the invisible captors who held me back. They shouted in surprise. It sounded like there were at least three of them. A girl growled, "Grab her!"

I sprang to my feet and bolted down the boardwalk back towards New Delos Prep. The campus was still hidden by fog so it was hard to gauge how far it was, but I at least had a good head start on them.

My shoes thundered on the wooden boardwalk, matching the thundering of blood in my ears. Three kidnapping attempts were three too many, and my luck would have to run out eventually.

And then, it did.

There was a sudden force around my wrist, like a giant magnet was pulling at the handcuffs clinked around my forearms. I fell head over heels, landing flat on my back with my arms in the air as something unseen continued to pull on the handcuffs.

It dragged me backwards, slowly at first and then faster. As panic washed over me, I flipped myself onto my stomach. The Winnie figure was changing again. Her hair crept back into her head and lightened to a brighter blond. Her cheek bones became more pronounced and her eyebrows heavier until it wasn't Winnie anymore. It was Andersen's friend, Skyler.

Four other figures shimmered into view. I recognized them all as members of Apex Team. There was Olivia and Freddie, who were both in my First Period class. Another girl I didn't know the name of, but I knew she was in the year ahead of us. The last one to take shape was Andersen. He grinned with his arm outstretched, summoning the handcuffs.

I fought against Andersen's pull, struggling to my feet as he pulled me closer. I dug my feet into the planks of the boardwalk but lost a shoe as Andersen pulled harder. He didn't stop until I was lying at his feet while his friends laughed behind him. I curled myself into a ball, sick with anger and shaking.

Naomi had warned me that Andersen was up to something. At least now I knew what he'd been planning.

"Let me go," I said, trying to keep my tone even.

"Oh, well, since you asked," Andersen shrugged. The cuffs pulled me to my feet. Andersen flicked his hand and sent me tumbling over the banister and into the ocean. He yanked up on the handcuffs before I hit the water, and I yelped in pain as the metal dug into my skin. My body weight was pulling me towards the water, and the handcuffs had slipped as high up my hands as they could go.

"Okay, great. You got me," I said, trying not to wince from the pain in my hands as I spoke. "What do you want? Your seat back in Fleming's class?"

Andersen smirked.

"We don't want anything from you! We're just welcoming you to the team, right?"

Skyler's face morphed into Naomi's.

"What, is this not fun for you?" Skyler taunted in Naomi's voice.

"Let me down, Andersen!" I kicked at him, casting my remaining shoe into the water below. The way I dangled by my arms made it difficult to breathe. "If you wanna fight, I'll show you a fight!"

"I thought you wanted to be part of the team," Andersen goaded. "Look at how welcoming we are!"

"I swear, if you don't let me go, I'll tell Jamie you're an Apex!"

Andersen's friends stopped laughing and looked at him. He glared back at me. He shook from the effort of holding me up. Something warm rolled down the back of my arm. The handcuffs continued to dig into my hands, and I'd started to bleed. The sight of the thick, red fluid running down my arms sent a renewed sense of panic washing over me, but I refused to give Andersen the satisfaction of watching me thrash as I dangled over the water.

"I swear I'll tell her," I repeated. "She doesn't know, right? How could she? She hates Apex, and so do her lawyer parents."

"You know what, Sammy?" Andersen spat my name. "I think you're nothing but a Beta, and Betas are just dead weight. You know what dead weight does?"

He glanced around him, as if waiting for an answer, but his friends didn't seem like they were playing anymore. I gaped at them, silently begging them to make Andersen put me down. They shuffled uncomfortably and looked away.

"No one? No one knows? What about you, Sammy? Do you know?" Andersen opened his shaking fist, and just before the cold waters rose up over my head, I heard him shout, "It sinks!"

16

Call Duty

Every muscle in my body contracted at once as the freezing ocean swallowed me. I gasped sharply, inhaling a lungful of burning salt water. I kicked upwards and coughed violently as my head broke the surface. I struggled to tread water with my hands still bound by the handcuffs.

"You can't leave her there," the girl I didn't know said. As I blinked the salt water from my eyes, I saw Andersen turn away from the banister to walk back down the boardwalk towards campus.

"Why not?" he shot. "She wants to prove herself, doesn't she?"

"She'll get hypothermia!"

"God, Carmen! I said she's fine!" Andersen snarled. "Come on."

The others glanced down at me struggling to stay afloat with the use of only my legs. The salt water stung the fresh wounds that circled my hands. Anger and pride almost kept me from calling out for help, but then Freddie and Olivia exchanged a look and turned to follow Andersen.

"Wait!" I spat water out of my mouth. "There's no ladder!"

"Andersen." Freddie hesitated, but Andersen spun around and got in his face.

"You want to join her? No? Good."

They all looked back at me bobbing in water one last time before heading back down the boardwalk.

The threat of hypothermia didn't bother me. Neither did the fact there was no immediately visible way to get back up onto the island. More than anything, I was angry.

It had been a cruel joke, tricking me out here using Wesley's face. It had been even crueler to then appear as Winnie. Leaving me to drown in the ocean was just the cherry on top.

How could I have been so stupid? So gullible? And after everything that had happened the past week! Sure, I might freeze to death but worse than that, I was embarrassed. Not to mention, if I managed to not sink to the bottom of the ocean first, Fleming would kill me if he found out.

I kicked over to the concrete pilings supporting the boardwalk. Salt water filled my mouth and eyes, but with my hands bound, it was difficult to keep my face very far above the surface.

With no ladder in sight, I had to find a way out somehow. I wrapped my legs around the piling and tried to shimmy myself up. The barnacles that had made their homes on the concrete beam dug into my thighs. I gritted my teeth and tried to keep going, but, again, no hands.

I splashed back into the water. Wet hair slapped across my face, covering my eyes. I struggled to wipe it away. The first flicker of panic flitted through my stomach. Without a way to climb out of the water, I was dead.

Luckily, the fog had mostly dissipated, forcing me to wonder if it hadn't been summoned by one of Andersen's cronies. It receded to reveal a floating dock, maybe thirty yards away. I could swim that far, assuming I didn't freeze first.

I felt heavier, though I wasn't as cold anymore. My whole body had gone numb except for a warmth that radiated weakly from within my chest. I was almost there, but my muscles were starting to cramp. The panic came rushing back, threatening to drown me just as much as the water.

I willed my legs to keep kicking. They were feeling heavier with every yard, up until my hands pushed up against the dock. I reached up and grabbed the edge, and the small amount of relief I'd found turned to dread. I wasn't sure I had the strength left to pull myself up.

But I kicked wildly, and with a final heave, I flopped onto the dock and curled into a ball, pulling my bare knees as close to my face as I could as I shivered. I was a good swimmer, but the cold and the effort to swim and then pull myself out of the water had left me out of breath. I wasn't sure I'd be able to walk all the way back to campus.

But I couldn't lie there. If I let myself be still, I'd never find the strength to get up. I struggled to my feet. Blood oozed from the scrapes the barnacles had left on both of my legs. The cuts that encircled my hands bled as well. They looked worse than they felt, but that might've been because I was too numb to feel anything.

A small ramp led up to the main boardwalk from the dock. I stumbled up the slope but slipped on the metal. Unable to catch myself with my hands still bound, I landed hard on my shoulder, and a loud, metallic clang rang out as I hit the gangway.

I couldn't move. I couldn't so much as shiver, and the darkness that tugged at me felt warm. I could sleep off the cold, wake-up feeling better and ready to kick Andersen's ass. The panic was gone now. The sleep tugging at my consciousness felt welcoming...my eyelids fluttered closed as I welcomed the dark.

"Holy crap, isn't that your sister's roommate?"

Two women huddled above me. One of them leaned closer, and Amanda's face swam overhead. Two fingers pressed against the side of my neck.

"Is she...?" The second woman didn't seem keen to finish the end of her question. Amanda answered her with a quiet curse.

I coughed up salt water, and they both leapt away.

"She's alive!" Amanda exclaimed. Her friend stooped to help me into a sitting position, but Amanda shooed her away. "Head back to campus, Brooke. I can handle this."

Brooke hurried back the way they'd come while Amanda pulled her jacket off and threw it over me.

"Who did this? Was it those creeps who took Winnie?"

She held onto my shoulders as I shook my head. Amanda exhaled, but I couldn't tell if she was relieved or frustrated by my response. She rubbed her hands together as if she were the one who was half-freezing to death. I was about to ask her what she was doing, but then I felt warmth radiating from her. When I found out she was an Apex, I assumed her powers had to be something that helped her swim career, like secret gills or retractable finger webbing.

But there were no webs between her fingers as she held out her hands. Instead, a tiny flame was cradled in her palm, and despite its small size, it was warming up the air around us.

"My parents told me you found out." She shrugged. "No point hiding it, especially if you might freeze otherwise. We passed some high schoolers breaking curfew back down the boardwalk. Was it them?"

"Y-y-yeah." The warmer I got, the more my teeth chattered. "Just some jerks from—"

I stopped myself. Amanda had been part of Apex Team, but I didn't trust her not to run to my parents and squeal on me.

"I recognized Carmen," she admitted. Carmen must've been the older girl I didn't know. "They were Apex, weren't they?"

"It was j-just a hazing. Please don't tell my dad, if he knew I was joining—"

"Joining?" she interrupted me. "Joining what? Apex Team? That's what this is about?"

"What else would it be about?"

"I don't know, I thought maybe they'd found out about...you know."

But I didn't know. Just like the last time I'd seen her, I had no idea what Amanda was talking about.

"You're gonna have to be more specific."

She squinted at me.

"Don't be stupid, you know exactly what I mean," she said, but she didn't sound sure anymore.

"No, I don't. But if there's something I should know—"

She shook her head.

"No, there isn't," she said firmly, but immediately followed it up with, "I can't believe it. I can't believe you don't know."

"Know what?" I pressed. The joke was getting old.

"I—" She glanced around. She looked almost afraid. "I'm sorry. I shouldn't have said anything. Come on, you're turning blue. You need to get back to campus."

Amanda helped me up, grabbing beneath my shoulders and guiding me up to the boardwalk.

"You don't happen to have unlocking powers, too, do you?" I held up my hands. The handcuffs clinked against themselves.

"No, but I'll take you to the prep school's base. Hopefully whoever is on call will be able to help."

Whoever is on call...

I didn't want Wesley to see me. I didn't want him to know I'd let Andersen best me like this. It was humiliating. But Wesley was working the call desk in the atrium. There would be no avoiding him.

"I'm sorry about Winnie, by the way," I mumbled as Amanda led me back down the boardwalk. She scowled.

"It's fine. Forget it." Despite their rocky relationship, the shadow that passed over Amanda's face told me it wasn't fine at all. She shifted the subject. "How are you joining Apex Team without telling your parents? Don't they have to sign something?"

I hunched my shoulders and looked away.

"I'm working on it."

Amanda barked a laugh and shook her head.

"Why don't you forge their signature if you're that freaked about telling them?"

I gawked at her.

"That's lying."

"So?" She rolled her eyes. "They lied to you, didn't they?"

I twisted my wrists in the handcuffs. Of course Amanda would suggest lying. She would probably do anything to get her sister back. It was my fault Winnie was gone in the first place. I needed to do whatever it took to save her.

When we reached the campus, we cut across the grass to get to the school building faster. Amanda balled her hands into fists, and her flame disappeared. The cold marine air overtaking us felt like being dropped in the ocean all over again. I hugged Amanda's coat tighter around my shoulders.

"Sorry," she said. "Can't be seen out in the open carrying fire."

"I–it's alright." My teeth clattered against each other.

The school wasn't particularly warm inside, but I sighed in relief as the stale air wrapped around us. Downstairs, Fleming's office was dark at the end of the hall, which was a little surprising despite the late hour. Fleming seemed to always be in his office.

Wesley was face down at the atrium desk with his arms folded under his head. He looked up groggily when the door clicked shut behind us, and his expression morphed from confusion into horror.

"Samantha!" He stood up so quickly that his chair clattered to the floor. "What happened? Was it Adrestus again?"

I shook my head. Now that we were under lights, I could see the dark gashes on my thighs, left by the barnacles. Blood ran down my legs and pooled around my bare feet.

I'd been okay when it was just me floating alone in the bay. I'd held it together when Amanda and her friend Brooke found me lying in a puddle of seawater and blood. But as Wesley grabbed my hands in his, green eyes wide with horror and concern, my throat constricted and my eyes burned.

Don't cry, don't cry...

"It was some of your teammates," Amanda explained. "I passed them before I found her."

Wesley grit his teeth so hard that a muscle jumped in his cheek.

"Was it—"

"Yes," I whispered. His grip around my hands tightened.

"Why were you out there?" he asked Amanda. "I heard you quit."

She shrugged.

"I can go on walks, can't I? There's no curfew in college."

Wesley hurried me behind the desk. He sat the chair upright and gestured for me to sit. He inspected the handcuffs and gave them a small tug, as if testing them.

"I don't know if I'm strong enough to break these. I think Everly might be in tonight. I can go get—"

"No!" I interjected. "I mean, I'm fine. I don't want a fuss, I just want to go to bed."

Truth was, I didn't want Fleming finding out what had happened. What if he kicked me off the team for being so naive? Or what if he punished Andersen and his friends, causing them to take it out on me?

"I can heat the metal," Amanda suggested. "It might make it malleable enough for you to break it apart."

"Worth a shot, but, Sammy, you should really have Everly look you over."

"Right now, I just want these off." I held up my hands and jingled the handcuffs at them. Amanda grabbed them by the chain in the middle.

"If the metal gets too hot, it might burn you," she warned. "Just say if it's too much."

However, the warm metal felt good. My jacket was soaked through, and, being unable to take it off as long as the handcuffs were on, it was keeping me cold. After giving Amanda a few seconds, Wesley grabbed both ends of the handcuffs.

"Try to relax your arms. I don't want to accidentally dislocate anything."

"Yeah, nothing more relaxing than the threat of my arm popping out," I smirked. He smiled at me, and with one sudden movement, the handcuffs fell apart in his hands.

"Everything still attached?"

I nodded and rubbed my wrists, careful not to disturb the cuts on my hands.

"Still have my arms. Thanks." I peeled my jacket off over my arms.

Wesley pulled a blanket from one of the desk drawers while Amanda looked at her phone.

"Are you alright if I go?" There was an unexpected protectiveness to her tone.

"Yeah, I'll be fine." I wondered if she saw Winnie sitting here instead of me. They didn't get along, but they were still sisters.

Wesley turned to me as the door shut behind Amanda. His face was grim and his jaw firmly set.

"What happened?"

"They tricked me." My voice shook. I cleared my throat to cover it, hoping Wesley didn't notice. "Skyler came to my room, but I thought he was you."

Even though I was still cold, the sudden warmth in my cheeks was unwelcome. Wesley looked like he'd just been hit in the stomach.

"You, or Skyler, I guess, said he'd found something about Winnie, and I know it was stupid. I shouldn't have believed him. You, or he, didn't seem like yourself so I should've known something was up. I'm really sorry."

"Then what?"

I went on to tell him how the others had been invisible and attacked me. I left out the part where Skyler had turned into Winnie. I'd really thought it had been her for a second. It had been their cruelest trick of the night.

When I told Wesley how Andersen had dropped me in the ocean and had told the others to leave me there, his mouth dropped open.

"Sammy, you have to tell Fleming."

"Why? Whatever he does to Andersen, Andersen will do to me ten times over. It was just some dumb prank, anyway."

"You could've drowned! Or frozen to death!"

I shrank back into the blanket.

"It's fine. It was stupid and Fleming would love an excuse to kick me off the team."

"It wasn't your fault."

"But I shouldn't have fallen for it." I hated the shame gnawing at my insides. "You have to promise me you won't tell him."

He shook his head at the ceiling but sighed.

"Fine."

I stifled a yawn and pulled the blanket up over my head.

"Do you want me to take you back to your room?"

"Can't I stay here?" The thought of my room was lonely. I would sleep better here, knowing I had Wesley.

"There're beds in the Sickbay, but I'd have to wake up Everly."

"No, that's okay." I got to my feet and untangled myself from the blanket. Wesley grimaced.

"You smell like the bay."

"Gee, I wonder why."

He sighed and took the blanket.

"There are towels in the locker room if you want to shower. There should be some sweats in there, too. We have an extra room with beds for when there's multiple people on call. I'll find the key and unlock it for you."

"Really? And Fleming—"

"Fleming will never know. Do you want me to text Naomi and reschedule training in the morning?"

I'd forgotten all about the training Naomi had planned.

"No, I'll be alright," I insisted. I staggered over to the locker room door. "Thanks, Wes."

He settled back down in the chair and started playing with the broken handcuffs.

"No problem. But I can't promise I won't kick Andersen's ass in training this week."

"I can't promise that either."

It felt like I had only just closed my eyes when there was a soft knock on the door. It pushed open from the outside, and Naomi poked her head in.

"Wesley said you were in here." She looked confused but didn't ask me any questions. She waved a granola bar at me. "Eat this, and get ready. We'll head to the track once you're out."

When Winnie had kept me awake all night at the docks, I'd felt like I'd been hit by a semi truck the next day. This time, I was more awake than I'd ever felt. I meant it when I told Wesley I'd kick Andersen's ass in training, and Naomi had already revealed Andersen was secretly afraid I'd best him. Now it was time to give him a real reason to be nervous.

"We're starting with the mile," Naomi said, reading from her planner as I met them at the call desk. "Then we'll do sprint times before going back inside for water treading—"

"We can skip that one. She's fine." Wesley yawned. He had dark circles under his eyes. Naomi narrowed her eyes at him but crossed it out.

"Okay, so then we'll go straight into the rope climb and then some strength tests."

As we went to leave the training base, the door swung open in front of us, and a couple of students filed in. Freddie and Olivia were among them. They flushed when they saw me and averted their gaze. Wesley looked as if he were about to stop and say something, but I gave him a shove from behind, and he kept walking. Naomi raised an eyebrow.

"I don't suppose either of you want to tell me what that was about?"

"It's nothing," I said. I found a small amount of solace in that Freddie and Olivia were too embarrassed to look our way. It didn't make me any less angry, of course, but it still felt good.

Running, however, did not feel good. After four laps on the track, I collapsed at Wesley and Naomi's feet, gasping for air.

"Nine minutes and thirty eight seconds," Naomi read off her stopwatch. "Also, you need to tell Fleming about last night."

I glared at Wesley.

"Why'd you tell her?"

"He didn't need to! I could feel half the story back at the training base when Freddie and Olivia came in." Naomi crossed her arms. "They're lucky you didn't drown or freeze to death."

"But I didn't die, so it's not a big deal." I sighed, still trying to catch my breath. "Nine minutes isn't great, right?"

"Need to lose over a minute," Wesley said.

"Hopefully you won't be half dead next time," Naomi grumbled.

I spent the next half hour doing push ups, crunches, and climbing ropes until Naomi was satisfied. I showered and got ready for class before meeting Wesley back in the cafeteria. Naomi was across the room, laughing with Jamie and Madison. I watched her grow stiff as Andersen joined them. She stood up and took her tray to the garbage and left without stopping by our table.

"Luckily the fitness stuff comes with the fight training," Wesley said through a mouthful of cereal. "You learn to fight, and you get strong in the process. Don't let Naomi freak you out, you'll pass this stuff no problem in a month."

I'd only passed two of the fitness tests that Naomi had put me through.

"It's not the fitness stuff I'm worried about," I admitted. "If I don't learn how to fight, I won't last the two minutes in the ring, and none of it will matter."

"Then we'll start with fighting today. Just so you know, I don't think you're giving yourself enough credit. I saw you tackle that lady at the docks, and you beat Hackjob. You're either some kind of crazy prodigy or you've been playing us."

We walked to class in silence. Andersen, Skyler, Olivia, and Freddie would all be in First Period. My insides boiled at the thought of them, but my anger evaporated when we walked into Fleming's room, and I saw the empty chair where Winnie usually sat.

"Do you maybe want to sit with me today?" Wesley asked quietly. Anthony's seat was empty, too.

I nodded. As much as I didn't want to sit in the front row, I wanted even less to be alone. I doubted Wesley wanted that, either, so I sank into Anthony's empty chair.

When Andersen walked in, hand in hand with Jamie, Wesley straightened up. I elbowed him.

"What?"

"Be cool, alright?" I hissed. "Like you said, we can get back at him during training."

Fleming hurried into the classroom and did a double take when he saw me in Anthony's usual spot. He deflated a little as he took his place at the head of the classroom. The room hushed before the bell had rung.

Fleming wrung his hands. He cleared his throat even though he already had everyone's attention.

"Unfortunately, I have to start the lesson with some bad news. As I'm sure you've all heard by now, there was an incident at the museum on Friday. I wish I could tell you more, but there's a lot we don't know."

Jamie's hand shot in the air.

"Was it Apex?" she asked without waiting for Fleming to call on her.

"Again, there's a lot we're not sure about—"

"I heard it was Apex," she insisted. "Serves Winnie right, always sticking her nose where she shouldn't. I guess they finally got fed up with her."

I balled my hands into fists under the table. I wanted to turn and scream at Jamie and her stupid Apex boyfriend, but Wesley reached over and placed his hand on mine. He gave me a half-grimace, half-smile, and I unfurled my hands.

"Talk like that about your classmates again, and you'll be in detention," Fleming shot at Jamie. She scoffed, but let it go.

No one dared interrupt Fleming anymore, and when class finished, the room was uncharacteristically subdued as we packed our notebooks.

"Samantha." Fleming beckoned me to his desk. My insides constricted. Was he going to ask about last night? How had he found out?

I skulked up to his desk, my hands thrust resolutely in my jacket pockets.

"You'll be in gym class downstairs starting today."

"Downstairs?" I repeated blankly. "You mean—"

"Yes," Fleming hissed, looking around as if I might have blown all of Apex Team's cover. "It's when you'll be doing most of your combat training exercises. Try to pay attention. You won't be able to rely on instinct every time you are in the field. And remember, I need that permission form still."

"Yeah, sure thing." I backed away, afraid if I lingered any longer he might guess I hadn't told my parents yet.

The morning passed slower than usual, probably because I was anticipating my first day in Fourth Period gym learning to fight with the sophomore Apex Team rather than playing badminton for the fifth day in a row.

Apex Team PE was taught by a woman with cropped, steel-gray hair and large pale eyes who introduced herself as Coach Reiner. She shook my hand after Naomi led me from the locker room to the training gym.

"Mr. Fleming warned me Alison Taylor's kid would be here today," she grinned. "Even if you didn't get her Apex gene, we'll find out if you at least inherited her hand-to-hand skills."

"Coach is the best fighter the team's ever had," Wesley said as Reiner left to help set up the other students trickling in. "That's her Apex power. She only has to try a move once before she's got it. She's been teaching combat here since Fleming was a freshman."

Andersen came in with Skyler from the boys' locker room. When the others weren't looking, Skyler morphed his face into Wesley's and made a face at me. I burned furiously, but turned away, refusing to give him any satisfaction. I did my best to lower my blood pressure before Naomi had the chance to feel my stifled rage.

The other students jumped straight into sparring. I looked at Naomi and Wesley helplessly, hoping maybe they'd start by fighting each other.

"You ready?" Naomi asked. Wesley stepped back as Naomi assumed a fighting position.

"Ready for what?" I looked around desperately. They didn't seriously expect me to just start fighting like it was no big deal, right?

"Just try it," Naomi prompted. "You've fought bigger than me already."

"With a sword!"

"I promise I won't hit hard."

"She's lying," Wesley interjected.

The sounds of grunts and bodies hitting the matted floor filled the room. I sighed and resigned to fighting Naomi. She wouldn't hurt me on purpose, but that didn't make the thought of going hand-to-hand with her any more appealing.

I tried to recreate the stance that Wesley had taught me yesterday. Naomi nodded encouragingly and did the same. I jabbed at her, but she swatted my arm away effortlessly and hit me square in the chest with an open palm.

I stumbled backwards and fell flat on my backside. Andersen guffawed from across the room.

Wesley spun on his heel.

"Hey, Lewis!" He marched away, presumably to make good on his promise to kick Andersen's ass.

"Sorry," Naomi blushed, extending a hand to help me back to my feet. "That was good. Just remember, even when attacking, you always need to be on defense."

I squared up, running the exercises from the day before through my head. Wesley had only taught me basic hits. Naomi would be able to counter all of them no problem.

Naomi struck first this time, catching me off guard. I recoiled and suddenly, I'm not sure how, Naomi was flat on her back, looking up at me in surprise.

"Are you hustling us?" she joked, getting to her feet.

"What? No! I don't know what just happened!" I said, but she laughed.

"That was really good!" she insisted, even though I still wasn't sure how she had ended up on the floor like that.

We faced each other a third time but were interrupted by Coach Reiner yelling at Wesley and Andersen across the gym.

"Lewis! Isaacs!" she barked. "No face shots!"

Naomi lunged while I was distracted, and again, I acted instinctively and ducked under her outstretched arm, tripping her as I passed by.

"Okay, you're definitely hustling us!"

"Do that again, Taylor." Coach Reiner had come up behind us to watch. "Sorry, I mean Havardson."

I tensed up, painfully aware that the students closest to us had stopped to watch. Naomi nodded encouragingly as I put my fists back up. She lunged.

I was back on the ground before I'd realized she'd hit me. There were a couple snickers nearby, but I ignored them. Coach Reiner tutted disapprovingly, but I was surprised when she turned her disappointment on Naomi.

"You're going too easy on her."

That was the closest thing I got to a warning. Coach Reiner threw herself at me, and I moved with each of her punches, parrying and blocking while stumbling backwards as my feet struggled to keep up with the action. She finally caught her foot on my ankle, and the room went sideways as I slammed into the mat.

"So your mom taught you some tricks after all," Coach Reiner said smugly. I shook my head as I pushed myself onto my knees.

"No, I didn't even know she could fight at all until Fleming said so the other day."

"Really? Those are definitely her moves. Maybe she taught you without you noticing." She must've been able to see my confusion because she laughed. "Maybe she didn't tell you her power set? I forgot you only just found out about her."

I blushed. The other kids were definitely listening now, with the exception of Wesley and Andersen, who were too busy trying to mop the floor with the other. It was embarrassing enough to be the only non-Apex in the room. Now everyone was finding out I didn't even know my own mother's abilities.

"I know she worked with Paragon," I mumbled, scrambling for anything that might give me more credibility.

"Your mom is an Inculcator."

I looked around, as if I might see a hint to what that might mean hiding somewhere in the room, but even Naomi looked lost.

"An Inculcator?" Reiner repeated. "C'mon, has Fleming really not taught you guys the Basic Abilities? Inculcators can implant thoughts and information in those around them."

My stomach churned. I wasn't sure what I had thought my mom's ability might be. Maybe I had been imagining something more on brand with the superhero image, something like levitation or laser beams. But planting thoughts in people? It sounded villainous. It was hard to ignore that half the class recoiled away from the conversation, pretending to have been training the whole time.

Great. Now not only was I a Beta, but I was the Beta with the creepy mom.

"So," I said slowly, putting the pieces together, "you're saying she secretly taught me to fight by putting fighting skills in my head?"

Coach Reiner nodded, but seemed less boisterous now. She must've also noticed the room turn cold at the mention of involuntary thought.

"You fight just like her, and you say you've had no training until now." She shrugged. "And it seems like it's instinctual, which would make sense if she just planted it in your subconscious. You wouldn't know how to fight until you had to."

I'd tackled the white-haired woman at the dock. I'd held my own at the museum. Even last night, I'd briefly escaped Andersen and his friends.

"That's good news!" Naomi's optimism sounded forced. "If we can just tap into whatever skills your mom put there, you'll be ready for the trials no problem!"

I grimaced. Maybe I should be thankful for the secret defense my mom hid in my head, and sure, she was probably just being a standard overprotective mom. I thought she'd been intrusive when she'd followed me into the bathroom on the ferry when I'd just wanted to puke in peace. But this? This was a whole new level of helicopter parent.

A crash across the room pulled Reiner's attention away. A rack of dumbbells had just soared across the space, scattering students.

"Lewis! Isaacs!" Reiner screeched as she stepped between Andersen and Wesley. "This is your last warning!"

"I'm sure your mom was just looking out for you," Naomi said.

"She could've at least asked for my permission before putting stuff in my head," I spat. "It's not like her powers are involuntary, like yours are. She knew what she was doing."

After the museum, in the Sickbay, Fleming had sounded accusatory when he'd talked to Mom.

"I didn't teach her sword fighting," she had said.

But that had to have been a lie, and Fleming knew it. Fleming knew I'd had things put inside my head without me knowing and didn't say a word about it. No wonder he didn't want to tell me what Mom's powers were.

"Fleming knew." I didn't mean to sound so angry. "It's my head, and he didn't even tell me."

Naomi stepped closer so the kids sparring around us wouldn't hear.

"It wasn't really his secret to tell."

"But it's not a secret at all, is it?" I gestured wildly at the room. "Reiner knew, and now everyone else either does or they will! I'm pretty sure Amanda knows, too. She's been real cryptic every time I've seen her."

I held back the impulse to hit something, even as everyone around me happily punched their partners.

"True," Naomi admitted slowly, "but maybe it wasn't really Coach Reiner's place to say, either, and she just messed up. Fleming was protecting your mom, and she was protecting you. You can't act like it hasn't come in handy more than once."

"But how am I supposed to know what's in my head because it's real and not because she put it there?" How could I trust anything anymore? Of course Naomi wouldn't understand. Intrusion on people's private feelings was normal for her. The idea that a mother could plant things in her own daughter's mind wouldn't seem weird.

But she sighed and put a hand on my shoulder.

"I get it, okay? My own relationship with my mom doesn't make sense because of my powers, but there's nothing you can do about it now." She half smiled. "Talk to Fleming about it later if you want, but right now, we get to figure out how to work with these mom moves."

"Please don't call them 'Mom Moves'," I groaned. She was right, but I still didn't have to be happy about it.

"And sure you have an incredibly invasive mom, but at least you aren't those guys." Naomi pointed across the gym, and I cracked a grin. Reiner stood over Andersen and Wesley, who were both serving a harsh sentence of push-up burpees.

Wesley caught my eye and smirked before double-timing his push ups. Andersen struggled to keep up, not ready to lose in any kind of physical contest. I still wasn't happy about how my fighting prowess had come to be, but Naomi was right. We could use it. Besides, my mom wouldn't be the only one with secrets, anymore. How hard could her signature be to forge, anyway?

17

First Mission

By the time I had finished training with Naomi and Wesley after class later that day, I'd managed to learn a couple of the fighting moves Mom had downloaded into my brain. Wesley, who was sporting a bruised chin from what he called a lucky shot on Andersen's part, was thrilled when we told him about my secret arsenal of moves. He came up with a plan to "Scare them out of me" by having Naomi fight me no-holds-barred and then repeat the same duck, pivot, or punch over and over until I'd learned it for myself.

I hurried to the library after training. Forging Mom's signature was easy. I still had a copy of the field trip permission slip she'd signed, and it was as simple as holding the paper form up to the computer screen, tracing, and checking to make sure the librarian wasn't watching. I slid the permission form under Fleming's office door when I was done. As good as it felt to be the one keeping secrets now, I still didn't want to look Fleming in the face as I handed the forged form over.

That week, whispers seemed to follow me through the halls to every class. While everyone had avoided Winnie beforehand, her kidnapping sent shockwaves through the school. No one had the full details as to what exactly had happened at the museum, so there was a lot of speculating. Each rumor was wilder than the last, but no one was eager to ask me for my account of the events.

Somehow, by Thursday, Wesley and I had found the time between training and class to throw together a rough draft of our industry project. Even though we hadn't had the chance to get all the material we wanted at the museum, it was still an okay poster outline. At the very least, it was solid B minus material, which was good enough for us both.

However, when we turned it in the next morning, Fleming gave it a single glance before writing us each a pass for study hour and saying, "My office, please."

"I didn't think it was that bad," Wesley muttered at lunch. His Study Period slip was crumpled in front of him.

"It definitely wasn't great, though," I said. It was a relief knowing Wesley had been called down to Fleming's office, too, otherwise I might've thought I'd already been caught in my permission form lie.

"What'd he expect?" Wesley shoveled cafeteria spaghetti into his mouth. "We were attacked on *his* dumb field trip! How are we supposed to make quality work if we can't take notes without worrying about being thrown through a display case?"

"You've had a whole week since then to finish it," Naomi pointed her fork at him accusingly. She'd taken to sitting with us at meals more since Andersen had thrown me in the ocean. When we asked if Jamie would be okay with it, she just shrugged and said she'd have to deal.

Wesley had a point, of course. Yes, we'd had a week to work on it, but, if I was being honest with myself, it was hard to sit down and look at it without thinking about the sound Winnie's body had made as she fell to the museum bathroom floor.

And then there was the fact that we'd been sabotaged by Andersen. We wouldn't have even been at the museum if he hadn't thrown out our drawings. I dropped my fork as I ran over the last couple weeks in my head. It was all so obvious, how had we missed it?

"What's up?" Naomi looked at me, her eyes squinting in suspicion. "You just got either very excited or scared, I can't tell which."

I leaned across the table. If I was wrong, I was going to sound so stupid.

"We were only at the museum because of Andersen. Me and Wesley, anyway," I said slowly. "And Andersen was on call duty the night I went with Winnie to the docks."

Naomi and Wesley glanced at each other, frowning.

"What are you saying?" Wesley asked.

"What if he knew something was going down at the museum and threw out our work to make sure we'd be there?"

"No, he's a jerk, but he wouldn't do that." Naomi shook her head.

"I don't know, he might," Wesley said.

"These are just coincidences," Naomi sighed. "You're both seeing what you want to see."

Wesley spun his spaghetti around his fork conspiratorially. He gave me a meaningful look.

"Right now, those coincidences are all we have to go on," he said.

"What about your powers, Naomi?" I whispered so that the nearby tables wouldn't hear. "How's Andersen been feeling lately? You'd be able to tell if he was up to something, right?"

She bit her lip as she thought about it. Her brow knitted together, and she shook her head.

"He's always up to something. He just threw you in the ocean, didn't he?" She shrugged.

I looked over at Andersen's table. Jamie played with his hair while he joked with Skyler and a non-Apex boy. Of course Naomi would give him the benefit of the doubt. She was friends with his girlfriend. Even though we both dropped it, the dark look on Wesley's face told me he wasn't done suspecting Andersen, either.

My phone rattled on the table, pulling me away from thoughts of Andersen. Dad hardly left me alone anymore, checking in multiple times a day.

Family dinner Saturday. Pick you up at 5?

It made sense they wanted to see me after all that had happened, but the sting of Mom's betrayal was still fresh. I hadn't gotten over how she'd secretly programmed self-defense in my head without my permission.

"What's wrong?" Naomi asked. She and Wesley stopped arguing about Andersen to look at me. I was learning that my privacy was limited, having chosen one friend that could sense every fluctuation in my mood and another who could hear the tiniest change in my breathing or heart rate.

"It's nothing," I said, shaking my head, before coming up with the perfect idea. "Actually, do you guys want dinner Saturday?"

"Dinner where?" Wesley asked. It would be hard for either of them to turn down the opportunity for free food that wasn't from the cafeteria.

"My parents' house."

Naomi squinted at me.

"Weren't they screaming at us last weekend?"

"No, that was Winnie's dad!" As angry as I was at my parents, I was offended she'd mix my dad up with Roy Hendricks.

"Yeah, we're in!" Wesley said.

"I'll go as long as you aren't just bringing us to buffer yourself from your parents." Like I said, as long as Naomi was around, there'd be little to no privacy.

"That might be one reason to bring you but also because you're my friends, and it would be fun to have you over. I haven't even seen their new place yet."

Naomi didn't look convinced but conceded with a shrug.

"Fine. Better be good food, though."

I grinned and texted Dad to let him know they'd be coming with me.

"And real quick," I said, chagrined, "they don't know about Apex Team and all this, so try not to mention it."

Wesley gave me an ostentatious salute, but Naomi narrowed her eyes.

"Didn't they sign off on your forms?"

I grimaced, and she looked towards the ceiling in exasperation.

"Yikes, the apple doesn't fall far from the tree, does it? What is it with your family and keeping secrets?"

She wasn't wrong, but it felt good to be the one with secrets to keep for once.

I continued to sneak glances at Andersen through gym class, and again during Sixth Period math, as if he might betray his allegiance to the mysterious Adrestus somehow during class. He only caught me staring once. I quickly looked away, but I knew he'd seen me.

It was a relief when Study Period came at the end of the day and I could escape the classroom, even if I was presumably walking straight into a lecture about academic excellence from Fleming.

"You don't think he's mad, do you?" I asked Wesley as we walked down the hall to Fleming's office. I shook my head violently. There was still water in my ear from being in the pool during gym.

"Why else would he call us down here? I hope you weren't counting on winning that scholarship."

I raised my hand to knock on the office door, but before I could do so, Fleming called out, "Come in!"

Wesley led the way but stopped abruptly in the doorway. I ran into his back. There were three chairs sitting opposite Fleming and one was occupied by a curtain of blonde hair. It spun around to reveal Remi's sullen, freckled face.

"Come in, sit down." Fleming gestured at the two empty seats.

"Hi, Wes," Remi murmured.

"Hey," he grunted, taking the seat furthest from her. I lowered myself into the middle chair. Their chat after froyo last week must not have gone well. I couldn't help but notice how they both angled away from each other.

"Is this about our project?" I asked, still not sure why Wesley's ex-girlfriend was there.

"No, we can talk about that later." Fleming frowned. "This is actually about your mission hours."

Both Wesley and I straightened up.

"Are we going scouting?" Wesley asked, leaning across the desk. "This is perfect, you'll get to play in the Night Games, now!"

"She can play in the Night Games if she completes three hours," Fleming reminded him. "Though, I don't see that being an issue with the mission I've chosen."

I wondered if I'd get to wear the gray and black helmeted uniform I'd seen Wesley in twice now.

Fleming slid a flash drive across the desk to us. I picked it up to inspect it, but there wasn't anything special about it.

"With Remi's help, we were able to get most of Winnie's pictures onto that," Fleming said, nodding at the girl.

Of course it made sense that Wesley's ex-girlfriend would be an Apex, although I hadn't seen her in the training gym.

"But Remi's not on the team," Wesley protested, answering my silent questions about Remi's absence.

"Name one person on the team who could decrypt six gigabytes worth of pictures," Remi snapped back.

"That's enough." Both Wesley and Remi fell back into their seats in a huff. "These pictures only go back the last couple of weeks, but, as Remi said, there are a lot of them. The council thinks there's a chance Winnie's pictures might have clues as to where the missing students might be or who might be behind the kidnappings."

It made enough sense. Even in our short week as roommates, Winnie had spent most of her free time either out taking pictures or editing them. Without any other leads, her photos could be the best bet at finding something that might lead us to her.

"So what will we be doing?" I asked.

"You'll be going through the pictures, looking for anything that might help us."

"Oh."

The images of me running through the city in the black and gray Apex armor dissolved in my head. My first mission was desk work.

"I know it's not the most illustrious of tasks," Fleming said, "but you and Wesley were the only ones at the dock with her, making you two the most familiar with the situation."

So far, I felt like the only value I brought to the team was having been closer to Winnie than anyone, and that still wasn't all that close. Now, my first mission was to go through her private pictures that had been taken from our room without her permission. I squirmed. Even if it did help save her, Winnie would be furious.

"How many pictures?" Wesley asked with a hint of unease to his voice.

"About three thousand."

Wesley deflated next to me.

"Forget getting in three hours before the Night Games!" he exclaimed. "We'll be doing this for three weeks!"

"I guess we all forgot that Wesley Isaacs is too good for desk missions," Remi snarled next to me. Fleming ignored their quips and nodded at me.

"Wesley will show you the computer lab. You'll have time to get started during Study Period, but are free to keep working until training later."

Remi stood up.

"Is it alright that I go back to class, Mr. Fleming?" she asked with a bite to her tone. "I have actual school work to be doing."

He waved her away, and Wesley exhaled in relief as she left the room.

We had to endure a five minute lecture on the importance of desk work and how it is just as important as field missions before Fleming released us to the computer lab.

I knew better than to ask about Remi as Wesley booted up a couple of computers. I'd only seen her on my dorm floor a couple of times, and it was odd she was an Apex who wasn't on the team, but still seemed to have privileges.

Wesley glowered as he jammed the flash drive into a USB port. Maybe I'd ask Naomi about it later. Maybe I'd drop it all together.

The first fifty or so pictures were of little things. There was a cup and saucer, a close up of a flower, and an artistic view of a skyscraper, looking straight up. I had thought that Winnie's pictures would all be strictly business— Apex creeping through the night and whatnot. But Winnie's pictures were surprisingly nice.

"What's wrong? You've been looking at that boat picture for a while."

I jumped at the sound of Wesley's voice.

"It feels weird to go through her stuff without her knowing."

Wesley sighed and leaned back in his chair.

"I keep forgetting you guys were friends back in elementary school."

"Honestly, I do, too."

I rapidly clicked through the next few pictures, which were all of sunsets, and grimaced as a dead mouse popped onto the screen without warning.

"Gross," Wesley winced. "What's she taking pictures of dead things for?"

"Why'd Winnie do any of the things she did?" I leaned in closer to the screen. "Although, I don't think it's dead."

"How can you tell?"

"She showed me a seagull picture she took. It was one of the paralyzed animals that've been popping up in the city."

"That doesn't explain why she'd be taking pictures of them."

"To sell to news sites maybe?" I guessed. She had called her photography her "Job", after all. If she ran into a paralyzed mouse, of course she'd take a few seconds to snap a quick pic just in case it raked in a few dollars down the road. "Hey, it's me!"

The Samantha on the screen sat at her desk, setting up textbooks on move-in day. I would've still been getting over my mystery illness when Winnie took this photo, and I was taken aback at how pale and gaunt I looked. It was a wonder Mom and Dad had left me at school at all instead of taking me to a hospital.

Wesley was kind enough to not comment on my half-dead appearance and continued to click through his assignment.

"All I have so far are ferry boats," he said, just as a picture of the Paragon statue popped up. "This one is actually kinda nice. It could be a postcard."

I thought Winnie would be more likely to sell a kidney before resorting to selling her photos for postcards, but what did I really know about my roommate?

Saturday brought an onslaught of rain that hinted at the end of summer. There was no official training on weekends, but Naomi insisted we wake up early to keep training, and after a drenching run outside, she recruited Heather to be my first real opponent.

I'd heard that Heather was a so-called "Heavyweight", like Wesley and Andersen, but hadn't yet seen her in action so I was caught off guard when she sucked all the light from the room, leaving me blind and vulnerable to her attacks. Even with my pre-programmed fighting skills, I didn't stand a chance.

By the end of the hour, it was hard to not despair over my prospects in the Final Trial.

"Don't worry." Wesley comforted me as I lay flat on my back in the center of the empty training room. Naomi and Heather had already gone to the locker room to change, but I had hung back to wallow privately in my anxiety. Wesley must've noticed because he stayed behind. "We'll throw a blindfold into practice just in case her name gets pulled."

"I can't prepare for one person, though!" I threw my arms over my face. "There are thirty different people I might get paired against! If I had to practice for each one, I'd only have a day for every student!"

Wesley fell back onto the mat next to me.

"Not really. There's a few you should worry about, but a lot of powers don't help fighting. Marcus is one of the captains, and all he can do is read heat signatures. How's that going to help him? Even heavyweights like Andersen are useless if you know how their powers work."

"Cotton, right?"

"Just wear cotton," Wesley confirmed. "He'll be useless. Unless you've got any metal plates we should know about?"

His gaze lingered on the scar that ran across my collarbone and up my neck. It was on full display when I wore tank tops.

"No," I murmured, rubbing a hand over the scar as if to check. "No metal plates."

"Good!" Wesley sprung to his feet and reached down to help me up. "In that case, the only person you'd never beat is me, and seeing as I'm not allowed to fight you, you're guaranteed a win."

"When do I get to fight you then?" I smirked.

"Maybe never." He made his way to the boys' locker room. "Which is good news for you."

A few hours later, we huddled in the front doors of the dorm, waiting for the family sedan to pull into the rotunda. Rain slammed against the doors with glass-rattling force. It was almost impossible to make out anything farther than a few yards away, and I pressed against the glass, watching for headlights.

When they flickered into view, we pulled our hoods up and sprinted through the downpour. Wesley and Naomi slid gracefully into the backseat while I took the front.

"Hey, kid," Dad smiled, the edges of his beard lifting upwards. "Staying dry?"

"No," Wesley replied from the backseat as he shook water from his bangs.

Dad glanced in the rear view mirror at Naomi and Wesley. I thought I saw a shadow cross over his face, but he covered it with a smile.

"Oh, you two are the friends."

He glared at me but didn't say anything about the two Apex I'd invited into his new home. It was hard to see through the rain, but I could tell he was driving us towards the northernmost part of the island where the ferry had docked. It was the most urban area of the island I'd seen so far, composed of corner shops and crowded townhouses. He turned up a narrow street, climbing a hill to a small cul-de-sac.

"Are we having salmon?" Wesley asked as Dad pulled the car into a tiny garage. Dad raised an eyebrow at him in the mirror.

"How'd you know?"

"I can smell it!"

Wesley led the charge out of the car, giving Dad a moment to roll his eyes at me.

"You can't be mad at me for having Apex friends now that I know you're married to one," I pointed out.

"Yeah, can't seem to get away," he grumbled.

Wesley and Naomi were already taking their shoes off in the mud room. Mom called from down the hall.

"Vic, is that you with the kids?"

"Yeah, it's us."

Now that we were inside, I could smell the baked salmon. My stomach growled.

"Nice," Wesley grinned. "I heard that."

Naomi tugged on my jacket sleeve and leaned in.

"Your dad's suspicious."

"Yeah, sorry about him. I promise he means well."

"Not of us," she hissed. "Of you!"

Of course. He knew both Wesley and Naomi were on the team. He'd seen them in the Sickbay. I knew that. Bringing them over would cue him into my new involvement with the team.

"It'll be fine," I insisted.

"I can hear him talking to your mom in the kitchen. Something about how they can't trust you at the school on your own," Wesley said.

"I'm not an Apex. Why would they think I'm on the team?"

"They know Fleming isn't an Apex, either, and he was on the team with your mom," Naomi pointed out.

Shoot.

"It's fine," I repeated even though it definitely wasn't fine.

However, any plans to quell my parents' suspicions were put on hold. The staircase above us thundered, and Avery came barreling around a corner.

"Sammy's home!" he cheered as he wrapped his arms around me. He unwrapped them almost as quickly when he noticed my friends. "Oh, hi."

"Hi, Avery," I grinned. He flipped his hair, still in dire need of a haircut.

"Yeah. Whatever." He looked like he was about to sulk back down the hallway but did a double take at Wesley and Naomi. "Wait, are these your museum friends?"

"What do you mean my—" I cut myself off. "Mom!"

I marched down the hallway, not taking any time to look around at the new family home. I barged into the kitchen where Mom was sautéing green beans while Dad whispered conspiracies about me joining Apex Team in her ear.

"Samantha!" She tried to smile warmly, but I could tell it was strained by the way it didn't reach her eyes. She opened her arms to me as I crossed mine resolutely across my chest.

"You told Avery about the museum?" I demanded. Mom's forced smile faltered, and she turned to Dad.

"We had a family talk about it, yes." She picked her words carefully.

"Not much of a family talk if a quarter of us aren't there for it!"

"If children of Apex are being targeted, he has a right to know."

"Sammy, did Mom tell you she was friends with Paragon?" Avery appeared behind me.

"Where was my 'right to know' for almost sixteen years?" I squawked.

"Told you we shouldn't have told him," Dad mumbled. Mom flushed red.

"If you want to discuss this later, I'd be more than happy to, but right now we have guests over and more on the way," Mom said firmly, going back to the green beans.

"Wait, who else is coming?" I demanded.

A doorbell chimed overhead, and Mom nodded at Dad to answer the door. He went to open it in the next room over, and a jovial voice boomed out, "Geez, Vic, any longer and we would've grown gills out here!"

I spun to confront Mom yet again at the sound of Roy Hendricks's voice.

"Winnie's parents are here?" I blanched.

"Of course, we invited them. What's wrong with the Hendricks?"

"It's nice to see you again, Mrs. Havardson," Naomi said behind me. "Your home is lovely."

Mom's face went slack for just a moment as she looked at Naomi and Wesley standing in her kitchen, and I was sure she was remembering Mr. Hendricks tearing into them as he made a scene in the Sickbay just a week ago.

"It'll be fine," she hissed at me as she walked past to offer a welcoming hug to Naomi. "Thank you both for joining us!"

"So are you both Apex?" Avery chirped from his corner of the kitchen.

"Avery!" Mom glared at him. "Don't be rude."

"You said some of Sammy's museum friends were Apex, so I was just wondering. What're your powers?" Avery shrugged unapologetically.

"Avery!"

"Mom says I might be an Apex, you know."

I whipped around towards Mom again.

"He what? How do you know that? What about me?"

"Enough, both of you."

Mom heaved a sigh and turned to greet the Hendricks as they came into the kitchen from the opposite room.

"Val!" She grabbed the bottle of wine from Mrs. Hendricks's hands before pulling her into an embrace. "How are you holding up?"

Mr. Hendricks lingered in the entryway opposite Naomi, Wesley, and me. He narrowed his eyes at us.

"I didn't realize it was going to be so crowded tonight," he said.

"The more the merrier, right?" Dad appeared behind them and clapped Mr. Hendricks on the back. "How about some of that wine? Amanda, you can just leave your coat there. I'll have Avery take care of it."

It was as if a dozen bricks dropped into my stomach. Why? Why did Amanda, yet another person who knew my secret, have to be here? I'd hoped I'd never see her again after having to shoulder the embarrassment of her finding me half-drowned a few nights ago.

She peered around the corner, lingering in the entryway. She glowered from under the bill of a baseball cap, which clashed magnificently with the burgundy lipstick she'd slapped on for the occasion.

"Let's get out of Mom's way," Dad said as he ushered us towards Amanda. "Avery, how about you show Samantha the house?"

We left the adults downstairs, and I tried to take comfort in the fact that Wesley would let me know if he heard Amanda telling them anything about my involvement with the team. Although, there was a chance Wesley would be too distracted. Now that we were free of Mom, Avery was grilling both of my friends on everything to do with The Apex.

"How old were you?" he asked.

"When I found out I was an Apex?" Naomi clarified. "About twelve, I think."

"But I'm twelve!" Avery looked nervous.

"We have someone on the team at school who didn't know until she was fourteen," Wesley said. "But I knew when I was six."

We came to the first landing of the staircase. There was a simple hallway here with four doors. Avery pointed to the one on the end.

"That's Mom and Dad's room," he said. "And that's the guest room. And that's mine, and that's yours."

"I get a room?" I felt stupid for saying it. Of course I got a room. Just because I lived at school didn't mean I *lived* at school.

It was the door closest to the landing. I pulled it open, but the small bedroom was filled with boxes. The window blinds were pulled shut, and even though they'd only been living there a couple weeks, dust had already settled on the desk that was shoved against the nearest wall. I hoped they'd at least put a bed in before Thanksgiving break.

Avery led us up more stairs to the top floor, which was an open living space with a high ceiling, a kitchenette, and balcony with a view of the water. I wondered if they'd be able to see the Paragon statue from the window on a nicer day.

Naomi sat down on a sectional couch and leaned back, rubbing her temples.

"What's wrong?" Wesley took a seat next to her. "Are you sick?"

She shook her head.

"Is it your powers?" Avery asked in a hushed tone, eyes sparkling with awe. Naomi managed a weak chuckle.

"Something like that," she admitted. "There's a lot of people in the house, and they've all got a lot of feelings."

"So do you always fight bad guys?" Avery pressed, undeterred by Naomi's apparent headache. "That's what the team's for, right?"

Naomi, in her infinite patience, laughed.

"Not usually. There haven't really been super villains since Paragon's days, but Schrader Industries keeps funding the Apex program, probably to help us learn how to handle our powers more than to actually benefit the city. Still, we do end up doing a lot of rescue work.”

“Like when I caught a runaway bus last year!” Wesley offered when Avery’s face fell.

“Is that what happened?” Naomi smirked. “I recall you getting hit by a bus and then pretending it was on purpose.”

“Samantha!” Mom called up the stairs. “Come help your father set the table!”

I looked at Wesley. I could feel the panic on my face.

“What’re they saying? Are they going to ask me about the team?”

“Why would they ask you about the team?” Avery asked. I swore under my breath. I’d forgotten he was still lingering in the room.

“Forget it. Get Naomi some water, would you?”

I slinked back to the kitchen on the first floor. Mom was taking the salmon out of the oven while Mrs. Hendricks had already made good progress on her glass of wine. She hiccuped through a story about Winnie.

I found the dining room down the hall. It had a high ceiling and overlooked a small patch of backyard through a bay window. Dad looked up from a dish-filled hutch.

“We need to talk.”

My heart rate quickened, but I did my best to look confused. He couldn’t feel my emotions like Naomi, and he couldn’t hear my heartbeat or breathing like Wesley. My feelings had been on my sleeve all week. It almost felt like an upper hand, now, knowing I’d be able to lie.

“About school?” I tried to sound blithe. I took the plates from him and began setting them around the table.

“Yeah, sorta,” he growled. He always became so surly when he was uncomfortable. “You doing okay? Since last weekend?”

“It’s been weird without Winnie. The room is kinda lonely now.”

“I thought you didn’t like Winnie.”

I screwed my face up at him.

"No," I said vehemently, "I did, she just got on my nerves."

"Huh." For a moment, the only sounds were the clinking of silverware and the pattering of rain on the bay window. "You don't seem lonely."

"I just meant the dorm is lonelier."

"And class is okay?" He was beating around the bush.

"Yes, Dad." I rolled my eyes. "Class is just great."

"Hey." He dropped a fork and knife onto the table. "I'm just making sure everything's been fine. You were almost kidnapped, remember?"

Correction: I was almost kidnapped twice, but I wasn't about to set the record straight.

"Yeah, sorry." I'd spent the last few days so angry at them for keeping secrets that I'd forgotten how the drama at the museum might have affected my parents. "I try not to think about it."

Dad's face softened, and his eyes crinkled above his beard. He set the rest of the silverware down in a pile and pulled me in. His beard tickled my forehead, but I let him hold me there.

"When Alex called us last Friday, I thought for sure..." He trailed off and heaved a heavy sigh. "Don't scare me like that anymore. That was enough adventure for the school year, alright?"

"No more scares," I gulped. They had lied to me my whole life, I reminded myself. I could lie, too. "Promise."

Dad pulled me away from his chest, holding me by my shoulders an arm's length away from himself.

"Then I need you to be honest about what I'm about to ask you."

Here it was. The question I'd been dreading all night. I rehearsed my answer in my head in the half-second before he asked it.

No, I'm not on Apex Team. Apex Team? Who? Me? Never!

"Samantha, tell the truth. Are you dating that Wesley boy?"

18

The Dinner

I could feel all the blood in my body rushing to my cheeks. Dad's face mirrored mine, glowing red under his beard.

"I know I have no room to talk," he gushed, "considering your mother is a, well, you know, but you need to know that dating one of them isn't easy."

Somewhere, deep within my overwhelming mortification, I found the ability to be offended.

"One of *them*, Dad? They're people, not aliens!"

"I know that!" he backtracked. "Obviously, I know that! But look what happened at the museum! Danger follows them, and if you are going to date one, you need to know how to keep yourself safe."

"First of all, what happened at the museum had nothing to do with Wesley! Those creeps were there for me, remember? I didn't need an Apex boyfriend to get that target painted on my back."

Dad scooped up the silverware and thrusted it onto napkins.

"Quite frankly, it doesn't matter if they have powers or not, you're too young to be dating at all. So whatever this is," he gesticulated wildly, "you need to end it."

I had never even considered myself the dating type, though my faith in that aspect of myself was admittedly shaken the closer I got to Wesley. Still, though. This was not something I wanted to explore in conversation with *Dad* of all people. I would've rather he'd just asked about Apex Team like I had thought he would.

"I'm not dating Wesley," I hissed. "And, just so you know, he can probably hear this whole conversation."

Dad's eyes grew wide, and he glanced up at the ceiling as if he might see through all the way to Wesley on the third floor.

"Damn Apex."

"Why would you think I'm dating Wesley?"

Dad shrugged and grunted noncommittally. I shouldn't have mentioned Wesley's super hearing. Now Dad was unlikely to say anything.

"He's my assigned project partner in Mr. Fleming's class," I explained. "And he's my friend. Naomi, too. I don't know if you remember, but I kinda saved their lives last weekend."

I grinned, trying to lighten the mood. I hadn't wanted to embarrass my dad, even though I was still secretly screaming on the inside from the sheer horror of him accusing me of dating Wesley.

He grunted again but smiled.

"So I've heard, but I'm not surprised. No one beats a Havardson in a sword fight."

"Right, I forgot you're a sword master who daylights as a linguistics professor."

He chuckled.

"Who knows, maybe I am."

"I wouldn't be surprised considering how many secrets you and Mom keep."

I was glad the conversation had strayed away from Wesley, and Dad was smiling now, but I wish I hadn't noticed the way his gray eyes had become watery. He turned away and brushed at his face with the back of his hand.

Luckily, Mom called from the kitchen.

"Everybody, wash up! Food's about done."

Dad turned back towards me, his eyes clear now.

"Go get your friends," he nodded to the hall. "But just so you know, I mean it when I say you're too young to date."

When Naomi and Wesley came downstairs with Avery, Wesley wouldn't meet my eye. Naomi sat between us at the dinner table, which worked out in Avery's favor since he wanted to sit on my other side to talk non-stop about his new middle school.

Mr. Hendricks sat directly across from me. He smiled awkwardly and looked like he was about to say something but instead cleared his throat and looked away.

"Watch your heads," Mom warned as she leaned between Naomi and me to set a large platter of salmon on the table. Wesley was tapping his fingers on the table listlessly, itching to dig into the food.

Mom took her seat at one end of the table, and Wesley didn't wait any longer. As everyone began loading their plates with salmon, Mr. Hendricks chuckled to himself, as if remembering something funny.

"You know, Alison," he wobbled his fork in her direction, "I was just remembering back when we were still on the team, now that we can talk openly about it."

Mom blushed, and Dad rolled his eyes next to her.

"That was a very long time ago," she said.

"We had fun, though, didn't we?" he said, still chuckling.

"Fun?" Amanda snorted. "I thought being on the team was about duty and diligence?"

Mr. Hendricks patted Amanda's shoulder but didn't pay her any more attention than that.

"Remember the exchange student from Italy?" Mr. Hendricks cackled. Mom snorted, trying not to laugh with her mouth full of food.

"That wasn't funny!" she said, although she had turned pink, and the corners of her mouth twitched as she fought back a smile. "I still feel bad about that."

Mr. Hendricks leaned back in his seat and looked around the table to make sure he had everyone's attention.

"We got a new student part way through the year, you see," he explained. "She was an exchange student from Italy, and a certain history teacher we all love took a liking to her."

Mom was openly giggling now.

"And someone who will remain nameless," Mr. Hendricks continued, looking pointedly at my mom, "thought it would be funny to convince him that he knew fluent Italian."

Naomi guffawed next to me.

"You didn't!" she said, eyes wide.

Mom nodded, unable to speak through the laughter.

"Alison used her powers on Alex so he was fully convinced he knew the language! Oh, you should've seen that poor girl's face when he walked up speaking complete gibberish!"

Even Dad and Amanda were chuckling now. I had to admit, the thought of Fleming walking up to a pretty girl and spewing nonsense was objectively funny. However, I was still smarting from discovering Mom had used those same powers on me, albeit in a much more useful capacity.

"To be fair," Mom said, finally catching her breath, "she thought it was cute! They dated until she moved back to Italy."

"Really?" Mr. Hendricks screwed up his nose. "I don't remember that."

"They were real cute, too," Mom said as her giggles subsided. "He wasn't too happy with me at first, but he eventually figured I'd done him a favor."

Dad turned to Amanda. She'd taken off her ball cap for dinner and glared around the table as if daring anyone to talk to her. Maybe he was just tired from all the Apex talk, but he was the first to take her up on the challenge.

"You enjoying sophomore year so far?"

"Best year of school yet." She glanced down the table at her dad as she said it. "I've never had free time before, and it's nice to finally get to spend the day doing what I want."

"Or," Mr. Hendricks said, "you could be out helping the search for your sister instead of running around with that *girl*."

"Her name is Brooke," Amanda growled.

"I don't care what her name is, she's a distraction," Mr. Hendricks retorted.

"You should've brought her tonight." Mom ignored Mr. Hendricks's fiery glare. "Vic only has good things to say about her."

Dad nodded.

"She's in my Intro class this semester. Great kid."

"Dating is a distraction," Mr. Hendricks interjected. "Especially when Winnie is still out there somewhere, and Amanda could be helping."

Mrs. Hendricks elbowed him and turned to Mom.

"The salmon is delicious, Alison."

Mr. Hendricks ignored his wife's obvious attempt at changing the subject.

"But, of course, I forgot," he smiled disingenuously at Naomi and Wesley, "you two have probably got it all under control."

"Sure do," Wesley said without missing a beat, his mouth full of salmon.

"How is Alexander doing these days, anyway?" He said it off-handedly, but I was willing to bet Naomi and Wesley were as unconvinced by his fake casualness as I was.

"You mean Mr. Fleming?" I asked. "He's great."

Naomi kicked me under the table.

"At-at least in history class, I mean," I stuttered. "I don't know about the Apex stuff."

I jerked my thumb towards Wesley and Naomi and shoveled green beans into my mouth so I wouldn't keep talking.

"He's good," Naomi nodded fervently. "Probably the best instructor the team's ever seen."

Mr. Hendricks snorted into his wine glass. His wife glared at him.

"I like Alex," Mom said, also glaring at Mr. Hendricks. "He was always the best of us."

"Oh, really? Tell that to Winnie."

Mom's face flushed. Food had lost its taste. It wasn't Fleming's fault Winnie was missing. It was mine.

"Come on, Roy, you know I don't like him much either, but that's not fair," Dad said. "How was he supposed to know that would happen at the museum? He's only human, after all."

"Exactly!" Mr. Hendricks waved his drink wildly. "Only human. When you're on Apex Team, you have to be better than that!"

"That's enough," Mrs. Hendricks said in a rare moment of conviction. She pried the wine glass from Mr. Hendricks's hand and set it on the table.

If Roy Hendricks talked about Apex versus non-Apex like that at home, I couldn't blame Winnie for her obsession with them. Looking at Amanda glaring at her beans and salmon, I couldn't help but to feel bad for her, too.

Mom cleared her throat.

"So, you have classes with Sammy?" She looked at Wesley and Naomi.

"We're all in Mr. Fleming's class together," Naomi said.

"Good thing, too," Wesley chimed in. "Without Sam, we would've been toast at the museum."

Naomi elbowed Wesley, but it was too late. Whatever tension had been briefly relieved from the room came rushing back ten-fold.

"Right," Mr. Hendricks said and the candles on the table seemed to glow brighter for a second. "I forgot that the Beta had to save the day."

"What's a Beta?" Avery asked.

"We don't call people 'Beta', Roy," Mom hissed with the world's fakest smile plastered on her face. Mr. Hendricks shrugged and wrestled his drink back from Mrs. Hendricks.

"But what's it mean?" Avery persisted.

"It's a rude way of saying a non-Apex," I said, wondering why my parents bothered hanging out with someone who was essentially an older version of Andersen. "He means me."

Avery's eyes widened, and he pointed his fork at Mom in accusation.

"You didn't tell me Sammy saved everyone at the museum!"

"You told him all the family secrets I was never allowed in on and that I was almost kidnapped, but you left out the part where I was super cool?" I leaned over my plate to get a better look at Mom and Dad.

"There's nothing 'super cool' about almost getting yourself killed," Mom snipped.

"I mean, it was probably at least a little cool." Dad winked at me. Mom gave him a warning glance.

"Maybe you should ask Alex about joining the team, then," Mr. Hendricks drawled. The way he stared at me felt like a challenge.

"No," Mom and Dad said in unison. Luckily, I'd just taken a large bite of salmon and couldn't stutter out a response.

"You are not joining the team," Dad said.

"Who said I was joining the team?" I said, thankful my voice didn't shake. Amanda smirked at me from her seat. I narrowed my eyes at her, silently threatening her. If they found out about the permission form, I was dead.

Avery came to my rescue.

"Mom, is there dessert?" He'd already cleared his plate. Any other night, I was sure Mom would have made him wait until everyone was done eating. However, she seemed eager to get away from the dining table. Her plate was mostly untouched, but she didn't like salmon anyway.

"Of course!" she chirped. She stood up to take his plate and kissed him on the forehead as she did. He scowled and shied away. "Anyone else done?"

It was a tough choice. I could stay at the table and listen to Mr. Hendricks get ruder and ruder, or I could follow Mom to the kitchen where she might continue an interrogation about my hypothetical involvement with Apex Team.

"You know, if it were up to me, Betas wouldn't even be allowed to try out for the team, let alone lead it," Mr. Hendricks said, making the decision a lot easier.

I followed Mom to the kitchen. She didn't notice me at first and leaned against the sink. She closed her eyes and sighed, her fake smile falling from her face.

"Did you need help?"

She jumped a little at the sound of my voice.

"Oh, it's you."

I felt bad for her for a half-second, watching her try to take a moment at the kitchen sink. She looked exhausted. I'd almost forgotten I was still a little mad at her, but something about the way she addressed me made me ready to bristle all over again. Maybe I was exhausted, too.

She went to the fridge and pulled out a decadent banana pudding.

"Wanna hand me some plates?" She nodded at the cupboard to my right. I pulled a stack of plates out and met her at the counter. She sized up her pudding, calculating the best way to scoop it out of the container without messing up the layers.

"Mr. Hendricks is kinda a jerk," I said. She sighed.

"He's worried about Winnie."

"I bet Mrs. Hendricks is, too, and she's not being rude."

A scoop of pudding landed on the first plate. Mom frowned at it and set it aside.

"I'm sorry if he is embarrassing you in front of your friends."

"He's not embarrassing me, he's offending me!"

"You just have to ignore it."

The second plate of pudding was a little prettier than the first, but Mom still didn't look satisfied with the presentation.

I boiled inside, but how was I supposed to tell her I already got enough flack at school for being a Beta? Now I had to come to the place that was supposed to be my home even though my bedroom hadn't even been set up yet, and take more verbal abuse at the hands of my parents' friend. It wasn't fair, but if I said something, it might clue her into my new extracurricular activities.

I found the dessert spoons and brought them to the growing row of plated pudding. I couldn't say nothing, though.

"I think you should know that I found out what you did to my head." The casualness that I tried to inject into my tone came off as strained.

Mom whipped her head to look at me, horror etched on her face. The plate she was holding slipped into the sink, pudding side down, and cracked down the middle.

"What?" she breathed.

I shrank away. Sure, what she'd done was duplicitous and invasive at best, but I hadn't thought she'd react so strongly.

"I mean, it wasn't hard to figure out," I said even though I hadn't really figured it out myself. It had been Coach Reiner that told me but, again, saying that would spell doom for my career with Team Apex. "I've never had a day of self defense classes in my life, and suddenly I can sword fight super-strong men twice my size? You could've at least told me you downloaded fighting skills into my brain."

Mom stared at me, blinking rapidly until she finally looked down at the broken plate in the sink.

"Shoot, they don't sell these anymore." She shook her head as if to clear it. "I'm sorry, Samantha, I didn't want to freak you out. You didn't even know about my powers, how was I supposed to tell you?"

"You could've just told me all of it." I shrugged. I pulled the broken plate pieces out of the sink so that I wouldn't have to look at her.

"What happened?" Dad appeared around the corner. "I heard a crash."

I held the two halves of the plate up. A glob of pudding dripped onto the floor.

"Mom broke a plate after I told her I knew she'd messed with my mind."

Where Mom's shock had been on full display, Dad was stoic. He looked between the two of us, looking so much like a man of stone that I thought he might have stopped breathing.

"She means how I taught her how to fight without telling her," Mom said quickly. Dad exhaled loudly through his nose.

"Thanks for telling me, by the way." I felt bad putting them on the spot, but I wanted them to know I was mad at them for the whole thing.

"Saved your life, didn't it?" Mom retorted.

"Just because it worked out doesn't make it okay you put something in my head without at least asking first."

She shook her head wildly.

"Okay, fine. We're sorry." She thrust a plate of pudding into each of my hands. "Now deliver these to the table, alright?"

I shouldered past Dad, who was still immobile in the doorway. I thought it would feel good to tell them I knew their secret, but I felt worse.

By the looks on Naomi and Wesley's faces when I entered the dining room, they were not enjoying dinner. Mr. Hendricks was at least talking about work now, so instead of listening to him slander our history teacher, they were being subjected to a lecture on European anthropology. They each raised their eyebrows at me, but I set down the puddings and shook my head, as if to say, "I'll tell you later."

I went back to the kitchen to pick up more desserts. Dad had disappeared so it was just Mom and me again.

"I can take it away if you like," she said gently. I shivered.

"You can do that?"

"Just the things that I put there. Like when I had to unteach Mr. Fleming fake Italian."

"No, it's okay. Might come in handy if I'm gonna be kidnapped again."

"That's not funny," Mom reprimanded.

"I wasn't trying to be."

I scooped up as many plates as I could. I should've stayed in the dining room and waited out Mr. Hendricks's ire. He could've ranted about Betas all night long. I would've preferred it to the weird confrontation in the kitchen with my parents.

Dad reappeared after dessert to drive us back to campus. Wesley stayed silent in the back seat while Naomi made polite conversation. It was still raining, and I focused on the splashing of the tires rather than listen to Naomi tell Dad about school.

He pulled up outside the dorms. As Naomi and Wesley opened the backdoor and bowed their heads against the storm, Dad put his hand on my shoulder.

"Wait a minute, alright?"

I waved at Naomi and Wesley to go on ahead and sank back into the passenger seat. Dad was silent a moment, and my stomach twisted in anticipation.

"I'm sorry we tampered with your head without telling you," he finally said. His voice was constricted, and there was a layer of pain to it.

"Oh," I said quietly. "It-it's alright. I'm mostly over it."

"It was wrong," he admitted.

"I'd probably be wherever they took Winnie if you didn't do it, though."

Dad's hands were still on the wheel, his knuckles turning white from the force of his grip.

"Ends never justify the means," he grunted. He let go of the wheel to pull me in. He held me there, and I felt his chest shudder. However, when he let me go, his face was clear, and he managed a smile. "I just need you to know I'm sorry for all of it."

I shrugged, opening the door.

"It's not a big deal," I insisted. "Just don't do it again. And don't do it to Avery."

He ruffled my hair before I stepped out into the rain.

"Be safe, alright?"

"You know me, Dad," I winked. "I'm always safe."

19

The Night Game

T he rain didn't let up all week. We weathered the storm by spending our free time cooped up in the Apex facility, running drills and dodges. Naomi finally gave us a well-deserved break from training on Sunday so Wesley and I were able to work on our project for Fleming's class. The next part was due at the end of the week, and I wasn't about to wait until the last minute to do it again.

We hadn't made much headway on sorting through Winnie's pictures, either, but had completed the minimum three hours for me to be eligible for the Night Game. Fleming signed off on my mission hours on Monday, though he didn't look too happy about it. Letting me run around the city after hours was probably a bit of a liability considering I'd almost been kidnapped twice.

The freshmen on Apex Team buzzed as they all reached three mission hours that week as well. On Wednesday, Fleming ended after school training by calling us all together and announcing the game we'd be playing that weekend would be island-wide Fugitive. One team would be driven across the island and tasked with returning to campus without being caught by the other team.

The room erupted in excited shouts and exclamations.

"As always, it is upperclassmen against underclassmen," Fleming shouted over the din. "Freshmen and sophomores will be the fugitives. If more than half of you make it back to campus, you win. Upperclassmen win if they stop enough of you. Losers will spend Sunday cleaning the locker rooms and gym equipment."

The locker room was full of strategy talk that night. The senior girls huddled in a corner, hatching plans for how they were going to catch us.

"Don't worry," Naomi whispered. "Most of their powers won't help them, and it's much easier to be a fugitive."

The rest of the school was also buzzing with anticipation the next day. Posters promoting the upcoming Homecoming dance had gone up overnight. I overheard Jamie talking to a group of friends.

"If I'm not voted Sophomore Queen, I'm seriously going to drop out."

"No, you'll get it for sure!" Madison said.

"Just have your parents sue the school if you don't," another girl joked.

I knew I had next to no chance of being voted anything, but anyone would be better than watching Jamie win.

By Saturday, it had finally rained itself out, and we saw the first patch of blue sky that we'd seen the whole week. Wesley insisted this was a good thing for the Night Games that night.

"Jeanie is invisible in rain and fog," he explained. "She's a junior, and she'll be at a disadvantage not being able to use her powers."

There were about twenty of us on the bus. The freshmen had taken the seats closest to the back, and their excitement was tangible. It was easy to forget they were all in the same boat as me. None of us were really on the team yet, but all of us were eager to prove ourselves.

"It's not really fair if you think about it," I mused in the front of the bus, fidgeting with the armband Fleming had fastened around my bicep. The other underclassmen each had one too. "Olivia can turn invisible, right? And she can turn her friends invisible, too."

"Don't worry," Naomi assured me. "There's a senior who can see heat signatures. Olivia can't hide from him. The only one with an easy ticket back to school is Heather."

Heather lounged in the bus seat across the aisle from us. She winked.

"Don't know why I even came along." She hadn't even bothered putting on running shoes. She was powerful, but I didn't understand how her powers would help her more than anyone else's would.

The bus shuddered to a stop in a parking lot overlooking the ocean. While the rain had let up, the skies were still overcast, making the night darker than usual. The bus door pulled open and Andersen led his friends off first. They looked ready to disappear among the buildings, but Fleming called them back.

"You've got a ten minute head start, and please remember, if your armband is removed, you're out. There's no fighting your way back into the game." He looked at Wesley as he said it. "Additionally, the idea behind the Night Game is teaching you how to effectively use your powers without causing a scene, so be covert, and don't let the public see you."

"Then why are Betas allowed to participate?" Skyler piped.

Fleming ignored him and waved at Heather as he closed the bus door. "Heather, since you'll beat me back to campus, man the call desk until I get there."

The others dispersed before the bus had even pulled away from the curb. Olivia faded from view while Skyler morphed into an old lady. Heather grinned at us.

"I'll see you guys back at school. Good luck."

She marched into a patch of shadows, outside of the glowing reach of the streetlights. The dark corner seemed to deepen and become even blacker, swallowing Heather. As it slowly faded back to normal, she was gone.

"What just happened?" I gawked.

"Heather's powers let her travel short distances if it's dark enough," Naomi explained. It was no wonder no one messed with Heather. She was a powerhouse.

Fleming had dropped us off on the far side of the island, not far from the docks. It was the industrial area of the island, and there weren't as many city lights overhead.

"Everest, you wanna stick with us?" Naomi asked. Everest was lingering nearby, coming up with a game plan. He half-smiled, but his eyes darted to me and back to Naomi.

"Groups aren't really my thing."

"Suit yourself."

I hadn't gotten the chance to get to know Everest, but he didn't blatantly dislike me as much as Andersen and his crew did. He was shy, so I wasn't surprised he wanted to go alone, though it was hard not to feel like he might've said yes if I hadn't been there.

Everest slinked deeper into the industrial district, headed towards the shadows.

"I vote we go towards downtown," Wesley said, pointing in the opposite direction of where Everest had gone. "People will be out, and we can blend in."

Naomi hesitated.

"I don't know, it'll be harder to tell if we're being followed."

"But we won't stand out as much as we would in the industrial district," I pointed out. I liked Wesley's idea, even if it was only because I was keen to avoid the shipping docks. If I had a run-in with the Adrestus people tonight, Fleming would never let me out on a real mission.

Naomi glanced at her watch and grumbled under her breath.

"Fine, but only because we're wasting time just standing here."

We half-jogged, half-walked along the waterfront, hunkering down to protect ourselves from the wind that blew in from the ocean. Naomi's watch beeped after a couple of minutes.

"That's ten minutes," she said. "The upperclassmen are on their way."

A mix of excitement and apprehension gnawed at my insides. This was it. I would make it back to campus and prove I belonged here just as much as anyone else did.

The darkened waterfront gave way to shops and restaurants. There were more people here, like Wesley had said there would be, but none of them took notice of us. We looked like three normal high school kids, out for a night after being cooped up all week by rain.

"Ugh," Naomi groaned and looked around. "I think Skyler might be nearby."

"How can you tell?" I looked around at the passing faces. If Skyler really was nearby, any of them could be him.

"He's got a pretty distinct emotional signature."

"That's fine, though," Wesley hissed. "He's an underclassman. We're on the same team."

"Are we, though?" Naomi sniffed.

The sidewalk had gotten progressively more crowded now that we were in the busy part of the city. I stepped closer to Wesley and held my arm with the armband close to my chest. It would be easy for anyone to brush by and pull it off.

"Gift shop, now!" Naomi hissed. She shepherded us into a gift shop and ducked behind a rack of novelty hats.

"Who is it?" Wesley and I asked at the same time.

She shook her head.

"I can't tell, but I know it's got to be one of them."

"Did they see us?" I pressed.

"I can't tell."

We slinked through the gift shop aisles, pretending to be interested in the magnets and snow globes that lined them. Naomi wouldn't let us leave until she knew it was clear outside, but I was getting agitated with every passing minute. The longer we stayed in the gift shop, the more time the upperclassman had to find us.

I chanced a peek out the shop window and grabbed Wesley's wrist.

"I think I see them."

I didn't know any of the upperclassmen very well, but I still recognized the twin brother and sister who lurked on the sidewalk just outside.

"Crap," Wesley swore, but his eyes lit up. The game had officially begun. "Naomi!"

Naomi came to our side and frowned.

"Desirae and Mike? They shouldn't be too difficult."

"What can they do?" I asked, a little embarrassed I didn't know, especially since I might have to fight either one in the Final Trial.

"They share a mental link," Naomi explained. "They can broadcast what they are seeing and thinking to each other. If one of them sees us, they both see us."

I peered out from behind the shelf we were crouched behind. Desirae tapped Mike's shoulder and jerked her thumb towards the gift shop. He nodded, and they made their way to the door. I clutched at my armband.

"We've gotta go," Wesley whispered.

"Should we split up?" I suggested.

"No!" They both hissed back at me.

Naomi led the way to a back exit that let out onto a boardwalk. She motioned for us to follow, but Wesley shook his head.

"Mike," he mouthed and pointed out onto the boardwalk. "I can hear him outside."

Behind us, a bell rang as the front entrance opened. We twisted around to see Desirae walk in. She locked eyes with me and grinned.

"Too late!"

I pushed Naomi and Wesley through the back door and straight into Mike. He lunged for Wesley's armband, but Wesley danced out of the way and tripped him. Mike landed on the wooden planks with a thud. Desirae knocked over a hat rack behind us as she jumped into the fray.

"Hey! Watch it!" A shopkeeper shouted from the register. "You gonna fix that?"

Desirae faltered and looked between us and the angry shopkeeper.

"And you kids! Close that door! It's freezing in here!"

We leaped over Mike, who was still sprawled out on the ground, leaving Desirae to deal with her broken hat rack.

"Keep going, Mike is following us!" Wesley warned. We sprinted out onto the street. An older woman squawked as we nearly ran her down.

"Sorry!" I called back over my shoulder.

We ran across the road and turned down an alley that was wedged between two shops.

"Dumpster!" I pointed up ahead.

"No way, this game is not worth it!" Naomi shook her head.

"Yes, it is!" Wesley sprinted ahead and threw the lid open. He crouched with his hands ready. Naomi hesitated so I hurried ahead of her. I ran at Wesley and jumped. He easily hoisted me into the metal container.

The smell hit me harder than the metal floor did. Trash must've been picked up earlier that day, but the stink that lingered was enough to make me gag. Naomi soared in and landed on top of me.

"You've got to be kidding," she moaned. Wesley slid in behind her, closing the lid as he did.

"You think it's bad? Try having a super nose."

Naomi tapped on her watch so that the glow of the screen cast a faint light through the dumpster. Wesley had his sweatshirt pulled up over his nose and mouth. He pressed his ear against the side to listen.

"He's getting closer," he breathed. Naomi smirked.

"But he's frustrated," she said. "He's lost us."

Wesley raised a finger to his lips. The slapping of shoes on pavement got closer and closer, and then farther and farther. Wesley waited another moment before he couldn't take it any longer.

He burst through the dumpster lid and vaulted back into the alley.

"Ugh, I can still smell it," he shuddered as Naomi and I climbed out behind him.

I looked back the way we came. There was a soft orange glow from the shop windows and street lights in that direction. The other way down the alley was much darker.

"Now what?" I asked. If we went one way, Desirae might be waiting for us. Mike was in the other direction.

"I think we should try the most direct route to campus at this point." Wesley shrugged. "They're everywhere, and I think I just heard Skyler get caught back at the waterfront."

I felt a hit of satisfaction at the news even though Skyler was on our team. If our team ended up losing, it might be worth it if it meant Andersen or his friends were to blame.

"I don't know," Naomi mused. "It'll only get more difficult as we get closer."

"Yeah, but that'll happen no matter what way we go to get there." Wesley began walking down the alley, farther from the shop lights.

"There's a park a few blocks that way that isn't very well lit. Cutting through will save us time."

"You don't think the park will be crawling with upperclassmen?"

"The whole city is crawling with upperclassmen! We'll just have to outrun them."

We ran on our tip-toes through the alleyway. I stumbled over the pavement a few times. It was easy to tell I was the loudest and least graceful out of the three of us. Luckily, Naomi and Wesley were patient enough to not say anything.

Wesley was the first to reach the main road. He poked his head out between the buildings and waved us forward.

"Looks clear." He gave each direction a second, precautionary look. There was no traffic this late. The only activity was several blocks away where a line of people stood outside of a club, but they were far enough that we wouldn't have to worry about them seeing us.

I followed Wesley out into the street, sprinting across the four lanes.

"Wait!" Naomi called behind us. I faltered and turned back to look at her, still standing in the alleyway with a hand outstretched towards us. The next second, I was bowled over by a sudden, powerful burst of wind.

I sprawled out across the pavement. Wesley shouted something, but it was impossible to hear. We were in a wind tunnel.

It subsided, and a girl ran out from the alley adjacent to the one we'd just exited. She sprinted at me full force. I tried to think of any of the moves I'd been practicing with Wesley and Naomi, but my mind was blank.

I stumbled backwards on my hands, searching for the sidewalk.

"Sam, you've gotta move!" Wesley shouted.

Naomi chased after the girl, who I recognized as a junior on the team. Naomi grabbed her arm, but she twisted away and pushed her to the ground before lunging at me.

Mom's back-up programming switched on. I kicked upwards, landing a foot square in her stomach.

"Ooof!" She fell backwards, and I felt Wesley's hands scoop me up under my arms to pull me to my feet.

"Don't look back!"

We ducked into the next alleyway just in time to avoid another torrent of wind. Naomi gasped for breath next to us.

"Who was that?" I demanded as we took off down the alley. I hadn't seen wind powers in my two weeks with the team.

"Isabelle," Naomi said grimly. "Her grandma was Lady Zephyress, one of the islands first big heroes."

"Lady Zephyress?" I looked at Wesley running next to me. "Didn't she have a statue at the museum?"

"Yeah," he said. "She was a big deal. She's Anthony's grandma, too."

There was a sudden roar behind us, and we stumbled forward as wind pushed at our backs. Wesley steadied himself against the alley wall. Naomi was closest to him, so he pulled her in to help anchor her. I was left to fall face first back to the ground.

I looked back at Isabelle. Her long, dark hair had come loose and whipped around her face in the micro-storm. She grinned at me and then sprinted towards us again.

"We saw her first!"

Mike barreled down the street behind Isabelle, tackling her to the ground.

"You idiot, you're on my team!" she shrieked. Desirae appeared behind them, leaped over them, and dove towards us. She had an armband wrapped around her bicep. She must've caught someone. I really hoped it had been Skyler.

I scrambled to my feet and let Wesley drag me towards the park. Naomi pulled a couple of trash cans down behind us, but they only delayed

Desirae for a moment. I could feel her fingers grabbing at my back, inches away from my armband.

Another wind blast knocked us all off our feet.

"I thought we were all on the same team!" Desirae shouted at Isabelle.

"You guys tackled me first!"

Their argument was enough to let us make our getaway. Wesley dragged us into the deep shadows of the park.

"Geez," Naomi said, rubbing her arm after Wesley finally let go. "Would it be easier for you if we got on your back?"

Wesley snorted.

"It might be, actually."

The walkway that weaved through the park trees was lit just enough so that we could see where the footpath was. A creek babbled somewhere nearby in the dark, and the glowing penthouse dome of Schrader Industries winked at us through breaks in the canopy cover.

"Do you think we lost them?" I asked, looking back apprehensively. I could still hear them shouting at each other in the distance.

"Hope so," Wesley said. "Did it seem like they were targeting Sam?"

"You think?" I retorted. It hadn't escaped my notice that both the twins and Isabelle had all but completely ignored Wesley and Naomi.

"It's a little weird," Naomi said. "I promise the three of them don't dislike you, but they did feel eager for some reason."

I groaned. It was weird how the closer we got to campus, the farther it seemed.

"It's already worked in our favor, though," Wesley pointed out. "They're self-sabotaging. It's like they'd rather get you and lose the whole game than let you go and win."

"That's fine." I shrugged. The path through the park was winding, and the babbling creek was getting louder. "If we get cornered again, we can split up. You guys will be able to get away and hopefully make it back."

"Come on, Samantha." I didn't look at Naomi's face, but I knew she'd be glaring at me. "We aren't using you as bait."

"Two out of three of us making it back isn't bad! If everyone does that well, we'll win."

"I think Naomi means we shouldn't split up," Wesley said. "Our best chance is staying together."

That sounded like a lie. Wesley and Naomi would probably be back at campus already if it weren't for me. They were faster, they were quieter, and no one was targeting them.

I was at least glad we weren't running anymore. It was peaceful in the park. The ocean winds didn't reach this deep into the island, and the brunt of the city lights was blocked out by the trees.

However, the peace didn't last. Naomi froze and grabbed my arm.

"We're being watched," she whispered. Wesley glanced around.

"I don't see anyone. Who is it?"

Naomi closed her eyes to concentrate.

"It's hard to say, but I think it's Marcus."

Wesley swore under his breath.

"Which one is Marcus?"

"I told you about him on the bus," Naomi said. "He can see heat signatures, which means even in the trees like this, he'll be able to spot us no problem."

"Keep walking," Wesley whispered. "If we stop too long, he'll know we're onto him. I'd hear him if he was getting closer so there's no use running yet either."

"But what if we're moving towards him?" I asked.

"Then we'll use you as bait?"

"We will not!" Naomi smacked Wesley's shoulder.

The walkway lights, which had seemed whimsical just moments ago, now felt sinister. Marcus could be anywhere, hiding just outside their halos of light. If he knew Wesley was here, he'd be careful not to move and give away his position.

"You can't tell how close he is?" I asked Naomi.

"No, it's not as simple as that. A weak emotion nearby might feel the same as a strong emotion that's far away."

There was a break in the trees up ahead. Streetlights seeped in through the branches, and the pathway was getting brighter. Wesley suddenly began sprinting to the park exit.

"He's on our left!"

Naomi and I bolted after Wesley, and something crashed through the bushes next to us. There was a faint whistling sound. Something looped over my head and shoulders, then tightened.

"A lasso?" I shouted, wriggling to get free. "Who the heck uses a lasso?"

Marcus burst through the bushes holding the other end of the rope. He was large for a high schooler. He towered over most of the kids at the school and had the brawn to match the height.

"Sorry." He pulled on his end of the rope, reeling me in.

I dug my heels into the ground and leaned away, but Marcus was too strong. I fell to the ground for the hundredth time that night. Marcus raced towards me, but Wesley beat him.

Wesley grabbed the rope and grunted as he tore it at the knot. Back on my feet, we chased after Naomi with Marcus in pursuit.

"Come on, that was my good rope!" he called after us.

For as big as he was, Marcus was fast. He remained on our heels as we sprinted across the street and tried to disappear between the buildings. My lungs burned. If I stopped, Naomi and Wesley would get away. They'd make it back to campus, and even if I didn't, I could take solace in the fact that I at least lasted longer than Skyler.

Naomi and Wesley were a half pace ahead of me. I saw a side road up ahead. I could dart down that way, and it'd be too late for them to turn back. I could lead Marcus away.

I braced myself for the decision.

"What are you up to, Sam?" Naomi shouted. It was too late. I banked right, forking away from them. Marcus's heavy footfalls followed me.

"I said no splitting up!" Wesley yelled.

"It's fine!" I called back. "I'll see you guys later!"

I led Marcus farther down the side street, then between two buildings into an alley, and finally, straight into a fence.

I slammed into the chain link. Marcus paused at the mouth of the alley to catch his breath. He might as well take his time. There was nowhere for me to go.

"I'm really sorry," he said between breaths, pushing sweaty blond hair back from his brow. "But you get it, right?"

"Sure." Of course I got it. I was the easiest target. "But where's the glory in picking off the weakest link?"

"I don't care about glory." He shook his head. "I just really need that night off."

I hesitated. I had no idea what he was talking about.

"I thought the prize was not having to clean?"

"Well, yeah, it is. But Andersen offered to cover Call Duty next month for whoever got you specifically."

I exhaled heavily. It wasn't surprising that Andersen had pulled a move like that, but, damn, did it make me angry.

"It's nothing personal," Marcus insisted.

"Of course not," I snorted. "What could possibly feel personal about that? What if I offered to cover your Call Duty for not taking my armband?"

Marcus laughed.

"Neither of us knows if you'll even be here next month."

I'd been ready to call it a night. I would've been fine with losing if it meant helping my friends. However, now that I knew Andersen had taken it upon himself to orchestrate my failure, I couldn't let Marcus take my arm band.

But he was huge, and he was a senior. Even if I managed to get away somehow, he'd have no problem finding me again with his heat-sensing vision. I steeled myself. I'd fought bigger.

Marcus wasn't expecting me to charge at him. His surprise worked to my advantage, and I was able to get around him using a dodge I'd worked on with Naomi that week. It had been a move Mom had put in my head, but I'd learned to execute it without relying on instinct.

"Hey!" he shouted, but I didn't look back. I ran back the way I'd come. Wesley and Naomi couldn't have gotten too far.

A hand wrapped around my mouth, and I was pulled off my feet into the shadow of another dumpster. I elbowed my attacker.

"Oof!" Wesley let go of me and doubled over.

"Careful, it's just us!" Naomi said.

"You guys scared the crap out of me!" I hissed. "And Marcus is right behind me, we've gotta go!"

"Exactly," Wesley said. He was clutching his side where I had elbowed him. "We're going down there."

I looked down at the gaping hole at our feet.

"The sewers?" I had thought the dumpster we'd hid in earlier had been gross enough. I wasn't sure if wading through sewers was worth winning the game.

"Not the sewers." Naomi grinned, getting on the ground and dangling her legs into the hole. A dim, orange glow emanated from its depths. "The tidal hydraulic system."

The industry project that Wesley and I had been working on might not have been A plus material, but I had learned enough to know about the rivers of salt water coursing beneath the city, powering the island and lifting and raising it as the tides changed.

"There's no way that's legal," I said.

"We can talk about it down there," Wesley said. "Marcus is catching his second wind so we've gotta get going."

Naomi disappeared down the hole, and I reluctantly followed. Wesley came down the ladder after me, and metal grated on concrete as he pulled the cover back into place.

"Won't he be able to see us with his powers, though?" I asked. The metal rungs of the ladder were freezing. I was sure our body heat would be unmissable from above.

"Not if we put enough concrete between us and him," Naomi explained.

"And is no one going to explain the lasso?" The tunnel brightened as we neared the bottom.

"His family owns a dude ranch," Naomi said. I heard her drop from the ladder and land on the pavement below. I tried to follow suit but stumbled on the landing. "His powers don't help much with combat, but he's had enough practice on the ranch to be efficient with a lasso."

We were standing on a pathway that ran alongside a massive, underground river. It gushed and gargled in an ebb and flow, as if it were breathing. The walls looked as if they were made of bronze. They reflected the light from the wall sconces, so the whole chamber glowed a soft orange.

Wesley jumped down on the pavement beside me. He rounded on me, and I was surprised to see he was angry. He pointed an accusatory finger at my face.

"We said no splitting up!"

"No, *you* said no splitting up! I had a plan, and it worked."

"You don't get to go rogue because you think your plan is best."

His voice echoed through the tunnel. I crossed my arms.

"My plan *was* best," I asserted. "You guys would've been fine."

"And you would? It's not like you have a great track record when it comes to being out in the city at night."

The chamber was cold before, but I swore it dropped another ten degrees.

"You don't have to protect me," I spat. "I'm on the team."

"You're *provisionally* on the team."

I bristled at Wesley's words. It had worked out, hadn't it? And no one had tried to kidnap me in the process.

"I think we should focus on getting back to campus and sorting this out there." Naomi put a hand on Wesley's shoulder, but he shook it off.

"Just don't run off again," he said.

"Whatever."I knew he'd been on the team longer and was used to all this, but it was still irritating that he thought he could tell me what to do.

"Great," Naomi said. "Now, which way towards school?"

Wesley sauntered down the walkway.

"It's this way. Straight shot."

We walked in silence, which was just as well. Not only was I mad at Wesley for blowing up at me, but it was also hard to hear at all over the rushing salt water. Every thirty yards or so we passed another ladder leading to the roads above. Wesley would pause at them and listen before continuing down the walkway.

There were off-shooting passages and doors that we passed every so often as well, but Wesley ignored them and stuck to the main walkway. It wasn't a very wide path, so we walked single-file. I glared at Wesley's back. Maybe this week I'd convince him to practice fighting with me. Maybe I'd convince him that I could hold my own.

I turned back to look at Naomi to ask her for the time. I couldn't tell if we'd been out for a half-hour or for the whole night. However, she was trailing behind us.

She'd stopped walking to lean against the wall. She grabbed at her head with one hand while steadying herself with the other.

"Naomi!"

I ran back to her and wrapped an arm around her to help hold her up. Her eyes screwed shut, and she trembled in my arms.

"What's wrong?" Wesley ran up behind me. Together we lowered Naomi into a sitting position on the ground.

"Is there an upperclassman who can do this to people?" I asked. Naomi shook her head.

"No, it's me," she whispered so she was barely audible over the water behind us. "I can feel someone nearby and—"

She shuddered.

"Are they okay?" Wesley asked. Naomi opened her eyes to look up at us, and they were glassy and bloodshot.

"No. They're not."

20

The Stray

The horrified look in Naomi's eyes sent a wave of fear running through me like electricity.

"Who?" Wesley demanded. "Where?"

She shook her head again.

"I don't know."

There was a side passage just ahead of us. While Wesley tried to console her, I crept along the walkway to peer down into the shadows.

The orange glow of the main chamber only reached a few yards into it before tapering off into darkness. However, I could make out the shape of a small, huddled mass lying at the base of the wall.

I tiptoed down the corridor and leaned over the shape. The bile rose in my throat. It looked like a dead animal. I resisted the urge to recoil away and leaned in closer, wondering if it had anything to do with Naomi's overwhelming fear.

A feeble hiss issued out from the creature, and two glowing eyes opened to blink up at me. It wasn't dead. It was a cat, and it was alive. It didn't seem able to move, and I knew it had to be affected by whatever had been paralyzing other animals on the island.

But the way it looked up at me felt familiar, like I had been here before, looking down on a paralyzed animal while it stared back. I saw Wesley swimming in my mind's eye, limp on the tiled floor of the museum, staring up at me as I brandished a sword.

"Hey!" I called out and pulled my jacket off to wrap around the cat's limp body. It hissed again. "I've found something!"

I carried the tabby out to them. Naomi was holding her head again, but Wesley looked up.

"I don't think now is the best time to be picking up dead animals."

"It's not dead," I said, "It's paralyzed, like the animals on the news."

"It's still not a great time to—"

"Remember at the museum?" I cut him off. Naomi peeked out from her hands to look at me. "They put a patch on you, and you couldn't move. I think they might've done the same to Winnie, and there are paralyzed animals all over the island."

"You think they're related?" Naomi asked weakly.

"I don't know, maybe? It's gotta at least be worth checking out."

Wesley left Naomi's side to get a closer look at the cat. In the light, I could see its orange stripes peeking out from a layer of dirt.

"They tested the patch they found on me," Wesley said. "Maybe if we get the cat back to campus before the paralysis wears off, they can test it for a match."

Naomi leaned away from me, eyeing the cat warily.

"I don't think I can go with you guys," she said.

"Is it that cat that's scared?" Wesley asked. "I didn't know you could pick up animal emotions."

Naomi shrugged weakly.

"If it's strong enough, I'd probably pick it up."

Wesley sighed.

"So much for not splitting up," he mumbled.

I held the cat out to Wesley, but he gave it the same wary look that Naomi had.

"I don't know how long the paralytic will stay in its system, but you have the best chance at getting back as fast as possible," I said. "I can stay with Naomi. We'll be right behind you once she's feeling better."

Wesley shook his head vigorously. He crossed his arms across his chest so that he couldn't take the cat.

"No, no way," he said.

"Come on, Wes," Naomi pleaded. "Just get it out of here."

He looked like he might throw up.

"No, Samantha should keep the cat," he decided. "You'll be okay on your own, right?"

"Once you get it away from me, I'll be fine," Naomi said. "Sooner the better."

Wesley straightened up, and I cradled the cat close to my chest.

"We'll see you back at school," Wesley said. He hesitated, and I knew he didn't like leaving her behind.

He nodded at me, and I held the cat tighter, silently willing it to calm down. The tunnel curved so that after a few minutes, when I looked back, I couldn't see Naomi anymore.

"The tunnel starts to lead away from campus here," Wesley said, stopping under a ladder. "We're only a mile from the school. I'll help you up."

Wesley crouched under the ladder and wove his hands together to create a step.

"What about the cat?"

"You'll have to climb with it."

Wesley boosted me up like it was nothing, and after I'd struggled up the first few rungs with a cat in one arm, I heard him clamber up behind me.

"You think there'll be more seniors this close to school?" I asked.

"Probably," Wesley said. "But if no one bothers us, we'll be back in under ten minutes if we run."

I tried not to think about running while holding a feral cat in my arms. What if the paralytic wore off half-way there, and it attacked me? My thoughts were interrupted as I reached the manhole covering the tunnel.

"Hey, we're at the top."

"Great, can you push the cover over?"

I juggled the cat, trying to hold onto the ladder with an elbow looped through the rungs. It was no use.

"I can't with the cat in the way."

"'Kay, hold still."

I made myself as small as possible against the ladder as Wesley climbed over me. The cover growled across the pavement, and a beam of light from a street lamp shone down on our faces. The cat hissed.

Wesley crawled out onto the street and reached down to help me out. We were back in another alley, but this one looked familiar. I looked up at the rickety fire escape hanging overhead. I could almost see Wesley disappearing up its ladders the day we escaped from the pier. That was back before I'd even known that it had been Wesley.

"Right, so we've got two choices," Wesley said. "We can go along the street, which would be the most direct, or there's the boardwalk—"

"No," I asserted. The humiliation of Andersen's hazing was too fresh for me to want to go back there. Besides, if we became surrounded, there'd be no way to escape. The cat twitched in my arms. I set off down the street in the direction of the school. "We need to hurry. I think the paralytic might be starting to wear off."

The streets and shops were busier on this side of the island. College kids milled around outside of bars, and the sound of karaoke mixed with the sloshing of car tires running through puddles left behind by the week-long rainstorm. We tried to blend in with the people on the street, keeping our heads down but our pace quick.

"Guess we won't be sprinting back to campus," Wesley muttered. I looked at the cat in my arms. It was hissing less and didn't look as frightened.

"So, are you afraid of cats or something?"

"What?" Wesley looked at me, confused.

"You wouldn't take the cat," I explained. "I thought maybe it was because you were afraid. Every hero has a weakness, right?"

Wesley frowned at my joke.

"I don't like small animals."

"Why not? They're cute."

He raised his eyebrow at the tabby.

"Yeah, feral cats are freaking adorable."

"They are," I insisted, knowing full well I'd seen cats much cuter than the filthy one I was holding.

"I just don't like them, okay?"

"But there has to be a reason."

"No, there doesn't," he said firmly. I dropped it, although small animals were a weird thing to be sensitive about.

A figure in a hoodie walked towards us on the sidewalk. Wesley glared at him apprehensively, but he shouldered past, pushing Wesley to the side.

"Someone's having a bad night," I grumbled.

"Watch out!" Wesley twisted around and threw himself between me and the passing figure, who had turned back towards us. His outstretched hand grabbed Wesley's arm, and he looked up at us from under his hood, grinning. "It's Justin!"

I recognized the senior Team Captain leering under the hood and stumbled backwards.

"Samantha, run!"

Justin stepped around Wesley, who made no effort to stop him.

"I'm surprised you made it this far." Justin pulled his hood back to reveal his closely cropped, bleached blond hair. His white teeth stood out against his dark skin. "I'm glad you did, though, so that I could be the one to catch you."

"Good luck using your powers," I teased. "This is a busy street. Someone will see you."

He raised an eyebrow at me and cocked his head.

"I'll be fine, they won't notice. You haven't, anyway."

I looked between him and Wesley. Wesley's back was to me. He hadn't moved since coming between Justin and me. My heart sank.

"What is that?" I asked, pointing at Wesley. "Some kind of stasis ability?"

Justin smirked.

"He'll be free in a minute, but by then I'll have both your armbands."

"Just run, Sam!" Wesley pleaded. "You need to get the cat to Fleming!"

I wanted to help Wesley. I didn't know how, but I was sure that I could get us both out of Justin's trap and back to school, where we could gloat to Andersen.

But the cat was twitching and struggling feebly in my arms. I didn't know how long it would take for the paralytic to wear off completely. I couldn't risk losing what might be the first big clue to finding Winnie.

"Listen," I pleaded and held out my arms so that Justin could see the cat. "We found this, and we need to get back to the school."

Justin looked at me dubiously.

"What're you rushing roadkill off to the school for?"

"It's one of the paralyzed animals." I pulled the cat back towards my chest. "I think it might be related to the paralytic patch the kidnappers used at the museum."

"You're joking."

"I need to get it to Fleming before it can move again."

"Even if that's true, the paralyzed animals are all over the city. You can find another one."

"Probably, but what if we can't? You're a team captain. Shouldn't finding the missing students be more important than a dumb game?"

Justin puffed his chest out importantly and grinned as if he had me cornered.

"Yeah, it should. So give me your armband, and I'll let you go with the cat. That way we all win. Besides, it's just a dumb game, right?"

My heart dropped. Great. Now I had to put my money where my mouth was. The only thing I wanted as much as I wanted to find where the kidnapped students had gone was to win, but Justin was right that I was right. One was more important than the other.

I scowled at him as I reached to rip my armband off. My pride was a small price to pay if this cat actually helped the mission. But just as my fingers wrapped around the fragile fabric, Wesley broke free of the stasis.

Justin didn't have time to react as Wesley knocked him to the pavement, pinning him down.

"Go!" Wesley bellowed.

I spun on my heel and ran and didn't look back. I didn't look back at the people on the sidewalk who complained loudly as I shoved my way through. I didn't look back to see if Wesley was able to get away from Justin. I just ran, keeping the cat bundled close.

I turned a corner, and the Paragon statue glittered dully at the end of the street, the dark silhouette of Schrader Hall looming behind it. I was almost there. It was just a sprint away.

There was a painful snap against my scalp, and my hair cascaded down around my face as my hair tie broke. My shoes caught on something in the dark, and I tripped. I curled myself around the cat as I fell and did my best to roll through the tumble.

"You seriously think you're going to make it back?"

I wouldn't have been surprised if Naomi was able to feel my rage all the way from here. It rose in me like a tsunami, and without either of my friends here to hide it from, I let the anger swell.

Andersen stood over me. He twirled my broken hair tie in his hand, and when I looked down at my unlaced shoes, I understood what had happened. Neither the elastic in the hair tie nor the plastic ends of my shoelaces were immune to Andersen's powers.

"We're on the same team, moron," I spat, getting back to my feet. I slipped out of my shoes as a precaution.

"You think taking those off will help you?" Andersen laughed. "I have two years fighting experience over you. Even without my powers I could easily—"

I planted one foot and twisted as hard I could to bring my opposite leg crashing into Andersen. One well-placed round kick was all it took to floor him.

I swore loudly. The human shin was not designed to smash into other humans at full force.

Andersen sprawled on the pavement, gasping as he tried to regain his breath and dignity. Movement caught my eye. Down the street, Justin had turned the corner and was barreling towards us. Andersen struggled onto one knee, but I kicked him squarely in the chest and ran.

My shin smarted, and the friction of sprinting in socks across pavement made the soles of my feet burn. The cat meowed angrily. I was so close, if I could just make it past the fountain...

Just before I passed the Paragon statue, I heard Andersen screech behind me.

"What about her!?"

I looked back as I crossed onto campus property, just in time to see Justin rip Andersen's armband. Sure, Andersen was on my team, but nothing felt better than seeing him lose.

"You made it!" Heather formed out of the shadows. I yelped in surprise. "Whoops, sorry. Where're the others?"

I pushed the cat into her arms, and she looked at it in bewilderment.

"What is—"

"You can take him downstairs, right? Through the shadows or whatever it is you do?"

"Yeah, but why—"

"Take it to Fleming. Tell him to test the paralytic. Fast!"

She nodded, took a step back into the shadows and disappeared. I took a moment to catch my breath, bending over with my hands on my knees.

"It helps if you hold your hands over your head."

Justin came up behind me. Watching him wave Andersen's armband made the sprint across the city entirely worth it.

"Good job, by the way," he continued. "I'm glad if I wasn't the one to catch you, no one did. I knew that cat bit had to be a ploy."

"What? Oh, I handed it off to Heather." I pointed towards the school building. I could see Andersen down the street over Justin's shoulder. He sat on the curb with his head in his hands. If it was anyone else, I probably would've felt a little sorry for him.

"It wasn't a trick?" Justin raised his eyebrows in surprise. "I feel a little bad for taking this, then."

He pulled an armband out of his back pocket. Wesley's name was scribbled across the fabric. The sweetness of victory soured a little in my mouth. Wesley had taken the fall for me.

"You could always give it back," I suggested, knowing perfectly well Justin would never give it back. He laughed anyways.

"Absolutely not. Besides, a game's a game, isn't it? If this cat thing pans out, you'll both get more credit than I will for catching a few sophomores."

I followed Justin back to the basement floor of the school hall. I figured I must have been one of the last people back if he was headed inside instead of back out into the streets to catch more of my classmates.

A group of freshmen pouted in the main atrium of the training base. They craned their necks to see if I was still wearing an armband. They elbowed each other and pointed when they saw it still secured around my arm. Skyler scowled at me from one corner. Olivia stood with him, her armband still intact.

"Alright, Havardson, why is there a feral cat in my Sickbay?"

Fleming must have followed us in from his office. He crossed his arms and stared down at me expectantly.

I quickly explained why I had just run across the city, and Fleming's eyebrows raised.

"That," he said slowly, "isn't a terrible idea."

I hadn't received too much praise since joining the team, but "not terrible" ranked up there for most positive feedback so far. I beamed at Fleming.

Upperclassmen trickled into the atrium. They pulled armbands from their pockets and slapped them triumphantly on the call desk.

"Who are we still missing?" Fleming called out to Heather. She looked down at a clipboard.

"For the upperclassmen? Isabelle, Penny, and Harvey."

"And the underclassmen?"

Heather glanced between her clipboard and the computer screen.

"Naomi, Freddie, Andersen, Chris, and Wesley," she counted them off. "But looking at the cameras, Freddie just made it back, and Wesley and Andersen should be walking in here any second."

Naomi was still unaccounted for. I hoped she wasn't still curled up under the streets. We had taken the cat away, and she had seemed to think that would make her feel better, but she wasn't back yet.

The door swung open, and Wesley ran in. His hair was ruffled so that it all stood out to one side. He looked around wildly until he found me.

"Did you make it?" He pulled at my arm and breathed a sigh of relief when he saw I was still wearing my armband. "Good. And the cat?"

"With Everly," I said. "But Naomi isn't back yet."

"Don't worry, she's gotta be just behind us."

Andersen slunk into the atrium after Wesley, looking sour. He hunched his neck and stuck his hands in his pockets.

"That's thirteen armbands for the upperclassmen," Heather announced dejectedly. "Even if Naomi, Freddie, and Chris make it back without getting caught, upperclassmen win."

A cheer went up from half the room. The twins Mike and Desirae high-fived, and Marcus lifted a blushing Justin off his feet in celebration. Andersen retreated to the locker room despite the fact that Fleming had wheeled out a cooler full of ice cream bars.

"Did we win?" Freddie burst through the door, looking triumphant, but his face fell when he saw the upperclassmen celebrating.

"Hey, Mr. Fleming?" Heather called out. She bent over the computer, straining to see what was on the cameras. "Can you come here?"

Wesley and I exchanged looks and ran to the call desk. Fleming beat us there and frowned.

"Go see if they need help," he said.

Three fuzzy figures walked across the security footage, two of them helping to support the one in the middle. I recognized Naomi's bun bobbing between them. A fourth figure appeared as Heather hurried to their aid.

"Get Everly," Fleming sighed. Naomi didn't look too hurt. She was at least walking, even if it was with support. Wesley hurried to the Sickbay, and Fleming turned to me. "What happened?"

"We thought it was the cat," I explained. My voice shook. We shouldn't have ever left Naomi. Why was everything always my fault? "Something had overwhelmed her, and she said it felt like fear, but the cat was nearby, so we figured that was the source."

"So you left her?" I'd never heard that dark of an edge to Fleming's voice before. I shrunk back towards the wall.

"She said to."

Heather burst through the door, preceding Naomi, walking with help from Isabelle and a junior named Harvey. Wesley led Everly into the atrium and rushed to Naomi's side.

"We found her by the Paragon Memorial," Isabelle explained as Everly led Naomi into the back. "She was shaking and could hardly move."

Fleming turned to look back at Wesley and me.

"So, it wasn't the cat," he said.

"She did mention a cat, though," Harvey added.

Fleming led the way back to the Sickbay. A crowd of curious students followed, but he only held the door for Wesley and me. Naomi smiled at us half-heartedly from atop a bed at the far end of the room while Everly took her pulse.

"I told you guys, I'm fine. It got better the closer we got to school."

"Where's the cat?" Fleming asked.

"In the back. He's sleeping, but I was able to get a blood sample for the lab," Everly explained. "But Naomi has more pressing news."

"Mr. Fleming?" Naomi's hands shook in her lap, but she looked at us with ice in her eyes. "I think I found the missing students."

21

Cleaning Day

My heart jumped into my throat.

"Wait, really?" Wesley looked between the two adults. Both men stared stonily at each other.

"I know what I felt," Naomi said. "That much fear in one place, plus if Sam's right about the cat..."

"How can we know for sure?" Everly asked. "The cat could be a coincidence, and anyone in enough distress could have overwhelmed Ms. Bradford."

"It had to have been multiple people," Naomi said quietly. "I've never felt anything that strong before."

"So we go get them," Wesley said, hitting his hands together. "We're all here, if we launch a massive offensive—"

"No," Fleming cut him off. He marched back to the atrium door, and Wesley followed in a huff. "Jacobi, contact the council."

Everly got up from Naomi's bedside and disappeared into his back office.

"What do you mean 'no'?" Wesley demanded, chasing down Fleming. "Worst case scenario, it isn't them, and we accidentally save someone else who is obviously in distress!"

A crowd of students waited for us outside the door, many of them holding melting ice cream bars.

"Is Naomi okay?" Heather asked from the back of the group.

"She's just shaken," Fleming reaffirmed, "but we need to move fast. Justin, Marcus, and Jen, suit up. Naomi will send street coordinates to your coms."

"That's all three team captains," Wesley hissed next to me.

The electricity in the room was tangible. The three team captains rushed to the locker rooms while the rest of the crowd stood waiting, desperate for information, hungry to be sent out, too.

"It may be nothing," Fleming started, "but we might have our first lead into the whereabouts of the missing students."

I watched Andersen carefully, but his face betrayed nothing. If he really did play a role in the kidnappings, he might try to sabotage the rest of the team. His eyes flicked away from Fleming and locked with mine. I quickly looked down.

"So we should go!" Wesley pressed. "If we're right, we could have them all back tonight."

"All we have to go off of is a feral cat and Naomi's ability," Fleming said, talking over Wesley. "We don't even have an exact location. We'll send out scout teams every night until we have enough information. When we do, and if it really was your classmates that Naomi felt tonight, we'll bring them back."

A determined murmur rippled across the crowd.

"Don't you think it's kinda convenient that the ones who were there the night they were kidnapped also happen to be the ones who supposedly found them?" Andersen shouted from the back. I blushed as the room turned towards Wesley and me.

"It's because we were there that we were able to put the pieces together!" I snarled. Only Andersen would be bold enough to imply I might be behind the kidnappings after actively sabotaging me all night. "If Wesley hadn't been paralyzed at the museum, I wouldn't have thought twice about the cat!"

"So you're saying it has nothing to do with how desperate you are to prove yourself?"

I pushed myself through the crowd, closing the distance between us.

"We wouldn't have even been at the museum if you hadn't thrown away our project!" I shouted as Heather stepped between us. "That's what seems convenient to me."

"Enough!" Fleming bellowed. "Both of you, stop, unless you want to clean the whole facility alone tomorrow."

I let Heather draw me away, but I stayed tense, secretly hoping Andersen tried to accuse me again so I could deal him another round kick.

"Everyone go get some sleep," Fleming continued. "We'll need all of you this week. Freshmen and sophomores, I'll see you tomorrow morning."

He disappeared back into the Sickbay. I caught Naomi's eye as the door swung closed. She looked apologetic with her eyes wide and frowning, which only made me feel worse.

"Don't mind Andersen," Heather insisted, pulling me further from the dispersing crowd. "He's just freaked out like the rest of us."

Or he's behind it all and knows we are about to catch him, I fumed.

Someone clapped me on the back.

"Good call on the cat," Everest said. It was the first time he'd ever spoken directly to me. "It'll be hard to not let you on the team if this pans out."

I saw Wesley walking out of the atrium over Everest's shoulder. He was alone with his head hung and his hood up.

"Uh, thanks," I said hurriedly. "Sorry, I've gotta go."

I chased after Wesley. He probably wanted space right now, but it stung that he'd leave without saying anything after the night we'd just had. I hadn't even had the chance to tell him about knocking Andersen on his butt. I caught up to him in the stairwell.

"Are you okay?" I asked. I wasn't sure what else to say.

"No." His honesty caught me off guard. "I'm not okay. You know that it had to be them, and we're doing nothing!"

We walked out into the cold, night air. I wrapped my arms around myself to keep warm. I hadn't gotten my jacket back from the cat.

"You saw Naomi," Wesley continued after a moment. "She was completely overwhelmed by what she felt, which means that someone else was having those feelings, and that someone else was probably our friends!"

"Anthony and Winnie are tough," I said. "It sucks, but they'll be okay. We're going to get them."

But I knew what he meant. The idea of someone as headstrong as Winnie being subjected to the fear I saw on Naomi made me queasy. It was hard to think of her being that broken.

"But they shouldn't need saving!" Wesley's voice cracked, and my stomach clenched when I saw tears welling in his eyes. "They're there because of me!"

I'd never felt so helpless before. Wesley's shoulders quaked, and I wanted nothing more than to calm him but had no idea what to say. What could I say? I hadn't been able to help our friends, either.

"At the pier, I was too busy being trapped under a table to help Lannie. Then at the museum, well, you know what happened!" Wesley raised a hand to his face and bowed his head. I heard students exit the school building behind us.

"Come on," I said gently before they could see something was wrong.

"Winnie's dad was right," he sniffed, allowing me to gently lead him across the grounds. I wasn't sure where I was taking us. "I should've done better."

"Winnie's dad is an ass," I asserted. "And shut up about the pier and the museum. I was there, too."

"Yeah, but it's not your job to protect anyone," Wesley argued. "At least it wasn't back then, anyway."

"And you're going to protect them," I insisted. We walked shoulder to shoulder now, crossing the field and heading towards the water. I held my breath as I deftly worked my hand into his. I wasn't used to consoling people and wasn't sure what else to do. I thought he might pull away, but instead he squeezed my fingers. "Besides, you did keep one person from being kidnapped."

"That's funny. I remember being limp on the floor while *you* saved *me*."

"Which I was only able to do because you held off Hackjob when he first showed up!"

"Only because I didn't want to get stuck working on the industry project alone," Wesley joked. We sat down on a bench overlooking the water. I let go of his hand but kept the tips of my fingers lying over his. The mainland lights twinkled like stars across the bay. "But I shouldn't have left Naomi alone tonight. I should've just taken the cat."

"That's not your fault, either." I rolled my eyes. "I could have taken the cat alone."

Wesley shifted uncomfortably.

"Actually, Fleming told us not to let you go off on your own."

Fleming's betrayal was hardly a surprise, though it did make a lot more sense why Wesley was so worked up about us not splitting up.

"Then let's compromise and blame Fleming, okay?"

"I might be able to work with that." Wesley smiled, but something about him still seemed dejected. He was quiet for a moment, and I let him stew in his thoughts.

"Wesley, why didn't you take the cat?" I asked softly. He'd snapped at me earlier when I brought it up, but now his shoulders sagged, and he frowned at the bay.

"I don't like small things," he said. "They're breakable, and I'm..."

"Strong?"

He made a sound somewhere between a laugh and a grunt.

"Sure."

"Have you hurt a cat before?"

"No!" He glared at me but then softened and fidgeted with the strings on his hoodie. "I broke my brother's arm when I was six. We were just playing. Not that that's an excuse. Even when I'm trying to keep my friends safe, they still end up hurt."

"I'm your friend and look at me! Unhurt and perfectly safe!"

He conceded a small smile as he looked out over the dark water. When he didn't say anything, I cleared my throat.

"So you have a brother? Why haven't I met him yet?" In all the hours we spent together the last few weeks, Wesley had never mentioned his family.

"He doesn't go here," Wesley grumbled. "My family doesn't live on the island. They only sent me here because of the Apex program."

"Oh." I bit my lip, sensing I'd stumbled across a sore subject. "I bet they'd be proud of you if they could see you."

He smiled and put his hand over mine but quickly recoiled.

"You're freezing! What happened to your coat?"

"It's with the cat, I think. It's alright, we should probably go to bed, anyway, since we have to be up for cleaning tomorrow."

We walked back to the dorms, and Wesley made half-hearted conversation about the industry project, though we both knew we'd be lucky to scrape by with a B minus with the amount of progress we'd made on it.

He stopped outside the girls' dorm.

"I'll see you tomorrow," he said. "Good job tonight, too."

"You haven't even heard about how I fought Andersen and won," I said coyly. Wesley gaped at me.

"Wait, really? You beat Andersen and didn't tell me?"

I laughed and welcomed the gush of warm air that spilled from the dorm as I pushed open the door.

"It'll give us something to talk about while we clean."

He smiled, then sighed a sigh laden with the weight of more than any kid should have to shoulder.

"We're going to get them back, right?" he asked.

"Absolutely."

He shoved his hands in his pockets and backed down the pathway.

"Thanks, Sammy. Goodnight."

"'Night."

He turned away to walk towards the boys' dorm. I lingered in the doorway for a moment, watching him until I realized he could probably hear me still standing there. I slipped into the building as quietly as possible, but thought I saw him turn to smile at me from under his hood.

Reggae music blasted from the backrooms of the Sickbay, and I bobbed my head to the beat as I pulled sheets off of beds. I'd been assigned to clean the Sickbay with Freddie, and while I was disappointed that I wouldn't be cleaning with Wesley or Naomi, at least I wasn't scrubbing locker room showers and toilets.

Freddie didn't make eye contact as he helped Everly unhook the white curtains that hung off of rails around each bed. Andersen had given him a hard time about being assigned to work with me. It was probably better we didn't talk.

Marcus, Justin, and Jen had returned from their scouting mission just before clean-up began. While they'd identified a few suspicious buildings, they hadn't found any solid leads. Neither had the squad the University team sent out.

I moved onto the next bed, and something brushed against my leg. I jumped away from the orange tabby staring up at me. I almost didn't recognize the cat from the night before. His coat had been cleaned so I could see his white chin and belly.

"Hey, it's the cat!" I exclaimed. I clambered onto my hands and knees to get a good look at him, but he bolted away to hide under a cabinet.

"Mr. Fleming's not too sure about how having a cat in the infirmary will affect our health standards, but he's not bad company so far," Everly said.

He coaxed the cat out from his hiding spot with a small treat, and he walked out purring with his tail high. Everly grinned in triumph and scooped the kitty into his arms. The cat batted at Everly's name badge with a white paw.

"Besides, I've already named him so Mr. Fleming can't take him away from me now." Everly scratched under the cat's chin. "It's Tonka, by the way. I should be getting his blood results back any minute."

Tonka leaped to the floor and chased a dust bunny across the linoleum. It was probably good for Everly to have a friend in the Sickbay. It must be lonely when the only people who came to visit were the sick and injured.

Everly sent Freddie to the laundry room in the back with the curtains and sheets and set me to organizing the cabinet Tonka had just been hiding under.

Several boxes of bandages toppled over me from the highest shelf as soon as I pulled the doors open. I pulled supplies out to organize them on the floor. I'd made my way through about half the cabinet when the Sickbay doors flung open. Dr. Weaver came strutting down the line of beds, her heels click-click-clicking on the floor. Her gray hair was pulled in a tight ponytail today.

She threw her blazer into a bedside chair and sat down on the one mattress Everly had left sheets on.

"You don't think you can do this any quicker than usual today, Jacobi?" she called out. "The council is supposed to meet in ten."

Everly pushed a cart up to her bedside.

"It'll take as long as it takes," he said patiently. She sighed and typed something out on her phone.

"Fine, then I hope you don't mind the room getting a little more crowded."

She looked up from her phone and locked eyes with me. I quickly looked away and made to look busy organizing bandages on the floor, but she clicked her tongue.

"Miss Taylor," she crooned. "I heard you might be the reason we find our missing students."

I looked up at her. She relaxed on the bed with her formidable looking heels crossed on top of the sheets while Everly fastened a tube to her arm near the elbow.

"Are you sick?" I asked before thinking and was relieved when she laughed.

"No, I haven't been sick in a long time. I come in every month for plasma donations."

"Dr. Weaver very generously lends her Apex ability to the rest of us to use in the Serum," Everly explained. I remembered Wesley hooked up to the IV after the museum. He'd explained how Apex donated plasma to make the Serum that had healed his broken leg. I wondered how many students had had transfusions of Dr. Weaver's plasma and if I had been one of them.

The door opened again, and Fleming entered with a familiar looking man in a police uniform.

"Officer Allen!" I exclaimed, recognizing the policeman who had driven Naomi, Wesley, and me back to campus after the disaster at the museum.

"I heard you're the reason we're having this meeting," he said as he and Fleming sat down on the bare mattress next to Dr. Weaver's bed.

"Meeting?"

Everly might as well have propped the door open because it swung open a third time. A woman I'd never seen before walked in, her box braids swinging with each step.

"Did we really have to do this here?" she asked. "You couldn't do this later?"

"We have meetings with the Schrader Foundation all afternoon for that god-awful industry project the high schoolers are doing," yet another newcomer said. He was dressed as sharply as Dr. Weaver and carrying a twenty ounce coffee cup. He tapped his foot as he convened around Dr. Weaver.

"How much of that is straight espresso, Trev?" Officer Allen asked. The man scowled and took a long swig from the cup in response.

"Who's missing?" Dr. Weaver asked with an impatient edge.

"Mickey can't make it," the woman with the braids chirped. "I guess the City Council has a meeting, too. Real quick, though, we all agree not to tell Roy anything until we know for sure, right? Because if that man shows up at my office one more time—"

"Roy is to know nothing," Fleming asserted. He looked around the circle as if daring them to come up with a good reason to let Mr. Hendricks in on whatever they were talking about.

Everly turned back to look at me sitting among the bandages on the floor.

"Samantha, why don't you go help Freddie in the back?"

I shoved the First Aid materials back into the cabinet and hurried to clear the room but was stopped when the woman with box braids called out.

"Wait. Samantha? As in Alison's Samantha?" She grinned, showing off a dazzling smile and hurried over to shake my hand. "Sounds like you've been putting in some good work! Keep it up, and maybe I'll see you in a couple years."

"This is Professor Parker," Fleming explained from his seat on the mattress. "She teaches at the university and is in charge of the Apex Team there."

"Can we please get this meeting going, Alex?" Dr. Weaver checked her phone as she spoke. "Again, I do have places to be later."

Seeing that as my cue to leave, I slipped into the back hall of the Sickbay. The door to my immediate left had the words "Nurse's Office" posted on the front. Directly ahead of me, the laundry room was open to machines rumbling violently through their spin cycles. To the right were two doors, labeled "Exam Room 1" and "Exam Room 2".

The door to Exam Room 1 swung open. Freddie startled when he saw me and mumbled an apology.

"Everly sent me back here to help," I explained. "There's a ton of adults in the main infirmary."

Freddie handed me a bucket of cleaning supplies and pointed to the second exam room.

"You can work in there," he said but hesitated after I took the bucket. I braced myself for whatever Andersen-coined insult he had ready for me. "Also, um, I'm sorry about that prank we pulled."

It took me a second to realize he meant the night at the boardwalk.

"Oh, it's okay," I said, even though we both knew it wasn't. I couldn't figure out why, but I felt sorry for him. I had every reason to be angry, but instead there was a hollow pit in my stomach where the rage should have been. "No one got hurt."

"We went back to look for you, you know," he continued, talking more to his sneakers than to me. "Olivia and I, I mean. As soon as Andersen went to bed, we snuck back out to make sure you were okay. Your shoe was still on the boardwalk, but you were gone. Olivia checked your room, but you weren't there, either."

"I stayed down here that night."

Freddie finally looked up from his shoes, his brow creasing in apparent pain.

"We thought you'd drowned," he said. "Olivia and I were up all night, figuring out what to do, and finally, we came here to tell Fleming what happened, but when we walked in—"

"You found me."

I still felt bad for Freddie, but a small part of me felt a thrill of vindictive pleasure. It would have been better if Andersen was the one who spent the night thinking he'd murdered me, but I'd settle for Freddie and Olivia.

"Yeah, well, I'm sorry about it." Freddie looked at me with sudden intensity. "But don't tell Andersen I said that."

I shouldered my way into Exam Room 2.

"Of course not," I promised. "Why would I let Andersen know he accidentally befriended a decent person?"

Freddie fidgeted uncomfortably but forced a smile.

"Thanks for understanding."

Inside the exam room, I could hear music blaring from the other side of a second door, and I swung it open to reveal the fighting arena. Naomi, Wesley, and a few others moved steadily back and forth over the mat with mops, their music blasting overhead.

Wesley waved his mop overhead in greeting. A freshman shrieked as dirty mop water rained down on her as he did so.

Cleaning wasn't so bad with friends in the next room over. We sang along with the music back and forth at each other, and at one point, Tonka snuck in to investigate the source of the ruckus.

I was about to go find a broom to finish up when the door on the far side of the fighting arena slammed open. Justin stood in the doorway and cut the music.

"Everyone in the atrium," he demanded. "Fleming's orders. The blood results are in."

No one spoke while we waited in the atrium for Fleming to emerge from the Sickbay with the results. If the results were negative, we still had Naomi's ability to work with, but that could have been caused by anything.

But if the results were positive, then there was likely a connection. And if there was a connection, then maybe we found where the missing students were.

News spread quickly to the juniors and seniors, who showed up in groups and joined the silent mass outside the Sickbay doors.

"Can you hear them?" Naomi whispered to Wesley. He screwed up his face in concentration, but shook his head.

"Yeah, but they're talking too quiet for me to make anything out."

The door swung open, and Dr. Weaver led the procession out of the infirmary. She stood to the side so that Fleming could move forward and address us directly. The other members of the council stood behind him.

"The university lab did find a type of neurotoxin in the sample of cat blood we sent last night," he started. His somber tone was hard to read, but he stared out over us resolutely, as if bracing himself. "They compared it to the neurotoxin found in the patch used on Wesley during the museum attack. We've got a match."

22

Scouting

The room filled with a chorus of inhales and "I knew it"s. Fleming raised a hand. I'd never seen a room quiet so quickly.

"We will monitor the sector of the island where the cat—"

"Tonka," Everly clarified behind him. Fleming scowled but continued.

"Yes, where Tonka was found. It is likely that the patches used at the museum are being developed in the city, and if we are correct, their production is polluting water runoff and paralyzing small animals. That, combined with Naomi's episode last night make us believe they are either holding the kidnapped students nearby or in the same facility."

"The police will continue to monitor the area," Officer Allen said, stepping forward. "We will take action once we've narrowed down the location and have assessed the situation."

"As will the university team," Professor Parker added.

"We want a team out at all hours and will work with the university team to ensure there is always someone monitoring the area," Fleming continued. "You will each get a chance to scout, but you will *only* scout."

There was a collective groan.

"Not fair!" Skyler protested. "We're the ones who found the cat!"

"It was Samantha who found the cat." Fleming glanced at me as he said it, and I thought there might have been something like pride on his face. "And we don't know what we are dealing with. You are all minors, and I won't put any of you in direct danger."

There was another mumble of dissent, but it didn't grow much louder under the stern eye of Dr. Weaver. We'd save our complaining for later. A few of the others shot dirty looks at me as if it were my fault Fleming wouldn't let us do more than scout.

"The schedule will be posted at the call desk. In the meantime, Carmen, Everest, and Isabelle, you'll be reporting to the 37th sector. Remember, surveillance only."

Carmen, Everest, and Isabelle ran to the locker rooms as the rest of us looked around, unsure of what was supposed to happen next. The adults dispersed, Dr. Weaver and the coffee-drinking man leading the way.

"Do we have to keep cleaning?" Olivia whispered wistfully.

Fleming caught my eye and waved me over. If he was about to tell me that I wouldn't be allowed to even scout, I wasn't sure what I'd do. Kick him in the shins, probably. I approached him cautiously with Naomi and Wesley close behind, and he surveyed me with tired eyes.

"I suppose it's time we assigned you a uniform."

Wesley's face broke into a grin, and he beamed at me while Naomi clapped her hands together quietly.

"A uniform? Does that mean I get to..." I trailed off, not daring to get my hopes up. Fleming sighed and ran both hands through his hair.

"Provisional team members are still team members," he said. "Just know that both our lives are on the line here because if anything happens to you, your mother will murder me."

I wondered if she had felt the way I did now when she finally got assigned a suit. I followed Fleming to a back closet in the main gym. A few heads turned as he opened the door to a storage room full of helmets and dark gray body armor.

"You've got two layers," he said, digging through a cardboard box. He stopped to look back at me and squinted as he sized me up. "Are you a tall size?"

He threw a pair of black leggings and a skin-tight black shirt my way.

"Anyway, two layers. That one, and then a light layer of body armor." He pulled a set of the body armor from another box and held it up. A black number "12" was painted on the shoulder. "Try all that on and come back."

Wesley patiently waited with Fleming in the storage room while Naomi coached me through the bathroom stall in the locker room.

"It's supposed to fit tight," she insisted as I leaned against the wall for support as I tried to wrestle the armor over my head.

"But how tight?" I said, searching for the head hole.

"Pretty tight. It'll feel okay once it's on, though."

She stepped away from the door as I stumbled out. She grinned while I wriggled my hands and feet into the boots and gloves she handed me.

I straightened up to look at myself in the mirror. My pale face blushed back at me, but I wasn't sure if it was from excitement or embarrassment. I had never looked so badass in my life, with the dark materials hugging my body, but I still felt a little bit like a poser.

Heather wolf-whistled at me from across the locker room.

"Hey, you're one good looking Apex!"

My chest ballooned with pride. I knew Heather was just being nice, but still, it meant a lot.

Wesley's face brightened when we walked back to the storage room while Fleming was stoic and unreadable. He procured another box, and Wesley dove for it before Fleming could open it.

"Nice!" He pulled out a glossy helmet identical to the one I'd seen him in. He slipped it over my head, and the room was thrown into sharp relief. The time blinked at me in the top corner of my vision. Weather conditions for "Sector 29" scrolled across the top of the visor.

"What's Sector twenty-nine?" I startled at the sound of my voice. It sounded electrical and robotic.

"It's here," Naomi explained. "The island is broken into forty sectors to help with navigating."

I gawked around at the gym through the helmet. Everything had a blue hue to it, but it was like my vision was enhanced. I wondered what it must look like to Wesley, who already had super vision.

"How's it feel?" Naomi asked.

"Really, really cool." I stuck my gloved and armored arm out in front of my face to get a good look at it.

"Great," Fleming said with a fake cheeriness. "Three miles, then."

He pointed at the treadmills.

"In this?" I asked. The armor was heavy, and the boots weighed on my feet.

"You've got to get used to it before one AM tomorrow morning," he said, putting the box away. "That's when you report for your first scouting mission.

I felt a little bad that I didn't get to help finish cleaning with the other underclassmen, but it was unlikely any of them envied me. Three miles on the treadmill was a long way to go in new boots and full body armor.

About halfway through the run, green text flashed onto my visor.

Hope you like my taste in music - WES

I smiled through my haggard breaths as music transmitted into my helmet from where Wesley and Naomi were mopping.

I marveled at how light I felt out of the uniform and how tight my calves were after dragging the boots for three miles on the treadmill as I walked to lunch with Naomi and Wesley.

"I'm scouting with you tonight!" Wesley said. "It's us and Isabelle. Looks like we're back on later in the week, too."

"What about you?" I asked Naomi. She smiled but shrugged sadly.

"I asked Fleming to keep me off scouting for a few days. I'm not rushing to feel what I felt last night, and if that were to happen again, I'm not sure what help I'd be in a pinch."

"Did you see when Andersen was scheduled?" Wesley asked. "I'll be so mad if he finds them before us."

"It's not about winning, Wes," Naomi chided. "It'll be good news if anyone finds them."

"I know!" he said defensively. "I'm just not convinced that Andersen didn't engineer this whole thing."

"He didn't!" Naomi glared at Wes, and he looked to me for back up. I grimaced noncommittally.

"I don't know, maybe he did, maybe he didn't," I wavered. I didn't want to upset Naomi by agreeing with Wesley, but I hadn't ruled out Andersen's involvement either. "Let's say he did—"

"He didn't!" Naomi hissed again. Her temper was rising.

"I mean, hypothetically!" I gushed. "Let's say he did play a part in the kidnappings. I don't think he'd help this Adrestus person just to turn around and betray him."

"Unless this was all for glory," Wesley pointed out.

"I don't think it would be," I admitted. "He's a jerk, but there's plenty of opportunity to make a name for himself without setting up his classmates. If he played a part in this, I think he'd be legitimately working for Adrestus."

"So if Andersen is part of the team that saves the students, we know he isn't working for Adrestus," Naomi mused.

"Unless he *is* Adrestus!" Wesley interjected. "Andersen, Adrestus, they even have some of the same letters in their name!"

We had reached the cafeteria and put our conversation on hold as we stood in line for chicken strips. I was chatting idly with Naomi about our industry projects when Wesley grabbed both our arms.

"What do you want?" Naomi said, still irritated with him. He pointed across the cafeteria where a TV was mounted over the tables. "You know we can't hear that from here, right?"

I squinted at the screen, only able to make out an important-looking man in a suit standing at a podium. Wesley scowled.

"'Prominent Anti-Apex attorney John Ratcliffe joins race for New Delos City Council'," he recited off the screen.

"Ratcliffe? Jamie's dad?" I looked to Naomi, who was the local authority on all things regarding Jamie. She gulped.

"You knew, didn't you?" Wesley accused. "Did Jamie tell you?"

Her dark cheeks grew rosy, and she shrugged.

"It doesn't matter, he won't win," she insisted. "There's too much support for Apex on the island."

Wesley didn't look convinced.

I was glad when lunch was over. Naomi and Wesley remained on edge with each other while we ate so once we finished, I mumbled about needing to go to the library and made my escape. However, Wesley hunted me down, weighed down with poster materials.

"This is due on Friday," he reminded me.

I looked up from my Spanish textbook and sighed. The Industry Fair was only a couple weeks away, and time only seemed to be going faster now that I had less of it.

"Won't Fleming give us an extension?" I asked. "He knows how busy we'll be this week."

Wesley laughed as if I'd just told a very funny joke.

"Fleming would sooner hand the Apex program over to Roy Hendricks than give anyone an extension, no matter what the reason."

We managed to get a good amount of it done in the few hours we worked. It was only missing a few subtitles and diagrams when Wesley looked at the wall clock.

"We should probably head downstairs soon."

"I thought we didn't have to report until one AM?"

"Sure, but typically, anyone assigned a time like that gets to sleep in the base. Otherwise people in the dorms might see you leaving."

"You have your first scouting mission tonight?"

Wesley turned pale and spun in his seat. Remi had crept up to our table between the bookshelves.

"Watch who you're eavesdropping on," Wesley snapped.

"You should be more careful if you're going to talk like that in a public space," she retorted but then smiled. I didn't like how pretty she looked when she did. She glanced over our poster. "You're only just finishing the poster? We finished those in Ms. Poplar's class last week."

The color rushed back into Wesley's face. Remi switched her focus to me, and I resisted the urge to shrink back in my chair under her analytic gaze. I wondered if she could read people the same way she could extract files from a computer.

"Your trials must be coming up, then?" she asked.

"In a couple weeks." I wished she would go away.

"What kind of powers do you have, if you don't mind me asking?"

"Oh, I..." I looked to Wesley for help, and he came to my rescue.

"You know that's a rude question," he grumbled. Remi shrugged, unabashed.

"I was just wondering. Fat load of good my powers did in the trial," she snorted. "I wanted to know if Samantha stood a better chance than I did."

Wesley swept his arm across the table, scooping as many poster supplies into his backpack as he could in one motion.

"I'd say her chances are good," he said. "C'mon, Sammy. We should head downstairs."

We stewed in awkward silence the whole five-story walk to the basement. Of course Remi had assumed I was an Apex. The last non-Apex to try out for the team was Fleming so why would I be one? But I was still filled with embarrassment at my inability to just admit to her that I didn't have any extraordinary powers. It had felt good to trick someone into thinking I was something special, but walking away, I only felt shame.

And Wesley's response to her? "Her chances are good." Why did that rub me the wrong way? Good was good, after all. But here I was, feeling like good was crap.

Luckily, the secret basement facility was alive with activity that quickly swept my thoughts far away from Remi. A few freshmen were suited up with their trainers, ready to head out with the next scouting team as the previous team reported to Fleming at the call desk. Others who weren't scheduled until the next day lingered throughout the facility, eager to stay in the loop.

"There are sandwiches in the Sickbay," Isabelle said, appearing between us. She had just come back from her first assignment and was still in most of her gear. "You'll want to eat something now since we're getting up so early."

"Weren't you just out, though?" I asked. Her face hardened, and she smiled grimly at Wesley.

"I'll be fine." She walked away towards the Sickbay to fuel up on sandwiches, and I turned to Wesley.

"Is she okay?"

Wesley shook his head.

"Anthony's her cousin. They're really close, too. I bet she volunteered for extra assignments."

In the Sickbay, Everly had a table set up with sub sandwiches. A crowd of seniors pushed at each other to grab napkins and plates, but it parted as we got closer. Justin looped an arm over my shoulder and cleared a path to the subs.

"First mission tonight, right?"

There was a round of whoops from his friends.

"You're really putting us in our place," Harvey said, pushing two sandwiches into my arms. "You like turkey? Here!"

Wesley scowled and took my wrist to pull me from the crowd. He plucked one of the subs from my arms as he led the way out.

"Bunch of suck ups," he muttered, jamming the sandwich into his mouth. "They all like you now that you found the cat."

The other students' newfound respect hadn't gone unnoticed. Since the night before, they'd all been nicer to me and a bit more willing to make eye contact and smile hello.

"I don't mind it," I laughed.

"Just remember, I thought you were cool before you started bringing strays in here."

"You're just jealous you didn't find the cat," I teased.

"Are you kidding?" He put on an air of fake indignation. "I sacrificed myself to Justin for you!"

"Yeah, but I did the hard part."

"You're right," he conceded. "I might as well offer you my spot on the team right now."

"Don't be dumb, if you gave me your spot, who would punch holes in the pier for me when I needed a quick getaway?"

He groaned and threw his sandwich wrapper at me.

"Are you ever going to let that go?"

"No," I smiled and bit into my sandwich. "Probably not."

I slept in one of the call rooms in the bunk across from Isabelle's. We lay in the quiet dark for a long time before I finally heard her breathing deepen as she fell asleep. Going to bed at six in a new place with the promise of my first real mission in just a few hours made it difficult to follow suit.

I must've fallen asleep eventually because when Isabelle's alarm went off at 12:45 AM, I was pulled from a dream where Remi was in charge of grading the industry projects.

It was easier wiggling into my uniform this time, and it was hard not to stare at myself in the locker room mirror. The previous scout team was coming back in, yawning and with nothing to report. A couple freshmen waved excitedly at me.

Wesley waited for us in the atrium with his helmet under his arm. He gave me a gloved thumbs-up and grinned.

"It still fits, then?"

I shoved him playfully, and Fleming cleared his throat from the call desk to bring us back to attention.

"I'm sending three addresses to you," he said. "The last group didn't bring back any news, but we're looking for any sign of activity. Anyone walking into unmarked buildings, any paralyzed animals—"

"We've got it," Isabelle cut him off. She scooped a ring of keys off the counter and nodded to the heavy metal doors that led to the underground parking garage.

Our boots echoed in the long corridor on the other side of the door. Isabelle was stoic and silent, but Wesley caught my eye and winked.

Isabelle led the way through the dark garage to a sleek, black car. I tried not to think about the only other time I'd been here, when Wesley had been loaded onto a gurney.

Wesley pulled his helmet on over his head before climbing into the back seat. I followed suit, though with a little less grace as I maneuvered my helmeted head through the car door. I barely had time to buckle my seatbelt before Isabelle threw us in reverse and shot up the parking garage ramp.

The car was just like the one that had picked Wesley and I up at the docks. There was a partition so we couldn't see Isabelle up front, and I clung to the seat as she whipped us around corners. Green text scrolled across the top of my vision. Fleming had sent the addresses.

Unfortunately, Isabelle's driving would be the most exciting thing to happen on our scout mission. After she parked us in a wide alleyway, we clambered out, and Wesley showed me how to stick to the shadows and avoid being seen, but the city might as well have been a ghost town at that time of night.

The three buildings we were supposed to patrol were all on the same block. We crouched in silence across the street, hiding behind a dumpster.

"You can't hear anything?" Isabelle whispered desperately after waiting an hour for movement. Wesley shook his head. His mouth peeked out under his visor, and his lips drew in a tight frown. "Fine. Let's shake this up. By the smell of it, garbage day for this block is tomorrow. They should have a dumpster out back. Twelve, go see what you can find."

It took me a moment to realize she was talking to me.

"You want me to dig through the trash?"

"Take Seven, too, if you don't want to go alone."

But as Wesley and I sifted through garbage, we found nothing in the trash. And there was nothing in the gutters. And when Isabelle finally got so frustrated that she tore off her helmet, marched right up the middle building's front window, and pressed her face against the glass, there was nothing inside out of the ordinary for a dingy apartment lobby.

She swore under her breath and jammed her helmet back on.

"Is patrolling normally like this?" I asked Wesley, back behind the first dumpster. He shrugged.

"Kind of. There's usually more ground to cover so there's more walking and less dumpster diving. A lot of times it is this boring. Other times you find your classmates locked in the trunk of a car." He flashed me a wry smile beneath his visor.

After several hours of waiting for something to happen, the city began to wake up. Lights flickered on in apartment windows, and early buses rumbled down the street. Defeated, Isabelle took us back to the car and re-parked us on the street outside the suspect buildings so we could finish our last hour of patrolling without worrying about being seen.

When the time display in the corner of my helmet visor read 06:05, another green message popped up.

ATTN: You have failed to report in on time. Please respond with mission status- F

Isabelle growled in frustration.

"We're on our way back." As she snapped the words, they appeared under the green text that had presumably been sent by Fleming. I quickly fastened my seatbelt as the engine roared, and Isabelle took us flying down the street, back towards campus.

The partition rose to separate us from Isabelle, but I thought I heard her choke back a sob just before it closed. I pulled my helmet off and looked at Wesley. He tried to smile back.

"Nice hair," he said. I attempted to tame my helmet hair with my gloved hands, but Wesley laughed.

"I know we'll find them, by the way," I said, trying to sound as matter-of-fact as possible.

Wesley set his helmet next to mine on the middle seat.

"It would be nice to have found them already." he shrugged. "Or to have not lost them at all."

Fleming was waiting for us in the parking garage. He glowered over the dark circles under his eyes. I held my helmet close, as if it might protect me from Fleming's ire.

Luckily, he turned on Isabelle. Wesley and I slipped past as he chewed into her about the importance of reporting in on time.

A crew of three more Apex lingered in the corridor, waiting for Fleming to finish telling off Isabelle. They glanced at us as we came in.

"Anything?" I barely recognized Heather's voice through the modulator in her helmet. Wesley shook his head.

My first scouting mission hadn't been bad. Nothing dicey had happened. No one was captured. We weren't attacked. It was a good first scout. But I still felt hollow, knowing we hadn't really accomplished anything, either.

After showering, I passed Isabelle on my way back to the atrium. Her eyes were red, and she threw her helmet at her locker as I skirted out the door. Fleming was back at the call desk. I was willing to bet he hadn't slept since before the Night Game.

I caught his eye and braced for a lecture, but he smiled.

"Good work this weekend," he said. "You've done a lot for the team."

I did my best to not beam in the praise, as good as it felt to hear. Instead, I shrugged, not sure how to respond to the kind words.

The rest of Sunday was a sleepy haze. After breakfast, I went to work on homework but woke up face-down in my chemistry textbook without having gotten anything done. Naomi advised me to not go to bed until a normal time, to try to keep a normal sleep schedule, and when seven in the evening finally rolled around, I crawled into my bed.

As I did every night, I tried and failed to not think about the empty bed across the room. I was still disappointed by the lack of progress in the scouting missions, although Fleming had sent out an email insisting we were getting closer. I guessed he was only trying to raise morale.

Wesley and I were scheduled to go back out on Wednesday night, and while I secretly longed for a second chance at scouting, it hurt to imagine three more days without Winnie. It had already been almost three weeks since she'd been taken.

I rolled over in bed so that I was facing her side of the room. Would she be happy when we rescued them? Grateful? Or angry that we had taken so long? And how was I going to keep my new role with Apex Team a secret from her when we got her back? Naomi shared a room with Jamie and managed to keep her secret, but Winnie was a lot smarter than Jamie.

I folded my pillow up over my face. I was getting ahead of myself. I could worry about keeping secrets from Winnie when she was actually here to keep secrets from.

23

The Memorial

The next morning, Naomi was still acting coolly towards Wesley, but she at least said hi in the omelet line before taking a seat with Jamie. I still didn't understand their friendship, and while it bothered me to see Naomi prioritize Jamie over Wesley and me, I at least understood wanting to appease her.

We sat far away from the clique in the cafeteria but couldn't avoid them in First Period. As students trickled into Fleming's class, I heard someone squeal when she saw Jamie.

"I saw your dad on the news again this morning!" Madison's voice was too shrill for seven in the morning.

I twisted around in my seat to watch Jamie smile and push her hair behind her ear in a show of fake humility. Andersen sat next to her, beaming at his girlfriend.

"If he wins, that makes you island royalty, right? I wish I could vote," Madison gushed. "I'd definitely vote for him."

Wesley snorted loudly, and Jamie's abashed grin melted into a sneer.

"Something funny?" she demanded. Wesley turned around to face Jamie, ignoring the warning glare that Naomi was giving us from her seat two rows back.

"Why would you vote for an Apex-hater like Ratcliffe?"

Jamie blushed bright red, but her eyes narrowed as she prepared for a fight.

"Does believing in equality make you an Apex-hater?"

Wesley threw his head back as he laughed, only making Jamie redder.

"Equality?" he repeated. "Is that the lie he's going with?"

"The Apex are a poison to society," Jamie hissed. She wrapped her arms around Andersen's.

"They *built* this society!" Wesley's voice rose. Naomi cleared her throat, maybe as a warning to Jamie. I glanced at the door, hoping to see Fleming walk in and force everyone to settle down.

"Yeah, off the backs of us normal people! They're born bad and are nothing more than public menaces. It's literally in their DNA. You can't change an Apex." She turned to Andersen for validation. "Right?"

Andersen stared motionless at Wesley with his mouth drawn in a tight line. The sleeve of his hoodie wrinkled where Jamie tightened her grip around his arm.

"Right?" she repeated. It sounded more like a threat than a plea for validation this time. Andersen loosened up and scowled.

"Apex are a public menace," he parroted back at her. "And the way you're defending them, Isaacs, I might start to think about why you want to defend them so badly."

Madison laughed derisively.

"Him?" she shrieked. "He's too scrawny!"

The ensuing laughter was loud enough to cover the sound of a splintering snap as the back of Wesley's chair cracked down the middle.

He'd gripped it too hard. Naomi met my eyes, her lips pressed together, then looked away.

"Imagine calling for help and expecting Paragon, but then someone like Wesley shows up instead!" Jamie giggled. Madison nearly fell out of her chair from laughing too hard. Naomi stared at her lap with her shoulders hunched.

"Everyone, settle down."

The laughter died immediately. Dr. Weaver took the spot at the head of the class in one of her signature gray pantsuits.

"Mr. Fleming had to call in sick last minute," Dr. Weaver continued. "Nothing to be alarmed over, he's just feeling under the weather."

She looked at Wesley and me in the front row meaningfully, and I figured Fleming was probably sleeping in after being awake all weekend facilitating scouting missions.

That class was the quietest First Period since the school year had started. Those on Team Apex were surely stewing over Andersen's betrayal and those not on the team seemed to be picking up on the tension. Wesley didn't bother opening his notebook. He stared straight ahead all period, not moving, leaning forward so the back of his shirt wouldn't get caught in the jagged crack in the seat back of his chair.

When the bell finally rang, he left as fast as he could. I gathered my things in my arms, not bothering to take the time to put them in my backpack. I'd almost caught up to him when someone tugged on the hood of my jacket.

"Hey!" I spun around, expecting Andersen but instead found Amanda looking very much out of place in the halls of a high school. "What do you want? Are you even allowed to be here?"

Amanda pushed me up against the wall so that she had me cornered against a display case.

"What's going on?" she demanded.

"I don't—"

"Did you guys find Winnie?"

The question took me by surprise, and I fumbled for the right words to say.

"I know something's up," she said. "All the kids on the university Apex Team have been working around the clock all weekend. Was there a break in the case? Where is she?"

"You know I can't tell you anything." Of course I wanted to tell her that we could have Winnie by the end of the week, but Amanda had left Apex Team, and I wasn't about to do anything that could get me kicked off. "If you wanted to be involved, you shouldn't have quit."

She glowed red, and I thought I felt the air grow at least five degrees warmer.

"Tell me what you know or I'll tell Vic and Alison what I know."

"You wouldn't," I said, although I knew she absolutely would.

"My next class is right next to Vic's office," she growled. "You tell me what's going on, or I'll tell him. You know I know you forged that permission form."

I juggled my notebook and history textbook in my arms.

"We haven't really found anything yet." It wasn't technically a lie, but Amanda still didn't buy it.

"Then what's going on?"

I looked around for an escape, but she had me trapped.

"You can't tell your dad," I mumbled.

"I would never tell him anything." She said it with so much disgust that I knew she meant it. Amanda may have been the favorite child, but she had no shortage of disdain for Roy Hendricks.

I glanced around the hall. The crowd of students was thinning. Passing period was almost over. I lowered my voice so I wouldn't be overheard.

"There's a part of the city where we think the missing students might be," I whispered. "All we have to go on is something Naomi felt, but—"

"Where?" she demanded.

"You can't go looking for her."

"I won't." This time, I didn't believe her, but it was clear she wouldn't let me go until I gave her what she wanted.

"Over in the 36th Sector." That wasn't true. It had been a few blocks over in the 37th Sector, but if Amanda got caught creeping around where we were looking, they might be able to figure out I was the one who'd given her information.

She half-smiled and took a step back so that I had room to pass.

"Thanks," she said, her eyes glittering as she began to scheme. "See you around."

"Don't do anything stupid!" I called after her. She waved without looking back.

The week passed at an excruciatingly slow pace. I stayed alert, listening in to reports when scouts would come back, hoping I wouldn't hear anything about Amanda slinking around the target buildings. However, if she was looking for Winnie, she was being discreet. There was no mention of her in any of the scouting reports.

Tuesday afternoon, there was a false alarm. Marcus had thought he'd found a secret lab giving off a strong heat signature, but it had turned out to be a faulty furnace in an old apartment building. He'd probably saved the building from catching fire, but it was hard not to be disappointed.

Wednesday morning, one of the freshmen thought he'd found another paralyzed animal, but Everly's professional medical assessment determined it was just a dead rat. He sent a blood sample to the university, anyways, presumably to make the freshman feel better.

I lingered in the gym after training that afternoon. Wesley and I were scheduled to scout with Mike and Carmen later that night. I had time to go eat dinner, but I wasn't hungry yet.

"Did you want to keep training?" Naomi offered when she saw me hang back by the free weights. "We could go over more combat moves in the arena if you like."

We started with some light sparring. Going through the movements with Naomi helped dissolve some of the pre-mission jitters, but twenty minutes in, she looked at the big clock on the wall and frowned.

"I've just remembered, I told Jamie I'd get dinner with her tonight."

"Why?" Wesley demanded. "Isn't this more important?"

Naomi blushed and shuffled her feet.

"I know, but look, she's my roommate, and if I make her mad, I'll have to deal with it all week."

I exchanged a look with Wesley. The fact that Naomi would want to cater to someone like Jamie at all was baffling at best. At worst, it was insulting. She at least looked genuinely embarrassed about it.

"But why do you want to hang out with her, especially after all she said to Wesley on Monday?" I asked, trying to keep the accusatory tones out of my voice.

"I just told you," Naomi sighed, gathering her bags. "It's not that I want to hang out with her, but it sucks when she gets in a mood. Besides, she gets suspicious when I'm down here too much."

"Right, but she's a bully. Who cares what mood she's in?"

"I care." There was a sudden, dangerous edge to her voice.

Wesley turned to me and shrugged.

"Sorry. Jamie's feelings matter more than you making the team, I guess."

Naomi glowered at Wesley.

"Why don't you spar with Samantha?" she asked. Wesley flushed red.

"You know why!"

"You aren't going to hurt her!" Naomi snapped. "And Jamie's feelings don't matter more than you, Samantha, but sometimes I've gotta do things for me, and, unfortunately, tonight that means eating dinner with my roommate."

She shouldered her bag and made her way to the door. She looked back as she pushed it open.

"Stay safe tonight," she added. "And I'm sorry."

Wesley pouted as the door swung shut behind her.

"I guess we can run some drills if you want to keep training," he said.

"Why can't we spar? Are you really afraid you'll hurt me?"

He raised an eyebrow so that it peeked out from behind the thick frames of his glasses.

"You've seen me rip the trunk off a car. You really think I won't?"

"It'll be fine. If anything, it should trigger my fight response even more. The trials are in a couple weeks. I need the practice."

Wesley juggled with the decision for a moment, biting his lip and bouncing on the balls of his feet. Finally, he let out an exasperated groan.

"Fine," he mumbled. "You have to wear your full gear, though. Helmet, boots, everything."

"Deal!"

I rushed to the locker room to suit up. I had done punching and kicking drills with Wesley, but this was the first time he'd been willing to spar. If I could fight against him, I would be able to fight against anyone in the Final Trial.

When I returned to the arena in my full Apex suit, Wesley was stretching in the middle of the room having changed into the black underclothes that went under the armor.

The material clung to his chest in a way that made me self-conscious about the speed of my heart rate. It was just Wesley, I reminded myself. There was no reason for me to be excited.

"If at any point you want to stop, just say so." He set his glasses aside and pushed brown, messy hair back from his eyes.

"Same to you." I smiled coyly and was pleased to see Wesley suppress a laugh. I threw my fists up and waited for Mom's pre-programmed fighting expertise to take over.

However, when Wesley came at me, I flailed helplessly and fell backwards onto the mat.

"What the heck was that?" Wesley asked, extending a hand to help me back up.

"I don't know! Usually with Naomi, something happens."

"What was all this, then?" He waved his arms around wildly, mimicking me.

"I did not look like that!"

"Yes, you did."

"I wasn't ready. Try again."

I took up a fighting stance. He attacked again, starting with a round kick this time. Again, no secret programming took over. I stumbled my way through a dodge that Naomi and I had eked out of my subconscious the week before, but Wesley stopped again.

"Are you sure we're doing this right?"

"You watch Naomi do this with me everyday."

We tried again, but this time I didn't wait for my arms and legs to respond without me. I dodged his attack and delivered an uppercut to his diaphragm. It was a move that would've knocked the air out of Naomi, but Wes hardly flinched before using a well-placed kick to send me reeling across the mat and tumbling over the low dividing wall in front of the bleachers.

"Sammy!"

I lay still for a moment while I waited for the room to stop spinning. Wesley leaped over the divider and crouched down next to me.

"I'm so sorry, I told you this was a bad idea."

"No, that was good," I insisted as I struggled to my knees. "I need to be able to fight anyone."

I pulled my helmet off and leaned back against the bleachers to catch my breath. Wesley continued to look at me with concern, so I knew he wasn't convinced I was okay.

"So, was that you or your mom?" he asked.

"That was me," I sighed. "I don't know why it's not working."

"What's different this time?"

I thought back to all the times Mom's fighting skills had taken over instinctually. There was the dock, when I'd tackled the white-haired woman. The museum had probably been the most notable display of Mom's programming, when I'd fought Hackjob. Outside of that, there was the time Andersen and his friends had lured me out to the boardwalk along with all of the times I'd sparred with Naomi and Heather in practice. This should've been like that.

"Maybe I'm getting too comfortable with fighting? Like I don't have to rely on it anymore so it's getting harder to trigger." I turned my helmet over in my hands. The only difference I could think of was sitting right next to me. This was the first time I'd fought Wesley.

Maybe instinct wasn't taking over because I knew Wesley wouldn't hurt me. Sure, I knew Naomi wouldn't either, but Wesley had been the one to face the crowd of protesters with me at the pier. He'd sprung me from that car trunk. He'd taken on Hackjob at the museum so that I could run away.

Mom's programming wouldn't take over against Wesley because it relied on a fight-or-flight response. The problem with Wesley was that he made me feel safe.

Wesley smiled and stood up.

"We'll stick to moves you already know, then. You've got a lot of them to work on, anyway."

I jumped back to my feet.

"You're just scared I'll beat you if we keep trying," I scoffed, but smiled. "Remember the combo Naomi and I were going over on Monday? Let's start with that one."

We practiced until Mike popped his head into the room to let us know Everly had more sandwiches in the Sickbay. I'd managed to get a few good hits in on Wesley, but nothing made him more than flinch. It was a wonder he'd lost to Hackjob at the museum. Even if he didn't look like much, Wesley was a tank.

Mike laughed as he handed me a sandwich.

"Were you planning on heading out early?" he joked, looking my armor up and down.

"No, just practicing," I explained.

"I wouldn't mind helping you practice sometime," Desirae said. She sat on a bed, picking the tomatoes out of her sandwich.

"You'd really do that?"

"Sure," she insisted. "Mike will help too, of course."

Mike's mouth was full of sandwich, but he gave me a thumbs up. I hadn't had the chance to practice against any of the upperclassmen yet. The other sophomores were talented opponents, but the older kids had more experience.

We jumped as Carmen burst into the room, her helmet under her arm.

"We're leaving early. The other team's reporting suspicious activity."

Wesley and Mike ran to the locker room to finish suiting up. Desirae scavenged Mike's discarded sandwich to relieve it of its tomatoes.

"I hope it's not another dead animal," she snorted.

Carmen shrugged.

"It's probably nothing, but Marcus saw three people on a rooftop. It's supposed to be an abandoned building, the one across from the Paragon Memorial."

"Oh, that *is* weird." Desirae frowned. "No one's been in those buildings for years. Do you think I should suit up just in case?"

"I'm still not convinced it's anything. Fleming said it could be construction workers, or even the Health Department. I wouldn't stray too far, though."

I followed Carmen into the atrium, shoving my sandwich into my mouth so I didn't have to talk to her. The only interaction I'd had with the Junior had been the night she had helped Andersen trick me on the boardwalk.

Fleming was in his new usual spot behind the call desk. A small crowd was forming, although it was nothing compared to how busy the atrium had been at the beginning of the week. The news that the scouting team had seen something suspicious had spread quickly, but morale was still too low to put much stock into it.

"Shouldn't you be sending someone with more experience?" Skyler stared at me from the corner of the room, as if daring me to oppose him.

"She has more experience than any of us with these culty weirdos," Heather snapped back before I could retort. To my relief and surprise, there were nods of agreement.

"Sit down, Skyler, before you embarrass yourself," Carmen said coolly. Skyler's eyes widened in betrayal.

"Weren't you saying the other day how Betas shouldn't be allowed to try out for the team?"

"Sure, but that doesn't change the fact that Samantha has done more in her three weeks here than you've done in over a year."

There was a small chorus of jeers, and Skyler turned beat red before sitting back down.

Wesley and Mike joined us at the call desk. Fleming looked up from the computer and stood up.

"The scouting team currently on patrol is reporting three figures on the roof of what is supposed to be an abandoned building," he recapped. "This is probably nothing, but the location is suspicious so the field team is requesting back-up to better survey the area. Mike is Team Leader. We'll keep Desirae on hand in case anything goes wrong."

After a half-second of confusion, I remembered Desirae, and Mike's twin-link. They could probably communicate faster than any messaging system.

Fleming looked us all in the eye, one by one, stopping with me.

"This is surveillance only," he reiterated. "Only engage in extreme circumstances and with my go-ahead."

It was difficult to keep up with the others as we walked down the long corridor to the underground parking garage. They half-walked, half-jogged down the barren hallway, eager to join the others in the field. My heart thundered under my armor in anticipation, but a part of me was afraid this would turn out to be a false alarm.

The first team had taken the main scouting vehicle, and instead we were left with a dark-gray sedan. Wesley and I squeezed into the back seats while the older two got in the front. There was no partition in this car, though the windows were just as dark.

"What's so suspicious about the Paragon Memorial?" I asked as Mike drove us out of the garage. He was a better driver than Isabelle, but not by much. Even with my seatbelt on, I had to hold onto the seat to keep from slipping as he took the corners.

"The Paragon Memorial is on an abandoned block, not to mention it's where Harvey found Naomi," Carmen explained. "It's a nice park and gets a lot of visitors, but no one has lived there since the fire, and as far as we know, there aren't any development plans for the area."

I gave Wesley a quizzical look, and he understood what I was asking.

"There was a fire in an apartment complex fourteen years ago," he explained. "Paragon was the first one to get to the scene. He saved everyone, but the building came down with him still inside. It's where he died."

It was common knowledge that Paragon was dead, but I hadn't given any thought until now as to how. He'd been on the team with Mom. Fourteen years ago, he wouldn't have been that old.

"And the whole block was abandoned?" It was strange to think that on an island with finite living space, a whole block would have been left empty for fourteen years. It absolutely seemed like the kind of spot a kidnapping cult leader would set up a home base. "Why hadn't we already checked these buildings?"

"We did," Mike said from the front seat. "That first night, Marcus swept the whole street using his heat-sensing. All he found were rats. No sign of people inside any of the buildings."

"They were only checking it again because we haven't found anything else," Carmen explained. The car rolled to a stop as Mike parked. I looked up at the buildings. It was still early enough in the evening for the lights in the windows to be lit.

"I thought it was uninhabited?"

"This isn't the building," Mike snorted. "We had to park down the road a bit to avoid looking suspicious."

Helmets on, we snuck into the shadows between buildings. Green text lit up my visor with coordinates. The other team knew we were nearby. The buildings got darker, and soon the only light came from street lamps.

There was a break in the brick structures up ahead that showed a sliver of ocean shining through the abandoned apartments. We crept between two buildings so we could walk along the water and out of sight of anyone who might be on the rooftops.

The Paragon Memorial sat on a square lot. The well-trimmed hedges and plants offered cover from any prying eyes across the street as we slipped deeper into the small park. At the park's center, a larger-than-life Paragon knelt on one knee. His cape draped over his shoulders, and his eyes were closed with his head bowed, but the metal face looked peaceful.

The flowers and lit candles at his feet were a testament to the fact that some islanders remained grateful for their Apex protectors, even while signs reading "New Delos's Greatest ZERO" sat nearby. Despite the Anti-Apex signs, the memorial was beautiful, but as I marveled at the garden and the candles, something about this new, solemn Paragon felt like a bad omen.

I tensed at the sound of approaching boots, but relaxed when Marcus, Justin, and a freshman girl I didn't know appeared around a hedge. They pulled their helmets off, safe in the privacy of the garden.

"Are they still there?" Carmen asked. Marcus nodded. Seven helmets tilted up towards the roof of the building directly across the street.

"Three of them," Marcus said. "Two men and a woman."

"What do they look like?" I asked.

"I can only see their heat signatures. They haven't come close enough to the edge for us to get a look, but they've been up there for almost an hour. The rest of the building is empty."

"I can't hear anything from here, either," Wesley sighed.

"We want to send Jessa and me up to the roof of the adjacent building, but we need someone in the alley behind the building as well as a team to stake out the area here in the front," Marcus continued. "Mike and

Carmen, if you want to take the alleyway, Justin can stay here with the sophomores."

"Sounds good," Carmen nodded.

"I might be able to hear them if I could get closer," Wesley protested. "Let me patrol the alley."

"We need you here." Justin put a hand on Wesley's shoulder. "If someone comes out that front door, you're our best bet on stopping them."

"Says the guy whose power is to literally stop people!"

"Which is why I'll be here, too," Justin said. Wesley's shoulders dropped in resolution.

"Fine," he growled. "But if anyone does come through those doors, I want first dibs."

As we split into our three teams, green text typed itself out on my visor. Marcus was updating Fleming on the plan and our positions. I'd spent so much time hoping I'd be there when the students were found that I'd been too busy to consider what that might actually look like. It felt just like it had when Andersen had thrown me in the ocean, with cold, darkness rushing in over my head.

"Are you alright?" The back of Wesley's hand brushed against mine.

"Yeah," I lied. "It's like Fleming said, right? It's all probably nothing."

I wished I could see Wesley's eyes past his visor.

"Probably," he agreed. I was glad to see Justin pretending not to hear us. "But if it's not, you'll do great. You always do."

"Thanks." I tried to smile back, but I still felt like the scared girl on the docks all over again.

It's probably nothing, I repeated in my head.

"They're on the roof," Justin said, reading the message Marcus had just sent. "What's the visual?"

Justin's words appeared under Marcus's.

Hard to see the men in the dark.
Tall, dark clothes, short hair -5

I pressed my finger to the button on the side of my helmet like I'd just seen Justin do.

"And the woman?" I demanded.

The words appeared as I said them with my suit number like Justin's had. My heart hammered in the few seconds it took Marcus to reply

Long white hair -5

My whole body went numb. I couldn't breathe. Wesley's fingers wrapped around my wrist. A message from Fleming flashed in front of my face.

DO NOT ENGAGE -F

"Do we know this lady?" Justin asked us.

"Do you not read the reports?" Wesley hissed. His whole body was tensed under his armor. Fleming's message flashed a second time before Marcus sent an update.

She's on the move. Downward, into the building -5

"It's an elevator," Wesley breathed. "I can hear it."

We snuck through the garden. I tiptoed down the path, hoping my footsteps were silent. The windows of the building were boarded, and the faded red paint on the double doors was peeling.

"If she comes out, we watch where she goes," Justin said, "but if she sees us, Fleming will kill us."

I waited for the woman from the ferry to appear at the top of the stoop, but she didn't. I threw a hazardous glance down the street, thinking I might see the car she had once shoved me into the trunk of. Wesley pulled me back down behind the wall.

Lost her -5

"What do you mean?" Wesley demanded.

Heat signature is gone. Any street visual? -5

"No," Wesley growled.

Nothing in the alley. -11

The last message must have been from Mike. He'd had the number eleven on his shoulder pads.

"She can't just be gone." I racked my brain, trying to think. We couldn't let her get away without seeing where she went. She could lead us straight to Winnie and the others. But Marcus couldn't see her heat signature anymore, so where could she have gone?

I inhaled sharply.

"What?" Wesley jumped and looked around.

"Remember how we got away from Marcus in the Night Game?" I whispered. "She's underground."

Wesley jammed his hand so hard against the button on his helmet that I wouldn't have been surprised if he'd concussed himself.

"She's underground!"

"Do you think they've got the students down there?" Justin asked.

DO NOT ENGAGE. Council has been notified -F

"We get it," I growled. Don't engage, don't get hurt, but Winnie could be just yards beneath our feet.

Wesley slid to the ground with his back against the stone wall. He slipped his helmet off and looked out towards the water.

"Put that back on before you're seen!" Justin barked, but Wesley ignored him. He stared out into the night and slowly raised his hands to cup his ears.

"Helicopter," he whispered. Justin looked out where Wesley was staring.

"There's no helicopter there," he sighed. "There's no lights."

"I can see it," Wesley insisted. "And I can hear it getting closer."

"Fleming, are there any helicopters cleared for travel into the city tonight?"

I held my breath while we waited. Five seconds, ten seconds, fifteen seconds, and finally-

OFFICER ALLEN SAYS NO -F

"You think it's theirs?" I asked.

"Why else would they be on the roof?"

"Then why would that woman go underground?"

Wesley's eyes widened. I raised a shaking hand to my helmet.

"They're moving them off island," I croaked, glad the text on the screen couldn't convey the quake in my voice. If Winnie was moved to the mainland, we might never find her.

I could hear the helicopter now. It started as a soft, pattering hum but was getting louder.

Someone's coming back up -5

I looked back at the building as if I might see what Marcus saw, but the bricks looked as benign as they had all night.

There's someone with them, lying down -5

Wesley was back in his helmet, his finger pressed against the button.

"If we don't do something, we might lose them." He sounded desperate. He was pleading. "Fleming, we need to do something. I can't just—"

He broke off, but I knew what he wanted to say. He wouldn't be able to bear it if he had to watch Anthony be taken away again.

We waited for a response, the helicopter getting louder behind us while we stood poised towards the red doors, ready to sprint and knock them down as soon as Fleming gave the signal.

"They'll be gone if we don't do anything," Wesley continued to beg the blank screen. Fleming had to give the go ahead. This could be our only chance, he had to see that.

"Fleming!" Wesley demanded into his microphone. There was a soft rustle behind us. Another helmet appeared between Wesley's and mine. Heather's jawline was tense under her visor.

"Fleming says go."

24

The Man in the Helmet

We were already halfway across the street when Fleming's official go-ahead flashed on the screen. Instructions were scrolling almost too fast to read them. Marcus and Jessa were to jump the roof and intercept the student already in the elevator. Heather would scout ahead, using her powers to jump to the lower levels. The rest of us would follow, using Wesley as a battering ram on whatever stood in the way. The names of the five missing students appeared in the screen corner. My heart twisted when I read Winnie's.

Heather vanished, jumping ahead to scout. The red lobby doors buckled under Wesley's force and clanged as they flew off their hinges.

The lobby was dark, but with the help of my helmet, I could see the dirt and animal droppings that covered the floor and the cobwebs that hung from the ceiling. The LED light above the elevator doors signaled that it was in use, glowing ominously in the otherwise decrepit room.

At Justin's signal, Wesley ripped the stairwell door off its hinges. It hadn't even hit the ground by the time he was hurdling downstairs.

The stairwell twisted down beneath the building, illuminated by small lights that ran along each step. Wesley kept several paces ahead of me, and when the sound of his boots on each step finally stopped, I knew we'd reached the bottom.

As the three of us lined up next behind the door, Lannie Bryce's name blinked three times and disappeared from the list in my visor.

We have Lannie -5

A shiver ran down my spine. Those three words electrified me. We'd been right. The missing students were here. *Winnie* was here.

Justin nodded, and Wesley knocked the door down with a single kick. It clattered to the floor, and our boots rattled over it as we rushed the hallway.

Doors lined either side of the wide, white corridor. Fluorescent lights hung from wires, but the hall was otherwise bare. A loud thud made them sway. A door slammed open, and a woman in a lab coat stumbled out, pursued by Heather.

Darkness spilled from the room and swirled at Heather's feet as she pulled the woman up by her coat collar. When the woman turned to look for help but saw us standing on the kicked in door instead, she shot a quaking arm up and pointed.

"They're that way, down to the left, please don't—"

Heather dropped her and beckoned us to follow her down the hall.

"What about this creep?" Justin pointed at the woman, who slid down the wall and stared at us between her fingers.

"I'll stay with her."

Marcus and Carmen had come down the stairs behind us. It had been Carmen who spoke.

"Lannie's with Seventeen and Eleven upstairs," Marcus explained, referring to Jessa and Mike.

Heather led the way down the hall while Marcus scanned the rooms for heat signatures.

"Anything?" I asked at the end of the corridor. Marcus shook his head.

"Just labs, by the looks of it." But then he pointed down the hall and shouted. "Second room to the right!"

Wesley didn't wait for orders. The door was locked but buckled easily as he dropped a shoulder and rammed it.

"Anthony!"

Anthony was pale and gaunt, and his breath rattled in time with the steady rise and fall of the blankets over his chest. Wesley rushed to the bedside, ignoring the man who cowered in the corner, and gently shook Anthony's shoulder. His head lolled to the side.

Wesley turned on the man in the corner.

"What's wrong with him?" he demanded.

"It looks like he's been drugged." Heather inspected Anthony. "Probably to make it easier to transport him."

Wesley didn't back down, though. I stood between him and the man, but Wesley looked right past me with his hands clenched into fists.

"Are the others down here?" I asked the man, hoping to deescalate Wesley. Instead, the man spat at me. Wesley howled in rage and lunged, but I held out my arms. "Don't!"

To my surprise, Wesley stopped. The man shrank back into the corner. Whatever courage it had taken to spit at me had already abandoned him.

"It's alright," Justin said. He pulled off a glove and grabbed the man's face with his bare hand. The man locked up. Justin had immobilized him.

"We've got Anthony," Heather said behind me, and the words appeared on my screen. His name blinked like Lannie's had and disappeared.

"I'll take him up," Wes said, returning to his roommate's bedside. "I'll bring him to the others upstairs."

"We need you here," Marcus insisted. "You're the only way to get past these locked doors. Twelve can take him."

They all turned to look at me.

"Wait, why me?" I protested. I hadn't found Winnie yet. I wasn't ready to go back up.

"Because I'm the mission leader, and I told you to," Marcus said. "The elevator is back the way we came. You shouldn't have any trouble."

I wanted to fight back. I wanted to argue. They were making me take Anthony because I wasn't useful. I couldn't knock down doors or freeze the bad guys. But I felt fingers interlace with mine, and I looked down to see Wesley holding my hand.

"Please," he whispered. "I don't trust anyone else with him."

The fight that had been building inside me disappeared.

"You have to promise to find Winnie and keep her safe."

His hand squeezed mine, and I knew he'd find her.

The bed was large and difficult to maneuver, but I managed to wheel Anthony into the hallway.

"Hey, guys?" Justin asked. "Who's that?"

He pointed down the hall at a cloaked figure waiting for us. His dark gray robes stood out against the sterile, white walls, and he stared at us from behind the blank, black eyes of a pearlescent Greek tragedy mask, its mouth drawn downwards in a grotesque frown. He stood perfectly still, as if waiting for us to make the first move.

"Two," Marcus hissed. "Make sure Twelve gets on that elevator."

Justin moved so that he was next to me. I could see the number "2" on his shoulder pad.

"Everyone behind me." Heather said, stepping forward.

The figure sprinted towards us. His dark cloaks disappeared as Heather sucked all the light from the hall ahead of her. I tore myself away, reminding myself that I was only running because they'd told me to. I would be back to help once Anthony was safe. The wheels of Anthony's bed squeaked as I rushed him down the hall. We turned the corner, slowing down to better maneuver the bed, and the sound of fighting broke out behind us.

"Don't look back!" Justin warned. "Keep going!"

I heard his footsteps that had been keeping time with mine stop. Despite his warning, I glanced over my shoulder. The masked figure had caught up, and Justin had fallen back to buy me more time.

The elevator was just ahead. I would make it. Justin would freeze the creep in the mask, just like he'd frozen the man in Anthony's room.

There was a grunt and thud, and I chanced another look back. Justin slumped against the white wall, and his head rolled forward. The figure turned his mask towards me as I punched the elevator call button. Anthony moaned in the bed.

The masked man ran at me, and I braced myself for a fight. He had gotten past all the others and had made quick work out of Justin. Hopefully Mom's brain software would be enough.

He was mere yards away when someone barreled out of a side door and knocked him off his feet. I had never paid enough attention to Carmen to see her fight in practice. I wasn't even sure what her Apex ability was. However, watching her now, there was no way she wasn't one of the team's best fighters. The masked man struggled to keep up with her, as if she knew his moves before he had the chance to throw so much as a punch.

The masked man tried to get around her, but she swept him off his feet, and he rolled to the ground in a flurry of robes.

"Get out of here!" Carmen shouted as the elevator doors opened. While she was distracted, the figure leaped at her and trapped her in a headlock. Carmen choked out a final command. "Go!"

I pushed Anthony into the elevator and repeatedly punched the door close button until they began to slide shut. I breathed a sigh of relief too soon. A white sleeved arm stopped the door at the last moment.

The woman that Carmen had been watching forced her way into the elevator, brandishing a hypodermic needle. She lunged at me as the doors closed behind her. I had enough time to grab her wrist with one hand as she pinned me between the wall and Anthony's bed.

The elevator shuddered beneath us and began to rise. The woman continued to press the needle towards my neck. She was much stronger than me, and I struggled to crane away from the needle point in her hand.

The elevator came to a stop, jolting the whole carriage as it did. I took the moment to free my other arm and delivered an uppercut to the woman's diaphragm. She gasped and doubled over, giving me time to pry the needle from her grip and plunge it into her shoulder.

Her eyes widened in surprise, and her jaw went slack. She tried to grab me but slipped to the ground as her eyelids fluttered closed.

I took a moment to move after the doors slid open, trying to remember how to breathe and hoping I hadn't just killed someone. I gripped Anthony's bed, hoping it might help steady my shaking hands.

A sea breeze rushed in through the open lobby doorway. Jessa smiled at me from the top of the stairs.

"We've got Twelve and Anthony," she said into the helmet mic before grabbing onto the bed rails. "I've got this."

Jessa lifted the bed up off the ground as easily as if it were made of styrofoam and pushed off the top step of the stoop. She drifted through the air to land lightly in the street as I stumbled down the stairs after them. Sometime in the last few minutes, Brent Todd's name had disappeared from the screen. Only Winnie and Lawrence Garcia were left.

"Where's Lannie and Mike?" I asked.

"Back here," Jessa said as we pushed the bed across the street and into the garden.

The garden felt too peaceful after the chaos of the underground facility. The hedges were kept tall so that the center of the garden felt cut off from the rest of the city. It was too quiet here. Mike sat at the base of the Paragon statue. Jessa parked Anthony's bed next to Lannie's.

"What's the situation down there?"

"I think Justin is down," I said, trying to catch my breath. "I don't know about the others. There was a guy in a mask, but last I saw him, he was fighting Carmen."

"Fleming and the university sent help," Mike said, "but there's a guy blocking the road."

"Just one guy? Why don't they run him over?"

Mike shook his head.

"It's that big guy from the museum by the sound of things, the one Fleming says you fought with a sword."

I wasn't sure if I should be relieved or not. Hackjob was able to beat even Wesley, but at least if he was busy blocking reinforcements, it meant he wasn't here.

"They got Lawrence!" Jessa announced.

Sure enough, Lawrence's name blinked away, leaving Winnie the only one on the screen. There was sudden static in my ears, and I jumped in surprise.

"You guys there?" I recognized Heather's voice in my helmet.

"Yeah, we copy," Mike said. I could hear him both next to me as well as in my ear. "You need back up?"

"Five thinks he sees two more prisoners. We're holding Brent and Lawrence in one of the rooms, but there's a lot of them now."

With the audio on, I could hear the grunts and thuds on the other end. Someone shouted for help.

"Two more?" I asked. "I thought only Winnie was left."

"We thought so, too!" Wesley's voice sounded strained, but it was a relief to hear him.

"Any word on reinforcements?" Marcus's voice asked. "Nine and Two are both down."

So I'd been right to assume Justin was out, and now it sounded like Carmen wasn't able to fight either.

"We're working on it," Mike insisted. "Unless you wanted one of us to come down."

"No!" Three different voices echoed on the other end. Jessa scoffed next to me.

"Sorry you got stuck on babysitting duty, Mike." Even though I couldn't see her eyes, I was sure she was rolling them.

I stared back at the building through the space between two hedges, the sound of breathing and grunting playing over the audio feed. The brick facade looked so harmless and quiet. Even though I had just come from the fray below the building, it was still hard to imagine the sounds I was hearing on my headset were coming from it.

A chill ran down my spine, and my eyes darted to the top of the building. A dark figure stood on the edge and looked as if it were surveying the memorial. Moonlight glinted off its head, and I knew whoever it was must be wearing some sort of armored helmet.

"Who's that?" I ducked farther behind the hedge, not daring to point.

Mike swore.

"I'm not sure," he admitted. "He wasn't there a moment ago."

"Do you think he knows we're here?"

Mike shook his head slowly.

"I don't think so. He's just standing there."

Static rattled on the other end of the audio feed, and someone shouted.

"Everything alright?" Mike asked.

"Any word on the reinforcements?" Marcus coughed in my ear.

"Desirae says they're still held up."

"What about the police?" Heather grunted.

"I-I don't know." Mike looked to Jessa and me for help. Jessa shrugged. I turned back to the building. The figure on the roof was gone, but that only made me more uneasy.

Something like an explosion threatened to blow out the audio in my helmet. All three of us threw our hands to our ears, even though the sound came from the headsets.

"What was that?" I demanded. No one responded to me. The three of us stood motionless, holding our breath as we listened to the sounds of struggle happening under the building.

"That thing is back!" Wesley's breath was labored as he spoke. "The one in the mask."

"Watch out!"

There was a crash.

"Look out, behind—"

My heart stopped when Wesley's voice broke off in a cry of pain. I hadn't even registered that I was rushing towards the street when Mike grabbed my arm and held me back.

"You need to stay here in case we have to move Lannie and Anthony."

I stood petrified, straining to make sense of the commotion happening in the audio feed.

"We lost Seven," Marcus choked. I tried to steady my breathing, and panic pressed down around me.

"What do you mean lost?" I kept my voice even.

"That masked freak took him!" Heather sounded like she was still fighting. I wondered how many she and Marcus were left up against. The white haired woman was still unaccounted for.

"Wesley?" I said his name quietly, as if it might keep the others from hearing me. "Wes, are you there?"

He had to have his helmet on still. He'd have to hear me, unless he was unconscious or...

"Wes, please," I begged. The only response I got was the sound of Marcus and Heather's ongoing struggle. I stared back at the solemn Paragon statue towering over us. How many times had he had to run back into the burning apartments to save everyone that had lived here? "I'm sorry."

"Samantha, don't—"

Wesley would be mad at me for leaving Anthony, but I'd rather have Wesley safe and angry than be a prisoner somewhere.

I sprinted at the building, but Mike was fast. He caught up half-way across the street and tackled me from behind, sending us both rolling across the pavement. He ended up on top, pinning me down in the middle of the road.

I struggled against his weight, but he was too strong. I kicked out and tried to arch my back to pry him off me.

"It's too dangerous in there, alright?"

"You'd go in if it were Desirae, wouldn't you?"

"She's my sister. It isn't the same."

"But you would."

Mike suddenly grunted in pain and doubled over, rolling off of me. He clutched at his helmet and curled up on the pavement, his teeth clenching beneath his visor

"What did you do to him?!" Jessa shrieked. She charged at me, but Mike held up a shaky hand to stop her.

"It's Desirae," he groaned, and then cried out. Jessa helped me to roll him onto his back. He whimpered. "She's been hurt."

I hadn't thought about their twin connection as anything but an advantage, but now I could see it was just as easily a weakness.

"Is she alright?" I asked. He nodded, but the muscles in his jaw jumped and tightened as he fought the pain. I looked at Jessa. "Get him back to the statue."

"You're going in there?" Her voice was small.

"I have to."

"No, you have to stay here," Mike groaned.

I ignored him and took the steps up to the front doors two at a time. The lobby was just as still as it had been when I'd left it with Anthony. I found the button on my helmet to silence the audio feed. The sound of Heather and Marcus fighting cut off, and the silence of the lobby gave no hint of the battle waging just a few floors below.

I could go downstairs, meet up with Marcus and Heather. I had no idea how far the basement hallways stretched or how many secret tunnels there were that Wesley could have already been dragged through. But the helicopter was on the roof, and they easily could have headed up.

I stood there, immobilized by indecision, and in the silence, I heard the lightest of thumping. I held my breath, listening. It was rhythmic, like something was hitting the stairs several floors above me. Like someone was being dragged up to the roof.

I moved to the stairwell, where the thumping echoed louder overhead. I wanted to yell for Wes. I wanted him to know I was coming. I would be there soon, just hang on. But as I sprinted up the steps, my boots began to feel heavier. My helmet was cumbersome. From the outside, the building looked about five stories tall. I counted them as I went.

Wes didn't leave me behind when I got lost in the crowd on the pier during the protest. He didn't leave me in that car trunk. He'd given me the chance to get away when Hackjob attacked us at the museum, and again when we were cornered by Justin in the Night Game. He was there for me every single time. I wasn't about to fail him when he needed me the most.

When I reached the roof-access door, I didn't hesitate. I only hoped Wesley would be on the other side.

The helicopter sat dormant in the center of the roof as two cloaked figures lifted Wesley's limp form into the carriage. They both turned at the sound of the heavy metal door clanging shut. The one in the Greek tragedy mask crouched, gearing up to lunge at me, but the other placed a hand on his shoulder.

The hilt of a sword protruded from beneath the tattered and frayed folds of his cloaks. His helmet was styled like a Greek warrior's, forged from black metal and decorated with a crimson plume. The way the moonlight bounced off it, I knew he'd been the figure Mike and I had seen from the garden.

Everything about him set every one of my nerves on end, and it was like the roof was electrified. I'd seen what a formidable foe the one in the tragedy mask was, but everything screamed that this new enemy was someone to be much more feared.

"We- Seven!" I stopped myself from shouting his name. "Seven, get up!"

"He can't hear you." The man's voice sounded hollow as it echoed off the confines of his helmet. "No need to worry, though. He will wake up in a few hours, rest assured. I was wondering how long it would take you to follow him up here. I'll admit, you were quicker than I had thought you would be."

I did a quick head count. There were these two, of course, plus a pilot in the cockpit of the helicopter. Yet another man bent over Wesley in the main body of the vehicle. He straightened up, and I bristled.

"You recognize Miles, yes?" the man in the helmet crooned. "Maybe you saw him at the museum? Were you there that night?"

It was the man with the force fields. He'd been the one to take Winnie away.

"Give me back my friend." The voice modulator helped me sound more intimidating than I felt.

"After Dion here worked so hard to bring him to me?" He tutted, and his friend hissed behind his mask. "Tell me, girl, do you know who I am?"

He said it like he was genuinely curious, and the question caught me off guard. I swept my eyes over the roof again. There had to be a trap here somewhere.

"You're Adrestus," I said. The costume made that obvious. "The one in the museum is taller."

Dion hissed again, but Adrestus still had a grip on his shoulder.

"So you do know me," he said slowly, as if savoring his words. "Then, tell me who you are."

He had to be stalling. Maybe he was waiting for someone else to come up the stairs behind me? I carefully circled Adrestus and Dion so that I had a clear view of them, Wesley, and the roof access door.

"Show me your face," Adrestus insisted. "It's alright, you can trust me."

"I just want my friend."

"Then show me your face."

"No!"

Adrestus removed his hand from Dion's shoulder, and Dion rocketed across the roof towards me. I braced myself, but he feinted at the last moment to hit me from the side. I wasn't ready for the blow and stumbled away.

"Bring me her helmet," Adrestus called. Dion slammed me into the ground. His mask pressed against my face as he tried to pin my arms. I kicked at him, but he must've had a good layer of armor on under his robes.

Naomi and I hadn't practiced much close quarter fighting, but Mom must have. I let instinct take hold.

There was a shout overhead. Dion and I were locked in a stalemate, but I was able to look up to see Miles soar from the helicopter. He landed in a pile on the ground and groaned, but didn't try to get up.

A dark shape leaped from the cab, but a swing of Adrestus's arm smacked it to the floor. Wesley struggled to his feet, awake but unsteady. The drug was wearing off. I watched Wesley waver and catch himself as Dion pressed my head into the concrete roof.

"Run!" I screamed. "Get downstairs!"

He faltered as he took in the scene. Adrestus swung at him, and Wesley at least had the sense to dodge it. However, instead of running towards the door, he began sprinting towards me.

Why did he always have to be the hero? Why couldn't he just run away? I struggled to break free of Dion without letting him get the upper hand but had barely begun to break his grip when Adrestus sprang after Wesley, grabbing him from behind, and flung him into the ground.

"Leave him alone!" I shrieked. I tried to get up, I had to get up, but Dion slammed my head back into the concrete.

Wesley stirred in a feeble daze as Adrestus grabbed the collar of his armor to drag him to the edge of the building. The toes of Wesley's boots scrambled to keep contact with the lip of the edge, and Adrestus leaned him out over open air, holding him there.

"No!" I finally found the strength to throw Dion off, and I charged at Adrestus. I would push him away, grab Wesley, pull him back, and—

My helmet collided with something solid, and I ricocheted backwards off the forcefield. Miles was still lying on his stomach across the roof but had stretched out a hand to throw a protective wall between his master and me.

"Wait, Dion. Leave her," Adrestus crooned.

Dion's boots tapped as he paced behind me. Wesley held onto Adrestus's wrist with both hands. He swayed in the wind as it rolled in from the ocean. I pushed against the invisible wall, but it didn't budge. Maybe Mike and Jessa could see Wesley dangling on the edge. Maybe they could find a way to catch him.

"I'll put him down if you do one thing for me." The metallic echo of his voice rang out over the rooftop.

"Just run," Wesley choked. Fat chance. I'd told him to run, too, but he hadn't listened.

"What do you want?" I asked.

"Let me see your face."

My heartbeat thundered in my ears. That was it? Show him my face and Wesley was safe?

But I had been one of Adrestus's targets. If he knew who was hiding under my visor, I'd be the one loaded into the helicopter.

Of course, he could just drop Wesley and overpower me, anyway.

"That's it?" I asked.

"No, don't!" Wesley yelled. Adrestus leaned him out farther over the street below.

"Just take off your helmet, and he won't be hurt."

"Why?"

"You've put up a good fight but show no Apex abilities, unless they are helping you in some undetectable way. I want to see your face because I want to know if you're like me."

"What do you mean 'like you'?" Red and blue lights danced along the facades of the buildings down the streets. The police were here. If I could keep Adrestus distracted long enough, maybe there would be time for help to find us up here.

"A non-Apex, I mean," Adrestus purred. "Or, some might say, a Beta."

A Beta kidnapping the children of Apex with the help of his Apex henchmen? But why? My head spun, but there wasn't any time to figure out why Adrestus was doing what he was while Wesley was a five-story fall away from doom.

"Show me your face." He said it more forcefully this time.

"I'll be fine," Wesley said. "Please, just go."

The police lights were below us now, sending Wesley's shadow flashing across the concrete roof. I pushed against the invisible barrier again, but it was still intact.

"I won't ask again," Adrestus boomed, and I knew he meant it.

I raised my hands up to my helmet.

"I'm sorry," I said, looking at Wesley.

I felt my hair swing down against my neck as I lifted the helmet off my head. Dion hissed angrily behind me. I blinked, trying to adjust my eyes to the dark. Without the help of the visor's enhanced vision, and with his robes whipping around him in the wind, Adrestus looked even darker and more foreboding.

"Your turn," I said and pointed at Wesley.

Adrestus chuckled, and for a moment I thought he might go back on his word, but he yanked Wesley up onto the roof and threw him to the ground.

He strode towards me, and the metal on his boots clanked with every step. Wesley tried to follow but was stopped by a new force field. He bounced off it, falling to the ground, clearly still weakened by the drug.

I stood my ground as Adrestus got closer. I threw my chin out in defiance. I wouldn't run away as long as Wesley was still on the roof.

"What is it they call you?" Adrestus was face to face with me now. I knew his eyes could only be inches from mine, but, despite the slit in his face guard, I couldn't see past the darkness that seemed to fill his helmet. Hot breath rolled out from inside. "What's your name, girl?"

"Don't answer him!" Wesley begged, still on the ground.

"I've seen your face, now tell me your name, or your friend is going to have to be scraped off the sidewalk. I won't give you a chance to think about it this time."

Wesley shook his head, but I ignored him.

"Samantha."

Adrestus growled.

"Not that name!"

"S-Samantha Havardson?" I stammered. "I don't know what other name you want!"

"No!" A leather-clad hand shot from the robes and wrapped around my neck, pulling me closer. I tried to push away, but he was too strong.

"Let her go!" Wesley slammed himself against the forcefield.

Sirens wailed below us. Shouts drifted upwards on the ocean breeze.

"Do you not remember me?"

"No? I'm sorry, I —"

His fingers tightened around my throat. I tried to force his hand away.

"Tell me your name!"

"Samantha!" I gasped. He let go of me, and I gulped for air. My knees were shaking, but I refused to fall to them.

"Fine," he whispered. "There's more than one way to find out if you are who I think you are."

His hands wrapped around my head. There was no time for me to react. Wesley's mouth opened in a scream, and I tried to focus on him as I felt Adrestus's muscles contract.

There was a crack. The world went dark.

25

Awake

The darkness lingered for what felt like both a couple of seconds and an eternity. No Adrestus, no Wes, no rooftop, no city lights, no sirens. Just nothing. It almost felt comforting.

But then, something in the back of my head flickered, like emergency lights blinking to life. Everything was still dark, but there was something, whatever that something might be.

I followed the sound of deep, shuddering breaths above me.

"On the roof, please hurry." Wes was talking as if he was trying to catch his breath between words. "Yeah, but she's not—"

He cut himself off with something between a cough and a dry sob. He was upset, I realized dreamily. Had we lost? Did Adrestus get away? I should've been faster...

I screwed my eyes tight before finally opening them, clearing the fog from my eyes and brain. Skyscraper outlines took shape above me. Wes was doubled over with his forehead resting on my stomach. He'd taken his helmet off so I could see his mop of messy brown hair ruffling in the ocean wind.

"Wes?" I croaked. It was hard to talk, like there was no air left in my lungs. His head snapped up, and he gaped at me.

"Oh my god, Sammy." He sat up. He was holding someone's hand, but I couldn't turn my head to see who else was there.

"Wes, your helmet." He shouldn't have taken it off. What if someone saw his face? What if Adrestus figured out who he was?

"It's fine," he assured me, clutching the gloved hand closer to his chest. I realized it had to be my hand, but I couldn't feel his fingers entwined around mine. I couldn't feel anything.

"Wes?" The panic was unmistakable in my voice. "It's-it's cold."

No, that wasn't right. It wasn't that it was cold, it's that there was nothing, as if when I'd woken up out of the dark nothingness, some of it had clung to me.

"I know." He brushed a lock of hair from my face. I could at least feel that, as his fingers grazed my cheek. It made me feel a little better.

I tried to gather myself. Adrestus had just been here, he couldn't have disappeared in just a few seconds. I did my best to lift my head and try to look around for any sign of him or his ghoulish sidekick, but my neck wouldn't move.

"I can't move," I rasped. "Wes, I'm—"

"It's alright, it's alright!" Wes tried to calm my rising panic. He set my arm down and leaned in close so he could look me in the eye. His ungloved hand gently rested against my cheek. It was trembling but warm. I clung to it. I hoped he'd never move it. "Sammy, I've got you. Help is coming."

There were tracts in the dirt that stained his cheeks. He must've been crying. Everly would be able to fix me, right? He had the Serum. The Serum could fix anything. So why would Wesley be upset?

There was a metallic slam somewhere to our right. Wes jumped to his feet, his careful composure crumbling.

"Over here!" he shouted. His voice shook, and tears began falling down his face. "We're over here!"

Heavy footsteps thundered against the concrete rooftop. Two new figures appeared over me. I'd never seen Fleming look so gaunt. He hovered overhead as Everly knelt beside me.

"She's alive?" Fleming gasped. "But you said—"

"Samantha, can you hear me?" Everly asked. I tried to nod, but my head barely moved.

"Yes," I said. Everly pressed the palm of his hand over my forehead. I felt the shudder run from the top of my head, but it cut off just under my chin. "Please don't tell my parents."

"What's wrong with her?" Fleming asked, though he didn't sound like he wanted to know the answer.

"Samantha, listen very carefully." Everly's voice was slow and low. "You have a broken neck at your C1 vertebrae. I can fix it, but I need to reset your spine."

"Reset her spine?" Fleming repeated. His bedside manner needed work. He didn't even attempt to hide the fear and skepticism in his voice. "I've never heard of that before."

Everly positioned himself behind me to place one hand under my head and the other under my chin.

"Shouldn't we do this back at the school?" Fleming hissed. Wesley stood behind him, looking like a little kid hiding behind a parent.

"No." Everly sounded resolute, but his voice shook a little. "Wesley, cover your ears."

Before I had the chance to ask Everly if he'd ever done this before, there was another deafening crack, and the nothingness returned.

I floated through the nothingness until flashes of dreams began to mix in my subconscious. They bled together in a tangle of images that changed faster than I was able to make sense of them.

Darkness faded into a hazy white. Something burned in my chest, and I coughed, fighting to see through thick plumes of smoke.

I was lying in a bed of moss on a clear, warm night. Someone's hand held mine, his thumb gently rubbing my knuckles.

I collapsed in a creek. The cold water stung my wounds and soaked through my clothes, but I didn't have the strength left to get up.

The smoke clogged my lungs, but I continued to scream.

I turned my head to look at him. His blue eyes smiled at me.

"Come with me," he said, and I wanted nothing more than to do so.

We were standing, face to face, blood oozed from between his lips.

The creek ran red with my blood. I watched it swirl and mix around the rocks. I was weightless. There was no pain.

He played with a strand of my hair.

I loved him.

I dug the blade deeper between his ribs.

I loathed him.

Their bodies lay in a neat row among the ashes. They'd been killed before the fire had been set. I only counted six. One was missing.

The cold water was turning my body numb. I could barely feel my injuries now, though a faint pain in my stomach was growing, shattering the scene.

The stabbing pains in my stomach slowly dragged me back into consciousness. I thought I might be dying, like I might have sustained the wounds from my dream, but then my stomach growled, and I realized I was just hungry.

The room was dark, but I recognized the tiled ceiling of the Sickbay. Hushed voices whispered nearby, but my view of the room was blocked by a white curtain around my bed. The images and feelings from my dream, however visceral they had been, were already slipping away.

But how did I get here? The memory of the rooftop came rushing back, and fear clawed at my insides. My neck was broken. I had been paralyzed. What might have been a comfortable Sickbay bed had been made uncomfortable by a stiff brace around my neck. My hand rested at my side on top of the white linen. I was afraid to try moving it.

But my fingertips twitched, and my arm bent at the elbow when I willed it to. I sighed in relief.

"Sammy?"

The curtains flew back. Wesley was still in his black underclothes but had at least washed his face. He pulled the curtains shut behind him and crouched down next to me.

"You're awake!"

"Barely," I croaked. He smiled through puffy eyes. I wondered if he had gotten hurt or if he'd been crying.

"Here, you're probably starving." He procured a fast food burger. It was cold. He must have been saving it for me, knowing how hungry the Serum would make me. He hesitated as he held it out, his eyes flickering over my hands.

I gave him a weak thumbs up, lifting my hand a few inches off the mattress. His shoulders relaxed, and he handed me the burger.

"You shouldn't have come after me." He put his head down on the bed. I fought the urge to comfort him by running my fingers through his hair.

"You would've done the same thing for me."

"And you shouldn't have taken off your helmet for him."

"He was about to kill you," I said, tearing into the burger.

"Sammy." Wes grabbed my wrist and raised his head. "Do you even know what happened? What he did to you?"

His lip trembled and his eyes glistened, but he kept his composure.

"Does it matter? I'm fine now, aren't I?"

Wes swallowed.

"Sammy, you died."

I'd heard of peoples' hearts stopping and having to be restarted, but it made me squirm to think about that happening to me.

"Oh," I said. "But you brought me back, obviously."

Or maybe it had been Everly? The memory was already getting fuzzy. Wesley stared hungrily back at me, looking as if I might disappear any moment.

"No," he admitted. "I don't know how you're even alive right now. Everly doesn't either."

I pressed two fingers against my wrist. The way Wesley was talking, I half-expected to feel nothing, but, sure enough, there was a steady pulse beating under my skin.

"He broke your neck," Wesley explained. He looked at the burger wrapper crumbled in my hand, refusing to meet my eye. "You had no heartbeat, and you weren't breathing, and then Adrestus and that *thing* ran, and I went to you, but you were already—"

His voice quaked. My apparent death had obviously shaken him, but he had to be mistaken. I was alive. Maybe he was confused because he had still had some of that drug in his system at the time. People just don't come back to life after having their neck snapped.

"I'm fine," I insisted, trying to convince myself just as much as Wes. "We're both fine."

But he shook his head.

"Even when you woke up, you weren't—"

He gulped.

"Weren't what?"

"You weren't really alive, which I know doesn't make sense, but I couldn't hear anything inside you. No heartbeat. No lungs working. And then Everly showed up, and the look on his face, it was like he knew you were dead, but how could you be? You were looking at me and talking."

"Right, and dead people don't do that," I snorted. I didn't want to believe Wesley. I didn't like what he was saying.

"I know that. But Everly reset your neck, which knocked you out, but after that, you started breathing again." He shrugged. "I don't know. It wasn't normal. He wasn't even sure you'd be able to move again. He had to get a special version of the Serum and inject it into your spinal column."

I winced, grateful I wasn't awake for that part. Wesley could believe I had been dead all he wanted. The fact was, I definitely wasn't dead now.

"Where's Winnie?" I asked, eager to change the subject. "I want to see her."

Wesley looked away from me again, and I felt my stomach twist.

"We didn't find her," he admitted. "Maybe they had already moved her or were keeping her somewhere else to begin with, but she wasn't in that basement."

"But I thought there were two other prisoners to rescue!"

Wesley shook his head.

"There were. We just didn't know they were missing in the first place because they're both from the mainland."

I was crushed. This was supposed to be it. All that work and surveillance for what? Of course the students we had been able to save were worth the work and the risk, but I had joined the team to help find Winnie, and she felt further away than ever.

"We have to go back." I ripped the brace off my neck and pushed the linens away as I struggled to get up.

"You need to stay in bed," Wesley insisted, but I fought my way to my feet. My knees buckled, and Wesley caught me under my arms and lifted me back onto the mattress. I collapsed against the pillow, out of breath and shaky.

The curtains slid open. Everly in his lavender scrubs raised an eyebrow.

"Oh, good," he said dryly. "You aren't paralyzed."

I glared at him.

"So can I go now?"

The curtain slid open further, and Fleming stepped inside, closing it behind him. He stared at me with wide eyes, as if he couldn't believe I was looking back up at him.

"Wesley, we need a moment with Samantha," he said softly. "Anthony's awake if you'd like to go see him."

Wesley looked between me and Fleming, torn between me and his roommate. I hadn't even asked him about Anthony.

"It won't take long," Everly assured him. I smiled at Wesley to show him I was okay, and he reluctantly disappeared back behind the curtain.

Everly took my hand, and I felt the familiar rush reach out along my nerves as he checked to make sure I was alright. He nodded approvingly, and Fleming exhaled.

"You'll have to thank Dr. Weaver when you see her next," Everly said, checking off boxes on his tablet screen. "She donated spinal fluid for the Serum. I'm not sure I would've been able to treat you otherwise."

Everly made me wiggle my toes, lift my arms, and put me through a few other tests to make sure the special version of the Serum hadn't caused any side effects. As he did, Fleming grilled me on the night's events. He shook his head as I explained what'd happened on the rooftop but didn't interrupt until I'd finished.

"First things first," he said when I finished. "No more field missions until after the trials."

"What?" I blanched. He couldn't be serious? "I saved Wesley! I figured out they were underground!"

"True," he conceded, "but you disobeyed orders from your mission leader. Mike told you to stay, and you didn't listen. There has to be a consequence for that."

"I got my neck snapped," I reminded him. "Isn't that a consequence?"

"You might be thankful for the extra training time," Everly said gently. "You weren't paralyzed for very long, but we aren't sure yet what kind of toll it will have taken on your mobility."

I wiggled my toes again, just to double check that they were still in working order.

Fleming went down a list of questions, and I did my best to answer them. I'd long since finished my burger, and my stomach was still growling. It was hard to focus when it felt like my stomach had begun eating itself.

"One last thing," Fleming finally said. "If you'll allow us, I'd like to take a blood sample to test you for the Apex gene."

"But I'm not an Apex."

Everly and Fleming gave each other an uneasy look. Fleming waved a hand, inviting Everly to take over. He ran his fingers over his bald head before speaking.

"How well do you remember what happened after Adrestus, uh, broke your neck?"

"It's a little fuzzy, but I know Wesley was there, and then you two showed up."

"Right, so, there's no easy way to say this," Everly continued. I felt a weight growing in my stomach. I already knew what he was going to say. "But, we think you were dead."

I glared at them.

"I already told Wesley, there's no way," I asserted. "I was awake and talking!"

"I know a dead body when I feel one," Everly said gravely. "And I'm never wrong, which is why we want to test you for the Apex gene. We aren't sure what other explanation there could be."

I might be an Apex. I wanted to laugh and puke at the same time. If it were true, what a twisted ability. Congrats, Sammy, you have the power to be killed horrifically over and over and bounce back every time!

"It's a little odd," Fleming said. "Most Apex abilities are well tracked and documented. Even if they differ a little between each Apex, many of them are related. This isn't one I've ever heard of before, though."

"That's not true!" I suddenly remembered. "Adrestus! The original one, I mean. Wasn't his name Adrestus the Unkillable?"

"And now *our* Adrestus has a special interest in Samantha the Unkillable," Fleming murmured. "So, is it alright if we run the test?"

"Yeah, that's fine."

"I'm surprised you aren't in our database already," he admitted while Everly pulled out supplies for the blood draw. "Many Apex parents have their kids tested at a young age. We keep a record of all of them, Apex or not."

"Is my brother in the database?"

"That's confidential."

I glared at Fleming, and then winced as Everly poked my arm. I watched the thin tube fill with red and was reminded of my dream, watching the water run with my blood.

"Is it normal to have weird dreams from the Serum?" I asked Everly. His brow furrowed.

"Not normally, although it wouldn't surprise me since we were repairing your central nervous system. It was injected straight into your spinal cord, after all, and that fluid does travel through the brain." He bandaged my arm and straightened up. "I've got to go make my rounds to the others. I'll send this to the university and will let you know when we have the results."

He disappeared, and I heard him move on to the next bed. Fleming hesitated.

"You aren't going to tell my mom, right?" I asked.

"I would really like to." His eyes looked glassy for a moment, but he blinked and they cleared. "But it would be a breach of privacy to reveal your Apex status, even to your parents. It'd be hard to explain to them what happened without me telling them you are likely an Apex. I'd encourage you to tell your parents, though. Alison was part of the team once. She'd understand."

"No, they'd kill me," I scoffed. "Not that I'd stay dead."

Fleming wasn't impressed with my joke.

"Right, well, I expect you in class tomorrow," he said. "Remember, the Industry Fair is in just over a week, and I expect you to keep up in class even with all this going on."

I settled back into my pillows. I'd given up on getting a good grade on the project a long time ago. There'd been so much going on outside of class before. Now I had to add dealing with the fact that I might be some kind of immortal Apex to the growing list of things to focus on instead of schoolwork. I closed my eyes. For now, I was still just Sammy. I could worry about being immortal after the test results came back.

Sleep was quick to reclaim me, keeping me wrapped in a sweet, dreamless nothingness until a flurry of movement and noise pulled me back from its clutches.

"Careful, she's sleeping!"

"Not anymore!"

My curtains flew back, and Naomi's arms wrapped around my neck. Her curly hair tickled my nose.

"I'm sorry," she cried. "I should've been there, I could've helped!"

I looked over her shoulder at Wesley, who smiled apologetically. His hair was ruffled from a recent shower, and the Sickbay was brighter now.

With the bed curtain drawn back, I could see how many of the beds were filled. Desirae was in the bed next to mine, typing away furiously on her phone. Mike sat at the foot of the mattress, eating the breakfast someone had brought her. Justin was on her other side, and the bed after him was obscured by curtains.

Heather waved at me from the bed directly across the way. Tonka the Cat was curled in her lap. Everest and Carmen talked to each other from their beds next to her.

"It's alright," I hugged Naomi back. "There isn't anything you could've done."

Mike snorted from Desirae's bed.

"Believe her, I tried."

I grimaced back at him. I felt bad for disobeying his orders, but I felt worse that Fleming had taken me off scouting missions when Winnie was still missing.

"We could all hear the audio feed," Naomi gushed, finally letting me go and sitting up. "When Wesley came on and said—"

I glared at Wesley as Naomi faltered.

"I said you were dead. Everyone heard." My cheeks warmed at Wesley's words, and I looked down at my hands. It was too late to keep it from the rest of the team, then.

"Fleming and Everly think..." I trailed off, but Naomi and Wes waited patiently. "They're testing me for the Apex gene."

It was embarrassing to say it aloud. Of course I wasn't an Apex, just a poser.

"We were wondering about that, actually." Naomi smiled. I looked at them in surprise, and Wes shrugged.

"You were dead, and now you're not. How else would that be possible?" Wesley tried to smile, too, but his eyes looked hollow. I wondered if he'd slept since the raid.

My stomach rumbled, and I looked over at Mike munching on Desirae's bacon.

"Wesley, go get her breakfast," Naomi snapped. He shuffled out of the room, ducking behind the curtained bed on his way out.

Naomi turned back to me.

"He was distraught, you know," she said. "He's playing it cool now, but Everly almost had to sedate him when you first got back."

"How's everyone else?" I asked, eager to talk about anything other than me horrifying my friends by dying.

"We're good, thank you," Heather called from across the room. "Broke an arm, but it's better now!"

She waved a hand to show off her mended arm, and Tonka pawed at it playfully.

"And you?" I asked Desirae. She smiled but winced.

"Mostly sore," she said. "That guy, what'd you say his name was?"

"Hackjob," Mike said through a mouthful of bacon.

"Right, Hackjob." She rolled her eyes. "He threw me into the side of a van. Same with Everest."

Wes returned with breakfast. My stomach growled loudly as he put the tray down on my lap.

"How is he?" Naomi asked. "I saw you stop by his bed."

"Awake. Isabelle's in there right now, though."

I almost jolted out of bed, and Wesley grabbed the tray to steady it.

"Anthony's down here?" I asked. "Why? Where are the others?"

"Unlike the others, he knows about the Apex Team," Wesley explained. "It's one of the reasons I got roomed with him. His family wanted him here instead of the hospital so that's where they brought him."

"Can we see him?"

Wes carried the tray of food for me while Naomi helped me to my feet. My knees quaked, but Naomi held on tight as I took the first shaky step forward. Everly had said my mobility might be affected, but other than one of my knees giving out half-way across the room, I felt fine.

"Anthony!"

He was awake and eating breakfast off a tray like mine. Isabelle sat in a chair next to him.

"Samantha!" Anthony looked just as gaunt and haunted as he had the night before. His skin was an even more sickly color under the bright fluorescents of the Sickbay, and it stretched uncomfortably as he pulled his face into a grin. "When I heard you were on the team I almost didn't believe it!"

"I told you, you could've joined," Isabelle teased. Seeing her next to her cousin, I noticed how her ears stuck out from under her long, dark hair the same way Anthony's did. "You don't have to be an Apex."

"Actually—" Wesley started, but Naomi elbowed him. There was no need to tell everyone I might be an Apex before we knew for sure. She took the tray of food from him and set it on my lap as I sat down on the foot of the bed.

"Is it true you were the one who got me out of there?" Anthony asked.

"It was a group effort," I blushed. "Listen. At the museum. I'm—"

"Don't," Anthony interrupted. "There wasn't anything you could do."

Somehow, that only made me feel worse.

"I hate to ask, but do you know anywhere they might've taken Winnie?"

"I never saw the others. I didn't even know Winnie had been taken until this morning." He shook his head. "I'm really sorry. I wish I could help."

Isabelle glared at me.

"He's already been interrogated," she snapped, and a mini wind flurry blew at her hair. I flushed, but Anthony smiled again.

"No, it's alright. You've been out so I know you've got some catching up to do."

"Out? What do you mean 'out'?" I looked at Wesley and Naomi. "How long was I asleep?"

"It's one in the afternoon," Wesley admitted. "It was just after four in the morning when you woke up the first time."

"Why aren't you guys in class?"

"Canceled," Isabelle said. "They were worried about a counterattack. All schools on the island were closed for the day."

Everly disbanded us after letting us talk with Anthony for a bit. He had begun releasing the others from the Sickbay but made me spend the afternoon running through physical tests to prove I'd regained my mobility.

"I'll let you know when we get your blood results back," he said as he finally signed me out on his tablet. He handed me a stack of forms as I prepared to leave. "And that is the post-incident paperwork everyone in the field is expected to fill out. Fleming wants it by tomorrow."

Naomi was waiting in the atrium with food she'd snuck out of the cafeteria for me.

"Any word on the Apex test?" she asked as we trudged across campus to the dorm.

"Not yet." I was trying not to think about the test. "Where's Wesley?"

"He went to bed. He hasn't slept since yesterday."

Naomi walked me all the way to my room. Winnie's cold bed was still empty. I stared at it from the doorway and choked back the bitter disappointment.

"I should probably go to bed, too," I said. Naomi put a comforting hand on my shoulder. "Thanks for all your help today."

My eyes burned. I tried to blink back tears, but instead they spilled down my cheeks, hot on my skin.

"I don't have to leave yet." Naomi ushered me inside and gently shut the door behind us.

I sat down on my bed and tried to wipe away the tears. I didn't like crying in front of my friend, even if she could tell how I felt using her powers. If I didn't cry, I could pretend to have privacy.

Naomi sat next to me, Winnie's empty bed staring us down from across the room.

"We all cry at some point," she said. "You don't have to be embarrassed about it."

I choked on a laugh through my tears. Of course she knew I was embarrassed.

"It's stupid," I sniffed.

"No, it's not. I cried just last night, you know. When I thought you were dead."

"You mean when I *was* dead."

"Yeah," she said quietly. "When you were dead. When we heard Wesley, the whole room just—"

She cleared her throat. She would've felt everyone's reaction to the news at the same time.

"I'll do my best not to die anymore," I said, leaning my head on her shoulder.

"Thanks," she laughed. "Maybe after the trials you can apply to be a weapon wielder. You were pretty good with that sword. I bet you'd get killed less if you had one of those."

I laughed, even as the image of me pushing a blade into a young man's chest in my dream played in my head as she said it.

"I mean it, though," she insisted. "Crying is okay."

"We saved six people last night," I pointed out. "And then I saved Wesley, and I might be an Apex after all. I should be celebrating."

"If there's one thing I know, there's never a right way to feel." She shook her head. "What happened last night was hard and scary, and you feel like you failed Winnie."

She hopped off the bed and threw me a box of tissues from the desk.

"Again," she continued. "We all cry. Even Andersen, believe it or not."

"That I don't believe," I half-sniffed, half-laughed. I fought the urge to ask how Andersen felt when I died.

Naomi climbed onto Winnie's bed and sat facing me.

"We'll find her," she insisted. "You'll pass the trials in a couple weeks, and you'll bring her home. Promise."

26

The Results

When I woke up the next morning, Naomi was curled up on Winnie's bed with my spare blanket draped over her. I'd thankfully had a dreamless sleep, so no more nightmares about smoke and blood.

I rolled off my bed gingerly, taking care to put one foot down at a time and test each leg before trying to stand. I was stiff and sore, but otherwise, I would have no problem getting to class.

As we walked through the cafeteria late that morning, everyone we passed seemed to be talking about the recovered missing students.

"I heard they didn't get them all," one kid was saying in the cafeteria line. His friend rolled her eyes.

"Of course they didn't, they're Apex, aren't they? They've been making things worse and worse ever since they blew up downtown."

"Who blew up downtown?" I asked Naomi. She scowled.

"That was a long time ago, and they never proved it was Apex."

I vaguely remembered something Wesley had told me the day of the festival about an incident that had spurred distrust of the Apex. I wondered if it was the same event.

The TVs in the cafeteria all played the same morning news. Anchors in nice clothes and perfect hair stoically delivered the story that all but one of the missing students had been found, but no names had been released. I wondered if they'd come back to school or if their parents would move them away. Charlie's had, after the museum incident, and he hadn't even been kidnapped.

"Any news yet?" Wesley asked when he found our table.

"You'll know as soon as I do." I rubbed the inside of my arm where Everly had drawn my blood for the genetic test. "I'm sure Everly will have news by gym class."

However, Everly didn't have any results to share when we arrived downstairs for Fourth Period. My heart skipped a beat when he walked into the room as we were warming up. He went to Coach Reiner and spoke with her in the corner. I spun towards Wesley.

"What're they saying?"

"He's telling her to make sure you, Everest, and Heather don't overexert yourselves today," he reported, tilting an ear towards them. "And now she's asking if you were really dead."

"No test results?"

He shook his head and Everly left the room without glancing my way.

My stomach was in knots for the rest of my classes. I thought I might hear from Everly during after-school training, but still nothing. By dinner, I was beginning to give up on the notion that I might find out my results, but then my phone buzzed.

"He's got it," I breathed, scanning the screen. "The test results."

Wesley was collecting our dishes in an instant. I tried to help and realized my hands were shaking.

"You go on ahead," Naomi insisted. "We'll catch up."

Minutes later, I was sitting in the chair opposite Fleming in his office, trying to make sense of the paper in my hands. Out of the nonsense on the page, I could make out a big, bolded EPSLN1—NEG", followed by, "EPSLN2—NEG".

"So," I said slowly, "this says I'm not an Apex?"

Fleming shook his head.

"You tested negative for both Epsilon genes," he confirmed. "More commonly known as the Apex genes."

"I didn't know there were two genes." I wasn't surprised by the results, like a part of me had known I couldn't be an Apex, but there was a weird mix of disappointment and relief swirling inside me.

"Epsilon One expresses the ability itself while the Epsilon Two works like an 'on' switch. You need both to be able to use powers." He pushed his glasses up his nose and looked over his own copy of the results. "Most children of Apex have at least one of the genes. I myself am positive for Epsilon Two but negative for Epsilon One."

"But I have neither."

"Yes, that can happen, too." He chewed on the inside of his cheek.

I stared at the paper. I wondered if Avery had both genes.

"How am I not dead?"

Fleming sighed and leaned back in his chair so he could stare at the ceiling.

"I wish I had an answer," he admitted. "Perhaps Adrestus is an Apex with the power to kill without really killing, but that doesn't make much sense."

"He's not an Apex, he told me so."

"The other one, then? Dion?"

I shrugged, but I knew Dion hadn't been the one to bring me back to life. He'd been nowhere near me when Adrestus had killed me.

But if I wasn't an Apex, what the hell was I?

"Does this mean you're going to tell my parents?" The paper crinkled as I tightened my grip around the edges. If I wasn't an Apex, Fleming was free to tell them what had happened. I was sure to be kicked off the team once they figured out I forged the permission form. I swallowed hard.

Fleming studied my face, and I was sure he could see my lie bubbling up to the surface. His eyebrows drew together, and his eyes narrowed.

"No," he finally said. "You're fine now. No need to worry them."

I was too relieved to question why he wouldn't tell them. Might as well as take the win and move on before he changed his mind.

"Is there any news about Winnie?"

"Not yet." I hated how sorry for me he looked. "Are you alright? We have counseling services—"

"I'm fine." I stood up and jammed the papers into my pocket.

I went for the door, knowing Naomi and Wesley would be waiting on the other side.

"Samantha," Fleming said, stopping me.

"Yes?"

"Try not to get killed anymore, at least not until we know what happened."

"I'll do my best."

Naomi waited alone in the hallway. She gave an apologetic smile.

"So the mystery continues?" she said.

"You already know?"

"Wes could hear the whole thing out here with me. He let me know. Would late-night training take your mind off it? No one's in the gym."

"Yeah, sure. I'd like that." I looked around. "Where'd Wes go, if he was here?"

"He thought you might want space," Naomi grimaced. "He went to check in on Anthony a couple minutes ago."

"Oh."

"Do you want to talk—"

"No," I cut her off. "I want to fight."

I marched down the hall and shoved my way through the door into the training facility. The Sickbay doors were open, and I could hear Anthony and Wes talking. I continued to the room with the arena and threw my bag against the wall before pivoting to face Naomi, my fists already raised.

"You've gotta take it easy, remember," she said.

"The trials are in a week," I reminded her. "They're in a week, and I have no powers, and Dion was literally wiping the floor with me, and I don't have time to take it easy, so come on."

She let her bag slide off her shoulder, sighed, and took on a fighting stance.

"From what I heard, Dion wiped the floor with everyone, but fine." She grinned. "Let's go."

Naomi fought me until she got a call from Jamie about Free Froyo Friday. She apologized as she left, and I insisted it was fine, even though it wasn't.

I stopped by the Sickbay on my way out, but Wesley had already left. Anthony was asleep, already looking better than he had when I'd last seen him. Tonka was curled up at his side.

I exited as quietly as I could, wondering why Wesley had left without stopping to see us in the gym. He'd made himself sparse ever since we'd faced Adrestus on the rooftop. I figured he was just nervous waiting for the test results. Now that I had them, I was disappointed he still seemed to be avoiding me.

The results didn't really change anything, after all. If they had been positive, it wouldn't have made me magically better at fighting. It was just information. I hoped Wesley felt the same way.

The walk back to the dorms from the training facility had become familiar by this point, but it was rare for me to be taking it alone. There were still plenty of students milling around campus, most of them carrying their free froyo back to their rooms. I heard a familiar laugh and looked over.

Wesley was walking with Remi and laughed as he tried to steal a gummy worm from her yogurt bowl. She pushed away playfully. I'd never seen Wesley so much as crack a smile when Remi was around. They were exes. I thought that meant they'd agreed to hate each other forever.

Remi looked up and saw me staring. I glanced away and sped up, but it was too late.

"Sammy?"

I stopped at the sound of Wesley's voice.

"Hey!" I forced the world's most awkward laugh. I didn't want to bring up the Apex gene results with Remi right there. "I was wondering where you went."

"We need to finish our Industry Project poster this weekend, right?"

"Yeah, we can figure it out later," I said, taken aback by Wesley's sudden interest in our project. "We've got a whole week."

"How about tomorrow afternoon?"

"Oh, sure." I didn't like how he was talking to me like we were just project partners. The way he spoke was stilted and awkward. I wondered if he was embarrassed to have been caught with Remi. "I'll see you then."

He waved goodbye and started walking away with Remi. He was allowed to hang out with whoever he wanted. Besides, I barely knew her. For all I knew, she might be a perfectly fine person.

He was just my friend. I had just died for him, but we were just friends. And I was fine with that. So why was I *not* fine? The sound of him laughing as he play-fought for one of Remi's gummy worms made me squirm. He hadn't done much laughing since the rooftop. I'd thought he was just shaken by the whole ordeal, but maybe it was just me.

I tried to push away thoughts of Wesley and Remi by mentally running through drills and maneuvers all the way to the dorm, through my shower, and until I was lying in bed, but the awkwardness of our interaction was still curdling inside me.

Things were supposed to go back to normal after the test results came in, but they were weirder than ever. He knew I'd just gotten back the test results, but he went to get fake ice cream with his ex-girlfriend rather than see me. Maybe it was because I wasn't an Apex but Remi was?

I pushed the thought away, but my chest tightened.

I'll see him tomorrow, I told myself. *Everything will be normal tomorrow.*

Turned out, Wes wasn't ready for things to be normal.

He'd booked a study room in the guys' dorm for us, but a heavy silence hung over the table.

Our poster was good, not great. Our five minute presentation was less than good, but could be worse. It probably would've helped if we talked at all while we worked. Instead, we worked on our respective parts, too afraid to be the first to break the silence.

Finally, Wesley took a breath.

"Should we talk about it?"

I gulped.

"What is there to talk about?" I shrugged. If he'd wanted to talk about the Apex test, then he shouldn't have run away to hang out with Remi last night. "I'm not an Apex, just like how I wasn't an Apex two days ago."

"Then what happened?"

He'd put down his marker and looked at me, his eyes wide behind his glasses.

"I don't know." I stared at the poster. I didn't want to say what I was thinking, but I'd kept the suspicion to myself long enough. "But, I think Adrestus does."

"What's that supposed to mean?"

I pretended to focus on the corner of our poster title, attacking a lifted paper corner with my glue stick.

"I don't think he meant for me to stay dead." It was hard to sound casual while talking about my own resurrection. "I think he knows me somehow, but wasn't sure so he snapped my neck to see if I'd come back."

"He kept asking who you were," Wes murmured, rubbing his temple. "But he didn't think 'Samantha' was an acceptable answer."

"Right. And the last thing I remember before he...you know...was him saying there were other ways to find out who I was."

Wes looked like he might puke. He'd turned a faint green color.

"It was a test?"

"I think so," I said quietly. "Which makes me wonder, why does he know more about me than I do?"

Wesley shrugged and stared at me from across the table. I was glad he didn't think I was crazy, but the fact that I had finally said out loud what I'd been thinking about Adrestus meant I had to reckon with what it meant. Adrestus knew me, but I didn't know him. What's more, he knew my death would be temporary.

"Maybe he's someone from your mom's time on the team?" Wesley suggested. "You could ask her."

"No," I said vehemently, though he had a point. She'd kept plenty of secrets from me. What was one more? "Anyway, I was thinking about heading to the gym after this. Naomi helped me with some extra training last night so I thought maybe I could give her a break today and train with you.”

He didn’t meet my eye as he started packing up our poster.

“I actually have plans.”

As he said it, his phone lit up on the table. He tried to pocket it, but I saw Remi’s name flash across the screen.

“You know the trials are in a week, right?” I didn’t care if he and Remi *were* getting back together. He’d already promised he’d help me make the team. “After this week’s set-back, I need all the practice I can get.”

His hands clenched for a moment, and he finally looked up at me. His brow had furrowed in anger, and his mouth was drawn into a tight line.

“Set-back?” he echoed. “You mean how you had your neck snapped?”

I recoiled at his sudden mood swing.

“You know what I mean.”

He shook his head and haphazardly swept the glue sticks and markers on the table into his backpack, and he regained his composure.

“Do you want to keep the poster with you or should I take it?”

“I can take it,” I mumbled. “So, when can we train? I’ve been working on a new maneuver I want to show you.”

Wesley paused in his clean-up and stared aimlessly into his open backpack. My palms were sweaty, but I didn’t know why. Dread crept up my throat.

“I’m really sorry, Sammy. I am,” he said quietly, “but I don’t think I’m going to be helping Naomi train you anymore.”

27

Random Draw

I dropped back into my seat in disbelief.

"You're quitting on me?"

"Shh!" he hissed, glancing around the study room. We were alone so I wasn't sure who he was afraid would overhear us. He turned back to me, and while I was relieved to see his expression had softened, mine certainly hadn't. "I'm not sure you should try out at all, actually."

"Excuse me?" I was standing again. "Where is this coming from? You were fine with it two days ago!"

"A lot has happened since then." He shrugged as he zipped up his backpack.

"Is this because I tested negative for the Epsilon genes?" I accused him. "You've barely looked at me since last night. You didn't even hang around after eavesdropping on my conversation with Fleming."

He flushed red and stepped back from the table, looking down.

"I just don't think it's a good idea," he said quietly.

"Because I'm a Beta? You thought for two seconds I might be like you, and when it turned out I wasn't, suddenly I'm not cut out for the team?" I raised my voice to better hear myself over the sound of my heartbeat pounding in my ears. "Sorry I can't be as extraordinary as everything else in your life, but nothing's changed! I'm still the same lousy Beta I was before."

"Everything's changed!" Wes exploded, and I shrank back. "Sammy, you died, and you don't even care! And I had to watch! I heard your neck snap, and I held your dead body. Even if you're alive now, that still happened, and we have no idea how you came back."

"But I'm still me," I insisted. "And I was trying to save you."

"That's the problem," he glowered. "I'd rather be prisoner than have you die for me, and I know you'll do it again. I won't let that happen."

He threw his backpack over his shoulder and turned away. I half-ran to the door to stop him from walking out. For once, could he not be the hero? And what the hell was this new surly attitude?

"So that's it? This is all over then?" Angry tears stung my eyes. I ignored them.

"For me, yeah. I already talked to Naomi, and she says she'll keep training you. She's better than me at that stuff anyways."

His words reeked of betrayal.

"When did you talk to Naomi about this?"

"Thursday, while Everly was clearing you to leave the Sickbay," he confessed. "I didn't think there was any way you couldn't be an Apex, but I told Naomi if you were negative, I was done."

"You don't get to decide if I join the team or not," I spat. "That's not your decision to make."

"No, you're right, it's not. But I'm not going to be complicit next time you get murdered."

I had half a mind to bash our poster over his head.

"That's not fair, so many of the others have powers that don't keep them safe! How would Naomi have been any safer on that roof? Or Freddie with his stupid fog power? Tell me how Marcus's heat vision would have stopped Adrestus from breaking his neck. Even you were helpless after they drugged you!"

"But Adrestus doesn't care about Naomi, or Freddie, or Marcus, or me!" Wesley pointed out. His voice trembled as he tried to keep it low so we wouldn't be overheard in the hall. "But it's you he's gone after over and over, and now he knows you're on the team."

"And I've got away every time!"

"You're not listening to me!" Wesley spun around to slam a fist on the table in frustration. "You didn't get away! How many times do I have to say that? You died. He murdered you, and you were there because of me."

"When are you going to realize not everything is your fault?" I stared at the space between his shoulder blades as I quaked with anger and disappointment. "I was up there because I decided to be. You do this every time! You blame yourself for everything, but, Wesley Isaacs, the world doesn't revolve around you!"

"It doesn't revolve around you, either!"

He spun back to face me, and we stood there, both red in the face. I was still blocking the door, but I knew I couldn't keep him there forever.

"It doesn't matter," he finally said. "I've made up my mind, and I've already told Fleming."

He pulled his phone from his pocket and scowled.

"I have to go," he mumbled. I stepped aside to let him pass. I wanted to yell and scream at him until he changed his mind, but I knew it was useless.

"Great, well, I'm not quitting!" I yelled after him.

He continued into the hall, pretending to have not heard me and leaving me with our poster to wonder what had just happened.

The week leading up to the Industry Project Fair seemed to drag on forever. As promised, Desirae and Mike volunteered to spar with me, along with some of the other upperclassmen. I should've been feeling optimistic and confident with the progress I was making, but my fight with Wesley hung over everything I did. I still sat by him in class, but neither of us acknowledged our argument. As angry as I was, I knew when I made the team, I'd have to work with him, and as much as I wanted to hate him, it was hard to muster up that kind of animosity toward someone who'd sobbed over your dead body just a few days before.

While I obsessed over the upcoming trials, the rest of the school's sophomores seemed to only talk about the Industry Fair and how the big Homecoming dance was approaching. Students had started seeking out dates, and Wednesday morning, we walked into First Period to see a mountain of flowers piled on Jamie's desk.

She squealed in delight as Andersen climbed onto a table to ask her to the dance while their friends clapped. I didn't see what the big deal was. They were boyfriend and girlfriend. It couldn't have been that much of a surprise.

Jamie carried her flowers to every class that day, even though Fleming had offered his classroom as a place to keep them until school was over. Watching her lug them through the hall, my stomach clenched as I imagined Remi carrying flowers throughout the school after Wesley asked her.

I shook my head. It didn't matter if Wesley did ask her to the dance because I didn't like Wesley that way. He deserved to be happy with whoever he wanted, and Remi probably did, too.

I still hated it, though.

I tried not to think about Wesley's rekindled friendship with Remi. Instead, I threw myself at my training with Naomi to the point where she had to remind me that she had schoolwork to do. After Winnie had been kidnapped, Naomi had gotten stuck finishing the Industry Project without a partner. I'd seen her poster. It was much better than the one Wesley and I had worked on together.

The worst part about training, though, was watching the patrols coming and going. After we had raided the secret hideout last week, Fleming had eased up on scouting missions. However, Winnie was still missing, and the abandoned building the others had been kept in yielded plenty of new leads to follow according to the incident report Fleming had handed out to each of us.

I scanned over the document, but my stomach churned where it outlined how the missing students had been tested on and drugged according to their interviews. They weren't able to remember details because of the drugs, but Anthony reported feeling something like electricity and fire coursing through his blood.

They still had Winnie, who was still enduring the same torture the others had been through. Every moment I wasn't out searching for her weighed on me, but, true to his word, Fleming wasn't allowing me in the field. Instead, I was stuck at the computer, clicking through Winnie's pictures with Wesley in awkward silence.

By Thursday night, the dorm hall was decorated with balloons, signs, and flowers as more and more of my neighbors were asked to the dance. They displayed the bounties they'd won from whoever had asked them on their doors.

As I came back after my second-to-last day of official training, I passed Bethany in the common room. Anthony, while he hadn't officially rejoined classes, had finally been allowed out of the Sickbay, and Bethany was retelling the story of how he'd come to her Fifth Period to ask her to the dance.

I waved at her as I passed, and she beamed back.

I pulled out my notes on the Industry Project when I got back to my room. Between my training, sorting through Winnie's pictures, and Wesley being out on patrols, we hadn't had much time to practice our presentation.

I had only just gotten through the introduction when there was a knock at the door.

"Sammy?" Wesley called from the other side. "Are you in there?"

"It's unlocked!" I called back. I pretended to be extra focused on my schoolwork as the door opened behind me.

"Do you have a moment?"

I glanced up from my work and twisted in my chair to look at him. He wavered in the doorway, his cheeks a deep red.

"You better not be here to tell me not to try out next week."

"No, but I still think you shouldn't."

I glared at him and turned back to my notebook.

"You can come all the way in, you know. No need to lurk."

He shuffled inside, and I heard the door click shut.

"When'd you get that?" Wesley asked.

"When'd I get what?"

He pointed at a plastic cup of water sitting on the windowsill. A brightly colored fish twisted and floated within its confines, its blue tail fanning out behind it.

"That's not mine!"

"It's in your room, so it's got to be yours." Wesley leaned in to inspect it. "Are we even allowed to keep fish?"

I joined Wesley at the window for a closer look.

"When would I have had time to go out and buy a betta fish?" Delighted confusion gave way to a pit in my stomach. I straightened up. "Oh, I get it now. Betta fish, as in Beta."

"It's not that clever," Wesley sniffed, trying to make me feel better. "They aren't even spelt the same way."

I attempted to smile back at him.

"It's fine. Free fish, anyway."

He didn't look convinced.

"If you tell Fleming, he'll—"

"If I didn't tell Fleming when Andersen tried to drown me, why would I tell him about this?" I snapped. "Why are you here, anyway?"

I turned away from the fish and sat on my bed. Wesley hesitated, growing red again.

Someone knocked on the door just as he opened his mouth, and Naomi stuck her head inside. She looked grim.

"Head's up," she warned. "Andersen's in the common room, and he felt a little too happy."

We both pointed at the fish without a word. She followed our fingers to the windowsill.

"Oh." She came into the room for a better look. "It's not that clever. They aren't even spelt the same."

"That's what I said!" Wesley exclaimed.

"What's Andersen doing in the common room?" I scowled. "And how'd he get a fish in here?"

"I can feel emotions, but I'm not clairvoyant." Naomi looked between the two of us, and her brow furrowed in suspicion. "What're you guys doing in here anyway? Other than looking at the fish."

"I was just asking Sam a question about the project fair this weekend," Wesley said quickly.

"No you weren't," I said. "You haven't talked to me about the fair all week."

Wesley turned an even deeper shade of red.

"Yeah, well, I was about to ask you about it, but there was a fish, and then Naomi showed up."

Naomi leaned back against the door.

"Sure." She continued to squint at us. "I'll leave you to it, then."

She slipped back out the door. As she closed it, I heard Andersen shout down the hall.

"Hey, Naomi, did she find it?"

"It really is a dumb joke." I shrugged. Wesley visibly gulped. "What did you want to say about the fair this weekend? I was just looking over my notes when you showed up."

"Oh, I—"

But he was interrupted again as my phone buzzed violently on my desk. Dad's name lit up on the screen, and I smiled sheepishly.

"Sorry, I should probably answer this."

Wesley nodded.

"Yeah, you probably should," he agreed, hurrying towards the door.

"But we can meet up tomorrow after training to go over the project more, if you like."

"The project, right." He continued to nod. "Yeah, tomorrow works."

He waved goodbye and backed into the hallway as I answered Dad's call.

"Hey, Dad."

"Hey, kid. How's everything going?"

It's been horrible.

"It's been alright."

"Listen, I'm sure by now you've figured that they didn't find Winnie last week. She was the only one they weren't able to find."

"Yeah, I know," I said quietly. "How's Mr. Hendricks?"

"Better than his wife, from what I've heard." Dad's sigh crackled over the phone. "I hadn't heard from you so I was just making sure you were holding up okay."

"Yeah, I'm good."

"Really?" he teased. "I had a whole plan to cheer you up."

"Did it involve sushi?"

"It might have."

"When will you be outside?"

"I can be there in ten, if you like."

"Yeah," I said quietly. "I'd like that."

We spent the drive to the sushi place in silence. Fleming wanted me to tell my parents about what had happened with Adrestus, but even trying to think of what words I'd use caused my stomach to twist painfully. I would have to tell them I was on the team if I did.

Dad wasn't even the best parent to tell first. He hated Apex. At least Mom was one and had even been on the team with a non-Apex like me. She might understand, even if she didn't like it.

If Dad found out, he might move the whole family off the island again.

"How are classes?" Dad asked when we sat down at our table at the restaurant. "You've got that big project going on, right?"

"Yeah, the Industry Project," I said. "You and Mom are coming this weekend, right?"

He grinned.

"I wouldn't miss it. Besides, this is the project you almost died for, isn't it?"

I rolled my eyes.

"Almost kidnapped for, you mean."

"Text your mom, tell her where and when, and we'll be there." He smiled.

We fell back into awkward silence.

"I'm sorry about Winnie," Dad finally said. I shrugged.

"We'll find her." My face flushed with heat. "I mean, my friends will."

Dad didn't seem to notice my slip-up.

"Those two who came to the house," Dad said. "Were they there last week?"

"Wes was," I said slowly.

"Is he okay?"

I swallowed hard.

"He's a bit shaken up. One of his teammates was injured pretty bad. He saw it happen."

"Will they be alright?"

"Oh, yeah," I said. "She's already better, but it was still scary."

Dad sighed and put his head in his hands.

"I don't know how Roy did it with Amanda," he admitted. "I can't imagine having a kid mixed up in all that. I'm gonna have to get used to it somehow, though."

My mouth fell open, and my heart jumped into my throat.

"How—"

"We've been meaning to tell you." Dad raised his head. The lines on his face seemed to have deepened over the last few weeks, as if the move to New Delos had him aging faster.

"How long have you known?" I couldn't believe it. The secret that had been eating at me wasn't a secret at all.

"A while now, to be honest." Dad chuckled. "All the signs were there, I just didn't want to see them."

I hadn't seen Mom and Dad too much over the last few weeks. Maybe I shouldn't have brought Wes and Naomi to their house. Letting Amanda in on the secret probably didn't help, either. I should have texted them more. I'd been so busy with training, I'd barely called to say hi.

"Does Avery know?"

Dad laughed, and my stomach loosened a little. If he was laughing, he couldn't be that mad.

"We thought about waiting to tell him," Dad sighed. "It didn't seem fair, though, so we had Alex come over and talk to him."

"You mean Mr. Fleming?" I nearly shouted. "Why'd you have him over, but not me? Don't you think I should've been part of that conversation?"

"I told Alison you'd be mad we left you out, but she didn't want to wait."

"And how'd Avery take it?"

"Oh, well, he's thrilled," Dad said, unable to hide his exasperation. "He hasn't stopped talking about it."

A waitress brought a platter of sushi to the table. Dad began piling his plate with fish.

"Really?" I couldn't help the surge of pride in my chest. The idea of Avery talking about his superhero big sister made me even more determined to make the team next week. The look on Dad's face brought me back down to Earth, though. Even with a plate of his favorite food in front him, he seemed crestfallen. "I'm really sorry, you know."

He shrugged and attempted a smile.

"That's what I get, marrying an Apex. She was bound to pass it down," he winked. "At least I've still got you."

I faltered and silently repeated his words in my head until they made sense. My insides did a backflip. He wasn't talking about me at all.

He was talking about Avery.

"Are you alright?" Dad asked. I quickly composed my face. If I revealed I'd only just put together what he was talking about, I might give away that I was on the team. It was a miracle Fleming hadn't said something about it when he went to see Avery.

"Yeah, it's just a lot to process."

I scraped a few rolls of sushi onto my plate.

So, Avery was an Apex. I'd be a senior by the time he was in high school and old enough to join the team. If Mom and Dad didn't know my secret by then, Avery was sure to tell them.

"So, what's he do?" I asked. "I mean, what's his ability?"

"It's a little abstract," Dad said, his mouth full of fish. "He's an Inculcator like Alison. While she can share information through touch, he can put thoughts and ideas in people's heads and make them believe they're their own."

"I don't understand how they're different."

"In layman's terms, your brother is very, very convincing. He can ask for an extra helping of dessert, and he'll get it because we think it was our idea to give it to him."

"Oh." I sank back in my seat. "That's actually kinda terrifying."

"Try being his parent!" Dad exhaled. "He's a good kid, but that's why we had Alex over to talk to him. He'll have to have specialized training, even if he doesn't join the team when he's old enough. It's a lot of power for one preteen to have."

I couldn't help but to feel a little jealous. I'd had to claw my way into Apex Team and still didn't have a secured spot. Meanwhile, Avery was already getting special training two years before he would even be able to think about joining. For him, the Final Trial would be as simple as telling his opponent to not fight him once they were in the ring.

I pushed the jealousy away. Even though I was doing everything in my power to get Winnie back, I wouldn't let myself become bitter like she had.

"I'm happy for him," I asserted, and I was. "He was all over Naomi and Wes when they were over."

"They'll be the ones in charge of dealing with him in a couple years, I'm sure."

Just tell him, part of me screamed. *He's already dealing with one kid being an Apex, this will be nothing on top of that.*

"Has work been okay?"

I couldn't do it.

"I've been covering a lot of Mr. Hendricks's classes," Dad said. "He's been pretty worked up over Winnie."

And we were back on Winnie. Dad must've seen the look that passed over my face at the mention of her.

"We don't have to talk about Winnie," he said quickly. "Have you thought anymore about what I said about that boy?"

I blushed furiously.

"You mean Wesley? I told you, we're just friends. Besides, I think he's getting back together with his ex."

"What?" Dad exclaimed, surprisingly loud. "What's she got that you don't?"

"Apex powers, for one thing."

"Eh," Dad growled. "I knew I didn't like him."

"I thought you wanted me to not date Wesley!"

"I don't! But he's an idiot to hang out with any girl other than you."

"I'm sure she's nice."

"Maybe, but there's a reason they're exes. I'm sure I'll get my chance to scare him off yet."

Dad drove me back to campus. He parked outside the dorm as he usually did and turned to me before letting me out.

"Listen, kid, I know all this business with your brother has got to be a lot." He cleared his throat before continuing. "But I'm really freaking proud of you, okay? More than you know."

He looked like he wanted to say more. His lips parted, and his eyebrows knit together, but he shook his head.

"I love you, alright?" he mustered.

"I love you, Dad," I said. "I'll see you Saturday, okay?"

He smiled and let me out after kissing the top of my head. The bristles of his beard tickled my forehead.

"I'll see you Saturday," he repeated. I shut the door behind me, and he rolled down the window to call after me. "And you tell that project partner of yours he better watch out for me when I get there!"

I hurried away from the family car before he could embarrass me any further, but his booming laugh followed me as he rolled the window up and drove away.

Everyone spent Friday gearing up for the project fair the next day while I remained hyper-focused on the fact that it was my last day of training. I glazed over in my classes, running drills in my head.

I systematically ran through the entire team, imagining myself against each one of them. There were only a few I was worried about and enlisted the help of Heather to get in a few more practice rounds against her. Even though we were friends, and I was sure Heather wanted me on the team, I knew she'd never go easy on me.

As after school training wound to a close, Fleming stood at the front of the gym.

"I want everyone in the sparring room in fifteen!" He pulled a cloth bag out of his jacket pocket. "If you're late, you owe me laps!"

"What's going on?" I asked Naomi.

"He's probably drawing names for the Final Trials."

"We're drawing names today?" I hissed at Naomi. "I'm not ready!"

"It'll be fine, it gives you a whole week to strategize against whoever you get paired with."

A wave of nausea rolled over me, and I swallowed the bile in my throat.

After everyone finished up in the locker room, we filed into the sparring room. I sat next to Naomi on the bleachers and did my best to not look at Wesley when he walked in with Everest.

Fleming stood in the center of the mat, his baggie in hand. He did a quick head count, and as the final student came hurrying in, he called for our attention.

"Just a quick reminder, there's no afternoon training next week, but you are all free to come and watch the trials. If your name is called to take part in the Final Trial on Friday, you need to be here and ready by four." He gave the baggie a dramatic shake. "And with that said, we'll start with Chris."

A freshman sitting right in front of me gulped audibly. Fleming reached into the bag and read the name.

"You'll be fighting Marcus."

Chris sighed in relief. Marcus wasn't a heavyweight. His relief only made me more nervous. There was one less name in the bag that I felt confident fighting.

"Danielle!" Another freshman tensed up down the bench when Fleming said her name. "You're up against Andersen."

Dang it. I would have loved to fight Andersen.

Luckily, Heather's name was drawn next, to fight Jessa. It was a small relief knowing I wouldn't be sparring against her. Jessa seemed nice, though. I hoped she felt more confident than I would have against Heather.

Fleming went down the Freshmen roster, one by one. I tried to keep track in my head of who had been called, but it was difficult since I was also keeping a running list of who I was hoping to be put against. Mike or Desirae would be easy. Freddie, too. Justin would be tricky, but maybe there was a way to turn his freezing powers against him.

Finally, Fleming locked eyes with me. His mouth tightened into a thin line. I thought he might be as nervous as I felt.

"Finally, our one Sophomore trying out, Samantha."

Everyone got quiet as Fleming reached inside the bag a final time. He looked at the name on the paper. I couldn't help but to feel like I noticed his shoulders fall a little bit.

"Wesley." He waved the paper dismissively. There was an uproar as the others began yelling in protest. I barely heard any of it. Blood roared in my ears, and I was glad to be sitting because my legs began to shake.

"That's not allowed!" Skyler was shouting. "He coached her!"

"He's gonna let her win!"

"How's that fair to any of the freshmen? They don't get to fight against their own classmates!"

I stared ahead blankly as Fleming tried to regain control of the room.

"Wesley gave up his training position!" he shouted over his students. "And I trust he'll give Samantha as fair a fight as anyone."

I chanced a glance in Wesley's direction. His face was stony, and his jaw clenched.

Even as the others yelled that he would go easy on me, I knew that Wesley Isaacs would never let me on the team.

Lucky for him, there was one person in the room I knew I couldn't beat, and Fleming had just drawn his name.

28

Industry Fair

Ａs soon as Fleming finished talking, I bolted for the door and pretended not to hear him calling me back.

"Samantha!"

He caught up in the atrium and stopped me with a hand on my shoulder. The other students filed past us. Even though they probably weren't, I felt like each of them was gawking at me.

"Come here." Fleming waved me through the door that led to the parking garage corridor. We were away from the rest of the team now, but I knew Naomi and Wes would still be able to find me.

"I'm sorry."

"You drew his name on purpose," I accused. "You don't want me on the team because you're afraid of my mom!"

"While your mom can be terrifying, I didn't rig it."

"Can't you redraw? Wesley trained me for most of the month! Isn't that a conflict of interest?"

Fleming ran his hand through his hair.

"That rule's in place to keep trainers from letting their trainees just walk onto the team. If Wesley was going to do that, I don't think you'd be asking me for a redraw."

I scowled and turned to walk away.

"Wait."

"What?" I turned back towards Fleming. He was leaning against the wall, and he bit his cheek, making it dimple.

"I had to fight someone close to me, too."

"So what?" I scoffed. "Even if I somehow beat Wesley, no one will believe it was fair. They'll all think he let me win, even after everything I've done to prove myself."

The deep lines of Fleming's frown told me he already knew all that.

"It was my brother," he said simply. "He was a Team Captain. No one on the team could beat him, although Alison might have stood a chance."

Fleming had never mentioned having a brother. Neither had Mom or Mr. Hendricks. The new information caught me off guard, but I continued to glower.

"But you did beat him, which is more than I'll be able to say about Wesley in a week."

"I had the benefit of knowing about a skiing accident when he was twelve. I knew exactly where to hit him to make him fall."

"Why are you telling me this?"

"I want to remind you what I said when you first came down here. No matter what you do, you'll lose, even when you win. I took my brother down in one hit and still get questioned about the legitimacy of my membership."

That I did know. I'd heard Mr. Hendricks talk about Fleming enough times.

"I'm not joining the team so that people like me," I asserted, though it made me sad as I said it. "I'm joining the team to find Winnie, and maybe a few years down the line, I'll get to give my own brother the chance to fight me for a spot on the team."

Fleming's eyes narrowed.

"So you've heard."

I shrugged.

"My parents aren't great at keeping secrets now that we know about Mom."

I thought Fleming's face darkened for a moment, but he cleared his throat and pushed open the door back into the atrium.

"Yes, well, hopefully down the line you realize you don't need to keep secrets from them either."

Even though I went to bed early that night, I didn't fall asleep until well after midnight. Until then, I ran through every possible way to take on Wesley in a fight, but even in my imagination, I lost every time.

When morning came, I tried to hide from the daylight and sounds of the rest of the hall getting ready for the fair by burrowing under my pillow, but was drawn out when I heard my door open.

"You really should lock your door at night, you know."

I leaped out of bed so fast that I made myself dizzy. Naomi stood at my wardrobe, her done-up hair and make up clashing with her jeans and old t-shirt.

"Holy crap, Naomi," I mumbled. "You might want to try knocking next time."

"I wasn't convinced you'd let me in if I gave you a choice."

I flinched as she opened the blinds.

"Watch out for Floundersen," I grumbled.

"Who?"

I pointed at the betta fish, swimming blithely in his new tank on the windowsill.

"You named him Floundersen?" she giggled. I grinned in spite of myself.

Naomi helped herself to my closet, throwing the doors open.

"My dress shirt has a hole in it," she said, flipping through the hangers. "You have anything that goes with navy slacks?"

She helped herself to a blouse and held it up for me to see.

"Yeah, that's fine," I yawned.

"You sure? What are you wearing?"

"That dress there." I pointed vaguely into the closet. I crawled back onto my bed and pulled my blanket up over my face. "We don't have to be on the bus until two, though. What's the rush?"

Naomi pulled the dress off the hanger to throw at me.

"You know it's past noon, right?"

"What!?"

I yanked my phone away from its power cord. Sure enough, it was already 12:30. My stomach growled.

"Get cute, and we can stop for lunch before heading to the bus." Naomi was surveying my closet again. "What were you planning on wearing to Homecoming, by the way?"

"This." I held the dress up. Naomi shook her head.

"I'm not letting you go to the dance dressed like you are headed to a board meeting."

"It's cute!"

"Sure, for career day. I've got some extra dresses from last year," she assured me on her way out the door. "You can try them on sometime."

I threw my outfit together, wiggling into the black, high collared dress and pulling my hair into a braid. Naomi was waiting by the elevators when I was done. She snorted as she watched me try to maneuver down the hall with both my presentation poster and notes folder.

"If I didn't know any better, I'd think you were trying to hide behind that poster," she said, tucking her own poster neatly under her arm.

I scowled, sidestepping into the elevator.

"I don't want people to talk to me."

"Good thing we're headed to an event where all you have to do to pass the project is talk to people."

"I can talk to strangers," I said. "It's the people I know that I'm avoiding."

The elevator doors slid open. The lobby was full of students in business-wear and carrying posters.

"You're going to have to talk to Wesley today," Naomi pointed out.

"All I need to do with Wesley is read off our presentation notes." I held my poster in front of my face while we walked. "That's all scripted so, no, I don't have to talk to Wesley."

"It's not his fault his name was pulled."

I scowled

"Doesn't mean he wasn't glad about it."

"He wasn't."

"Then he shouldn't have quit on me."

As we walked across campus, I was already wishing I'd worn my sneakers. My dress shoes were rubbing against my heels.

"I don't think he thought it through that far, to be honest," Naomi sighed. "Try to be nice today, okay? He's just as upset as you over all this."

It was hard to imagine that stony, stoic Wesley with his clenched jaw and brooding expression had any feelings about the whole thing.

"Not that anyone would've been able to tell."

"Except me."

I rolled my eyes but couldn't argue.

"I'll be nice if he's nice," I said begrudgingly.

"I'm sure he'll be perfectly pleasant. He cares about you, probably more than anyone else on the team."

I wrinkled my nose at her but felt my heart soften a little bit.

"Don't be dumb, he cares a lot about you, too."

"True, but he cares more about you."

"Don't say that!"

"Why not? It's true, and I'm okay with that. He cares a lot about me, like you said, but he's already been through more with you than he has with anyone."

"Then why doesn't he want me on the team permanently?"

"I can tell you people's feelings but not why they feel them," she laughed. "But, find a way to beat him, and it'll be his problem, not yours."

I shot off a few texts to my parents as we ate lunch, reminding them what time the fair started. By the time we made it to the rotunda in front of the main school hall, most of the school's sophomores had already gathered under the Paragon fountain. The history teachers stood at the front of the crowd, each of them waving a clipboard as they tried to corral their students.

Several school buses waited at the curb along with squad cars from the city police.

"What's with the cops?" I asked.

"Security at this thing is going to be insane after everything that's happened," Naomi explained. "Fleming assigned most of the seniors to patrol around the Schrader Hotel, and there's probably more students from the university scouting, too."

Fleming began reading names off his clipboard and filing us into one of the buses. When he called my name with Wesley's, I was forced to leave Naomi's side and meet Wes at the bus door.

"Oh, good, you brought the poster," he said, attempting a smile. I tried to smile back and was sure it looked more like a grimace.

He sat down in the bus seat next to me. The poster sat awkwardly between us, forming a barrier.

"Are your parents coming?" Wesley asked from his side of the poster.

"Yeah." I forced myself to sound amicable. "They should be there right when it starts."

With the last students taking their seats, the bus shuddered beneath us, and with a lurch, we were headed out of the rotunda. Wesley wrestled the poster to the floor. He grinned at me when he'd finally gotten it out of the way. His hair had been carefully combed earlier in an attempt to look nice, but it was already sticking out in odd spots.

I swallowed my pride and reached over to flatten them with my hand.

"Did it get messed up already?" Wesley asked. He tried to catch his reflection in the window next to me. He frowned and began fussing with his tie.

"It looks fine, don't mess with it."

"Easy for you to say! You look—" He cut himself off abruptly and looked towards the front of the bus, his cheeks glowing. We fell back into an awkward silence while the rest of the bus buzzed with excitement. Fleming yelled at someone to stay in their seat.

"So," Wes said, cutting the silence, "are we gonna talk about it?"

"Nope."

The bus came to a stop in. the part of the city where the buildings were the tallest. We were out front of Schrader Hotel. A big banner hung across its extravagant glass doors, welcoming the island students.

Fleming herded us into the main lobby. I gawked up at the high vaulted ceilings and the splashing water features. The marble floor met with opulent walls decorated in gold gilding. I imagined it was usually full of fancy business people, but today it was overrun with teenagers in ill-fitting button-ups and poorly tied ties.

"Everyone, please stick together!" Fleming shouted, leading the way down a side hall toward "Ballroom A".

The ballroom was just as fancy as the main lobby with the same marbled floor and gold gilding, but the grandeur was undercut by rows of rickety fold-out tables, already filling with poster projects. A temporary stage had been put up on one end of the room. A salt-and-pepper haired man was talking to a sharply dressed gentleman in a navy suit. He had sandy hair that was neatly gelled back, and he towered over his friend.

"Is that Adrian Schrader?" I asked. Wesley followed my gaze, and his eyes widened.

"Yeah! It is! I didn't know he'd be here!"

Adrian Schrader looked exactly like the kind of man whose family would own half an island. Even from across the ballroom, his wide grin was infectious.

"Isn't that the museum guy with him?" Wesley added.

"Museum guy?" I squinted at the shorter man. "Oh! Dr. Cunningham!"

The last time I had seen Dr. Cunningham, he'd been unconscious on the floor of his own exhibit. It was nice to see that, at least from this distance, he was doing alright.

We found our assigned table near the middle of the room, situated among the other students from New Delos prep. Naomi stood alone at her poster a few tables away. Heather and Madison were directly across from us. Their poster was beautiful.

I sighed and looked back at our display. The pictures we'd pasted on the board were already coming up at the corners.

"It could be prettier," I admitted. Wesley shrugged.

"Considering everything that happened with this project, I don't think the goal was ever to pass it, but to survive it."

More and more posters went up around us as the rest of the city's sophomores filed in and found their spaces. I pulled my phone out of my purse to see if Mom or Dad had texted back yet, but they hadn't.

I shot them another text, telling them where in the room we were, and shoved the phone back in my purse.

"Miss Havardson," someone behind me said, "I was hoping I'd run into you today."

I turned around to find Dr. Cunningham. His blue eyes glittered as he approached our table.

"It's good to see you're doing well," I said politely.

"Thanks to you both," he replied. Wesley shifted next to me, and I wondered if he was feeling guilty again for being bested at the museum. "I've been wanting to thank you for your brave efforts at the beginning of the school year. I know I was out for most of it, but I've heard you did incredible things to keep your friends safe."

"It was nothing," I said, looking to Wesley for help. Dr. Cunningham was just as awkward to talk to as ever, and it was hard to take praise knowing Winnie was still out there somewhere.

"Of course, I hear one of the students still hasn't been found," Dr. Cunningham said, as if reading my mind. "But that doesn't mean you shouldn't be proud. Same goes to you, Mr. Isaacs."

"Thanks," Wesley muttered.

"I'm sure Mr. Schrader would love to meet you both," Dr. Cunningham continued. "When I see him next, I'll direct him this way."

"You don't need to do that!" I flushed. I'd rather not be talked up to the most powerful man in New Delos just for him to come by and see my lackluster poster.

Dr. Cunningham's laughter reminded me of something, but I couldn't place what.

"Such a hero-type, ever humble," he said.

"Oh, I'm not—" I glanced at Wesley again, but he was looking around the room, presumably for a way out. "Thank you, I mean."

A speaker system crackled overhead, and a woman's voice echoed around the room.

"Welcome, students, to the fourth annual New Delos Industry Project Fair!"

There was a half-hearted spattering of applause. Dr. Cunningham looked up at the stage.

"That's the superintendent," he said, as the woman continued to welcome us all and began outlining the format of the fair. "They'll need me up front. I'll be by again with the judge's panel."

His eyes flickered over our poster as he left, but he kept his carefully composed smile when he saw it.

Madison was squinting at us suspiciously from her and Heather's display.

"What did he mean by 'incredible things'?" she demanded. "What happened at the museum the night the others got kidnapped?"

"Calm down," Heather rolled her eyes at her partner. "They were attacked, you know that. No need to remind them."

"Why did he call you a hero-type?" Madison pressed.

"I'm not an Apex, if that's what you're getting at." Now it was my turn to roll my eyes at Madison.

The superintendent finished her welcome speech, and the fair officially began. We stood at our poster, reciting notes and facts to anyone who bothered to stop by. The benefit to having an ugly poster was that not many people were interested in asking about it.

Mom and Dad would be arriving soon. I wondered if they'd bring Avery. I looked over at Madison. I couldn't trust Avery to keep quiet about his newfound identity as an Apex, and I definitely couldn't trust Madison not to listen in. I didn't care if she ran back to Jamie and told her I was one, but I wasn't about to ruin Avery's shot at anonymity right off the bat.

I glanced over at Wesley. For his sake, I wanted his tie on straight when Dad came by. His hair was messed up again, but I let it be. It looked better that way.

Wesley cleared his throat. I stiffened. If he was about to bring up the trials, I would walk away.

"Do you think after all this today, we can talk?"

I crossed my arms and refused to look at him.

"Depends on what you want to talk about."

"Nothing bad!" he said quickly. I looked around at the empty walkway.

"Why can't we talk now?"

He blushed.

"We're busy right now."

"Yeah." I nodded solemnly. "We're absolutely slammed at the moment, aren't we?"

"Okay, I just don't want to talk here."

Madison was still glaring at us from across the way.

"Why not?"

"Wesley! There you are!"

I clenched my fists and plastered a fake-welcoming smile on my face for Remi as she approached us.

"Hey!" Wesley lit up. "Where's your poster?"

She jerked her thumb over her shoulder.

"Back there. Bethany's watching it for us, but the judges shouldn't be coming around to our section for another half hour at least so I thought I'd come say hi."

She grabbed his hand, and I felt myself bristle.

"This'll look better if you roll these up." She giggled and began rolling his sleeves for him.

I didn't understand. Almost every other time I'd seen them together, they'd looked ready to murder each other, but they'd been on-off boyfriend and girlfriend according to Anthony. Maybe they were wading back into "On" territory.

"Hey, if the judges aren't going to be here for a while, I'm gonna go find the snack table," I said dryly. Wesley's eyes widened.

"Wait—"

But Remi had him trapped by his other sleeve now.

The snack table was against the back wall and covered in an array of cheese and crackers. As I loaded my plate, I tried to distract myself from thoughts of Wes and Remi by wondering if my family had arrived yet instead. I had a clear view of the main doors and kept glancing over, thinking they could be walking in any moment.

"Cheese break for you, too?" Naomi appeared at my side. "What's up? You feel funny."

"There's just a lot of people here," I lied. "Dr. Cunningham came by our table."

"Really? How is he?"

"A little awkward, so, as far as I can tell, normal for him."

"I hope that's not my curator you're talking about."

We both jumped as Adrian Schrader himself loomed over us. He was handsome, with sandy hair and a neatly trimmed beard. He extended a well-manicured hand for a handshake. I accepted it clumsily.

"No, Dr. Cunningham is..." I looked to Naomi for help, but she was frozen with a confused look on her face. "He's really nice, I'm sorry."

Adrian Schrader laughed. It was a charming sound.

"I'm only messing with you both. Samantha Havardson, I presume? Of course he's told me about both of you, and I've watched the security footage." He winked. "Both of you are excellent fighters for being so young."

Naomi smiled politely, but her eyes were cold.

"Thanks, but we've got to get back to our posters."

"What's the rush? I almost forgot to introduce myself! Adrian Schrader." He went to shake Naomi's hand next. She took it tentatively. "Naomi Bradford, right?"

She smiled, but didn't confirm her name.

"We really need to get going," she insisted.

"I can't argue with students who are enthusiastic about their work."

Naomi scowled as soon as we turned away.

"You lecture me on being nice to Wesley, but could you have been any ruder? Doesn't the guy bankroll the whole school?"

Naomi frowned at her cheese and crackers.

"Something was off about him," she said quietly.

I looked over her shoulder at Schrader, who was now talking up a group of teachers. They laughed at something he said.

"What kind of 'off'?" I asked, suddenly much quieter. "Fun, quirky off? Or up-to-something kind of off?"

Naomi shook her head and squinted as if she was trying to do math in her head.

"No, like, empty?" She shrugged and came out of her reverie. "He's a blackhole. I can't feel him."

"A sociopath?" I looked back at the charming billionaire. Naomi snorted.

"Sociopaths still feel. This guy, though, it's like he's not even there."

"Maybe he's an Apex?" I offered. "With an ability that cancels or blocks other abilities?"

Naomi shrugged.

"Might be, but I thought Schrader was a non-Apex," she mused. She held up a cracker to mine as if she were toasting with them. "I'm sure it's nothing, I just don't like being around people that I can't read."

I looked around the crowded ballroom. I would've thought a person she couldn't read would be a relief in what was sure to be a caterwauling of different emotions. If she wasn't worried, though, I shouldn't be, either.

"Oh, hey!" She lit up and snickered. "Someone just got bad news. I'm not sure where, but I can definitely feel it. I wonder if the judges gave someone a bad score. Gives us a better shot at winning if they did."

My heart sank. If they'd come by our table while I was grabbing snacks, would they have docked points for my not being there?

"You're fine," Naomi sighed, and I glared at her even though I was getting used to her intruding on my feelings by now. "Head back, though. Remi's gone. She's why you're over here, isn't she?"

"Shut up," I groaned, and Naomi laughed as I hurried away from the snack table, back to Wesley.

He and Heather had taken up a game that involved throwing paper airplanes at each other's posters while Madison looked on disapprovingly. Heather tossed a plane, and its nose hit our main diagram dead center.

"Ha!" She pumped a fist in the air. "How many points is that?"

"Points?" Wesley scoffed. "We didn't decide on points."

"Ok, so fifty to me?"

Wesley perked up when he saw me walking towards them.

"You're back!"

"You're just excited because you think I'm going to give you some of my food."

Wesley helped himself to a mini cheese-and-cracker sandwich off my plate.

"Were you not?" he asked with his mouth full.

I looked up and down the aisle at the row of students and their posters. Teachers and family members intermixed as they wandered from project to project.

"Have my parents come by yet?" I asked.

"I haven't seen them." Wesley also scanned the row. "This thing goes for two hours. They're probably not here yet."

I dug my phone out of my purse. No new messages. I went back and checked to make sure the texts I'd sent had gone through, but they looked like they had.

"Yeah, you're probably right," I said, even though it was weird they hadn't even texted me back.

A teacher from a different school came by, asking about our posters. Wesley and I straightened up and read to her from our notes. She nodded approvingly before moving across the aisle to Heather and Madison.

"That wasn't so bad," Wesley sighed. "Still hope no one else comes by."

"Except the judges, you mean," I reminded him.

"I wouldn't mind if they skipped us."

I watched Heather and Madison flawlessly navigate the teacher's questions about their poster. As much as I disliked Madison, I hoped they won for Heather's sake.

"Weaver incoming," Wesley hissed. I immediately straightened up and glanced down the aisle. Dr. Weaver was smartly dressed in a black pantsuit with her gray hair pulled into a fancier twist than her usual bun. Her expression was dark, with her mouth drawn into a tight frown, and her brow furrowed.

I looked up at our poster. Dr. Weaver already looked in a bad mood. I didn't need her seeing our shoddy work. As she got closer, I could hear the furious click-click-click of her heels on the marble floor. She stopped in front of us and glowered down at me.

"Samantha, I need you to come with me."

"What did I do?" I blurted. Was this about disobeying orders last week when I went to save Wesley? Or maybe my poster really was that bad?

What if Adrian Schrader had complained to her about how rude Naomi and I had been?

Dr. Weaver's expression softened, and my hands clammed up as I realized she was looking at me with pity.

"Not here," she said, and her gentle tone made my chest tighten. "Follow me, please. Grab your things."

"What's going on?" Wesley asked. "What about the poster? The judges haven't come by yet."

"You'll have to manage on your own, but Samantha, you need to come with me."

The students at nearby tables had started staring. I grabbed my purse and handed my notes to Wesley.

"Sorry," I mumbled. Dr. Weaver was already walking back through the rows of posters. I chased after her.

She led the way out of the ballroom and back into the hotel lobby, only stopping when we reached the front doors. She glanced out onto the street and then at her phone.

"They're sending a car," she said.

"Where are we going?" I asked. "What's happened?"

She looked around the lobby before handing me her phone. A picture of an office took up the screen, but books and papers had been scattered across the desk and floor haphazardly. The window was broken, and shattered glass covered the scene. A shelf had cracked and splintered, sending its contents flying, leaving the wooden board hanging on the wall by a single nail. I was about to ask what I was looking at when I saw the nameplate on the desk, knocked askew but still readable.

"Vic Havardson, PhD," I read. Dr. Weaver took the phone back.

"His office was found like this this morning," she said. "No one has seen him since yesterday. I'm so sorry, Samantha."

Dad was gone.

29

Alone

The lobby spun. My stomach lurched. I needed to sit down, but Dr. Weaver was already shepherding me out the front doors to the curbside and into the backseat of a car.

Dad was missing? His office looked ransacked, but who would be stupid enough to try to attack a man that looked as terrifying as my father? I had just seen him the other night, how could he be missing now?

"Mr. Fleming is already back at the school," Dr. Weaver said while typing out an email on her phone. "Your mother is there, too."

"But what happened?" I felt empty and lost and angry and small. I wanted to scream, and I wanted to disappear.

"Security footage has been tampered with, of course," Dr. Weaver sighed. She hit send on her email and looked at me from across the middle seat. "But we were able to identify a woman named Mira Aimes on campus earlier in the day yesterday."

That name meant nothing to me. I continued to stare at Dr. Weaver blankly, waiting for more.

"You've met her before, when your roommate snuck you both to the docks. She secretes neurotransmitters, giving her complete control over her victims if she's able to make skin-contact."

The white-haired woman. The one Dad had been so wary of on the ferry.

This was my fault. I had shown Adrestus my face. He knew who I was, and now he was going after my family. My family who I should've been honest with.

"Why?" I croaked. Dr. Weaver only shook her head.

We drove into the campus parking garage. By now, I was familiar with the winding drive down beneath the school to the heavy door that led to the Apex Facility.

My mom was down there. I didn't know how I'd be able to face her. If Avery was with her, how was I supposed to look him in the eye and tell him I got Dad abducted?

I numbly got out of the backseat and followed Dr. Weaver into the long corridor. Her brisk footsteps echoed off the walls and in my head. Isabelle was at the call desk. She looked at us with wide eyes when we came in. She pointed wordlessly towards Fleming's office.

Dr. Weaver wavered outside Fleming's door. There was a slam from the other side, as if someone had hit the desk.

"Dammit, Alison! What aren't you telling me?" I'd never heard Fleming yell like that before. I wondered how long we'd been at the fair by the time he'd received the news and came back to campus. "Stop playing games!"

Dr. Weaver cleared her throat and knocked before inviting herself in.

Fleming and Mom stood on opposite sides of the office. Black streaks of mascara ran down Mom's cheeks, and her eyes were red and swollen. She sobbed when she saw me cowering behind Dr. Weaver and made to pull me towards her.

"Don't touch her," Fleming growled, and Mom hesitated.

"Mom?" I tried to move past Dr. Weaver to get to her.

"Samantha, stay back," Fleming snapped at me without taking his eyes off Mom.

I didn't understand. This was all my fault, so why was Mom being treated like the bad guy?

"I'm leaving the island," she said. She was looking at me. "It's not safe."

My heart sank. Leave? We couldn't leave. I was so close to joining the team for real. I would find Dad, she just had to give me the chance.

"When?"

"Right now," she said. "The Hendricks already have Avery safe on the mainland. I'll meet up with them as soon as I leave here."

"But," I struggled to come up with words, "what about my friends?"

"She's not taking you with her." Fleming's tone was harsh, and he continued to glare at Mom. Relief mixed with betrayal and confusion. She was abandoning me?

"Why not?"

Mom glared right back at Fleming. Her whole body shook.

"Tell her, Alison."

"You don't know what you're talking about," she hissed.

"If you don't, I will."

"You— I mean, I don't—" Mom stammered.

Fleming pointed a finger at me.

"Did you know your daughter can't die?"

I flinched away. Fleming had told me he wouldn't tell my parents about the rooftop. I glanced between him and Mom, panicking. I didn't know what I expected. Anguish, maybe? Confusion? But she looked stony and resilient and grim. She didn't even blink.

"Mom, did you know?" My pulse quickened. More secrets from my parents.

Only her eyes moved, flickering between Fleming and me.

"We tested her," Fleming continued. "We thought it had to be the Apex gene."

"You what?" It was Mom's turn to look panicked. "You had no right!"

"Samantha has every right!" Fleming was yelling again. "Of course, you already know she tested negative."

"Stop yelling at her!" I shouted. Why was Fleming so angry? Mom hadn't done anything wrong.

"Tell her."

"Alex, don't do this!" Mom wailed.

"If you're going to leave her behind, she deserves to know why!"

Mom tried to move towards me again, but Dr. Weaver stepped between us.

"It's not my secret to tell," Mom croaked.

"Who is she, Alison?" Dr. Weaver asked.

The question sent a chill through my body. What kind of question was that? They knew who I was. I could see Adrestus standing on the rooftop, asking me the same thing before breaking my neck. It was getting harder to breathe inside Fleming's office. Dad was missing. Why weren't we focusing on that?

Mom pressed a quivering hand over her mouth and shut her eyes.

"She had no matches in the Apex Database when we added her blood sample." Fleming looked at me as he said it.

"You had no right," Mom repeated in a whisper. "She's my daughter, Alex."

"I believe you." Fleming switched to a gentler approach. "But we need to know who she is."

"But she just answered you!" Why did I sound panicked? Was I panicking?

"A daughter can be a lot of things," Dr. Weaver said coolly. "But where did she come from?"

Mom opened her eyes to look at me.

"I'm so sorry," she rasped. "Samantha, look, I'm so sorry."

"What's happening?" I demanded. I was growing frustrated. All these adults were talking around me, but not to me.

"She's Vic's." Mom turned to Fleming. "He already had her when we met."

Everything turned ice-cold, and my head felt light.

That's how they knew I wouldn't be an Apex like Avery. That's how I was double negative on the Apex Gene test. But as those things clicked into place, everything else in my head began to unravel. Nothing made sense.

"Mom?" As I said it, I felt like I didn't recognize the woman in front of me. So many secrets, but I never would've guessed this one.

"You're still my daughter," she insisted. The corners of her lips quivered. I wanted to reach out to her and run away at the same time.

"That's it?" Dr. Weaver clicked her tongue. "There's nothing more to the story? Why can't she die?"

Fury rose and twisted inside me. Why wouldn't they leave her alone?

"What else do you want?" Mom spat. "I've just told you! She's Vic's."

The last words echoed in my head. I'm Dad's, but Dad was gone, and now Mom was leaving because she wasn't really my mom. It felt like the earth was giving way beneath me.

"Alison, Samantha died last week." Fleming's voice was low. "If you know how it is she didn't stay dead, she deserves to know."

Mom shook her head.

"Did you even know she'd joined Apex Team?"

A heavy weight settled in my stomach. How long had Fleming suspected I'd forged the permission forms?

Mom looked at me with wide, watering eyes, but they narrowed with stony resolve.

"Yes."

I tried not to look surprised, but her lie caught me off guard. She can't have known I was on the team, so why would she cover for me? Fleming grunted, clearly unconvinced.

"I've told you everything I can. I need to catch the next ferry, I don't have time." She straightened up. "Let me say goodbye to my daughter."

Fleming and Dr. Weaver passed a look between them, and Dr. Weaver begrudgingly stepped aside. Mom wrapped me in her arms, but I stayed rigid at her touch. I could feel her mouth near my ear.

"I'm sorry, Sammy," she said. "I'm so sorry."

Images began flashing in my mind, as if I was dreaming and remembering all at once. I could see Mom and Dad's townhouse, I was in the front room, then, my bedroom, full of boxes. There was a manila folder. I was pulling it from one of the boxes, and I shook the contents into my hand...

The images stopped, and Mom's face swam inches from my own. Her eyes looked nothing like mine.

"Find Vic. Find your dad. Please." Her fingers cradled my cheeks. She tried to smile and let me go before grabbing a large duffel bag from the floor. "Alex, take care of her. You're all she has left. I don't know how long I'll be gone."

I tried to find the words to say goodbye, but they got lost somewhere in my throat. She was abandoning me, somehow with more questions than ever before.

Then the door clicked shut, and I realized she was gone. Dr. Weaver had left with her. Fleming was looking at me with apprehension, but I was trying to grab onto the images Mom had left in my head before they slipped away. It had to have been a message from her. There was something I needed to go find in the townhouse that she didn't want Fleming knowing about.

"You can have a seat if you like." Fleming's voice was raspy from yelling.

I fell into the familiar chair across from his, and he tentatively took a seat, too.

"My dad..." I was too numb to cry. "I just saw him on Thursday."

"I promise we are doing everything we can—"

"The same way you're doing everything you can to find Winnie?" I interrupted. Fleming took a long, shuddering breath.

"Yes, just like that."

Dad missing. Mom gone.

Mom...

"So, my mom isn't..." I swallowed. There was a sharp pinch behind my face, and my eyes began to sting. The numbness was seeping away as reality set in. "She's not my..."

"No, she's not."

Why hadn't she told me?

"And you knew?"

Fleming shrugged helplessly.

"I figured when you didn't genetically match her in the Apex database."

Had she left me behind because I wasn't her real daughter?

I pushed the thought into the farthest corner of my brain. No, she had still raised me. She left me because she knew I was dangerous. I'd shown my face to Adrestus, and Dad was abducted because of it.

This was all my fault.

"I'm sorry," I whispered. "This is because of me."

"No." Fleming's voice was hard, and I flinched away. "Don't you dare put this on yourself."

"I shouldn't have joined the team! I wasn't ever supposed to! I've gone and endangered my family, and it's driving Wesley away, too! My dad was taken because of me! I just wanted to find Winnie." I shook my head. "That's all, but I haven't found her, and now Dad is gone, too."

"Your parents kept secrets," Fleming pointed out. "Those secrets are what got us here, not anything you did."

He tossed his glasses on his desk.

"You've done more for this team than most of the kids who've been on it for years," he continued. "And you've been here four weeks."

His words did nothing to lift the weight that had settled in my stomach.

"Fine." He leaned back in his seat. "What if it is your fault? What can you do about it?"

"I can quit the team," I said. I felt hollow.

"And then what? Wait for your friends to do the work? Adrestus isn't going to return your dad just because you quit. Alison won't bring Avery back to the island. The only difference it'll make is you won't be able to help."

"Maybe I shouldn't help."

But even as I said it, the thought of leaving Dad's fate in the hands of the team was unbearable. Sure, Naomi and Wes would fight to get him back. But Andersen? And Skyler?

Maybe this was why Mom had lied about the permission form for me. She wanted me to find Dad.

"What's done is done," Fleming said. "All that's left now is finding your dad and Winnie. You can't let yourself be immobilized by guilt."

The glass case stood behind Fleming. The picture he'd shown me of him with Mom, Roy, and Paragon standing on the steps to the school glinted behind the glass. Paragon's elbow rested on Fleming's head.

"What was Paragon's real name?" I asked. Fleming frowned.

"Why would you ask that?"

I didn't have an answer. Fleming stood up abruptly.

"I'm sending you over to Nurse Everly before you're free to go," he said.

There was no fight in me to object. I picked up my purse. I felt so stupid in my nice presentation clothes in the midst of all this.

There was little that Everly could do for me outside of letting me sit with Tonka in my lap. He brewed a mug of tea as well, but I hardly touched it.

I pulled out my phone and dialed Dad's cell. I listened to it ring before inevitably going to voicemail. His gruff voice played on the recorded message.

"This is Vic. You know what to do."

I hung up as the recording tone beeped in my ear. I dialed again, just to hear him tell me I knew what to do.

I knew I had to go find the folder in the townhouse like Mom had shown before she left, I knew I had to pass the trials this week, and I knew I had to somehow beat Wes on Friday.

Then I would find Dad.

I scratched Tonka under the chin, and he melted into a pile of orange fur on my lap, purring blissfully. Too much had happened in the last few hours. It left me stripped of emotion, and I basked in the numbness.

The Sickbay doors swung open. Naomi and Wesley hesitated in the doorway. Tonka leaped away and darted under a bed.

"I was just about to leave," I said. Naomi closed the distance between us in two strides and pulled me into her.

"We're gonna find him," she said.

"I know," I mumbled. I didn't want to talk about it. It still didn't seem real, and I didn't want the fact that my dad had been abducted to sink in. "How did the presentation go?"

Wesley half-laughed, half-grunted.

"It was fine," he grimaced. "I wouldn't get your hopes up for a good grade, though."

I pried myself away from Naomi and threw my purse over my shoulder.

"I wasn't hoping for much to begin with. I think I'm gonna go to bed. You guys mind telling Everly I've gone?"

Naomi's shoulders fell. Wesley looked down at his feet.

"Yeah, sure," Naomi smiled. "You go on ahead."

I shouldered past them, through the door and into the atrium before pivoting on my heel.

"Wait, Wesley, you wanted to talk after the fair, right?"

His face flushed, and he shrugged.

"It wasn't anything important. It's fine."

I had bigger things to worry about than Wesley. I tried to smile goodbye, but it felt awkward on my face.

30

The Townhouse

I welcomed the sleepless dark of my dorm room. I didn't even bother getting under my covers. I knew it was futile as my mind raced, formulating a plan. I went through the steps over and over, keeping thoughts of missing dads and secret step-moms at bay, until I must've fallen asleep.

I woke up sprawled out on top of my blankets, birds chirping outside the window. For a fraction of a moment, I'd forgotten everything that had happened the night before, but then the memories came crashing down on me, twisting my stomach.

The hall sounded quiet. Everyone must've been sleeping in after a busy day at the fair. Good. No one would bother me on my way out.

I slinked down the hall and slipped into the stairwell. I could hear the showers running in the bathroom, but I was able to go unseen. I kept my head down all the way to the cafeteria so that the few students already milling around campus didn't bother me.

As I ate my cereal, I looked up the university campus map on my phone. The only time I'd been there had been with Winnie when we stole Amanda's car to go to the docks, and she hadn't exactly given me a grand tour of the place.

However, using the university directory, I was able to figure out the building Dad's office was in. I gulped down the rest of my cereal and marched back outside into the morning fog.

A lazy Sunday morning lull hung over the buildings of New Delos University, which was next door to the high school, but stretched on for much further. The humanities building where Dad worked was clear across campus.

A student carrying a bag filled with textbooks swiped his keycard into the humanities building, and I followed him inside. He disappeared into a computer lab while I found the stairs.

It was a cool building, with exposed brick walls and industrial metal staircases. A large art piece made of blue glass hung from the ceiling on the top floor, visible from the three floors of walkways below it. The walls were decorated with student paintings and the head shots of professors and Deans.

On the second floor, my pulse quickened. Down the hall, yellow police tape cordoned off an office. The office to my immediate right had Roy Hendricks's name slapped across the door.

I pulled my phone from my back pocket and pulled up the contact my parents had insisted I put there in case of emergency. I hoped she was awake.

I hit the call button and held the phone up as it rang. Just as I started to worry she wouldn't take the call, Amanda answered.

"Who is this?"

"I'm at my dad's office." I tried to force authority into my voice. "Meet me in ten."

I hung up before Amanda could say no or ask questions. She owed me, I told myself. I tipped her off when we were narrowing in on the missing students. Plus, her sister was still missing. She'd come just to see if I had more information for her.

I fixed my eyes on Dad's office. I hadn't worked up enough willpower to get my feet any closer to it yet. I clenched my jaw and moved forward. Even though Dr. Weaver had shown me the picture of his desk, I needed to see it for myself.

When I was a few feet from the door, I realized it was open. A tall woman stepped out, ducking beneath the police tape. She looked at me in surprise.

"Samantha!"

I'd only met Professor Parker once, but I recognized the head of the University Apex Team immediately. Her long braids were coiled in a neat bun on the top of her head, and she donned a casual t-shirt and jeans.

A student stepped out behind her, eyeing me with curiosity.

"Sorry," I said, blushing furiously. I was about to turn heel and book it out of the humanities building, but the professor sighed and gave me a sympathetic smile.

"Don't be," she stepped aside. "Although, I hope you let someone know you left campus."

"I talked to my floor assistant," I lied, hoping Professor Parker wouldn't look into it.

She lifted the police tape and beckoned me forward.

"I understand why you'd want to come," she said before turning to her student. "I want the report by this afternoon. Get going."

He hurried away, but not without looking over his shoulder at us.

The picture on Dr. Weaver's phone screen couldn't have prepared me for the mess inside. Everything had been left in disarray. Broken glass covered the floor. Textbooks lay open facedown, their spines caving inwards. Dad's chair was on its side, and his computer had been knocked off his desk. The bookshelf behind it looked as if something heavy, maybe Dad himself, had been thrown into it.

His name plate glinted on the desk.

"Try not to touch anything," Professor Parker said quietly.

A framed picture had been knocked behind the desk. It was the last picture we'd taken as a family, a group selfie Mom had forced us to take after getting on the ferry a month ago. Dad looked sullen and wary. Avery was pretending to pout. My face was pale and gaunt with sickness, but I was forcing a smile. It was strange that this was the picture Dad would choose to display on his desk. I wanted to laugh and cry at the same time. I fought the urge to pick it up and dust it off.

All three were gone. They'd abandoned me.

No, they were taken, I reminded myself, although I knew Avery and Mom had left of their own accord.

"Thanks," I said to Professor Parker. She smiled warmly again and led me back into the hall.

"The entire University team is on the case," she promised. "We'll find him. They're especially eager for a win after you and your team found the students first."

My cheeks warmed, and I shrugged bashfully.

"There's still one missing," I reminded her.

"We'll find her, too."

Professor Parker made her exit back the way I came. I hoped she didn't run into Amanda on her way, because that would definitely stir suspicions. However, Amanda appeared at the top of the stairs on the opposite end of the hall.

Her hair was jammed into her favorite ball cap and her sweatpants had a tear at the knee. She crossed her arms at me, glaring furiously.

"What were you doing with Parker?"

"I didn't know she'd be here," I said, all the confidence I'd had on the phone seeping away. Even in her less-than-Sunday-Best, Amanda could destroy anyone with her withering stare. "I need your help."

Professor Parker had closed the door to Dad's office, but Amanda looked at it with apprehension.

"I'm sorry," she said, and she sounded like she meant it. "Thing is, I've already got one missing person to find."

"If we find one, we'll find them both."

Amanda barked a single, dry laugh.

"You would've thought that would've been the case when you found the others." The bitterness in her voice was undeniable, and I felt myself deflating.

"I know," I said quietly. "But I have a lead on my dad already, and it's the closest thing I've got to helping Winnie at the moment, too."

Amanda glared at me in silence, and I thought she might decide to chase me off the university campus. However, she sighed and rolled her eyes, looking so much like her younger sister when she did.

"Fine," she mumbled. "What've you got?"

"I'll tell you in the car. Did you bring your keys?"

Amanda had to move several stacks of old homework and coffee cups off the front seat and into the back when we got to the parking lot. She'd grumbled the whole walk there about how I was just using her for her car, and, yeah, that was partially true.

"I could've taken the bus," I pointed out. She glared in response.

She climbed into the driver's seat and jammed her key in the ignition.

"Great. Where're we going?"

"My parents' house."

She grumbled under her breath but started the car and peeled out of the parking lot. I clutched my seat, now knowing who must've taught Winnie to drive.

I explained the message Mom had left me, and Amanda scowled at the road.

"How's an old folder going to help Winnie?"

"I won't know until I find it." I said.

"And why didn't you just tell Fleming this and go with a group from your team?"

The idea had occurred to me, too, but I shook my head.

"Fleming was right there when Mom showed me where to go. If she'd wanted him in on it, she would've said so. Besides, I'm banned from field missions until I pass the trials."

Amanda threw her head back as she laughed. The car swerved a little, and I watched the road nervously.

"How'd you already get taken off field work?" she cackled. "Do you know how hard that is to do?"

My face grew hot, and I shrugged.

"I might've ignored an order and got myself killed," I mumbled. Amanda stopped laughing and looked at me.

"Killed?" she repeated.

"I don't want to talk about it," I said and turned my attention out my window.

"No, tell me what happened."

"Why? It doesn't matter because I'm not dead anymore."

"Obviously, but I think..." She thought for a moment before continuing. "I think you've been dead before."

My stomach flipped. Amanda still knew secrets that I didn't. Was that the reason she was so standoffish at the beginning of the year? Because she knew I was some kind of weird zombie monster?

"Why would you think that?" I tried to keep my tone casual but was betrayed by a quiver in my voice. Amanda sighed.

"I don't know for sure," she mumbled uncomfortably, "but that night on the boardwalk, you seemed dead."

I thought back to the night Andersen and his friends had ambushed me. I had been so cold when I'd collapsed on the small dock.

"But I was awake," I said.

"Yeah, but you were blue and not breathing. You didn't even shiver until I started warming you up." She shrugged. "When we found you, we thought you were dead."

When Fleming had told Mom I wasn't able to die, she didn't even blink. I couldn't shake the feeling that she knew. Maybe what I found at the house would hold more answers.

"I almost forgot someone was with you," I mused. "What was her name again? Brooke?"

"None of your business," Amanda glowered, but her cheeks tinged pink, and she bit back the tiniest of smiles at the mention of Brooke's name.

She pulled her car up to Mom and Dad's townhouse, and we clambered out. I led the way to the porch and pulled the birdhouse down off its hook. The base twisted in my hand, and a silver key fell out.

"Let's make this quick," Amanda said as I unlocked the front door. "I've got a bad feeling about this."

Despite the good weather, the inside of the townhouse was dark. Curtains blocked every window, and even though I knew Mom and Avery had just been there yesterday, it was easy to imagine no one had been home in a while.

"Check the upstairs," Amanda hissed. "I want to make sure we're alone."

I hadn't considered that Adrestus might have someone lurking in the house. The idea of it made me angry. He'd already taken my dad. What more could he want?

I tip-toed upstairs and systematically checked behind every door and curtain between me and Amanda. My heart skipped a beat when I swung open the door to what was supposed to be my room.

It was still filled with boxes, like it had been a few weeks ago. Like it had been in the images Mom had put in my head the night before. Had she never set up my bedroom because I wasn't really her daughter?

"Upstairs is clear," I said to Amanda as I met her in the kitchen. She stood over the sink with a funny look on her face.

"They didn't even have time to do the dishes," she said. Plates and pans, sticky with syrup and butter, rested at the bottom of the sink.

"Mom was pretty freaked out last night. I'd never seen her like that before."

Amanda started the sink and searched under the cabinet for soap.

"Actually," I continued, not sure why I was going to tell Amanda this, "I found out she's not really my mom."

Amanda grunted.

"How about you go find what we're here for while I take care of this?" She scrubbed thick syrup off a plate as she pressed her lips together.

"You already knew, didn't you?"

She glared at me from under the brim of her ball cap.

"Is that why you don't like me?"

"I don't want to be involved. I'm here to help Winnie, so go find your clue or whatever before I leave."

I knew Amanda would never budge. I left her in the kitchen to go back to what was supposed to be my bedroom, biting back a frustrated retort.

The number of boxes piled in the extra bedroom was overwhelming. I sat down next to the one closest to the door and tried not to breathe in too much dust. I closed my eyes, trying to recall the images Mom had shown me.

It was the same feeling that took over whenever I fought on instinct, like someone else was in control. Muscle memory that didn't belong to me brought me to a box in the middle of the room. I had to shove other boxes out of the way to reach it.

The envelope was near the bottom of the box, hidden in an accordion folder. Old receipts and birthday cards sprinkled onto the floor when I pulled it out.

The envelope felt empty except for a small rectangle nestled in one of its corners. I shook it out into the palm of my hand. It was a flash drive.

"That's it?"

I spun around at the sound of Amanda's voice. She was in the doorway, drying her hands with a kitchen rag.

"There's a computer upstairs," I remembered. "If we plug it in and—"

Amanda held up a hand, cutting me off. Her eyes lit up as she crept towards the window. She used a finger to pull down one of the blinds.

"Crap," she sighed. I tripped over boxes to join her. On the curb below, an older black car had parked behind Amanda's beater. The trunk was bent in and held down by bungee cords. A man in a black suit slowly walked around Amanda's car, scanning over the exterior and peering into the backseat windows. He straightened up and looked towards the house.

The last time I'd seen him, I'd been begging Adrestus to spare Wesley's life. I gripped the windowsill to steady myself. It was Miles, who had kept Wesley away while Adrestus murdered me. The man who'd kidnapped Winnie. His car looked like the one I'd been shoved into at the docks, the trunk mangled by Wesley.

"Do you recognize him?" Amanda asked.

"Yeah," I said through gritted teeth. I wanted to fight him. I wanted to hurt him. But it was most important for me to get this flash drive back to campus so I could see what was on it. "We need to get out of here."

I knew if I told Amanda this was the man who'd kidnapped her sister, there would be no chance of us getting away without a fight.

"And go where? My car is out front, where *he* is," Amanda hissed.

I stepped over boxes on my way out of the room. A leather photo album fell to the floor. Even in my hurry to escape, I couldn't bear to leave it there. I bent down to scoop it up, but Amanda held out an arm to stop me.

"No, we've gotta go."

We escaped downstairs and into the garage, hoping to exit through the door into the backyard, but as we passed through the mud room, we froze at the sound of the front door knob jiggling. Thankfully, Amanda had thought to lock it behind us.

"We'll sneak out back and loop around through the neighbors' yards after he's gone," I whispered, leading the way through the garage and to the small patch of well-maintained grass that was the backyard.

Something solid knocked against my forehead as I tried to step out onto the lawn.

"What the hell?" Amanda held a palm up, pressing it against what should have been empty air.

My fists clenched, and I scanned the yard, but there was no sign of Miles.

"He knows we're here," I growled.

"This is him?" she asked, knocking on the force field as if to test it.

"Would you take a look at you!" Miles sang as he came around the corner. A smirk danced across his face. "Walking around with your neck unsnapped."

A hot gust of air blew my hair back as Amanda attacked the force field with a wall of flame. Miles threw his head back and laughed.

"And you must be the other Hendricks girl!"

The air around Amanda crackled with heat. The grass at her feet withered and died, emitting tiny plumes of smoke.

"You know my sister?"

Miles stuck a hand out and leaned against his invisible wall. His sneer was only inches from Amanda's face on the opposite side of the barrier.

"Oh, yeah. She's mentioned you a few times, you know."

Amanda threw her entire weight into the force field. Flames spread across the barrier before dissipating in waves of heat.

"Tell me where she is!" Amanda demanded.

Miles laughed and straightened up.

"Tell you what, I'll consider telling you where she is if you hand off what it is you found in that house."

I was gripping the flash drive so tightly in my fist that it dug into the skin of my palm.

"You did find something, right?" Miles asked coyly. A wicked grin crept across his face. "Our newest prisoner wasn't exactly forthcoming, but we thought it might be here."

My blood howled in my ears, but I wouldn't give Miles the satisfaction of throwing myself at his wall like Amanda had.

Focus, I told myself. *Lashing out won't help Dad.*

But focusing was hard. Every fiber of my being called out for Miles's blood. The heat radiating off of Amanda didn't help, either.

We could retreat back through the garage, but Miles would surely follow and seal the exits. As long as we had him in the backyard, we at least had some room to move and could keep him busy before he had the chance to call for backup.

Amanda put both hands up against the barrier. The air around them distorted and warped from the heat.

"Good try, but you can't break it," Miles taunted, though he looked wary.

I looked back in the garage for anything that might help. A red, plastic container sat on the floor near a workbench.

"Where are you going?" Amanda demanded as I disappeared inside. The container wasn't full, but I could tell by the way the liquid sloshed around inside when I grabbed it that it would be enough. Amanda's eyes widened when she saw me bring it out. Miles stopped smiling.

"Throw it and go!" she yelled, just as the barrier shattered into nothingness. I hurled the gasoline container towards Miles. Amanda shot a well-aimed flame and it burst in the middle of the backyard.

Miles had thrown up a barrier to protect himself, but the force of the small explosion knocked him back. We were running through the garage before we could see how he landed. I punched the button to lift the carport door, and we rolled underneath into the main driveway without waiting for it to rise any further.

Amanda fumbled for her car keys while I repeatedly tried to open the locked passenger door until she finally found them. I looked back at the house as she peeled out of the neighborhood. Miles stumbled out of the garage, coughing into his arm, his black clothes smoldering.

"Please tell me you still have it," Amanda said. Her ball cap was still smoking.

I opened my fist to show off the flash drive.

"Better be something good on this if Adrestus wants it, too."

"Adrestus?" Amanda repeated. "Is that the name of the guy behind all this? Like the old Adrestus the Unkillable story?"

"Yeah," I cringed. I'd forgotten Adrestus's name wasn't public information.

"But it sounds like you are the one who's Unkillable."

I sank back in the car seat.

"Seems that way."

Amanda was quiet for a moment.

"Was Adrestus the one that killed you?"

I rubbed my neck thinking about it. I could see Wesley's mouth open in a scream as the crack rang out across the rooftop.

"Yeah."

Amanda pulled over as a fire truck going the opposite direction passed.

"That flash drive better have answers," Amanda scoffed. "I'm ready to be done with this crap."

31

The Trials Begin

I woke up Monday morning with a knot in my stomach and the mysterious flash drive at the forefront of my mind. Unfortunately, the computer lab had been closed all afternoon the day before, so I hadn't been able to investigate the drive any further.

I snagged a Study Period pass for the library so I could use the computer lab at the end of the school day. The flash drive felt like a cinder block in my backpack, and even with the first round of trials looming over me, I could think of little else for the first half of the day.

However, as I walked into the training gym for PE, my stomach clenched at the thought of the trials starting after school. I just about doubled over when I reminded myself that if I failed, I'd be off the team and less able to help Dad.

Naomi and I retreated to our usual sparring corner while Wesley paired up with Everest across the gym. Every time he went off to practice with someone else, the sting of his betrayal returned.

"So, what's your plan?" Naomi asked.

"Plan for what?"

"For fighting Wesley. We know he won't go easy on you. I've got some tips, but I want to know what your plan is first."

I exhaled heavily and looked back at Wes. Everest had the ability to change his density, making him one of the few kids on the team who could withstand Wesley's hits. They were exchanging heavy blows, and I thought I might puke.

"I'm thinking my plan might revolve around dodging."

Naomi laughed and squared up.

"Not a bad plan, honestly. You don't have to beat him, just last the full two minutes without hitting the ground."

She came at me, and I sidestepped her without a problem. She was starting easy.

Her next attack was quicker, and she clipped my shoulder as I ducked around her. Her third attack landed me on my back. I groaned but got back to my feet.

"Don't worry about relying on whatever your mom's put in your head," Naomi suggested. "No one would blame you for using it."

The unease in my stomach doubled at the mention of my mom. I hadn't yet told my friends that I wasn't Alison Havardson's daughter.

"I can't rely on that, though," I said. "Not for the trials."

"Why not? Anyone else would if they had programming. Besides, how else are you supposed to level the playing field against a room of Apex?"

"It's not my pride that won't let me," I snapped. I looked back at Wesley again. He'd only sparred with me that one time, but I knew it hadn't been a fluke. "It doesn't work against him."

The benefit to being Naomi's friend was that I rarely had to explain myself. My cheeks burned, but Naomi nodded.

"That's fine." Her careful smile was slowly slipping into a disappointed frown. She was realizing what I had known since Friday. I was screwed. "We'll just have to be creative."

"It's going to be hard to be creative when he helped teach me everything I could throw at him in the ring," I pointed out.

"You'll figure it out," she insisted. "Remember, you can bring things into the ring as long as they aren't weapons."

I hadn't considered bringing anything in with me. Maybe I could bring in Floundersen and simply hold him in his cup. Wesley wouldn't dare hit someone holding a fish, would he?

It was a dumb idea.

"Freddie can make fog," Naomi reminded me. "When we were trying out, he brought buckets of water in with him. Filled the whole room with a fog cloud. His opponent never even hit him because he couldn't find him."

"How does that help me, though? I can't make myself invisible or hide. Plus, Wesley's got superhuman senses."

Naomi shrugged and took up a fighting stance.

"You'll think of something," she assured me. "For now, we better practice your dodging."

It might have been easier to dodge Naomi's attacks if I hadn't been distracted by the thought of the flash drive hiding in my backpack. Whatever was on it must've been important if Adrestus had sent one of his top people to check the house for it.

When I finally handed my library pass to Mrs. Young at the end of the day, I practically jogged down the halls. I tried to find a computer in the corner, away from prying eyes.

My fingers quaked as I logged on, and I tapped my foot impatiently while the computer loaded. I held the flash drive ready in my hand. It was hard to press the drive into the USB slot, my hands were shaking so hard.

An icon appeared on my screen, and I hurried to click it.

A red error box glared angrily at me, the black letters taunting me: "Recovery Form Invalid".

"What?" I hissed, causing several heads to turn and look at me. I ignored them, scowling at the screen. I punched the words into the computer's search engine. The first hit on the internet was about encrypted files.

I was gutted. I didn't have the first clue of how to decrypt files. A few more internet searches didn't help. I couldn't understand any of the jargon and was lost just a few sentences in, no matter which article I clicked on.

I carefully ejected the flash drive, and, despite wanting to hurl it across the library in frustration, I zipped it back in the front pocket of my bag.

I had the full Study Period ahead of me with no way to view the files on the flash drive. Maybe the computer lab in the training facility would have special programming for encrypted files.

For now, I was stuck in the library. I'd much rather be spending this time downstairs, practicing for my fight against Wesley in a few days.

Unable to do anything else, I tried to focus on strategizing against Wesley. I had to be creative. Fleming said he'd beat his brother because he knew about his secret weak spot. But Wesley didn't have any weaknesses. He was a classic super-human.

But maybe that was the trick? Maybe I could get him to punch a hole in the wall and get stuck there?

I smiled to myself. That was dumber than my Floundersen idea, but the thought of Wes stuck in the wall made me want to laugh.

No, my plan would have to be more graceful than getting Wesley to use too much strength. He had other powers, after all.

My smile widened, and I clicked back into the internet. I had a plan.

The chlorine smell burnt the inside of my nose, and I shivered in my black one-piece swimsuit. I was surprised at how many of the other students had come to watch the trials. Andersen sat on the top tier of the small set of bleachers next to the pool.

The freshmen were all lined up next to me, freshly showered and ready to have the first set of trials behind them. Fleming talked at us, explaining the importance of being able to swim when tasked with protecting an island.

I ignored him and scanned the bleachers. Naomi gave me a thumbs up. I smiled back at her weakly. Wesley hadn't come. It would probably be easier for him if I failed before Friday so that he wouldn't have to fight me.

There were three parts to the Trial, starting with treading water. It was the easiest of the three tests as the bare minimum required to pass was to not drown. I'd been able to tread water in the ocean while handcuffed and scowled at Andersen for a good portion of the test. He'd had a better chance at seeing me drown when he pushed me off the island, and he wasn't going to get the satisfaction here.

The pool only had six swimming lanes so the second test had to be done in two groups. Naomi brought me a towel while I waited for the first group to finish.

"He's not avoiding the trials," she said as soon as I opened my mouth.

"I don't care if he is," I lied, scrambling to get my emotions in check. "Besides, Wesley wants me to fail, and I already have enough people cheering against me."

"No one's cheering against you," Naomi insisted, though we both knew that wasn't true. "Andersen would rather see you lose to Wesley than a swimming pool. He wants you to pass today!"

"How comforting."

Fleming lined up the second group of swimmers. Chris was in the lane next to me and grimaced as he forced webs to form between his fingers. I was one of the best swimmers out of the sophomores, but I would look lousy swimming next to a kid with amphibious powers.

Fleming blew the whistle, and I dove in the water. Three minutes later, I emerged from the pool having only been beaten by Chris. It wasn't a race, but it still felt good to show off in front of people who didn't like me.

The final task was rescue themed. Justin and Isabelle took turns sinking themselves to the bottom of the far side of the pool while, one after the other, we leaped in and swam them back. Being the only sophomore, I was last to go. I adjusted my swim goggles. As soon as Isabelle was settled at the bottom of the pool, Fleming blew his whistle, and I was back underwater.

There was a painful snap on the side of my face, and my vision filled with burning chlorine water. My goggles had broken, and my swim cap snapped off with them. I forced my eyes open. I could still make out Isabelle's shape across the pool and struck out to reach her. Once I had my arms under hers, I shut my eyes against the chemicals and pushed off the pool floor.

We broke the surface, and my hair fell around my face. It didn't matter, I knew where the edge of the pool was. I blindly swam Isabelle back to Fleming and pulled myself out of the water. My feet slapped against the floor as I marched over to the bleachers.

"What the hell, man?" I shouted at Andersen. He was laughing so hard that he nearly toppled over the back of this seat. Skyler guffawed next to him.

"What now?" Fleming came to stand between us, but I continued to stare down Andersen. If I'd had my goggles still, I would've thrown them at him.

"He broke my goggles!"

My eyes still stung from the chlorine, but I pointed at the pool where my broken goggles and swim cap floated on the surface.

"Did not!" Andersen protested, unable to hide the grin smeared across his face.

"They were perfectly fine until I was underwater!" I shouted. "This is the Night Games all over again!"

"What happened at the Night Games?" Fleming asked.

"He messed with my shoes and my hair tie!" It sounded stupid as I said it, but I was too mad to care.

"That doesn't sound like me," Andersen sang.

Fleming turned to me and tried to lead me away.

"You passed, that's all that matters," he said.

"He sabotaged me!" I protested. "And you're doing nothing because I passed?"

"I'm doing nothing because it won't do you any favors in the long run to have me fight Andersen for you," Fleming grumbled. "Trust me, I'd know. Besides, I can't really prove he did anything."

Naomi rushed to my side with my towel.

"You're giving him what he wants by yelling at him," she said.

"Good!" I shouted, stomping back towards the locker room. "Let him have it!"

I knew I shouldn't be yelling, but when those goggles snapped, so had I. Naomi chased me to my locker.

"You passed!" she reminded me. "I know Andersen is a jerk, but that's never going to change."

"Yeah, you're right." Sarcasm dripped off me like pool water. "I should just put up with him, and I should just put up with my dad being kidnapped by my murderer while I'm at it!"

"Sammy." Naomi reached out and placed a hand on my shoulder, but I batted it away and began ripping my clothes out of my locker.

"Why stop there? My roommate's been missing for a month, my brother's an Apex, apparently, so there's that. But, oh!" I punched the locker next to mine. The metal rang out in the empty locker room. "Don't worry, because he's only my half-brother because my mom isn't even my real mom, which she didn't bother to tell me until right before leaving me behind in this stupid city!"

The locker room door opened, but the freshmen who wanted to come in quickly retreated.

"Sammy," Naomi said again. She wrapped my towel around my shoulders and as she did so, wrapped her arms around me, too. I was shaking with pent up fury, but she held me tight.

"Moms are hard," she said after I stopped shaking. "Even fake ones. I'm really sorry. I had no idea."

I sniffed.

"Really? You of all people had no idea?"

"I already knew you were going through a lot," she laughed kindly. "You didn't need all the extra stuff to validate how upset you've been."

I pulled myself away and began picking up my things.

"Thanks," I muttered. Now that my rage was subsiding, embarrassment was rushing in to take its place. "You said once that your relationship with your mom is weird, too."

Naomi fidgeted uncomfortably as she sat down on a metal bench.

"Yeah. It's a little different, though." She must've wanted to avoid the subject of her mom because she changed gears. "Wesley showed up, you know. For the last part. He watched from the gym."

I took a moment. I wanted to pretend to be mad at him still.

"And?"

"And he felt proud."

I turned away so Naomi wouldn't see the smile that had crept over my face.

I stopped by Fleming's office early before class the next day. I needed to get into the facility's computer lab to see if those computers did better than the ones in the library at reading my flash drive.

"We still haven't gotten through all of Winnie's pictures," I explained to Fleming when I told him I needed a pass for Study Period. "I don't have much time to work on them with the Trials happening this week."

"Very well," Fleming sighed. "You and Wesley stop by my desk after class, and I'll have the passes for you.

"Oh, I don't think—"

"Wesley was assigned to this project, too," Fleming cut me off before I could finish my protest. "I know it might be uncomfortable given you have to fight him in a couple days, but last night proved you need practice working with people who make you angry and upset."

"Wesley is not the same as Andersen."

"Perfect. Then you'll have no issue working with him."

I internally kicked myself. I'd just argued against the point I wanted to make, but it was no use now.

"Also," Fleming faltered and looked at me with worry. My insides constricted, which was a very familiar feeling at this point. "There was a small fire reported in your parents' backyard this weekend."

I did my best to not look relieved. I already knew about the fire. I'd helped start it, but if Fleming found out, I could say goodbye to field work for the rest of the year.

"Do they know how it started?" I asked, trying to sound concerned.

"They said it looked like it might've been arson, but since there wasn't a lot of damage, they didn't do an extensive investigation."

I nodded solemnly. I was relieved to hear the house was fine, but I tried to continue to look passive.

"It was probably just neighborhood kids messing around," Fleming assured me. "I'm sure it's nothing to worry about."

Except it was something to worry about. Adrestus had sent someone there to find a flash drive that I had in my backpack. I bit my tongue. I would let Fleming know after I had a chance to look at it. By then I might have a good enough story to explain how I'd found the flash drive without incriminating myself.

I hurried away to meet Wesley and Naomi for breakfast, where Wesley pretended not to have come to the trial the night before. Naomi and I told him about Andersen trying to sabotage my rescue test, and it was nice to have something to be angry at *with* Wesley. I'd gotten tired of being angry *at* him.

In gym class, I let Naomi in on the plan I'd come up with for the Final Trial. Her face lit up, and she clapped her hands together, insisting it was perfect. We practiced more dodging since if Wesley was able to land even a single blow, I'd be down for the count.

At the end of the day, Mrs. Young waved me away without even looking at my pass. I already had the flash drive in my hand, ready to jam it into the computer as soon as I sat down in the hopes of pulling the files up before Wesley had the chance to arrive.

As I had hoped, the private computer lab in the basement was empty. I sat down in my seat too fast, almost spinning out of it, but I steadied myself on the desk and logged in. As soon as the desktop was loaded, I had the drive in the port.

"Dammit!" I smacked the table. The same "Recovery Form Invalid" message flashed at me.

"Something wrong?"

Wesley dropped his backpack in the seat next to me and leaned in to look at my screen.

"It's nothing," I insisted, ejecting the drive. I had been so sure this would work.

"It doesn't look like nothing," Wesley said, taking his seat. "It looks like you're trying to open encrypted files."

I scowled at him and pulled up the folder with Winnie's photos stored inside. We still hadn't made it through all of them, and it was hard not to mindlessly click through them without really looking.

"It's not your business," I said coolly. My phone buzzed on the desk. I reached for it, but not before Wesley read the text that appeared on the screen.

"Why does Amanda Hendricks want to know if you've opened the files yet?" he asked. I snatched my phone off the desk.

"It's rude to read other people's messages."

Wes wasn't about to give up, though.

"Sammy, what's on that flash drive?" He sounded apprehensive now, like he didn't want to hear the answer.

"I don't know," I sighed. "I haven't been able to open them."

Wesley picked up the flash drive to inspect it.

"Where'd it come from?"

I gritted my teeth.

"My mom, before she left."

"And she didn't tell you it was encrypted?"

"Obviously not."

"And Amanda knows about it because...?"

I furiously clicked through several more of Winnie's photos. Sunset, boat, tree, dead mouse.

"Where were you Sunday, anyway?"

"Just drop it, okay?"

"You could've lied and said your dorm room, but now I really want to know, where were you?"

He wasn't going to leave me alone until I told him. I pushed myself away from the desk and spun the chair so that I faced him.

"Mom didn't give me the drive, but told me where it was and didn't seem like she wanted Fleming to know. I asked Amanda to drive me to my house so I could find it."

Wesley frowned.

"I would've gone with you."

I shrugged and looked away, not wanting to meet his eye.

"Amanda has a car. I didn't think she'd want to drive extra people," I lied.

"Don't you think it was a bit dangerous going back to your parents' house after all that's happened?"

I gritted my teeth. This is why I hadn't wanted to tell him.

"So what? It's dangerous for me to be anywhere."

"Adrestus might be watching their house! You could've been ambushed!"

"I can take care of myself," I snapped. "I don't need your permission to go to my family's home, and I don't need you to protect me! I did fine on my own."

I gulped and turned my attention back to the computer, hoping he didn't catch the last part. No such luck.

"What do you mean you did fine on your own?" Wesley asked slowly. "Don't tell me..."

"It was just one of them," I grunted. "We've beat him before."

"Who!?" Wesley's voice cracked.

"The guy with the force fields. Don't worry, Amanda barbecued him."

Wesley reached over and grabbed my wrist, pulling my hand off my mouse. I was surprised by the gentleness of his touch.

"Sammy." His eyes were wide and green, and I refused to be melted by them. "At least let me know you're going somewhere next time."

"I'll consider it." I pulled my hand away, and his fell into his lap. I wanted to dislike Wesley so bad. He wasn't the boss of me, and I didn't need anyone's protection. But he was my friend, as mad as he'd made me in the last week. I knew he didn't want me to get hurt, but why couldn't he just trust me to take care of myself?

The rest of Study Period passed in a blur of amateur photography. I shouldered my bag and tried to smile at Wesley.

"You coming to the Trials?"

He looked miserable.

"Probably not."

Figured. I couldn't blame him. Watching me run the mile with eleven freshmen wasn't how I imagined anyone wanted to spend their afternoon, but it still stung that he'd be skipping again.

There were less students gathered to watch the Trials today. I glanced around for Andersen, but Naomi shook her head.

"Don't worry, I convinced Jamie they were due for a date. He won't bother you this time."

I exhaled in relief. I'd been afraid I'd have to run the mile barefoot to keep Andersen from tangling my shoelaces.

Fleming gathered us around him down on the track. A cold October wind blew in from the bay, but I knew I would be thankful for it once I started running.

Naomi stood on the sidelines during the mile and clapped for me each time I passed her until I'd finally completed all four laps. I was nowhere near the best runner, but it was enough to pass.

Fleming took us back to the main gym and ran us through a gauntlet of strength and endurance tests. We ended with a hanging pull up, and my muscles shook with exhaustion.

The final whistle blew, and the twelve of us dropped to the ground with a collective exhale.

"Great work," Fleming called out to us. "Remember, tomorrow is the written test so we'll be meeting in my classroom."

I wiped the sweat from my face and shook out my arms. I should've been feeling proud of myself with half the trials completed. Instead, there was a knot in my stomach that, no matter how deeply I breathed, I couldn't untangle.

"Good job today," Jessa smiled at me as we made our way to the locker room.

"Thanks, you too." My face grew warm as residual post-explosion embarrassment from the night before returned.

I threw my laundry in the locker room hamper, and my phone buzzed in my back pocket. I hadn't texted Amanda back, and guilt washed over me.

However, the text was from Wesley asking to meet in the library. I frowned at the screen wondering why he'd want to meet there. We'd finished our project together, so I knew he didn't want to build posters.

Naomi had already left by the time I was done in the locker room so I headed to the library alone. There were a few tables with studying students, but I didn't see Wes until I looked in the computer lab. Remi sat next to him looking nervous.

"What did you need?" I asked as I approached them. Remi didn't meet my eye, instead messing with the watch on her wrist.

"Did you still need that drive decrypted?" Wesley asked. "Because Remi said she'd help."

"You told her?" I hissed. Remi glared at me.

"He only said you were having a problem with a USB," she said. "That's all I know."

I wanted to be mad at him for dragging Remi into the search for my dad, but if she could make the files readable, it would be worth it. I pulled the drive out of my backpack and handed it off to her.

"This'll only take a second," she said, enclosing the flash drive in her fist and shutting her eyes. I shifted my weight from one foot to the other uncomfortably. What if she somehow damaged the files?

"Don't worry," Wesley insisted. "She's done this plenty of times."

Her closed eyes moved back and forth, as if she were reading something on the inside of her eyelids. She frowned slightly and bit her lip.

"There's a lot of data on this," she muttered, her eyes still closed. "A lot of...personal information."

She finally opened her eyes, blinking them rapidly to clear them. She opened her hand to give me back the drive and then revealed a second drive in her other hand.

"That drive is still encrypted, but you should be able to view it all on this one." She blushed as she passed off the second flash drive to me. "I'm sorry. I tried not to look at anything on it."

"Thanks," I said and was surprised to find that I meant it. Wesley stepped aside to make room for me at the computer.

There was no error message this time.

"I should really go," Remi said quickly. "I hope you find what you need."

I barely noticed her hurrying away. The mouse hovered over the folder that had popped up on the desktop. I swallowed hard. Wes read the folder name out loud.

"'Samantha'. I guess it really is for you, then."

I double clicked, and the screen exploded in a mosaic of folders. They were named everything from "Family Trip to Grand Canyon" to "Grandpa Max's Funeral". There was a folder for each year of school I'd been in and a folder for each major holiday of every year I'd been alive.

"What is this?" I mused out loud. "Some kind of digital scrapbook?"

"Why would your mom want you to find this?" Wesley asked. "Is this supposed to help? She knew going back to the house would be dangerous for you."

I clicked on Grandpa's funeral first. I'd been very young when Mom's dad had died, but still had a vague memory of the church service that was held for him.

A series of pictures scrolled across the screen. The front of the church, the pews, the closed casket covered in lilies. They all looked just how I remembered.

I closed out and clicked on "Christmas 12". A document listed off the presents I had gotten that year next to a picture of Avery under a dark Christmas tree, barely eight years old and grinning in the light of a camping lantern. I smiled.

"I remember that year," I said. "Mom insisted on only using gold tree ornaments because of a picture she'd seen in a magazine. There was a big storm, though, and—"

"And the power went out five minutes into opening presents," Wesley finished the story for me.

"Yeah!" I laughed. "Did I tell you that story before?"

He shook his head and pointed at the screen.

"No, it says it right there."

Sure enough, at the bottom of the page, there was a short paragraph outlining the power outage and how we had to use camping lights to open presents in the dark.

My smile faltered. I went back to click into a new file. This time, it was the one titled "Seventh Grade".

There were more folders inside of this one, and I clicked on the one called "New Student Orientation". I hit play on a video at the top of the page.

I recognized the halls of my middle school. I remembered orientation night. Dad had walked me through the rows of rooms, showing me where each of my classes were. The camera panned over, and there he was, smiling. It made me ache to see him looking so carefree.

"Your first class will be over here," he said, waving a schedule at the camera.

"And what's the teacher's name?"

I scowled in confusion. It wasn't my voice behind the camera, but Mom's.

"Does it matter?" Dad was scowling, now, too.

"Every detail matters, Vic!" Mom reprimanded him.

I shook my head.

"That's weird," I half-laughed. "I don't remember Mom being there."

Wesley had gone silent next to me.

"But I remember this!" I said. "Look! There's a stain on Dad's shirt. He had spilt his coffee in the car on the way to the school."

The video on the computer was grating against my memories. There was a dull throb in the back of my head. I ignored it and clicked into the next folder.

It was a bullet point list, outlining orientation. The first bullet said, "Vic spills coffee in the car".

"Sammy, I can go if you like," Wesley said. I shook my head at him and continued to click into folder after folder, each one outlining every detail of every day I could remember.

I made it to third grade. The class picture was the first thing that came up. I remembered the teachers lining us up on the bleachers, trying to get us to stand still long enough for the picture. I had wanted to stand next to Winnie but was too tall. They put her in the front row, and I was in the back.

She stood in the center of the picture, her round cheeks rosy and stretched into a grin. She looked just as self-assured as she was now. I scanned the picture, looking for my face. I wasn't there.

I wasn't anywhere .

Every folder, every file, had every detail of my life, but there wasn't a single picture of me.

"I don't get it," I said. Did I need to go back to the house? Maybe there was another flash drive for Avery.

"Why would your parents record all this?" Wesley asked. I wished I had an answer.

I scrolled to the bottom, zooming past what felt like a hundred different folders. The very last one was titled "Birth Certificate". My gut clenched. This must've been the folder Mom wanted me to find. My birth certificate would have the name of my real mother, and if I could find her, she might have answers.

My trembling fingers clicked into it, and I scanned the document hungrily, looking for my mother's name. A fresh wave of confusion engulfed me. Alison Taylor was listed as my birth mother.

But she couldn't be. The genetics test hadn't matched us as family, and she'd admitted to not being my birth mom.

"What is it?" Wesley asked. "What's wrong?"

I leaned back in the chair and gestured hopelessly at the screen.

"All of this is wrong!" I said. "This was supposed to answer my questions! This was supposed to tell me why I can't die or why Adrestus cares enough about me to kidnap Dad. But this information isn't even correct."

Wesley squinted at the birth certificate.

"What's not correct?"

"That's not my mom! She even said so!"

She'd lied to me my whole life, and even now, as I read through dozens of documents outlining every detail of my being, she was still somehow lying to me through the screen.

"Oh." Stark realization dawned on me as the pieces all began to click together. "Oh, no."

"What?" Wesley was no longer looking at the computer, but at me. "Sammy, what is it?"

The room spun. My forehead erupted in a sheen of sweat, but I kept clicking through the pages, desperate for something that would prove me wrong, something that would quell my fear.

"When I was thirteen," I said, trying to keep my voice even, "I rode my bike into the side of my dad's car."

I typed "Bike" into the search bar as I spoke.

"It left a dent in the door, and he was furious. It was so small, though, that he didn't notice it until a few days later. I never told my parents it was me."

Several search results appeared. I clicked into the result for the file "Eighth Grade".

"Okay," Wesley said slowly. I knew he hadn't figured out where I was going with this. "But if you never told them, it won't be here since they didn't know about it."

"Exactly," I breathed. I'd just found the picture of Dad's car. The dent was barely visible, but I still felt guilty about the damage I'd secretly done. Except it wasn't a secret. There was a whole paragraph outlining how I'd careened into the car and then tried to hide the damage.

They'd known. I'd never told them.

"Alison is an Inculcator," I reminded Wesley. I couldn't bring myself to call her "Mom" anymore. I felt hollow. My hands had gone numb, and there was a lump in my throat that I couldn't get rid of. "She can invent memories. Memories like denting your dad's car."

"No." Wesley grabbed my shoulder and turned me in my seat to look at him. "Don't even go down that road."

He was finally catching on.

I should have known after I found out she'd put fighting instincts in my mind. Why would she stop there? But if I really was Vic's daughter like she'd said, why would he have let her invent an entire life to cram inside my head? I scrambled across the computer lab to a trash can and retched, but nothing came up.

"Your memories are real." Wesley came up behind me to hold back my hair even though my stomach was empty.

"Those files go all the way to just before we moved here." I held myself up on the lip of the trash can with trembling arms. I'd been so sick that week. I thought it had been a summer bug. I wasn't so sure anymore. "Adrestus knows me, but not as Samantha. Wesley..."

I looked back at him. His wide eyes glistened behind his glasses.

"Don't be ridiculous."

"Wesley, I don't think Samantha Havardson is real. I'm...*I'm* not real."

32

Reflections

My whole world, the only life I'd ever known, was collapsing around me. Campus was quiet tonight, and as I charged across the grounds, unsure of where I was even going, I almost expected it to start fading away, as if it never existed. Like me.

"Sammy, come back!"

Wesley followed me across the yard. I refused to look back. I could barely hear him, anyway, over the pounding in my ears. He grabbed my elbow, and I spun around to face him. I'd expected him to look angry. After all, I'd abruptly got up and left him in the library, leaving him to scramble to gather both our things and chase after me.

Instead, his eyes were soft, and the corners of his mouth turned down in a frown. I bristled at him all the same.

"Leave me alone!" I spat. I needed to work this out. I had to be wrong.

"Why?" he demanded. His tone was as forceful as his face gentle. I pulled my elbow away from his grip but stood my ground. "So you can work yourself up and go do something stupid again?"

"Again?" I hissed in indignation. "What's that mean?"

"Going to your parents' house," he said, holding out a finger. He put up another. "Chasing after Dion. Literally getting yourself killed."

"I'm not going to do anything. I'm going to bed."

"I'm not letting you go to bed thinking your whole life is a lie."

I hated how sad he looked, and I hated how guilty it made me feel. Why should I be feeling bad? I didn't know what was real anymore, and here I was feeling like an inconvenience.

An icy ocean breeze ran between us, knotting my hair across my face, and I hunched my shoulders against the cold.

"Let's go inside," Wesley insisted. "We'll figure this out."

I nodded. I didn't know what else to do. Standing out in the cold with my entire existence in question, Wesley was the only thing I was certain of anymore. I let him lead me to the boys' dorm, up the stairs, to the study room we'd had our fight in not too long ago.

"Wait," I said, patting down my pockets in a panic. "Where'd it—"

Wesley waved the flash drive at me, and I snatched it from his hands. I turned it over in my fingers as if doing so would make the collection of folders it housed make sense.

"I don't exist," I said simply. It sounded ridiculous out loud. Of course I existed, but if my sixteen years of memory had been fictions invented by Alison and Dad, what had I actually been doing?

"You know that's ridiculous," Wesley said, taking a seat on the old couch in the corner of the room. I paced in front of him.

"Why else would they have this flash drive?" I asked. "It's my back-up software!"

The thought made me wrap my arms around myself to keep from shivering. Had there been other Samanthas? Each one of us picking up where the last one left off?

"Whatever you're thinking, stop it," Wesley said. "Let's say for a moment that your mom—"

"Alison," I interjected. The title of "Mom" was a lie, just like everything else.

"Let's say Alison did use her powers to give you a lifetime of fake memories." Wesley's words were careful, but his voice shook just slightly. "That doesn't account for any of the people who have memories of you."

I mulled over what he was saying for a moment and felt the pain in my chest loosen. He was right. Avery knew me to be his sister. Winnie and Amanda remembered me from elementary school.

Unless Alison had gotten to them, too.

The tightness came back, making it harder to breathe.

"Let's look at the facts," Wes said. "What do we know?"

Nothing. We know nothing. I shook my head.

"We know your— Alison wanted you to find those folders. She kept them for a reason."

"And we know Adrestus wants them," I added.

"Right." Wesley nodded. He was forcing himself to sound positive, but his eyes were a little too wide. "We know that the folders are a record of your life."

"And they include forged documents," I said, reminding him of the birth certificate. "If that's a lie, why shouldn't it all be? Why else keep it all unless it's to keep their story straight?"

Wesley stood up and grabbed my shoulders, grounding me to the Study Room with his sincere, green eyes.

"Because I know you," he said. "Because you know you."

"But so does Adrestus." My voice cracked. "And he knows things about me that I don't. All I wanted was to find Winnie."

I fell back into a chair and cradled my head in my hands. How had I gotten here? This was going to be a normal year of normal school before

I'd been shoved in that car trunk. I was starting to understand why Dad hated New Delos so much.

"I want to find her and just be normal," I repeated. "I wanted to help, but now I don't even know who I am anymore!"

"We'll find her," Wesley said, parroting the same words I'd heard over and over again the last few weeks.

"Will we?" I spat, turning my frustration on him. I couldn't help it. "Or will you?"

He was silent but continued to look at me.

"I have to make the team on Friday."

"I'm not letting you win."

"I'm not asking you to," I said, offended he'd think I'd ask that. "But this would be a lot easier if you hadn't quit on me."

"I did what I thought was best." His voice was soft but strained, and he sat back on the couch.

I put my head down on the table. The cool wood felt good against my forehead.

"Do you still think it was best?" I already knew the answer, but my heart still broke when I heard it.

"Yeah, Sammy. I do. I'm not going to watch you die again, even if you do come back."

The coolness was quickly seeping away, but I didn't want to look at Wesley, and I didn't want to have another fight in this dumb study room.

"Sammy?" He sounded nervous. "I know your fighting skills don't work against me."

I clenched my fists in my lap.

"I won't need them."

"It's just—" He faltered, searching for the right words. I immediately became guarded. "You know you won't be able to win, right?"

I lifted my head so I could glare at him. He'd been the first person to say it out loud, and as much as I hated him for those words, I respected he'd been the only one to be realistic with me.

"We'll find out on Friday, I guess."

"I hate to ask but—"

He stopped, already regretting what he was going to ask.

"What?"

"It's just, since you can't beat me, maybe you should drop out."

The rage and indignation was strong enough to push thoughts of everything else aside.

"You want me to quit? Just give up after everything I've done?"

Wesley shrank back into the couch cushions and looked around wildly as if the correct words to say might be posted somewhere.

"No, I just don't want to have to fight you. Wouldn't it be easier for both of us if it didn't happen if we both know how it's going to end?"

"It would be easier for you," I pointed out. "Adrestus has my dad, and I bet he has answers about this flash drive. I'm not going to tap out just to make you feel better."

"Right," he said meekly. "Sorry."

I didn't have any fight left in me, and as the flare of anger subsided, every worry came rushing back. Dad, Alison, Winnie, my identity and how I was connected to Adrestus...

It was exhausting.

"We'll figure it out," Wesley insisted. I nodded. We would. Even if I didn't make the team, I wasn't going to rest until I had Dad back and I knew who I was.

The furious scratching of pencils filled Fleming's classroom the next afternoon. The written part of the trials may have been the most boring test so far, but it was my favorite. No one was watching me. Andersen couldn't intervene. I didn't have to run. All I had to do was regurgitate information on the page, and all that would stand between me and being a permanent member was Wesley.

I was one of the first to bring my completed test to Fleming's desk. He raised an eyebrow at me as he took it.

"If only I could get you to study for your history tests, too."

Naomi was waiting for me in the hall, wanting to get dinner. I would've preferred to sneak off to the library and scroll through the flash drive folders again, but my stomach growled loudly, and I knew I should eat.

I felt my phone buzz in my pocket as we walked, but I ignored it. I'd been putting Amanda off all day. She wanted to know about the flash drive, and I wasn't sure what to tell her.

There was a commotion in the cafeteria where a group of students stood under the mounted TV, craning their necks to look up at the screen.

I did a double take when I noticed Jamie in a neat pantsuit smiling on the news between two adults. I recognized them as Ratcliffe and Ratcliffe, attorneys at law. All three of them were beaming.

The banner at the bottom of the screen read, "Ratcliffe projected to win City Council position".

Naomi swore under her breath.

"What's wrong? Isn't she your friend?" I asked. "Shouldn't you be happy for her?"

Naomi rolled her eyes.

"Maybe if her parents weren't anti-Apex freaks," she said in a hushed tone. "Besides, if you thought she was full of herself before, she's going to be unbearable now."

"Jamie? Unbearable? No way."

"Her dad's going to try to usher in anti-Apex laws," Naomi said, ignoring my sarcasm.

I knew Jamie's father being on city council could only mean trouble, but with everything else going on, it was hard to take it seriously. For one, he hadn't actually won yet, and sure, it sucked, but it wasn't quite My-Dad-Got-Abducted-By-My-Murderer level of suck.

And it didn't really compare to the fact that I might be a nobody built on a flash drive of lies, either. I pushed that particular looming question out of my mind. I hadn't told Naomi about the flash drive at all, let alone what its contents might mean. I didn't even know where I would start if I did.

"It'll be okay," she said, scooping soup into a cup. She could probably sense some kind of distress coming from me, but with everything that was going on, she'd never be able to guess what was bothering me at the moment. "Adrian Schrader still pretty much owns the city, so there's not much Ratcliffe will be able to do."

"I thought you didn't trust Schrader, either," I said, following her to a table. Naomi made a face.

"I didn't like that my powers didn't work on him," she explained. "That's an issue with me, not him. I'm sure he has all sorts of security, probably including things that stop Apex powers."

I shuddered.

"That doesn't sound like a man who is pro-Apex," I pointed out. "Or at least not one who trusts them."

Naomi sighed and shrugged at her soup.

"Either way, I trust him more than I trust that guy." She jabbed a thumb towards the TV screen, where John Ratcliffe was now addressing the crowd in front of him. I couldn't hear him from our table, but I was sure that whatever he was saying wasn't good for the Apex hiding on the island.

Jamie came back to the dorms late that night but made sure everyone heard her. Madison started chanting, "Ratcliffe! Ratcliffe!" Only a few others joined, but Jamie basked in it all the same. Her dad had won the vote, as expected.

"You know he's a civil servant and not the freaking king of the island, right?" A very tired Remi retorted from her doorway. There were a few stifled giggles, and Jamie looked like she'd been smacked. For a moment, I thought maybe Remi wasn't so bad, after all.

Renee chose that moment to exercise her Resident Assistant authority and sent everyone to bed. Jamie scowled but didn't argue. Naomi held the door to their room open for her and gave me a look down the hallway before disappearing after her friend.

I slinked back to my own room, dreading what kind of scene Jamie might make in First Period the next morning. Thoughts of her fell away as I drifted to sleep and the nightmares I'd had after Adrestus snapped my neck came back. I'd mostly forgotten them, having chalked them up to side-effects of the specialized Serum that Everly had injected into my spinal cord, but now they were rushing back in a fog of blood and smoke.

I stumbled through underbrush before collapsing in the dirt. A creek babbled nearby, and I pressed my fingers against my neck in an attempt to stem the flow of blood bubbling out. I was going to die, there was no avoiding it now.

But first, I needed to hide it. I could feel its smooth edges clasped in the palm of my free hand. The stream...

I crawled towards the sound of the brook. My vision was fading. I could drop it in the water, and maybe it would carry it away.

Or maybe it would sink, and when they found my body, they'd find it next to me.

I could throw it, but I knew my strength was fading.

I pulled myself all the way into the water. It was ice cold, running from the glaciers, but I only felt it for a moment before everything started to go numb.

I unfurled my fingers. They were sticky with blood. Mine? Or his? Maybe it was both. But my prize rested in the palm of my hand, small and round, turned red by the blood.

I flipped onto my back and felt the stream tug at my tawny hair. There was one place I could hide it. One place it might be safe from him. It would hurt, but I was dying anyway.

I raised my hand to the wound that ran down the base of my neck to my broken collarbone. I screwed my eyes shut. I hoped my brother would be okay...

I pulled at the cut, widening it. I kept from yelling out in agony as I pushed it deep into the wound, wiggling it into the tissue.

It was too much, and I went limp, staring up at the sky, water and blood seeping into my clothes like the darkness seeping into the corners of my vision...

"Samantha?"

The voice pulled me out of the dream. I sat up in bed, drenched in sweat and breathing heavy. It took my eyes a moment to adjust to the dark, but I didn't see anyone else in the room. Winnie's bed was just as empty as it had been for the last month. I ran a hand over my neck and shoulder to check the wound from my dream wasn't real. All I found was the raised line of scar-tissue from my bike accident years ago.

If that bike accident had actually happened.

I settled back into my pillow and closed my eyes after deciding I must have only dreamt someone calling to me, but then, I heard it again.

"Samantha!" a young man's voice said in a lilting whisper.

I sat up again, looking around the room wildly, my heart in my throat. A dark-haired young man, not much older than me, grinned from the other side of the floor length mirror on the back of the door. His blue eyes were radiant against his porcelain skin.

"Ah," he crooned. "There you are."

I leaped from the bed in a swirl of blankets. He kept grinning even as I drew back a fist and let it fly at the mirror. His manic smile shattered into pieces at my feet.

There was a sudden knocking at the door. I gasped and opened my eyes, back in my bed. I looked back at the mirror. It was in one piece, and no one was staring back at me from the other side. It had been another dream.

The knock sounded again, and I jumped, slapping a hand over my mouth to keep from yelping out loud.

"Sammy?" Naomi asked from the other side of the door. "Are you okay?"

I got up to open the door for her. Her pajamas matched the silk bonnet she wore over her curls, and she frowned with concern.

"What's up?" I tried to ask casually.

"You tell me," she whispered. "I could sense you all the way down the hall."

I stepped aside to let her in.

"Yeah, sorry," I mumbled. "It was just a nightmare."

"What happened to your hand?"

I held my hand out in front of me. Small cuts raked across my knuckles.

"Oh." I closed the door to look back at the mirror, double checking that it was still in one piece. My pale, sweat-shone face gaped back at me.

"Must've been some nightmare," Naomi mused. She still looked concerned, but her shoulders relaxed a little.

I turned on my desk lamp and dug a band-aid box out of one of the drawers.

"Yeah, it was."

"Do you want to talk about it? That helps me. You say them out loud, and you hear how ridiculous it sounds."

"I'm okay," I insisted, crawling back onto my bed. The dream was already fading away, though I could still see the smile of the boy in the mirror. I could hear him calling my name. I rubbed the scar on my neck.

"O-Okay," Naomi smiled kindly. "I'll let you sleep. Sorry I bothered you."

"No," I said, too quickly. "I mean, you can stay. If you want."

I didn't trust the boy in the mirror to not come back if she left. She pulled my extra blanket off my bed and crawled onto Winnie's covers.

"I don't mind," she said. "Jamie's phone keeps buzzing, anyway."

I left the desk light on, just in case.

33

The Final Trial

I avoided looking in the mirror as I got ready for class the next day. I didn't want to see those blue eyes looking back at me.

There was no trial to keep me occupied that day. Instead, I had to stew in anticipation for my fight with Wesley while I dodged texts from Amanda, which were becoming increasingly frustrated. I half expected to see her in the halls, ready to corner me again.

Meanwhile, Jamie was just as obnoxious as I'd thought she'd be with her dad being newly elected to City Council. She strutted around school, loudly warning any Apex that might be listening that "their kind" better watch out. Andersen beamed at her proudly, obviously overlooking the fact that Jamie was threatening him and his closest friends.

The weight of the upcoming trial doubled as I woke up on Friday. By the end of the day, either me or Wesley would be victorious. I hadn't talked to him since the other night when he'd asked me to quit. I couldn't wait to make him eat his words.

I signed up to go through more of Winnie's pictures during Study Period to keep myself distracted in the last hour of the day, and Fleming was kind enough not to give a pass to Wesley this time. It would have been torture to sit with him in the hours before the trial.

Without Wesley there, I plugged the flash drive back in, continuing to pour over the contents, determined to make the folders tell me why Alison had wanted me to find them. I found the folder with the details of the bike crash I'd broken my collarbone in. Most days it was easy to forget about the scar it had left me, but after the nightmare I'd had, neck wounds were on my mind.

The details in the folder were scarce, which was disappointing, since I didn't actually remember the crash all too well. I went over the handlebars and hit my chin on the pavement. I'd tried to break my fall with my left arm, resulting in my clavicle snapping in the middle.

There was a picture of my neck, shoulder, and collarbone, showing off the long, jagged scar that ran across the skin. I traced it with a finger along my skin as I looked at the picture. It all added up. It couldn't be fake, could it?

The door opened behind me, and I jumped.

"Samantha?" Naomi said. My stomach knotted. My palms were already slick with sweat. "It's time to get ready."

Wesley glowered at me from across the ring, and any hope of him going easy on me evaporated. Naomi tightened my arm guard, pulling my attention back to our side of the room.

"Remember, you just have to last the two minutes," she hissed. "Don't get any stupid ideas about actually trying to fight him."

"Right," I agreed. "But it might be nice to get just one hit in, you know? Just so everyone knows—"

"That you're an idiot?" She smirked and moved to tighten my other arm guard. "Don't worry, we are all very aware."

Fleming was taking his place in the booth. All eleven Freshmen had already fought, and all eleven Freshmen had lasted the full two minutes. Even Jessa had managed to avoid Heather by drifting weightlessly to the ceiling and hanging out there for two minutes.

Fleming tugged on his tie nervously, and I realized that not everyone here wanted to see me fail. Was it his own personal stake since he'd been through the same thing, or was he the only person who actually wanted me to join the Apex? Or maybe he was just queasy at the thought of all the paperwork he'd have to fill out if Wesley accidentally killed me.

Although, maybe he wouldn't have to do paperwork if I rose from the dead.

The other students filled the bleachers. The freshmen had joined the crowd as they passed their trials. Every member of the team was there to watch. Everest looked bored, and Heather gave me a nervous thumbs-up, but everyone else was ready to see me get wiped across the floor. Andersen was back in the top row of bleachers again. I was starting to feel as nauseated as Fleming looked.

"It'll be fine," Naomi assured me. "Your plan's a good one. Just don't try to prove anything more than you have to."

She gave me a final pat on the back and took a seat next to Heather.

Fleming cleared his throat. The students behind him shifted in anticipation.

"Are both opponents ready?" He looked at me as he said it. I stepped forward and raised my fists in front of my face like Wesley had taught me on my first day. Some students laughed. "Samantha, you have two minutes to remain standing. Your time starts now."

The red digits on the wall clock began counting down from 2:00. Wesley stared at me pleadingly from across the ring.

"Samantha, please don't make me do this," he begged.

I didn't respond. We'd already had this conversation, and my mind hadn't changed. Wesley hadn't even bothered to take off his glasses. Why would he? There was no way he'd need super-eyesight to fight some teenage girl who'd only been training for a month. Still, he could at least give me the dignity of acting like he did.

I shuffled forward, bouncing on the balls of my feet, ready, wanting him to come at me. But he wasn't moving. The clock ticked past 1:30. Irritation washed over me as I realized he was going to wait out the clock as long as possible, just to give me as much of a chance of backing out as he possibly could, before knocking me flat in the last few seconds.

Thing was, that could work for me. Naomi would want me to wait. Maybe I should...

"Take her out, Wes!" Skyler called from the seats. Wesley ignored him.

"Yeah, Wes," I jeered. "Take me out. Or are you scared of being beat by a Beta?"

He was still leaning against the low barrier, but his eyes narrowed. The timer ticked 1:15.

I danced closer to him on the balls of my feet, hands still raised in fists in front of my face. The crowd was getting impatient.

"I'll give you twenty bucks if you knock her out with your eyes closed!" Andersen yelled. His friends laughed.

Wesley was getting impatient, too. He straightened up.

"Please, Samantha," he said. "I don't want to hurt you."

Someone was booing behind me. Wesley bit his lip. 1:00. He looked towards Fleming, as if asking for help.

"So, you're gonna drag this out?" I goaded.

"I'm not the one dragging it out!"

"You're the one not fighting me! You haven't even taken off your glasses yet!"

Wesley flushed red. He tore his glasses from his face and flung them to the ground.

"There! I'm facing you like a real opponent. Now, please," he lowered his voice and walked towards me carefully, "Samantha, it's okay if you don't do this."

0:45.

"And it's okay if you do," I said. He frowned. Up close and without his glasses, I could see his eyes glimmered with pity and desperation.

"Sam, I—" he was speaking softly now so that the jeering crowd couldn't hear him. "I don't want to embarrass you."

My fist made contact with his face before I'd even realized I'd thrown the punch. A collective cry rose from the crowd, but I couldn't tell if it was in my favor or not. I didn't dare look at them, but instead kept my eyes on Wesley, who looked as stunned as I felt, but his brow quickly sharpened into a glare. He wiped a stream of blood from his nostril with the back of his hand.

I had drawn blood!

"Ha!" I yelled in elation. I didn't just land a punch on an Apex, but I drew blood, and on a heavyweight at that! My pride withered as quickly as Wesley's expression turned dark.

0:25.

I revealed the small flashlight I'd been hiding in my closed fist just as he lunged. I clicked it on. He cried out as I aimed the beam square in his face.

"Dammit, Sam, you idiot!" He grabbed at his eyes. His super-sight wouldn't have done him any favors in this fight to begin with, but now it was helping me. He should've kept his glasses on.

"Hey, I heard Andersen say he'll give you twenty dollars if you beat me with your eyes closed," I grinned. "Now you'll have to take him up on that."

0:14.

Wesley kept his eyes shut tight, but turned to face me. He was about to attack again, but, again, I was ready for him. My other hand was hiding a thin, silver whistle, and I brought it to my lips. Just as Wesley swung at me, I ducked out of the way and blew into it.

It was barely audible, but Wesley, along with a few others watching, cried out in pain. He clapped his hands over his ears.

0:11.

"A dog whistle?" he hissed in indignation. He lunged again. As I blew it a second time, he tore it from my hands and bent the metal in his fist.

0:08.

I stumbled backwards. My fists were raised in front of my face again. Wesley leered through squinting, watering eyes.

0:05.

"Samantha, please..."

0:03.

I swung another fist. This time he was ready.

0:02.

He grabbed my arm and pulled me in.

0:01.

A swift uppercut to my diaphragm. Sharp pain in my knees as I dropped to the floor. The mat pressed against my face.

0:00.

The buzzer was harsh and rang in my ears. There was cheering and laughing, and I couldn't remember how to breathe.

"Sammy." Wesley rolled me onto my back. "Are you okay?"

I struggled to push him away and inhale at the same time, but, for some reason, my lungs didn't want to work.

"Don't," I gasped, "call me Sammy."

Fleming appeared above me, but his outline was out of focus. Something lurched in my stomach, and then in my throat, and then—

I rolled onto my hands and knees, and the Cheerios I'd forced down for lunch splashed across the ring. There was a mixed cry of disgust and delight behind me. Even worse, I could feel hot tears welling in my eyes. I quickly brushed them away under the guise of wiping vomit off my face.

"Great, now the whole room's gonna stink of Beta!" Andersen taunted.

"Not since you're going to clean it," Fleming shot back. He grabbed me under my arms and guided me to my feet. "You know where the mop is."

My mind raced as Fleming led me to the exam rooms on the far end of the ring. Maybe time had run out before Wesley had hit me. Maybe they'd make an exception since I had fought so cleverly. Because that month of running and training and being hit over and over couldn't have been for nothing. I'd worked too hard to let Wesley of all people be what stopped me.

I shouldn't have thrown that last punch.

Everly met us at the door of the office. Wesley and Naomi trailed in behind us. Everly must've been watching the fight because he immediately instructed me to lie back on the exam table so he could check for bruising.

"I'm sorry, Sammy— I mean, Samantha." Wesley quickly corrected himself. He was still holding the dog whistle. I winced as Nurse Everly laid his hand over my abdomen. Unnatural warmth radiated from his fingertips.

"Slight internal bruising, nothing serious. And a hairline fracture on your left tenth rib. Nothing to do but wait for it to heal, unless you wanted to use the Serum."

"No Serum," Fleming said quickly. "Ice will do fine."

As Everly left to get ice, Fleming turned towards me. He had the same look that Wesley had just before I'd hit him. Fleming felt sorry for me, and that could only mean one thing.

"Samantha—"

My cheeks burned, and I felt a tightness behind my eyes. *Don't cry...*

"You did very well out there." His tone was low and careful. "Turning your opponent's strengths into weaknesses like that, it really was clever."

"Save it." I'd meant to come off gruff, but my voice cracked. Fleming bowed his head and ran both hands through his hair. It was amazing he wasn't bald for the number of times I'd seen him do that.

"You didn't make it the whole two minutes."

"I could have kept fighting!" I insisted. "He knocked me down, sure, but time ran out, and I could've kept fighting. I just wasn't given the chance!"

"Samantha—" Wesley tried to interject. Naomi shot him a warning glance, but it was too late.

"Oh shut up, Wesley!" I ignored the pain in my ribs as I got to my feet.

"Don't get mad at me!" he spat. "You're the one that played dirty! And I said I didn't want to do it."

"No, you just dragged a fight on for two minutes and then made me puke my brains out!" The tears flowed freely now. "You didn't even have the decency to treat me like a real opponent!"

"Because you aren't a real opponent!"

It was as if he'd hit me again. Fleming stepped forward.

"Wesley, that's enough." He put a warning hand on Wes's shoulder before turning to me. "Samantha, you did fight like a real opponent, but the rules are in place for a reason."

Naomi tensed up, and I was sure she could feel my anger just as strongly as I could.

"Come on," she said to Wesley. "We should leave."

"Take him to the next room," Fleming sighed. "Everly needs to check his eyes and ears for any damage."

It was hard to feel bad for any injury I might have caused Wes when I'd just been told that he'd fractured one of my ribs. I refused to look at him as they filed past. I was pretty sure he was refusing to look at me, too. Everly held the door for them as he came back into the room.

Fleming took the ice from Everly and nodded after Wesley and Naomi. Everly took the hint and backed out of the room once again.

I took the ice begrudgingly and held it against my left flank as I sat back down, this time in a spare chair rather than on the exam table. The cold was sharp against my body, but I welcomed the distraction. If I was lucky, it would numb my thoughts as well as the rib pain.

"Moving forward, you're still a person of interest to Adrestus, so you'll continue to be involved with Apex Team, just in a slightly different role." Fleming cleared his throat.

"You mean as a helpless civilian?" I snorted. Fleming fidgeted uncomfortably.

"Obviously I agree it would've been better to have you actually be on Apex Team, but given the circumstances—"

"The circumstances?" I glared at Fleming. "You mean because of the arbitrary and completely changeable rules you are refusing to change?"

"They aren't arbitrary, and I understand you're frustrated, but if a team member can't defend themself, they become a liability to the rest of the team."

Ice water dripped onto my leg. I had been gripping the bag of ice so tightly that my fingernails had bore a hole in the plastic. Melted water was oozing out.

"But it isn't fair," I mumbled. "You could've drawn any name. I could've beat Freddie or Everest. I could've beat Andersen! I'd love to beat Andersen!"

Fleming sighed.

"The rules were the same when I was undergoing the trials." He sounded full of regret. "And it was the same for me. Apex have never wanted Betas on the team."

"I know, you already told me. You had to fight your brother."

If Fleming's brother had been so great, where was he now? Why hadn't he swooped in to save Winnie or my dad? Maybe it was just the ice pack, but a shiver ran through my body. Fleming's brother couldn't be...

"I had to fight New Delos's greatest upcoming hero," Fleming said with a surprising amount of bitterness. His shoulders hung heavy. "He was just a kid, but the whole city already knew who he was."

"Paragon."

Fleming looked away.

"It's like I told you before. Everyone thought he'd let me win because no one had known about his knee but me. It took years more than high school had to offer to earn their respect as a team member," he sighed. "Paul Fleming was unbeatable, after all, so how could his Beta brother have won?"

"But you did," I pointed out. "Which is more than I can say about me and Wesley."

Even as I said, it didn't feel real. I couldn't have lost. I had to be on the team still. I was still down here, wasn't I? I wasn't done fighting. They couldn't just kick me out.

"I'll have Naomi clear your locker," Fleming sighed as he stood up. Almost every statue and picture of Paragon showed him smiling triumphantly. Fleming only ever seemed to frown. It was no wonder I'd never seen the family resemblance.

I was glad to not see any Apex on my way up to my room. I winced as I lowered myself onto my bed. I covered my face with my pillow, blocking out the ceiling. Nothing made sense anymore. I couldn't reconcile the image of awkward, nervous Fleming with that of his brother, the larger than life Paragon.

And I couldn't come to grips with the idea that my search for Winnie was over.

Because it's not, I told myself. Dad was still out there. Adrestus would still be looking for me, even Fleming had admitted so. I had the flash drive. They didn't. Amanda wasn't part of the team, but she was still searching for her sister. Why shouldn't I?

I would find them, team or no team, even if I had to die over and over to do it.

34

Wesley's Question

I woke up in the clothes I'd fought Wesley in. My pillow had fallen to the floor sometime in the night, and there was a massive knot in my neck. However, that was nothing compared to the throbbing in my ribs. I lay in bed for at least an hour after waking up. It was Saturday, so I had nowhere to go and nothing to motivate me to get out of bed.

Besides, I thought bitterly, outside of my room, I was just another civilian in danger for the Apex to protect.

I pressed my palms against my eyes, as if that might force away the bitter disappointment that had only grown overnight. If it hadn't been for the knock at my door, I might have lain there all day.

"One second," I mumbled as I rolled gingerly off the bed. I bit my tongue to keep from groaning. The pain in my ribs was ten times worse now that I was standing.

I recoiled when I opened the door. Wesley held up a toaster pastry wrapped in a paper towel.

"You weren't at breakfast, and I wanted to make sure you were okay, but boys aren't allowed in until after ten."

I glared at him and momentarily considered slamming the door in his toaster pastry, but my stomach was growling just enough for me to drop my pride.

He stepped in when I stood aside. I hoped he didn't expect me to thank him as he handed me the paper towel. He sat down at Winnie's desk. It was still set up the way she had left it, other than the light layer of dust that had settled over her things.

"Floundersen looks good."

Floundersen the Betta Fish was swimming circles in his tank. I'd upgraded him from his small cup a few days ago.

"Huh," I grunted as I bit into the pastry. The middle of the filling was still cold even though the edges were warm. I didn't care.

Wesley held his hands neatly in his lap, playing with his thumbs. I leaned against my desk and took another bite of pastry without looking away from him. He forced a smile back.

"How are you feeling today?"

"Fine," I said with my mouth full.

He waited patiently for me to say more, but I wasn't going to give him the satisfaction. Besides, he'd come here. There had to be a reason. His face was inexplicably turning a deeper red the longer he sat there.

"So," he said, clearing his throat. "We're, uh, all good, right?"

I glared at him over the toaster pastry.

"Sure. We're all good," I said dryly. "But I bet you wouldn't be saying that if I'd won."

His nostrils flared, but he kept his cool.

"You're my friend, Samantha. I hoped we'd be good no matter what." There was the slightest hint of a bruise under his left eye. I wondered if I'd put it there in our match.

Don't feel bad, I reminded myself. *You're mad at him.*

"Yeah, well, it's easy to say that since you got what you wanted."

"What I want is for us to be friends still."

I sat down on my bed, eating around the coldest part of the pastry. Every tiny movement sent pain shooting across my left side. The ice pack Everly gave me was in the freezer down the hall. I could make Wesley get it for me, but I didn't dare let him see that I was in pain.

"And I wanted to say that I'm sorry."

I finally met Wesley's eyes. He gulped.

"You're sorry?" I laughed. "I guess that fixes everything, huh?"

"I didn't mean—"

"You meant you're sorry that you feel bad and you want to feel better. So you bring me a half-toasted pastry and a half-formed apology and cross your fingers it'll work."

"I'm sorry I hurt you," he spat, suddenly defensive now that I was attacking him. "I'm sorry you're mad at me, and I'm sorry we're in this stupid situation! But I've already told you, I wasn't going to be responsible for the next time you die!"

"And I've already told you it's not your job to protect me!"

He rose out of Winnie's chair, shaking so hard that his glasses quaked.

"Can you try to pretend that this isn't all about you, just for a second?" he said. "I get that Adrestus has it out for you for some reason, but what about the rest of us? What about me? I still hear it, you know. The joint in your neck splintering. I hear it every night when I'm trying to sleep. I hear it every time I see you practicing with Naomi. It doesn't matter that you came back because I keep thinking about you lying on the roof with your head twisted in the wrong direction. And have you stopped for even a second to imagine what that was like?"

His words stung. They made me mad at myself, which only made me madder at him. I hadn't had time to think about what Wesley might be going through, but that's because I was going through my own things. Did that make me a bad person?

Maybe not, but it didn't make me a good friend, and even after yesterday's disappointment at the hands of Wesley, I knew I still wanted to be friends with him.

"Great," I sneered. I couldn't let him see that his words had gotten to me. "So did you come to apologize or to yell at me?"

"I came here to ask you to Homecoming!" he shouted.

I felt all the color drain from my face as Wesley's cheeks burned bright. His eyes went wide behind his glasses.

"Oh," I said, my voice now three octaves higher than before. I tried to think of something to say, but my brain only gave me static. "B-but, well…"

"It's fine, I'll leave."

He made a break for the door, and for a moment, I was too stunned to stop him.

"W-wait," I stammered, his hand on the door knob. He twisted around to look at me. His eyes were still wide, as if he were staring down an oncoming train. My mind remained blank. "Uh, thanks for the breakfast."

"Sure thing." He yanked the door open and fled into the hall, leaving me alone in my room, too stunned to move. My heartbeat roared in my ears.

Who did he think he was, showing up, knowing I was already mad at him, just so he could make me feel bad about myself and then drop that bomb? It wasn't fair, and it infuriated me.

I jumped up and doubled over in pain. I scowled as I stumbled to my door. I refused to let him have the last word. He didn't get to make me the bad guy and then run away.

"Oh, my god, you look like crap," Madison whistled as I passed her in the hallway.

"Thanks," I mumbled, bracing one hand against the wall as I trudged towards the elevator.

By the time the lobby doors slid open, Wesley had made it across the room, about to push through the main doors.

"Wes!" I called after him. He spun around and immediately began blushing again. It was his fault I wasn't on the team. It was his fault I couldn't even breathe without feeling immense pain in my side. I was too angry to care if I was about to cause a scene. "Fine!"

I faltered, and Wesley turned redder.

"What?"

"I'll go with you."

What was I saying? This wasn't the plan.

"Are you sure?" Wesley asked. "It's okay if you don't want to."

"But I do want to go," I said. "With you, I mean. Only if you want to, though."

"Of course I want to!" He crossed the lobby to stand with me. "But not if, you know, you hate me."

Hate him? How could I hate him?

"I don't hate you!" I insisted, maybe a tad aggressively. He grimaced. "Yeah, I'm really mad at you, but it's like you said. I still want to be your friend. Only if *you* don't hate *me*, though."

My face warmed as I said it, but Wesley's grimace turned into a tentative grin.

"You're annoying, but I don't," he said. "So, you'll go with me?"

"I just said that I would! Don't make me say it again."

His grin widened.

"Perfect! I mean, good. Also, are you okay?"

I was leaning against the wall and trying to breathe as shallowly as possible. Each breath was like a knife in between my ribs.

"Yeah," I insisted, straightening up despite the pain. "I'm fine. Homecoming. Okay, cool."

He was the worst.

"Yeah." Wesley sighed in relief. "I'm mostly glad you don't hate me."

"I'm glad you don't hate me, either. I'm sorry, by the way. I'm still mad at you for keeping me off the team, but I get it. I'd probably do the same thing if I were you."

"I promise, I'm going to find them, okay?"

I looked down at his shoes, not wanting to meet his eye. If anyone on the team could bring Dad and Winnie home, it was him. I was bitter I wouldn't be there to help, but at least I knew Wes would do everything in his power to keep his promise.

"I'm going to have to find a dress, aren't I?"

"Only if you want to," he said. "I'm sure you'll look nice in whatever you wear."

His cheeks glowed again, and he backed towards the door.

"Anyway, I'll see you Saturday." He was half way out the door. "But probably before then. For like, class and stuff."

"Right," I smiled. "I'll see you in class. And stuff."

Wesley gathered himself enough to send a single finger-gun my way and disappeared out the door.

Truth was, while it sucked I wasn't on the team, I was already formulating a plan. As I stared at the ceiling, clutching an ice pack to my side, I knew one thing for sure. I didn't need the team. I could work with Amanda, if I was ever brave enough to tell her the flash drive was a dead end. Wesley and Naomi were sure to let information slip, too.

The pile of homework waiting in my backpack forced me to finally get up on Sunday. If I finished it fast enough, I'd have enough time to continue skimming through the flash drive folders.

It still hurt to even breathe, but I was getting used to it by now. A large bruise had spread across my left side, and I ignored the sharp pains as I loaded textbooks into my backpack, preparing to trek them up to the library. I double-checked the front pocket to make sure the flash drive was there and felt my whole body go numb.

It was gone.

"Crap-crap-crap-crap!" I ripped everything out of the backpack in a blind panic. I tore through my notebooks and papers and shook the bag upside down, but the flash drive wasn't there.

I fell back against the desk, grabbing at my hair. Where was it? Had someone taken it?

I screwed my eyes shut, trying to picture the drive in my head, trying to see where I'd had it last.

The computer lab in the Apex Facility. I groaned. I was relieved to remember where I'd had it, but why did I have to leave it in the one place I wasn't allowed anymore?

I gathered my things back into my bag and hurried out of the dorm and across campus to the main school hall. The basement floor used to be an exciting place. It was somewhere I had felt I belonged, but now I felt like an intruder.

My key card had already been deactivated. A small red light blipped at me when I tried it on the door, and I scowled. I was locked out. I looked down the hall to Fleming's office, but it looked dark. For once, he wasn't there.

I raised a fist to the door and gritted my teeth nervously as I knocked. It was humiliating.

The door swung open, and Everly looked down at me in his lavender scrubs.

"Samantha? Is everything alright?"

"Sorry," I tried to smile. "I realized I left some school things in the computer lab, and I was hoping I could grab them."

Everly stepped aside to let me in.

"I'll take you there," he said. I needed an escort just to grab my things.

Jessa sat at a computer near the one I'd been using. I couldn't help the surge of jealousy that washed over me. Why did Jessa get to sit there while I'd been kicked out? I'd done more than her in the month we'd been on the team.

The knot in my stomach loosened when I saw my flash drive under the chair I'd used the other day. I scooped it up and inspected it for damage, but it appeared untouched. I shuddered to think about a drive full of my life's information in the hands of someone like Andersen.

"Hey, Samantha," Jessa said. "What're you doing here?"

"Just grabbing my things," I replied coolly.

"Oh." She sounded disappointed. "I was hoping maybe they'd changed their minds."

Everly waved from the computer lab door, signaling for me to hurry up. I turned to say bye to Jessa, but her screen caught my eye.

"Are those Winnie's pictures?" I asked.

"Yeah, Fleming assigned them to me now that you're...you know."

If I hadn't been so transfixed by the picture on the screen, I might have found the energy to be hurt that Fleming had reassigned Winnie's pictures so quickly. However, I only had attention for the black car in the photo. My heart rate quickened. I knew that car. I recognized the way the trunk bent inward and had to be held shut by bungee cords.

"Can you run those plates?" I asked.

"Samantha, it's time to go," Everly warned.

"I've seen that car."

"I don't think I can run license plates," Jessa said softly. She leaned in towards the screen, examining the car.

"Can you?" I turned to Everly. "Can we call the police and ask them?"

"You don't have clearance to be looking at these pictures anymore," Everly reminded me. I ignored him.

"One of Adrestus's men, Miles, drives that car," I explained. Winnie would've had to have taken the picture the day between our dock misadventures and the second museum trip.

Everly sighed but must have decided it was easier to placate me than it was to get me to leave. He slid into the seat next to Jessa's and logged in.

I turned the flash drive in my hands impatiently as I waited for the system to load for Everly and then as he typed the plate number into a program.

We held our breath as the cursor spun in circles as the database searched for matches. A match popped up. Everly shook his head.

"It's a company car for Schrader Industries," he said. "That could be anyone on the island."

"It doesn't say who it's issued to?"

"Just that Schrader's company owns it. I'm sorry, but now it's really time for you to leave."

He rose from his seat, but I held my hands out.

"Wait!" I said, trying to think fast. "Isn't there an employee directory for Schrader Industries? We can search for men named Miles and–and maybe..."

"That's a good idea, but you aren't on the team," Everly said.

"The docks!" I exclaimed as a bolt of inspiration struck. "Who owns the docks on the northwest end of the city?"

"There are a lot of docks, owned by a lot of different companies," Everly pointed out.

"Then look up Wesley's mission report from the first weekend after school started!" I insisted. "The docks where Adrestus had his people first try to kidnap me."

Everly hesitated but sat back down begrudgingly. Jessa and I watched as he pulled up another program.

"Schrader Industries," he read. "But they own most of the island."

"Most of the island," I repeated, watching the pieces fall together in my head. "Like the Museum? And the underground waterways where we found Tonka?"

"Be careful jumping to conclusions," Everly warned.

"Where's Fleming?" I demanded.

"It's Sunday."

"Doesn't matter, he's always here. Where is he?"

Everly stood a second time and towered over me.

"Should I write up a report?" Jessa asked quietly.

"Mr. Fleming is meeting with the Council at the moment," Everly explained. "He won't be free for at least another hour, but, again, you aren't on the team anymore. This is Jessa's assignment. She'll take care of it."

His words stung, but they wouldn't stop me.

"Okay," I nodded. "I'll leave, then."

Jessa could write up her report, but if the Council was meeting, they would hear from me first.

"You sure you have everything this time?" Everly asked, escorting me back to the hallway outside Fleming's office. "I won't let you in again."

"I've got it all. Thanks." I did my best to look innocent and not at all like I was up to something. Jessa was a good team member, but I wasn't going to leave finding my dad in her hands.

I hobbled up the stairs to the third floor of the school hall, regretting not asking Everly to fix my rib while I was downstairs. I usually would have taken the stairs two at a time but was now forced to lean against the handrail with every step.

Dr. Weaver's office was at the far end of the third floor hall. Her name was painted on the double doors, and I could see figures shifting behind the distorted glass.

I ran through the details in my head as I approached. Schrader owned all the places where there had been attacks. Schrader's company owned the car of the man who'd just ambushed me a week ago. Schrader himself was hiding the mysterious ability to negate Apex powers like Naomi's.

He was stealing the children of Apex when his family's legacy was built on creating a safe place for Apex to live. Had this been the plan all along? Draw in Apex families and harvest their non-Apex children?

I didn't bother knocking and pushed my way into Dr. Weaver's office. A large window behind Dr. Weaver's desk looked across the school fields and over the bay. It was a spectacular view, especially on a clear fall day like today. Dr. Weaver sat behind her large desk of polished mahogany. Framed diplomas hung on the wall next to her.

Five extra chairs had been pulled around her desk, each one occupied with a different member of the Apex Council, who all stared at me in varying degrees of surprise and anger.

"Samantha," Fleming said, shooting out of his seat. "What are you doing here?"

I stared back at the six pairs of eyes that were trained on me. My mouth was suddenly dry. Why was I there, again?

"I think I know who's behind the attacks."

"Really?" the man closest to me said. I recognized him from the day the Council had met in the Sickbay. He was wearing the same smart suit and was sipping from the same massive coffee cup. "That's funny because Alex just debriefed us on the trials, and maybe I didn't hear him correctly, but it sounded like he said you didn't make it."

My cheeks burned in indignation, and I instinctually looked to Fleming for help. He stared back in embarrassed horror.

"Enough, Trev," Dr. Weaver warned. "Samantha, we're in the middle of a Council meeting. Perhaps Mr. Fleming could spare you a few minutes after class tomorrow for any concerns you might have."

"I know who Adrestus is," I insisted, more forcefully this time.

"You know?" Dr. Parker from the university raised an eyebrow at me. "Or you think you know?"

"Adrian Schrader," I said, trying to force as much confidence as I could muster into my voice.

The man named Trev laughed so hard that he almost spilled his coffee on his nice suit.

"Should I include this in the notes?" he asked Dr. Weaver. "Let Adrian know the one kid who didn't make the team burst in and accused him of being the bad guy?"

Weaver pursed her lips.

"What do you mean?" I asked. Why would Adrian Schrader get meeting notes? He wasn't even an Apex. "Why does he get to know anything?"

"Who do you think bankrolls this whole operation?" Trev sneered. "Without Adrian, the Apex Teams wouldn't even exist."

It didn't matter. He wasn't stealing kids on the team, he was stealing kids who weren't.

"Why do you think Schrader is involved with Adrestus?" Fleming asked. I could tell he was mad. His frown threw sharp lines across his face.

"There's a car." I knew I sounded stupid.

"Miss Havardson, we'll look into it, in the meantime—"

"One of Adrestus's top men drives a Schrader Industries company car," I cut Weaver off, having finally gathered my thoughts. "It's the same one they tried to kidnap me in, and I saw it again last weekend when..."

"When what?" There was a warning edge to Fleming's tone. I gulped.

"I went to my parents' house to pick up some things after they...you know."

A vein throbbed in Fleming's forehead.

"And?" he hissed.

"And that guy Miles showed up, and we just ran the plates, and it's a Schrader company car."

"What do you mean 'showed up'?" Fleming demanded.

"I mean he came to the house, but Amanda and I—"

"Amanda Hendricks?" Dr. Parker interjected.

"Well, yeah." I shrugged. "She's the only person I know with a car."

"The fire in your parents' backyard." Fleming sighed and put his head in his hands. "Samantha, you should've told me!"

"When you say 'we ran the plates', who do you mean?" Officer Allen asked from his seat.

"Does it matter?" I asked, not wanting to get Everly in trouble.

"Yes!" Half of the adults chimed back at me.

"Schrader Industries owns every location there's been attacks at," I explained, pressing past the question of who ran the plates. "The docks, the museum, the pier where the festival was."

"Adrian Schrader's family built this island," Trev said. "You'd be hard pressed to find somewhere he doesn't own."

"And that makes him innocent?" I asked.

"Miss Havardson," Dr. Weaver clipped, "your concern is noted, and we realize you have a lot of personal stake in this matter, however you are no longer a part of the team. I assure you we'll look into it, but in the meantime, you need to trust us to do our jobs. Alex, see her out."

Fleming crossed the office and stood between the others and me.

"It's time to go," he said. "We'll take care of it."

Trev snorted loudly, but I turned away. Fleming opened the door for me and followed me out into the hall.

"Are you kidding me?" he seethed. "Why wouldn't you say anything about Miles? And why would you leave campus to begin with?"

Fleming was in a perpetual state of anxiety so it was rare to see him angry. Now he fumed in a way that made me glad he couldn't assign me running laps anymore.

"It didn't seem important at the time."

"But now it's important enough for you to burst in on a Council meeting? And accusing Adrian Schrader of being Adrestus?" Fleming threw his hands in the air. "Honestly! You want us to lose our funding?"

"Naomi didn't trust him," I said quietly, and I was surprised when Fleming wavered.

"Why not?"

"We met him at the Industry Fair," I recounted. "She said she couldn't sense him, like he was blocking her powers."

"But Schrader isn't an Apex," Fleming said. I shrugged.

"Doesn't change what Naomi felt," I said. "Or, I guess, didn't feel."

Fleming ran his hands through his hair.

"We'll look into it, alright?" he said, but I felt like he was just placating me. "Just promise me you'll stay on campus. Students shouldn't be leaving without permission, anyway."

"Yeah, alright."

"And Samantha," he said, his hand on the door knob to go back to his meeting. "Vigilantism will be met with expulsion. Try to keep that in mind when you hang out with Amanda Hendricks."

"Yes, sir." I gulped.

He frowned, and I knew he didn't believe for a second that I would stay out of trouble. However, he sighed and went back to his meeting. As the door opened and closed, I could hear voices discussing John Ratcliffe's appointment to the City Council, all talk about Adrian Schrader forgotten.

35

Guardianship

Monday morning brought my first school day as a normal student since the museum incident. I trudged into class, and Andersen leered at me from his seat. I ignored him and hurried to my usual spot next to Wesley but stopped in surprise when I realized it was already taken.

"Anthony!" I exclaimed. "You're back for good?"

Anthony grinned up at me from what had been my desk for the last month.

"Finally got cleared this weekend. I moved back in with Wesley yesterday!"

Wesley glanced at the seat on his other side, but it was already filled.

"Sorry," he grimaced. "I didn't think to save you a spot."

"That's okay." I shrugged. "I'm just glad Anthony's back."

The bell rang overhead.

"You're late if you aren't sitting when the bell rings," Andersen jeered. Wesley mouthed "sorry" again, but I waved him off. It was probably best I didn't sit by him anyway, with the combined awkwardness of me failing the trial and the upcoming dance.

I made my way to my old spot, where I had only sat for a week. Naomi smiled encouragingly at me from her seat next to Jamie. It was hard to smile back.

Andersen turned around in his chair.

"Beta luck next time." He winked.

Fleming called me up front after class. My heart rate doubled, and I wondered if he had an update on my Adrian Schrader theory. However, when I reached his desk, he handed me a copy of my class schedule.

"What's this?" I asked.

"You'll be back in your old gym class for Fourth Period today," he said flatly.

I deflated. The idea of playing half-hearted badminton while my friends learned elite combat skills made me want to drop-out all together.

"And Schrader?" I prompted. Fleming scowled.

"You'll get news when there is news that pertains to you."

I jammed my class schedule into my jacket pocket, crumpling it into a ball before stalking out of the classroom.

Even if he had reclaimed his seat in Fleming's class, it still made me smile to see Anthony back in classes. He waved excitedly when I entered the cafeteria for lunch, and I sat down with him and Wesley. It reminded me of the first day of school when he'd invited me to their table.

"Wesley told me about you two." Anthony grinned.

"What about us?" I asked.

"Homecoming!" He clapped Wesley on the back. In return, Wesley looked like he was trying to disappear behind his meatball sub sandwich. "You guys should come with Bethany and me! We're gonna grab burgers before the dance."

"That'd be fun," I said, though I wished Wesley would stop looking so uncomfortable.

I watched Wesley and Naomi meet up at the end of lunch, preparing to head to training with Coach Reiner. I couldn't help the bitterness and jealousy that rose in my throat like bile. It was hard to enjoy gym knowing what I was missing out on, and it didn't do me any favors that I could hardly move without pain radiating from my ribs.

The feeling of being excluded got worse as the day went on. I passed Justin in the hall before Sixth Period, and he gave me a sad smile. I wished he wouldn't. When the final bell rang for the day, I sat at my desk, wondering where I was supposed to go.

I couldn't go to training, but that's where my friends would be. Winnie was still missing, and while Anthony and Bethany were nice, it was hard not to feel like a third wheel with them.

The worst part was, at the beginning of the school year, when I felt this lonely, I could still text Dad. Now, all I had of him was his voicemail message. I dialed it, just to hear his voice.

"This is Vic. You know what to do."

Even with the upcoming dance, I spent the week wallowing in loneliness and self-pity. I was exiled back to my old seat in Fleming's class and was stuck wincing my way through a normal gym period each day while Andersen fired off as many jabs at me that he could in normal school hours. Jamie would laugh at them even though she had no idea what they meant.

With no training after school, I spent hours clicking through my flash drive, but the search only yielded more confusion and more memories that I thought had been secret. All the while a little voice whispered in the back of my head, *you aren't real.*

I told it to shut up.

Wednesday evening, after another two hours of searching through file folders, I finally gave up and went back to the dorms. The bruise on my side had started to yellow, and I was still too sore to condemn myself to walking up four flights of stairs. I scrolled through my phone as the elevator took me up to the top floor. When the doors slid open and I looked up, I froze.

Amanda scowled at me from down the hall where she stood in front of my dorm room door.

"Havardson!" She marched down the hall towards the elevator, pushing girls out of her way as I continuously punched the "door close" button, begging it save me from Amanda's fury.

The doors slid shut just in time, nearly clipping her outstretched fingers. I held my breath as the elevator sank back towards the lobby, but she was waiting for me, out of breath after running down the stairs.

She forced her way into the elevator and hit the button to take us back up.

"How long were you planning on avoiding me?" she asked. Last I'd seen her, she looked like she'd just rolled out of bed. Now, her make-up was done flawlessly, and her clothes looked like they could be brand new.

"I was hoping forever," I admitted as we reached the top floor again. I led the way to my dorm room knowing there was no escaping her.

She made herself comfortable on Winnie's bed and glared.

"I could've died helping you get that drive. What's on it?"

I could lie. I could tell her I grabbed the wrong one, it was just family pictures or financial records. But then she'd drag me back and tell me to find the real clue, and we'd be in danger for nothing.

I tossed her the flash drive in defeat.

"Nothing," I admitted. "Nothing useful, anyway. It's some kind of electronic diary, I think."

Amanda wrinkled her nose.

"For who?"

"Me."

"You made me take you to your parents' so you could grab your diary?" She grabbed Winnie's pillow, and I flinched, thinking she might throw it.

"Here's the thing, though!" I said quickly. "I'm not the one who wrote it! It's full of my life's details, including things I thought were secret, but I didn't put them there!"

The pillow dropped to the floor, and Amanda went white, making her red lipstick stand out against her pale skin.

"Dammit," she whispered. She punched the mattress and put her hands over her face. "That's what this is about? I said I didn't want to be involved!"

"What do you know about it?" I pressed but she shook her head.

"Nothing."

I knew she was lying.

"If it could help find Winnie and Dad—"

"It won't help anyone, alright?" she snapped. "It's not my job to clean up after your family."

Amanda knew why the flash drive existed. She got up from Winnie's bed, but I leaped between her and the door to keep her from leaving.

"Tell me where it came from," I demanded.

"It's not my business."

"Amanda," I pleaded. "Am I real?"

She gulped. That was not the response I wanted to a simple yes or no question.

"Listen, I just want to find Winnie, okay?" she said. "I'll keep searching on my end, and you let me know if the team finds anything."

"I'm not on the team," I said quietly.

"Oh." Her eyebrows raised a fraction. "I hadn't heard. I just assumed..."

"It's fine," I lied.

"You're not missing out on much, trust me."

That was easy for her to say. She'd actually made the team.

"I know you're hiding something from me," I said. "At least tell me why Alison wanted me to find that flash drive."

"Honestly, I don't know why she would. It'd be best if you just forget about it." She shrugged. "Focus on finding Vic, and I'll focus on finding Winnie."

"Amanda, please tell me what you know."

She pushed past me and yanked the door open.

"Bye, Sam," she scowled. "Tell me if you find anything."

"Wait!"

"I'm serious. Drop it."

"It's not that," I promised. "It's just, I think I found something."

Amanda was much more interested in my theory about Adrian Schrader than the Council had been. She helped herself to a notebook on my desk and began jotting down notes. She ripped the paper from the spiral rings and neatly folded it.

"Who else have you told?"

"The Council," I admitted. She laughed derisively.

"They won't investigate Schrader as long as he's bankrolling them," she said.

"Yeah, I kinda got that feeling from them, too."

"Keep your head down, alright?" Amanda insisted, her hand back on the door knob. "I'll look into it and let you know what I find."

As she left, I couldn't help but to feel grateful that she was willing to work with me, even if she was withholding information. To her, it didn't matter that I was a Beta, and she didn't care enough about me to be overly concerned about my safety. It was the perfect team-up.

I thought I might have some time to myself, but Naomi peeked her head in the door, grinning ear to ear.

"I have a surprise." She pushed her way into the room so I could see her arms laden with dresses. "I heard Wesley asked you to the dance, and I'm not letting you wear the dress you wore to the project fair."

Bethany trailed in behind her before I was given the option to say no.

"Try the blue one first!" she insisted.

"How do you have so many dresses?" I asked as Naomi laid them out on Winnie's bed.

"I like them." She shrugged.

Bethany picked out each dress for me to try. She was fun to have around and told me why each dress looked best, but I couldn't help but to suspect Naomi of inviting her as a buffer. I couldn't ask about Apex Team with Bethany around.

I looked at each dress in the mirror on the back of the door, trying not to think about the young man's face I'd seen leering from the other side in my dream the other night.

"Anthony and Wesley found a burger place a block from campus," Bethany said as I inspected a red dress that I knew must've looked a thousand times better on Naomi. "We're thinking about going there before the dance. Naomi, you should come, too."

Naomi smiled, but shook her head.

"I already told Jamie I'd go with her group," she explained, though she didn't look too excited about it. "She'd kill me if I bailed."

"Or you should do whatever you think sounds more fun." Bethany passed me the next dress. "She has Andersen, doesn't she?"

I settled on the blue dress that I'd tried on first after trying about half of Naomi's collection. It hurt to wiggle in and out of dresses with my fractured rib.

Bethany left for dinner while Naomi hung back to gather her dresses.

"I'll make sure to find a matching tie for Wes," she winked, and then frowned. "What is it?"

I shrugged. Nothing got past Naomi.

"Is Wes even excited for the dance?"

I'd barely had time to talk to him, and I never saw him outside of class anymore. He was busy with training and scouting, things I wasn't allowed to partake in.

"Of course he's excited." Naomi sat back down. "He's a little nervous, but don't tell him I told you that."

"Nervous?" I blanched. "What's there to be nervous about? He fights bad guys on the daily. This is just a dance!"

Her curls bounced as she laughed.

"The difference is he's used to fighting bad guys. The last time he danced with a girl, it didn't end well for either of them."

"He doesn't need to be afraid of me," I said and Naomi laughed again.

"I think he might be terrified of you, actually. You have punched him twice now." Naomi's smile faded, and she looked at the floor. "Can I ask you something?"

"Sure," I said, suddenly nervous.

She fidgeted for a moment, using her hand to flatten the wrinkles of the dress on top of her pile.

"How do you know if a friendship is bad?"

My heart sank, and my mind raced. Had I done something to hurt Naomi? Her eyebrows rose, and she looked at me in surprise.

"Not you!" she insisted. "You're a good friend. Just, I don't know, in general."

I sat down on my bed, thinking. I didn't know much about friendships, to be honest. I only kept a few of them. If Mom really had invented my whole life, she hadn't spent much time inventing friends for me.

"I guess if you have to even ask the question, it's a bad sign," I finally said. Naomi clicked her tongue.

"Yeah, I thought so." She sighed and stood up. "Thanks. It's good to hear someone else say it."

"You're welcome to change your mind about dinner before the dance whenever," I said.

Naomi laughed again.

"No offense, but with my powers, sitting through a dinner with you and Wesley before a dance sounds like hell."

"What's that supposed to mean?"

She shrugged coyly and draped her dresses over one arm before disappearing into the hallway.

Friday night brought more nightmares, although none of them were coherent. It was just flashes of blood, smoke, and the blue eyes of the young man I'd seen in my mirror.

I woke up Saturday morning with sweat-soaked pajamas and my heart hammering, feeling like I was being watched. I looked at the mirror, but it was empty.

I rolled out of bed and lifted my shirt to inspect my bruise. The skin was mottled with yellow and green. It still hurt to make even the slightest movement, although I was getting used to it by now.

My phone buzzed on my dresser, and I dropped my shirt back over my bruise. My heart stopped when I read the message on my screen. Fleming wanted me to come to his office. Maybe they'd found Dad or maybe they'd finally looked into Schrader?

I rushed to get dressed and minutes later stood in front of Fleming's desk. He took off his glasses where he stood opposite me to rub his face. He looked like he'd just pulled an all-nighter in his office.

"Take a seat." He gestured at the chair. I gingerly lowered myself into it. "Are you adjusting alright?"

"What do you mean?" That hadn't been what I'd expected him to say. I wanted updates, not a heart to heart.

"I know it must be difficult trying to get back into a rhythm."

"Yeah, it's fine," I lied. "Have you looked into Schrader yet?"

"I told you I'd let you know if we learned anything that pertained to you." Fleming frowned.

"Yeah, but doesn't it all kind of pertain to me?"

As I said it, I remembered Wes yelling that it wasn't all about me.

"Samantha, it's important that you try to find a new normal routine."

The word "normal" struck a nerve.

"What could be normal about this? My dad's missing, my mom's not even my real mom, I can't die, and no one knows why, and I might not even be—" I might not even be real. I stopped myself before I said it out loud. "Why did you call me down here, anyway?"

"Paperwork." Fleming braced himself. "We need to deal with the issue of your guardianship."

"Guardianship?" I screwed my face up at him. "My parents aren't dead!"

"But they aren't here, either."

"It's a boarding school! No one's parents are here!"

He pushed some forms across the desk.

"You know what I mean. Alison sent these over. If you aren't okay with it we can look into alternative solutions, but this is the only way to guarantee you stay at the school."

I skimmed over the documents, not making sense of most of it except for one key detail.

"*You?*"

Fleming turned red. On top of all the insanity I'd been mixed up in, Fleming somehow becoming my legal guardian was the cherry on top.

"Again, there are alternatives but—"

I scribbled my name across the bottom of the form. Fleming sighed in relief. As a teacher, he was already the boss of me. Nothing much would change, and I'd be able to stay at New Delos Prep.

"It's temporary, of course." Fleming cleared his throat. "That's all I needed, unless there was anything else I can help you with."

My side screamed for attention, and I smiled cautiously.

"You don't think I could have any Serum?"

"The Serum is reserved for the team," he said.

"Yeah, but it's not like I fell down the stairs," I pointed out. "I broke it doing official team business. The dance is tonight, and my rib is still broken so I was hoping maybe I could get something a bit stronger than an ice pack."

"Honestly, Samantha," Fleming sighed, "I would say yes if I didn't think you'd immediately run off to investigate Schrader yourself."

"So you're keeping me injured to keep me on a leash?"

"Like I said, it's time to embrace normal. Even if 'normal' feels like a bit of a stretch."

I scowled. I'd just signed papers allowing my history teacher to be my guardian. Nothing was normal.

"Whatever. You're a lame dad, you know that?"

I scooped up my things to leave before I could let him have the last word, but I thought I saw him smiling as I closed the door behind me.

36

The Dance

I did my best to sit still while Naomi came at my face with a make-up brush.

"Are you trying to make me look nice or blind me?" I winced as the brush pressed against my eyelids.

"At this point, whichever is easier," Naomi said through gritted teeth. "You need to stop moving."

I opened one eye to check on her while she ran the brush through the eye shadow pallet. She was already dressed for the dance in a deep purple dress that made me feel silly in the blue one I was borrowing. She was gorgeous, with her curls surrounding her head like a halo and her make-up perfectly done.

I'd insisted on doing my own make-up, but she'd insisted harder that she do it. We were sitting in my dorm room, and I wondered if she was trying to put off joining Jamie for whatever their pre-dance plans were.

"Don't worry, I'm almost done." She shuffled through my make-up collection, which wasn't much. "When are Wesley and Anthony headed over?"

"A few minutes, I think." I glanced at the time on my phone before Naomi came at my face with another brush. "You sure you don't want to go to dinner with us?"

Naomi laughed and shook her head.

"Alright, you're good," she said. I leaned forward to look at myself in the door mirror.

"You think he'll even recognize me?" I asked. Naomi had done an excellent job, but I felt a little silly, like I was pretending to be someone I wasn't.

"You think a little make-up is going to fool his super senses?"

My phone buzzed. Wesley was outside. My stomach worked itself into a knot, but I didn't know why.

"You'll be fine," Naomi said, double-checking her curls in the mirror. "I'll see you guys at the dance, alright? You better come find me."

Bethany bounced with excitement where she waited in the hall.

"Wait until you see the decorations!" she gushed. "It took us six hours, but it looks amazing!"

We crammed into the elevator with several other girls. No one felt like walking down four flights of stairs in heels. I looked down at my high-top sneakers. My nice shoes had given me blisters at the Industry Fair.

In the lobby, Wes stood near the doors with Anthony. His hands were jammed in the pockets of his dark jacket as he scanned the crowd of girls. Naomi must have been able to find him a blue tie because Anthony was reaching over to straighten it.

Wesley caught my eye and grinned.

"I feel like I haven't seen you in forever," he said.

"You just saw me at lunch yesterday."

"True." He shrugged, his hands still in his pockets. "It's just different, you know?"

He went red as he said it.

Bethany shrieked in delight next to us. Anthony fastened a bright pink corsage to her wrist, and Wesley visibly gulped.

"I didn't get you one of those," Wesley said quickly. "Is that okay?"

"It's fine." I smiled. "I didn't get you one, either."

Anthony and Bethany walked a few paces ahead of us, leading the way to the burger place down the road. Wesley finally pulled a hand from his pocket.

"I did, uh, I got this," he said, turning cherry red. He dangled a silver chain in front of him. A bent-up piece of metal swung from the end. I grabbed it for a closer look and laughed, ignoring the pain that erupted in my side as I did. Wesley had strung the dog whistle I'd used during the trial into a necklace. "You don't have to wear it if you don't want to."

I took the whistle in my hands, grinning as the stilted awkwardness between us seemed to melt away.

"No, I like it!" I insisted. I clasped it around my neck and turned to Wesley to show him. His eyes darted from the whistle to the scar running down my neck and to my collarbone. The dress I was wearing showed off the whole thing.

I turned away so Wesley couldn't see it anymore.

"I don't want things to be weird for us," he murmured, so that Anthony and Bethany couldn't hear. "I feel like everything is going back to normal, though."

There was that word again. Normal. Things for Wesley probably felt that way. He had his roommate back. He wasn't worried about me getting murdered at any moment. His life was moving on.

"Yeah, we're good," I said.

"Would you guys hurry up?" Anthony called from up ahead. They'd put more distance between us. I winced as we sped up.

The burger place was full of girls in dresses and guys in suits, but Anthony was able to find us a table. We laughed as we ate, and I was surprised to find I was actually having fun. A small part of me felt bad for it, though. What right did I have to be enjoying myself while Dad and Winnie were missing?

As happy as Anthony looked, I couldn't help but to notice the way he jumped and gripped the table when someone came up behind him to say hi, and when the conversation lulled, he got a far away look as he stared aimlessly out the window. Whatever was haunting him, I knew Dad and Winnie were going through the same thing each minute they were left unfound.

Bethany hurried us out as soon as we were done, eager to get to the dance as soon as the doors opened. She led the way back to the school gymnasium, bouncing so hard in excitement that I thought she might break a heel.

Streamers, paper, and balloons covered the gym. Twinkling lights were strung into a tunnel at the entrance. Bethany beamed proudly at the decorations she'd helped put up.

The music blared from the far corner of the gym, and the kids that were showing up were already flocking towards it. A pile of shoes sat under each table as girls immediately shed them to better dance. Someone threw glow sticks into the growing crowd, and a teacher hurried over to yell at them.

"Can you even hear anything right now?" I shouted at Wesley over the music. He winced and nodded.

"I'll have a headache tomorrow, but I'll be fine."

Bethany and Anthony disappeared to the voting table to cast their ballots for Sophomore Homecoming royalty. There was a rustle behind me, and I jumped as Heather appeared at our side. She'd chosen a long red dress, and for the first time, she wasn't wearing a bow in her dark hair.

"Wesley, I'm stealing your date."

"You shouldn't be using your powers here," he warned. "Most people aren't used to their classmates appearing out of thin air."

"No one's paying attention." She rolled her eyes and took my wrist. "We're doing a picture, come on."

"What about me?" Wesley protested as we left him behind.

"Girls only!" Heather called back.

Naomi and Olivia were already by the photo booth and pulled me in to pose with them. It made me happy that they still wanted to include me in their picture, even if a part of me was suspicious they were only doing it to be nice.

"I thought you came with Jamie?" I asked Naomi after our photo was snapped. She scowled and nodded towards the voting station.

"She's overseeing Homecoming Queen votes."

Jamie leaned against the table with the ballot boxes. I couldn't hear her over the music, but she talked animatedly. Andersen nodded along with her, though I doubt he heard anything she was saying.

"Hey, come here," Naomi said, pulling me back into the photo booth line. Wesley had caught up with us. "We have to take one of the three of us!"

The gym was filled with students now, most of them conglomerating on the dance floor. One kid lifted his friend onto his shoulders before teachers swooped to bring an end to it.

"Should we go vote?" I asked.

"No, Jamie's over there." Wesley wrinkled his nose.

"But I want to go vote for anyone that's not her."

Naomi and Wesley followed me to the table. Mrs. Young watched over the ballots and handed us each a paper with "Sophomore" printed across the top.

"Hey, guys," Jamie exclaimed, as if just noticing us. She smiled sweetly. "Wow, Samantha, you look really pretty."

"You can stop," I snorted. "I'm not voting for you."

Her smile turned sour.

"In that case, fine. The best you could do were hand-me-downs, and Naomi looked better in that dress anyway."

"That's enough," Naomi warned. Jamie's eyes widened ever so slightly.

"I was wondering where you went." She glared. "I thought you came to the dance with us."

"I'm not going to third wheel all night while you tell anyone who will listen about your dumb dad," Naomi said.

"You don't talk to her that way!" Andersen said, stepping in.

"You know what, Lewis?" Naomi spat. "How about you go suck up to someone that actually gives a crap about you for a change? Because I can promise you, Jamie doesn't."

She shouldered her way to the table and scrawled her own name across the ballot as big as she could. She made a show of flashing it at Jamie so she could see and then folded it up and dropped it in the box.

"You know how badly I want this!" Jamie screeched.

"No fighting," Mrs. Young said from her side of the table without looking up from her phone.

Naomi grinned and pulled Wesley and me away before we could cast our votes, but I didn't mind.

"Naomi, that was amazing!" Wesley exclaimed. Naomi shrugged, beaming brighter than ever.

"It was a long time coming," she said. "Hey! I like this song!"

She ran to the dance floor, and we stumbled after her into the throng of students. They all shouted along to the music, but I didn't know the lyrics. I nodded in time to the beat, unable to do more with my fractured rib, and as the songs changed, the people around us did, too.

Different members of the team would stop and dance with us before moving onto their next group of friends. It was easy to pretend I was still one of them.

The music slowed and became softer. There was a collective groan as girls grabbed their dates and pulled them to the dance floor while half the students already there quickly vacated.

I froze. I would rather face Wesley in the arena again than turn and face him now as the slow song came on.

"Did you want to...?" Wesley mumbled.

"Sure!" I tried to recover from my panic by forcing myself to sound overly chipper. I cringed.

I glanced at the other couples, all of them already with their hands on each other's shoulders and waists, swaying with the music. I followed suit, placing my hands on Wesley's shoulders, but kept them balled in awkward fists.

Wesley put his hands on my waist. Where was I supposed to look? I kept my eyes dead ahead so that I was staring at Wesley's chin. I knew enough to know that I wasn't doing any of this right. Why couldn't Alison have put dancing abilities in my head, too?

"Are you okay?" Wesley asked. I dared to raise my gaze from his chin to his eyes. He looked like he was holding in a laugh.

"Yeah!" I lied. "I'm just not sure I've ever danced before."

"You didn't find anything on that flash drive about you dancing?"

I snorted.

"Not yet."

I became hyper-aware of my balled fists on his shoulders. One at a time, I stretched my hands and laid them flat on his shirt.

"I hope you're having fun," Wesley said.

"Me, too."

He looked at me funny, and I quickly backtracked.

"I mean, I hope you're having fun, too," I stammered. How long was this song?

I looked around at the other dancers and was relieved to see many of them looked as awkward as I felt, with the exception of one couple whose faces were locked together.

"You look nice, by the way," Wesley said. "I don't know if I said that before."

"You're just trying to get me to vote for you for King," I teased. "But thanks. It's Naomi's dress."

"And this is Everest's tie," Wesley admitted with a crooked smile.

"The shoes, though," I said seriously, "they're one hundred percent mine."

Wes peered down at my high-tops and laughed.

"Very practical choice."

Just as I was beginning to enjoy dancing with Wesley, the music picked back up, and a surge of students rushed the dance floor. Wesley's hands dropped from my waist, and it took me a moment to realize mine were still at his shoulders. I quickly drew them away.

"How we doing, New Delos Prep?!" a voice called out over the speakers. The crowd roared in response. "Are you ready to crown your class King and Queen?"

I turned to Wesley. My side was throbbing from standing for so long. If only Fleming had given in when I'd asked for Serum.

"I'm gonna go sit down for a minute," I said, shouting again to be heard over the music and cheering. He nodded, and I wove between bodies to get back to the table where we'd dropped our stuff.

"Freshmen!" The voice on the speaker called out. "I give you King Donnie Hart and Queen Jessa Davidson!"

I smiled to myself as I pulled my phone from my bag. It was nice that Jessa was as well liked outside of Apex Team as she was amongst team members.

I frowned at my screen. Amanda had texted twelve minutes ago.

I'm in the park across from Schrader Industries. I have something you need to see.

So she'd taken me up on my tip about Adrian Schrader. My mind raced, wondering what she might have. I quickly typed back a response.

You can't come to me?

No. Hurry. It's urgent.

"Sophomores! Welcome your King and Queen, Anthony Schultz and Bethany Valente!"

I wanted to feel happy for my friends, but my heart was hammering louder than the music. I looked up for Wesley but couldn't see where he'd gone.

"If you're looking for your fake boyfriend," Andersen sneered behind me, "he's over there."

Andersen dropped into the seat next to mine, and I set my phone down before he could see Amanda's texts. I looked where he was pointing, and my heart fell. Wes stood at the punch bowl, laughing with Remi. She reached out and fixed his tie for him.

"So what?" I shrugged. "They're friends."

"They were friends a few times last year, too," Andersen goaded. "I wonder if he would've asked her instead if he didn't...well...you know."

I bristled but refused to let Andersen see he'd hit a nerve.

"Don't you have to go console your girlfriend?" I snapped. "They just called Sophomore Queen, and it wasn't her."

"Eh." He shrugged, tilting back in his chair. "She's mad at me. But at least she came here with me because she wanted to."

I didn't understand what Andersen meant so I ignored him. I picked my phone back up, making sure to angle the screen away from him.

Can't you tell me what you've found before I come?

"Wait, wait, wait," Andersen said quickly, falling forward in the chair so all four legs slammed to the gym floor. "Do you not know?"

Amanda's response blipped across my screen.

Not over text. Get here. Now.

"Go away," I said, gathering my things. I'd show Wesley the texts. We would figure out how to get to Schrader Industries together.

"Careful," Andersen warned in a sing-song voice. "You wouldn't want to bother Wesley while he's on a mission."

"Mission?" I looked at Andersen. "What mission?"

Tonight was supposed to be a night off. Even though I wasn't on the team anymore, I would've hoped Wesley would trust me enough to let me in on anything he was assigned to.

"Don't take it too hard." Andersen shook his head. "I would've volunteered, but I already had a date."

I dropped my phone into my lap and looked back at Wesley and Remi. She was still holding onto his tie while he told a story with lots of hand movement. She tilted her head back in a laugh.

"I'm the mission?" No, that couldn't be it. Wesley had asked me to the dance because he'd wanted to, because we were friends, not as an assignment.

"Big school event like this was sure to draw attention," Andersen explained gleefully. "Fleming wanted to make sure you'd be safe in case something happened so he asked the team if anyone would volunteer to take you to the dance. Trust me, I would've if I could've."

I'd thought Wes and I had been having fun together. It was supposed to be a good night, and so far, it had been. But now I knew that he was just my babysitter. Even now, he was talking to the girl he'd rather be here with. My lip quivered, but I had no way to tell if it was from bitter disappointment or anger since both were raging inside me.

"So, again, while Jamie might not be the most caring girlfriend in the world, at least she came here with me because she wanted to and not because someone made her." Andersen stood up and stretched. "Enjoy the dance with your chaperone."

I would've loved nothing more than to punch Andersen in his smug face, but he was already walking away. I looked back at Wes. He scooped punch into a cup for Remi. He wouldn't miss me if I left.

I grabbed my things and didn't look back. I shouldn't have been surprised. Why would the guy who'd actively worked to keep me off the team want to immediately turn around and go to the dance with me? All that crap about wanting to still be friends...I'd fallen for it because it was what I wanted.

The October night air sent a chill through me. I should've worn a jacket over the dress. I would have to stop at the dorms before going to meet Amanda.

I angrily threw the dress across my dorm room, wincing in pain as I did so. I should've known about Wesley. Fleming had admitted to not letting me have Serum in an attempt to keep me out of trouble. Even when I had been on the team as a provisional member, he'd made Naomi and Wesley keep an eye on me.

So what was he more worried about? Adrestus attacking me or me looking for trouble?

I smiled wryly to myself as I threw on jeans and t-shirt. I grabbed my zip-up jacket on my way back out of the dorm.

It would take almost an hour if I walked to Amanda. If it was as urgent as she was saying, I didn't have that kind of time. I looked up the bus route as I walked past the gym.

I could hear the music all the way out here, and technicolor lights flashed in the windows. I wondered if Wesley had even noticed I was gone or if he and Remi were still making eyes at each other over the punch bowl.

A light drizzle had started to fall over the darkened city streets. I pulled my hood up and shoved my hands in my pocket as I waited for the bus. I glanced around nervously, sure that Wesley would show up at any moment to stop me.

I scoffed to myself when the bus rolled up and he hadn't shown. Either he hadn't even noticed I was gone, or he didn't care. I shoved a few dollars in the fare box and found a seat near the back.

I kept my hood up, watching the city pass. Rain clung to the window, distorting the street lights. Had Naomi known Wesley only asked me because he was told to? Did I actually have any friends?

My phone buzzed in my pocket. Amanda was wondering where I was. The Hendricks sisters didn't make the best company, but at least they trusted me.

The closest stop to the Schrader Industries building was a block away. I hunched my shoulders against the rain and stepped off the bus. The domed penthouse at the top of Schrader Industries shined bright, but the rest of the skyscraper was dark.

Streetlights illuminated the park across the street from Schrader Tower. As I got closer, I could make out the wooden frame of the gazebo that sat on its border. A figure hunched on a bench under it, protected from the rain. Amanda didn't acknowledge me as I approached but continued to look resolutely forward.

A leather album sat on the bench next to her.

"What is this?" I picked up the book and took the seat next to her. She didn't respond. "Is this what you wanted me to see?"

The first page showed an old picture of my family home, the one we'd lived in before moving to the city. A "For Sale" sign had a red "SOLD" sticker slapped across it. Dad grinned at the camera, a young Avery in his arms, clinging to Dad's neck.

"The photo album," I sighed. I'd seen it in my bedroom when I was searching for the flash drive but hadn't had the time to grab it. "You went back to my parents' house for this? Why? And why did we have to meet here?"

Amanda remained taciturn, and I closed the album. My heart hammered in my chest. I'd pushed away the idea that "Samantha Havardson" was a made-up character shoved into my brain by Alison's powers. I didn't want to think about that possibility, but I knew Amanda had brought me the answer. I just had to open the album.

I listened to the rain pattering on the gazebo roof while Amanda waited. I raised a trembling hand and flipped to the middle of the book. There were pictures of Avery's birthdays, holidays, vacations, Dad pulling a scorched homemade pizza from the oven, Mom teaching Avery how to do a cartwheel...

They were all things I remembered, but there was no record of me being there. But Alison had even said to Fleming that I was Dad's. Had that been a lie, too? If not, where was I?

"This doesn't prove anything," I said. "I-I was camera shy. There's got to be one..."

I tore through the album now, flipping through pages as fast I could until I reached the leather-bound back cover. I gripped it so hard that my knuckles turned white in the dim light.

The reality of what I'd been afraid of settled over me. I wasn't real. I didn't have a family. I was alone. Even my friends only hung out with me because Fleming had made them.

No, I told myself. *You have Dad.*

"You could've shown me this anywhere," I said. "So why are we here?"

But Amanda stayed silent, still looking forward. A sharp, bitter smell made me wrinkle my nose.

"Is something burning?" I asked, leaning away from Amanda. It was only then that I saw her hands quaking, straining against something I couldn't see. "Amanda?"

I pulled her hood back to reveal a thin stream of smoke rising from the nape of her neck. A white patch clung to her skin just below her hairline, and it was catching fire.

"R-run," Amanda stammered, straining to look at me through the corner of her eye as gloved hands wrapped around my face.

37

Behind the Mask

It was a set-up, and Amanda was the bait.

I twisted away, managing to break my assailant's grip. Amanda tried to get up, but the paralytic patch on her neck kept her from getting far. She crumpled to the ground in front of me, still trying to burn through the patch, as a familiar Greek tragedy mask materialized in the darkness beyond the bench.

Dion leaped over the bench, and I dealt him a kick while he was still airborne. The movement made my ribs feel like fire, but I managed to knock him to the ground.

I bent over Amanda and scrambled for the patch. I ripped it off, singeing my fingers against her skin. She gasped in relief as the paralytic released her, and she pushed me aside to shoot a column of flame at Dion, who was staggering to his feet.

I grabbed at my ribs as Amanda fended off Dion's next attack. I tried to regain my breath and formulate a plan, but each inhale of air felt like a knife in my side.

Dion was skilled, but so was Amanda. They sparred in a mess of flames and fists. Dion's cloaks must've been made of a special material, because they didn't seem able to catch fire.

Someone grabbed my wrist, and my whole body locked up. I tried to call out for Amanda, but my mouth couldn't form the words. Long, white hair tickled the side of my face. Tears of helpless panic welled in my eyes.

"It's been a while," the white-haired woman purred. What had Dr. Weaver said her name was? Mira?

Amanda turned at the sound of Mira's voice. Flames shot across the gazebo floor and licked across my arm. I shouted in pain as my skin burned, but I was free of Mira's grip.

Amanda and Mira stared each other down, both knowing the danger of touching the other, unsure of how to attack. I scrambled to get away from them, cradling my burnt arm against my chest. Something splintered and cracked above me. I looked up to see the gazebo ceiling engulfed in fire.

But where was Dion?

I glanced around and spotted him, already halfway across the street, sprinting through the rain towards the museum.

"Amanda, the other one—"

"Just go!"

I heaved myself to my feet and jammed my hand in my pocket for my phone. I'd been an idiot to leave the dance without Wesley and Naomi. I dialed Wes's number as I struggled to the sidewalk. I pressed it against my ear. Part of my jacket sleeve had burned away, leaving my burnt, blistered skin vulnerable.

I gripped the phone and listened to it ring. If Andersen had just left me alone, I wouldn't have run off like that. If he had just been able to go one night without making me miserable, I'd have my friends here with me.

Dion paused at the top of the stone steps and turned his mask towards me. The museum behind him was dark, but he stood out against the glass door. Lights from the street bounced off his grotesque mask.

Andersen knew I was at the dock the night I was shoved in a car trunk.

Andersen threw away my homework, ensuring I went to the museum the night it was attacked.

Andersen had thrown me in the ocean where I *died*.

And Andersen had made me mad enough to run into danger just as Amanda had texted me to meet her.

"The voice message box you're trying to reach is full," a cool voice said over the phone.

I hit redial and stared back at the mask, shaking in anger and pain. It couldn't be Andersen. We'd run into Dion when we'd rescued the missing students.

But where had Andersen been that night? He wasn't on the mission. Maybe he'd been back at the facility, but I couldn't say for sure.

"The voice message box you're trying to reach is full," the voice said again.

I stepped out into the street, my shoes soaking with rain water. The gazebo continued to burn behind me, and orange light danced across the puddles on the pavement.

Rain drops glistened on the mask, which was still staring at me from the front of the museum. A cool determination overcame me.

It couldn't be him...

But it had to be.

I knew Andersen hated me, but we'd still been on the same team, fighting the same enemy. He hadn't just betrayed me, but his friends and his teammates, too.

I'd been an idiot to fall for another one of his tricks.

I redialed Wesley. I knew who was behind that mask, and I'd beat him before, but that had been without a broken rib or burnt arm.

"The voice message box—"

I hung up before the voice finished her message and shoved the phone back into my pocket. I stared back at the mask, steeling my nerves with a few shaky breaths. My side and arm hurt, but nothing was going to keep me from stopping Andersen.

Dion turned away as I began running across the street, splashing with each step. He slipped into the museum just as I reached the bottom of the stairs. I took the stone steps two at a time. My ribs screamed in protest. I ignored them.

For more than a month, Andersen had watched me search for Winnie and my dad, and all along he'd been the one behind it. I wouldn't be surprised if he'd lied about Wesley taking me to the dance as part of a mission. He wanted me angry, and he wanted me here.

I caught my breath on the top step and pushed my way inside. The door slammed shut behind me, and there was a loud, metal click. I tugged on the handle. It was locked.

"I know it's a trap!" I called out. Dion had vanished, leaving me alone in the vast museum foyer. The large fountain gurgled in the center, its splashes echoing across the empty marble floors.

"Well, as long as you know," a voice called out. It wasn't Andersen's. It was lower, more grown-up. I recognized it.

I looked around the darkened museum, searching for Adrian Schrader.

"That's too bad," he mused softly. "I liked that gazebo."

Dull, orange light flickered ominously across the floor, streaming in from the windows, but I still couldn't see where Schrader's voice was coming from, or where Andersen had gone.

"I want my dad back," I demanded, crossing the foyer to the fountain. "And Winnie Hendricks."

Schrader chuckled softly. The sound bounced around the open room.

"I heard you made a scene at the Council meeting the other day," he said. "You think I'm Adrestus, which, I have to admit, is cute."

"I know you are," I said. "Give me who I came here for or—"

"Or what?" he laughed. "You'll burn down my other gazebo?"

I hit redial on my phone. The fire outside would at least draw the fire department, but the museum was dark. They'd have no idea I was locked inside.

Wesley's phone began to ring again, and Adrestus tutted.

"We can't have that," he said.

Something tackled me from behind and knocked my phone from my hand. It landed in the fountain with a soft splash. I elbowed my attacker and spun to hit him with a right hook, but he easily sidestepped it and swept my feet out from under me in the same motion.

Dion was back, looming overhead, his mask frowning at me. When he reached down to grab me, I kicked up, landing both feet in the middle of Dion's chest, and catapulted him over my head, into the fountain.

I scrambled to my feet and made a break for the nearest exhibit. I didn't know where Schrader was speaking from, but I could at least draw Andersen away to face him one-on-one.

"It's useless trying to get away from me." Schrader's disembodied voice sounded from somewhere among the tapestries that decorated the exhibit wall. His voice was too clear to be coming over a speaker. He might have been right next to me for how he sounded.

"You're an Apex!" I accused.

"Wrong again," he chimed. "But you better hurry. Dion's coming."

I slid behind one of the tapestries. I held my breath as I listened to heavy bootfalls creep into the exhibit. Andersen wasn't even trying to be quiet. I squeezed my eyes shut as if it might help me listen better.

He was getting closer...

When I could hear him right outside my tapestry, I screamed and pulled the tapestry down over his head. I wrapped my arms around him, trapping him under the material.

He thrashed in my arms, but I held on tight, clasping my hands to make my hold harder to break.

An elbow swung hard into my left side. I heard a crack and howled in pain, stumbling away.

All the air had left my body. It had been hard to see in the dark room before, but now my vision swam with tears. Andersen was still struggling to get out from under the heavy tapestry.

I couldn't fight like this. I was sure my rib was properly broken now. I bit down on my tongue to keep from crying out in pain and forced myself to hobble into the next room as quietly as possible.

"Oof," Schrader's voice sighed. "That looks like it hurts."

I gritted my teeth and leaned against a corridor wall. Ceiling signs pointed towards different exhibits, restrooms, and elevators.

Elevators.

Even if Andersen figured out where I'd gone, the museum was four floors. He'd have no idea which I was on. I found them down the hall and stumbled into the nearest one. I pressed the button for the fourth floor. If I could find offices, maybe I could find a phone.

I never should have let Andersen get under my skin. Hot tears of agony slid down my cheeks as I squeezed my eyes shut against the pain in my side. Mistake after mistake had brought me here. There was no one to blame but myself.

The doors opened with a ding that I hoped Andersen wasn't able to hear on the floors below. I limped into the hall and fumbled through the dark for the first exhibit I could find.

Ancient Greek helmets stared at me from their cases. They glinted in the green glow of the illuminated exit sign over the doorway. I shied away from them, as if one of them might be Adrestus himself, back to snap my neck again.

"What, do you not like my collection?" Schrader asked. I scowled. Of course he was up here, too, but I ignored him.

I kept moving through the darkened exhibits, coming to the cafe Wes and I had eaten at on our field trip at the beginning of the year. There was a case for sandwich displays and a few small tables for seating. A glass door with the words "Viewing Deck" led out to a terrace.

I stepped around the counter to get into the kitchen. I breathed a sigh of relief and scrambled for the phone on the wall. I began dialing 911 before I even had the receiver up to my ear, but silence sounded on the other end, and it was like being elbowed in the side all over again.

"Ooh, tough luck, love," Schrader sighed. "We thought you might try the phones and disconnected them before you got here."

"No," I whispered, hanging up the phone and pulling it back to my ear. Still silent. I punched in the numbers a second time, but there was no change. "No, no, no, no!"

I slammed my hand against the number pad, but it was useless. The phone was dead.

A melodic ding from down the hall signaled the elevator's arrival. I slapped my hand over my mouth to keep myself from making a sound. There was a whole floor for Andersen to search. I still had time.

I slipped from the kitchen and to the dining area. If there was a viewing deck, there might be a fire escape. The door to outside was unlocked.

It was still raining, and the glow from the fire in the park intermingled with red and blue siren lights. I stumbled to the edge of the terrace, leaning out over open air.

Firefighters and police milled around the park, putting out Amanda's flames, but there was no sign of her or Mira. I waved, desperately wanting to scream for help, but knowing that'd give away my location.

The workers below were too busy with the fire to notice the girl waving frantically from the terrace four floors above them. Even worse, there was no fire escape on the deck. I was trapped.

I hung my head in defeat, and a piece of silver slipped from the collar of my shirt to dangle from my neck. I'd forgotten to take off the necklace Wesley had fashioned for me out of the bent-up dog whistle.

Wesley...

I hadn't even given him the chance to explain himself. I'd left him at the dance because of something Andersen had probably just invented to get me mad.

Now he might never see me again.

But he'd see Andersen on Monday. They might even get put on the scouting team to look for me together. There was nothing I could do, no way to warn Wes, and it was no one's fault but my own.

I looked out towards the edge of the island where I knew the school was, where Wesley was probably wondering where I'd gone. I clasped the silver whistle between two fingers. I knew Wesley had superhuman hearing, but just how good was it?

I raised the whistle to my lips and blew as hard as my broken rib would allow. The sound it made was barely audible to my normal-human ears. Even if Wes did somehow hear it, he'd have to then recognize what it was.

I kept sounding the whistle until I started to get lightheaded. I let it drop around my neck and looked out over the sleeping city as if waiting for a signal from Wes that he'd heard me. But what was I expecting? It wasn't like he was going to stop and light a fire to send a smoke signal.

I backed away from the railing. It was only a matter of time before Andersen found me, and, even though Adrian Schrader's disembodied voice hadn't followed me out onto the terrace, there was nothing to stop him from telling Andersen where I'd gone.

A shuddering breath racked my body and sent pain shooting up my side. I clenched and unclenched my fists. There was one last thing for me to try.

A four story fall might not kill me, but if it did...

Well, I'd come back before.

It would hurt, though, and I could count on Fleming barring me from a quick, Serum-induced recovery. But Andersen was going to bring me to Adrestus, I was sure of it, and Adrestus had killed me once without batting an eye. I didn't want to find out what else he would do.

Besides, the firefighters were down there. They'd see me fall. They'd be able to help as soon as I hit the pavement.

I closed my eyes and counted down from three in my head. I was shaking, but I didn't know if it was from pain or fear.

The first running step towards the railing was the hardest, but then I was sprinting, and my hands were on the banister, vaulting me over into the air, and—

My jacket tightened around my throat, and I fell back into the deck as someone grabbed me from behind. My head collided with the tiled floor, and stars burst in my vision, making it hard to look at Andersen's Dion mask looming over me.

I hurt too much to move, and my head was spinning. The world turned at an angle as Andersen hoisted me unceremoniously over his shoulder. The armor beneath his cloak dug into my rib cage. I groaned. Andersen hissed.

"You can drop it," I said, my words slurring together. "You don't need to act all creepy and mysterious anymore. I know who you are."

I felt him tense under me, but otherwise, he didn't respond. The exhibits were still dark, bathed only in the eerie green glow of the exit signs. I blinked to try to steady my vision.

I only had a half-second to make a grab at the wall-mounted fire-extinguisher as Andersen passed it. I latched onto the edge of its metal container and heaved myself off of him as I opened the door to grab the extinguisher.

Andersen barely had time to register where I'd gone before I'd pulled the safety pin and expelled white, powdery foam from the canister. He shouted and stumbled back, and I launched myself at him, swinging the heavy metal at his head.

He raised his arms to protect himself from the attack, but it still knocked him off his feet. Dion collapsed in a flurry of robes.

The mask skittered across the floor.

Strawberry blonde hair swung forward from under Dion's hood.

"Honestly, Sammy," Winnie hissed, wiping her bloody nose on her sleeve. "You should have just stayed in the trunk of that car."

My brain rushed to try and make sense of what I was seeing. In the dull glow of the exhibit, I could see the bags that hung heavy under Winnie's eyes. Maybe it was the lighting, but she looked paler than before. Even in all the times I'd seen her angry or irritated, I'd never seen such deep loathing etched across her face.

I'd been looking for her since she'd been taken. I didn't know what I'd expected to find when I finally found her, but this wasn't it.

"Winnie," I said in disbelief. It didn't make sense.

My knees buckled, finally giving out from shock and pain. Winnie got to her feet.

"I don't get it," I said, just before her boot made contact with my face, and the exhibit hall went dark.

I came round to the sound of the elevator door sliding open. Blood had dried on my face, and I raised a hand to wipe it away. I looked up at Winnie from where I was slumped in the corner.

"Why?" I mumbled.

Winnie grabbed my ankle and dragged me out into the hall. I was too dazed to resist, and all the fight had gone out of me when her mask had come off.

"I've been looking for you." My words slurred, and she looked over her shoulder to glare at me.

"I know."

Why did she look so angry?

I watched the ceiling as Winnie continued to drag me down the hall. There was more light here, wherever we were. It streamed across the ceiling tiles ahead of us.

We passed under a familiar archway. The words "The Hall of Heroes" stretched above me. My chest tightened. It was the exhibit where I'd fought Hackjob with a sword.

Winnie brought me to the middle of the room and dropped my leg. I struggled to my knees. My head spun, and the larger-than-life statues swam around me. I blinked to steady myself.

A man stood with his back to me. His cloaks were dark and tattered, and he held a gleaming, black helmet under one arm so I could see the back of his curly, salt-and-pepper hair.

My stomach clenched. Adrestus stared at the statue of his namesake, apparently too engrossed in the carving to notice our arrival.

"I've always thought the likeness wasn't quite there," Adrestus said, still staring at the statue. Everything went numb. I knew that voice. "Maybe it's the clothes. I haven't dressed like that in over a millennia."

He turned to face me, and every ounce of my being filled with dread. Dr. Cunningham's blue eyes lit up, and he shifted his Spartan helmet to his other arm.

"There you are, Samantha, I've been waiting."

38

In the Shadow of the Statues

Cunningham couldn't be Adrestus. If he was, then his own men had attacked him the night we'd been ambushed at the museum. But here he was with Adrestus's cloak and helmet. Maybe Winnie had kicked me in the face too hard, but I couldn't get it to make sense in my head.

Others were there, too. I recognized Esther, who'd been at both the docks and museum. She stood with a man I hadn't seen before. His receding blond hair was slicked back, and he looked at me with a jaunty grin.

"Good work, Dion," a voice purred to my right. Mira stood between the statues of Sir Francis Drake and Queen Elizabeth I. The ends of her long, white hair had been singed in her fight with Amanda. She held my family's photo album in one hand while the other was clamped firmly over Amanda's wrist.

Amanda couldn't move, but her eyes, already wide with terror, widened further at the sight of her sister. Winnie scowled back, and her grip tightened around the mask in her hand.

"I'd been wondering when you'd come back to see the museum," Dr. Cunningham said, just as casually as if I'd waltzed in on an ordinary afternoon and wasn't on the floor bleeding. "The Scourge Queen is back on display, and I was hoping to show her to you."

I'd already seen Eydis the Scourge Queen the night we were attacked, but Cunningham had been unconscious. Unconscious and definitely not Adrestus.

"She's marvelous, isn't she?" he continued, turning to look up at her. "Although, I can't say she looks quite like the real thing, either, wouldn't you agree?"

"Why am I here?" I asked, drawing his attention away from the statues. He looked at me in surprise.

"You have something that belongs to me. I believe you took it from Vidar's house."

"Vidar?" I repeated the name. I knew that name, but how? I shook my head, trying to clear the fog that had settled over my brain since Winnie's kick.

"Right, I forgot." He waved a hand. "Vic."

I had never heard anyone call Dad "Vidar" before, nor had I ever heard anyone speak his name with such disdain.

"I don't know what you're talking about," I lied.

"I know you know *exactly* what I'm talking about," Cunningham snapped, his cool demeanor slipping away. "You nearly torched one of my best men when I sent him to retrieve it. Well. 'Best' is probably a stretch, but Miles is loyal at least, and I prefer him unburnt."

I didn't want to know why he wanted a flash drive with every detail of my life outlined in its files, and I wasn't about to hand it over. I needed to stall. Maybe Wesley had heard the whistle. Maybe he was on his way.

"Where's Schrader?" I asked. Cunningham raised an eyebrow.

"Not here." He gestured around the room. "I'm afraid he couldn't make it. He's a busy man."

The blond man snickered, enjoying some private joke.

"So are you by the looks of things," I said. "How do you find time in the day to run a museum and terrorize the city?"

He frowned, and readjusted his grip on his helmet.

"I'm saving this city. I built this city. Hell, I've built this whole world!" He whipped around so that his back was to me, once again staring up at his namesake's statue.

"Do you know the story of Prometheus?" he said, switching back into a calmer demeanor, more fitting for a museum curator.

"Not really," I said carefully.

"He was a titan in Ancient Greek myths," Cunningham explained, still looking up at the marble Adrestus. "The gods had invented fire and didn't want to share it with the humans. Prometheus, however, loved the humans, so he stole fire from the home of the gods and gave it to them against Zeus's wishes. Do you know what happened next?"

He twisted to look back at me. I shook my head. I needed to keep him talking.

"The humans flourished. Prometheus had given them light, warmth, protection! But the gods were angry. They tied Prometheus to a rock, where eagles would eat his liver, only so it could grow back and be eaten again the next day and the next day and the next day."

He stalked across the exhibit hall towards me, his heavy boots echoing with every step.

"I've always liked the story of Prometheus because I see myself in it," he mused. "But instead of fire, I gave humanity powers. I'm the father of all Apex, and every single one of these heroes is mine, as are their achievements."

I snorted loudly, and Cunningham narrowed his eyes at me.

"You've been spending too much time staring at your statues," I said. "The Apex Father was just a legend, and even in that story, he was killed."

"So were you." He knelt down so that his blue eyes were on the same level as mine. His gloved hand grabbed my chin, and I tried to recoil away. "I felt you break in my hands, and yet here you are."

My head spun. If what Cunningham was saying was true, then he was almost two thousand years old. But what could a two-thousand-year old man who'd found the secret to immortality possibly want with a teenage girl?

I tried to piece it together in my head, but Winnie's kick had made thinking harder.

"You said you're like Prometheus," I said, "but I don't see any eagles trying to get at your liver."

Cunningham's, or rather, Adrestus's mouth twisted into a snarl and once again the curator gave way to the villain underneath.

"Oh, you don't?" he hissed. "I die a little more with each passing day. There may not be eagles ripping at my insides, but I assure you, I am decaying."

"You're not decaying!" I forced a laugh, putting on the bravest face I could muster. "You're aging! If that's what you consider eagles eating your liver, then everyone is Prometheus. You think you're a titan, but you're just a human like the rest of us."

"I am nothing like the rest of you!" Adrestus howled, straightening up so that he towered over me. "I've seen every major nation rise and fall since the Romans! I've watched the world grow from the shadows, prompting it along, helping it, placing my Apex warriors where they needed to be. I refuse to age a day more, and I refuse to die."

"Yeah, well, I'm the one who can't die," I pointed out. Adrestus's lip curled.

"Exactly."

"Is that why you want...?" The pieces were finally falling together. I couldn't die. I might even be immortal. Adrestus knew this somehow. He'd known on the roof, and he must've known when he had his men attack us on our field trip. They'd even offered to let everyone else go if I stayed.

And now he wanted my secret, which is why he kidnapped Dad, and when he didn't talk, why Miles was sent to the house to find the flash drive detailing my whole existence.

The room echoed with the sound of my laughter. It made my ribs ache, but I couldn't help it.

"What's so funny?" Adrestus snarled.

"Nothing," I cackled. "It's just that thing you were looking for is useless."

"What?" He grabbed the collar of my shirt. "What do you mean?"

"I mean that it's all a lie. Nothing on those files is real. I'm not even sure who I am. You should've looked in that album you set out with Amanda. I'm not even in any of my family pictures."

Adrestus dropped me back to the floor and growled.

"I don't want files," he said. "Who said anything about files?"

I faltered.

"You want what I took from my dad's house. It was just a flash drive filled with lies."

Now Adrestus was laughing.

"A flash drive of lies, then? Sounds like you found your back-up hard drive and figured out what it meant."

I curled my fingers into fists on the marble floor.

"Then what do you want?"

"The Magnum Opus," he said, throwing his arms wide. "The Lapis, my crown jewel that you stole from me!"

I didn't understand half the words he was saying, and my confusion must have registered on my face. He scowled in frustration.

"How about the question I asked you on the roof, hmm?" He was pacing now, his cloak whipping around his heels each time he pivoted. "Who are you? You know who you aren't, but do you know who you are?"

"I'm still Samantha," I insisted.

"No!" He threw his helmet to the floor in a sudden rage. It clanged loudly and rolled across the tiles, coming to rest at Winnie's feet. I still hadn't figured out how she had fallen into all this. "You are not Samantha, you were never Samantha. She is a lie. So who are you?"

"Samantha!"

"Liar." It was Winnie who spoke this time. I looked up at her, but she stared ahead, shaking in anger. If Samantha really was a lie, then it had been one fed to Winnie as well. But how could she blame me for something Alison had done?

"Winnie, please," I begged. "Our friendship was real! I cared about you."

"More lies," Adrestus said. His eyes lit up as he looked past me towards the exhibit entrance. "But why ask me when Vidar can tell you the whole story."

"Dad?" I twisted around on the floor to see Hackjob leading my dad into the exhibit. His face was swollen and bruised under his beard, and he was limping heavily. A ghastly pallor washed over him when he saw me. "Dad!"

"Sammy!" He struggled to get away from Hackjob but as big as Dad was, Hackjob was bigger. I scrambled to my feet, and Winnie grabbed the collar of my jacket to hold me back. "What are you doing here?"

"She's not Sammy though, is she?" Adrestus said, clicking his tongue as Hackjob positioned Dad next to Amanda. "We're trying to figure out just who this girl is and thought you might help us."

"Dad, I'm sorry." My voice cracked, and tears mixed with the dried blood on my face.

"Not quite 'Dad', though, right, Vidar?" Adrestus teased. But he had to be wrong. Alison had said he was still my dad, even if she wasn't my mom.

"Vidar is dead," Dad growled.

"No, Havard is dead," Adrestus said matter-of-factly. "Along with Erika and Gunhild and Knut—"

"Stop!" Dad broke free from Hackjob, but Mira was ready, dropping the photo album to grab him. He locked up.

"Leave his face free, Mira," Adrestus drawled. "We need him to talk. Where was I? Oh, right. Hjordis is dead, as is Solveig. Even Sammy here was dead pretty recently."

"You killed her?"

I hadn't known Dad could get any paler, but he looked as white as the marble statues that flanked him on either side.

"Snapped her neck." Adrestus shrugged. "You didn't tell him?"

"I'm sorry," I croaked again. I should've been honest. I should've told him about the team, about everything.

"It was a couple weeks ago, when her and that tiresome team of traitors came to free their classmates."

"You joined the Apex Team?" I was thankful for the tears that swam in my eyes. They kept me from seeing the betrayal I was sure was on Dad's face.

"It doesn't matter, I didn't make the cut."

"We moved here so they could protect you, not so you could join them!"

"I'm sorry!"

"And who did she need protecting from?" Adrestus interjected. His blue eyes twinkled. He already knew the answer.

"You," Dad spat.

"Imagine my surprise when my most loyal follower came to tell me Alison Taylor's daughter was going to be her roommate when I hadn't even known Alison Taylor *had* a daughter. And then she tells me that they've known each other since they were both seven." Adrestus continued to smile. "Of course, I didn't know right away who she actually was, but I still needed her since she was the Beta child of one of my Apex. And then she came here."

He spread his arms out as if greeting all the statues in the hall.

"I'll admit, I thought it couldn't be her. I hadn't seen her in a thousand years, after all. I thought maybe I was finally going crazy. But the resemblance was uncanny."

One thousand years? Adrestus *was* going crazy. I was barely sixteen.

"I told Dion to bring her to me that night. We almost had her, but she had a lucky break."

All this time I'd thought Andersen had been the one setting me up, but it had been Winnie.

"Dion fixed the situation and came up with a plan to capture three Betas all at once. They came back to the museum, and we would take them then. I had to be unconscious, of course," Adrestus snorted. "First, to keep me looking guilt free and second, to keep that irritating Empath from figuring me out."

He was right that Naomi would've felt he was up to something, just like she had with Andersen so many times. Even though Winnie was her project partner, any suspicious emotions probably felt normal for Winnie and wouldn't have raised alarm.

"But it didn't work," Dad laughed derisively. "Sammy beat you."

"Yes," Adrestus scowled. "Things went sideways after my idiot men kidnapped Dion by mistake. She led Samantha into a dark corner to be taken away, but got herself taken instead. My man didn't realize it until it was too late, at which point, we had to pretend Winnie had been captured, too."

"Winnie, your parents are worried sick about you," Dad said.

"They don't care about me," Winnie spat. "I was never special enough for them."

She glared at Amanda, who was still petrified by Mira's powers, but even Mira couldn't stop the stream of tears falling down Amanda's cheeks.

"Your father is far from perfect, but he loves you," Dad insisted.

"Why would I believe you? You stuffed lies in my head, and then you told her about it!" She pointed a shaking finger at Amanda. "She knew the whole time but didn't tell me my one friendship wasn't even real!"

"I'm real," I said quietly. It made sense now why Amanda had hated me. My parents had filled her sister with lies, and she had thought I was in on it. I kind of hated me for it, too.

"And those lies are what bring you here now, Vidar," Adrestus said. "You see, while that night at the museum was a disaster for everyone involved, I learned something very important. Samantha didn't just look the part, but she could play it, too."

Adrestus unsheathed the sword buckled at his side, pulling it from his cloak. I recognized the pummeled hilt and engraved blade immediately. It was the same sword I'd used to fend off Hackjob.

Dad inhaled sharply at the sight of it.

"You recognize it, yes?" Adrestus said in a coarse whisper. "It's the exact blade you gave her. I kept it as a souvenir after she put it in my gut. But now—"

He turned to point the blade towards me, placing the tip of it just below my chin.

"Tell me again. Who are you?"

"Leave her alone!" Dad bellowed. Adrestus raised an eyebrow at me. His eyes were a familiar, piercing blue.

In my head, I remembered the feel of the sword handle as I pressed the blade into his stomach. I remembered seeing those blue eyes widen in shock and pain.

"Who are you?" Adrestus asked again.

"She's Samantha Havardson!" Dad shouted. His voice broke. I'd never heard it do that before.

But I couldn't look at him. I couldn't tear myself away from Adrestus's sharp, blue eyes. The nightmare face I'd seen in the mirror had been younger, but the eyes were the same.

"Who are you?"

The name rose to my lips from somewhere deep within my subconscious. I didn't know how it was possible, but I knew it was true. I raised my gaze to meet Adrestus's and clenched my jaw.

"I'm Eydis Solveigsdotter," I said. "The Scourge of The Apex."

39

Lapis

My statue stared down at the scene in front of her, and as I looked back at her, I had to agree with Adrestus. The resemblance wasn't there. For one, she looked to be a full-grown adult. Her face was distorted in a war cry, and I was certain I'd never looked like that.

"I'm so sorry," Dad said. Tears ran down his cheeks into his beard. "I'm sorry."

"It's okay, Dad," I whispered. It was like grasping at a dream that was already slipping away. Fuzzy images and memories danced just out of reach. "Really, I'm alright."

Adrestus's whole body shook.

"You haven't aged a single day," he said, venom seeping from every word.

"Don't ask me how because I don't know," I said simply. "I can barely remember my own name."

"That's alright." Adrestus dropped the sword. "Your brother knows how, doesn't he?"

"Leave Avery out of this! He has nothing to do with either of us!" I spat.

"He means me." Dad scowled at Adrestus from under his beard. "He murdered your real dad— our real dad."

"You were supposed to die too, you know," Adrestus said, polishing the blade on his cloak. "But you got away. I don't know what you did to Eydis's memories, but I'd like you to give them back."

"They're gone," Dad— no, Vidar said. "I don't know where to. We found her bleeding out in a river. She should've died, but she didn't. She screamed to be put out of her misery, but death never took her. At least, not permanently. Eventually one of our Apex put her to sleep so she wouldn't feel it anymore. Even then, she stayed alive."

Adrestus's eyes glinted, and he broke into a hungry grin.

"But you figured out why, I assume?"

Vidar looked at me. It felt weird to call him that, even in my head. The name felt foreign and familiar at the same time. Even as the memory of Vidar Havardsson, my brother, clawed at the back of my mind, I still saw my dad.

"No, and I never did. And as long as I'm with her, I don't seem to age, not at the normal pace at least. A thousand years and I never found the answer."

"Liar," Adrestus spat. "You can't keep it from me forever!"

"Why can't I remember any of that?" I asked. The river sounded familiar, at least, but I was missing a thousand years of memories.

"The Apex who put you to sleep was killed when Adrestus had his men raid our town looking for you. We didn't have anyone who could wake you so I kept you safe until I could find an Inculcator who could."

"Alison," I breathed. "It took you that long to find one?"

"I found her after she graduated from New Delos University. It took a week to prepare to wake you up, but when she did, you'd been asleep for too long. You didn't remember anything, and you panicked. We had to put you back under. The kindest thing we could do was construct new memories for you. It wasn't too long before we had Avery, and after we got married, we decided the best course of action would be to build your memories around our family, make you one of us."

Hot tears splashed on the tile. As awful as the story Dad was telling me was, relief washed over me. Even if I'd been asleep in the basement the whole time, I'd still been with the family. They were still mine. Avery was still my brother, even if he was technically my nephew. Vidar was still every bit my dad. Even Alison had spent more than the last decade painstakingly reconstructing me so I could have a chance at a normal life. After Dad had been taken, she'd tried to warn me by leading me to the flash drive.

But there was still a hollow feeling deep in my gut. My only real memories were the ones from the last two months. Was that why I had been so sick at the beginning of the school year? Sleeping for a thousand years must've taken a toll on my body.

"But why Winnie?" I asked. "Why involve her?"

Dad looked at Winnie, regret etched in every line on his face.

"The only other people who knew were Roy and Valerie. Roy and Alison were old teammates. They offered Winnie to be your friend when the time came to wake you. Winnie, I'm so sorry. We never meant to hurt you."

Winnie stood as still as the statues.

"Master," Esther spoke suddenly from her corner. "There are people in the Museum."

"What?" Adrestus spun around to face her, and then back to me. He lifted me by my jacket collar and held me close to his face. For a moment, I felt like I was back on the roof with his hands around my throat. "Tell me where it is."

"I don't know what you're talking about!"

"I've already told you! The Lapis! Where is it!?"

"I don't know!"

"I know you've got it, how else could you be alive and no older than you were back in Iceland?"

"Master!" Esther warned again.

"Send Hackjob," he snarled. "Miles should be down there already."

Adrestus's blue eyes were inches from mine, and I wondered if he might break my neck again.

"What's the Lapis?" I asked. I needed to keep him talking. If people were in the museum, then help was here. If I stalled long enough, it'd give them time to find us.

"You really don't remember? Maybe your new memories are in the way of the old. Maybe if I erased them, you'd know where my Lapis is."

The man with the slicked blond hair stepped forward. The malicious grin on his face, and his ill-fitted suit made him look every bit like a dirty used car salesman.

"Whatever an Inculcator puts in your head, any other Inculcator can take away," Adrestus explained. "While Alison is gifted at what she does, Gregor here is second only to her."

"No," I begged. I squirmed, trying to get away as the blond man came closer.

"Leave her alone!" Dad shouted.

"Mira, I'm done with him. You can shut him up now," Adrestus said. Dad's mouth clamped shut, and Adrestus refocused his attention on me. "The question is, should we start small or take all of it at once?"

Even if my memories were fake, Samantha Havardson was all I had. I couldn't lose her. I swung my foot hard into Adrestus's shin, and he dropped me in surprise.

I fell back to the floor, landing hard on the stone tile. Adrestus glared down at me.

"All of it, then," he snarled. "Gregor, you—"

Adrestus froze. His eyes went wide, and he pointed the sword down at my neck. He used the tip of the blade to push aside the collar of my jacket. His hungry eyes feasted on the sight of the long scar that ran to my collarbone. There was a crash downstairs, but Adrestus didn't seem to notice.

"My men did that after you tried to kill me," he murmured, tracing the length of the gray scar with the blade. I shivered at the touch of the metal. "And you thought you could hide it from me."

I looked to Winnie desperately as I realized what Adrestus was about to do.

"Winnie, please," I begged her. She was the only one who could do anything to stop him.

Winnie looked down at her feet. Adrestus smiled and placed his heavy boot square on my chest, not that I had the strength to get up anyway.

"Winnie knows you don't mean anything to her, she won't help you." He leaned over me, bracing himself with his hands against his knees. "There is no one to help you this time."

He cast the sword aside, and it clattered onto the floor. He pulled a long knife from his belt. The tip of the blade brushed past my neck and to my shoulder, where Adrestus gingerly hooked it on my shirt collar. He tugged the fabric down over my shoulder, exposing my long, gray scar.

He exhaled sharply, and his lips tightened.

He gave me no warning. The blade felt almost familiar in my shoulder as he plunged it into my flesh. I could hear someone screaming. It might've been me. My back arched off the marbled tiles as he dug the knife from one end of my scar to the other. I couldn't see Winnie anymore. I couldn't see anything.

The knife clattered next to me. Adrestus sat on my stomach, his visage blurring. He tried to wipe the gushing blood away from my shoulder, and then...it was like something was scraping against me from the inside, tearing at me as he pulled it from my wound.

Finally, it was free. He held it up to his face with shaking hands, but I couldn't see what it was.

The floor beneath me was getting colder. My vision shifted in and out of focus.

"Is that it?" a far away voice asked.

"Yes," Adrestus breathed. He wiped something off on his cloak and held it up to inspect it. He held a small, deep purple stone between two fingers. "The Magnum Opus. My Lapis."

I held a hand over the wound in my neck, but it did little to stem the sticky flow of blood. I would die if I didn't get help soon.

"Do you even know what this is?" Adrestus mused as if I wasn't bleeding out in front of him. "Some call it the Stone of Life. Many have tried to create one for themselves. Few have come close. Even fewer have succeeded. It's what kept you alive all this time, whether you knew it or not. It's what I used to create The Apex, and it's what I used to create the elixir that has sustained me over the years. This is what I used to create the world as we know it, and you stole it from me!"

"Winnie, help," I gasped.

"You could've been Blessed," Adrestus continued. "You and I would've shaped the world. Think of the wars and plagues we could've prevented together. But instead, you stole my youth. I was going to give you fire, but you would rather chain Prometheus to the rock and leave him to the eagles! And now that I have what's mine, it's your turn. I will watch you die every day until you know the pain you've put me through!"

There were more sounds outside, getting closer now. I could hear the thundering of boots in the hall, but that might have also been my heartbeat pounding in my ears. I rolled onto my stomach and pushed myself to my knees, brandishing the knife Adrestus had dropped.

"Sammy!"

Even with the voice modulator, I recognized the sound of Wesley's voice. I fell forward in relief, catching myself on the tile. Adrestus dove for his black helmet and jammed it over his head. Winnie leaped away, securing her own mask and stood over me, challenging the newcomers.

I looked towards the entrance to see Wes in his Apex Armor, the number seven emblazoned on his shoulder. More came in after him, at least three, but it was getting hard to count. They were led by someone wearing red and white armor, identical to the others in everything but color. He was wearing Paragon's colors, and instead of a number, the Greek symbol for Alpha shone on his shoulder.

One of the Apex raised his hands, and there was a series of crashes. Several statues crumbled to the ground where they cracked. Mira jumped back against the wall, and Dad and Amanda broke free.

"You idiot!" Amanda screeched, and for once, she was mad at someone who wasn't me. A pillar of fire shot across the floor. I found the energy to scramble away from Winnie, who threw her cloaked back to the flames. Of course she had a fire-proof costume. She knew she'd come face-to-face with her sister someday.

Big hands scooped me up from the floor. I recognized the feeling of Dad's beard on my forehead.

"Take her!"

Armored arms wrapped around me as chaos engulfed the room. Statues fell around us, collapsed by unseen forces. The archway crumbled overhead, bringing down the exhibit from the floor above as it collapsed in on the hall entrance.

"Watch it, Eight!" the man in red and white shouted. "We need a way out of here!"

"I've got you," Naomi said in my ear. I was relieved to see her but wriggled from her arms to stand on my own. The stone Adrestus had just pulled from my shoulder must have left lingering effects. It was a miracle I was even still awake, let alone able to stand.

On any other day, I would've been able to climb over the rubble to escape the room, but in the condition I was in, Naomi had no choice but to help me to the floor with my back to a slab of stone. I still held the knife tightly in one hand.

"Watch her!" Dad commanded. He looked down at me, his face a mixture of pride and grief. He placed his hands on my face. "Sammy. Eydis. I'm so proud of you, and I'm so sorry."

"Don't go, I came here to get you!"

He smiled sadly.

"I know, and you did. You'll be okay for now, but Winnie won't."

Winnie. Winnie wasn't his daughter, or sister, or whatever. *I* was.

"Are Alison and Avery safe?"

"Yes."

He gave my forehead a final kiss and dropped his hands to run back into the fray. Naomi stood with her back to me, ready to fight anyone that came near us, but everyone else was stuck in combat.

Winnie and Amanda were locked in a battle of fire and cloaks. Dad ran to intercept them, but they only had eyes for each other, ducking around his outstretched arms.

Two other armored Apex double-teamed Mira, careful to not get too close to her. Rubble flew across the room at her face, but she batted away the smaller pieces and dodged the larger ones. The only team member I could think of with powers that could do that was Andersen, but it couldn't be him. Half an hour ago, I'd thought he was Dion. If my math was right, that had to be Wesley fighting side-by-side with him, something I was sure neither of them would ever do.

In the center of the room, the white and red figure went hand-to-hand with Adrestus. Cunningham had always come off as frail and a little quirky, but now he was the most agile fighter in the room. He hardly threw a punch, letting his adversary do all the work.

"Naomi," I groaned, my hand plastered to my neck by the blood I was trying to hold there. "Is that Fleming?"

Even if the man in white and red wasn't able to land a hit on Adrestus, his form was flawless and didn't give Adrestus much room to maneuver.

"Yeah. What the hell were you thinking, Sam?"

"I'm sorry." My head was getting lighter.

"Just stay with us, alright?"

I blinked to clear my eyes. The smoke from Amanda's fire, and the dust from the rubble made it hard to see. Dad was still trying to wrestle Winnie and Amanda away from each other. I would've liked to believe they wouldn't hurt him, but now I knew how naive that was.

The smoke became thicker, and something buzzed near my ear. Naomi swatted at something near her head. A fly landed on my knee, and I shook it away, but when I looked up, a whole cloud of them had descended on the room.

I watched in horror as the others stumbled through the mass of bugs, trying to escape. But where had they come from? Naomi backed up, nearly stepping on me. A bug crawled across the open wound on my neck, tickling the flayed skin.

Mira had Andersen by the neck, and Wesley tried to fight her through the horde of flies. Amanda paused in her offensive against Winnie to fire flames into the air around her.

This had to be an Apex ability, but it didn't match what I knew the Apex in the room to be capable of, unless it was possible to have more than one power. Mira could control people with touch, maybe she could control bugs at a distance?

Near the back of the exhibit, Gregor grinned maniacally. Esther stood just behind him, and neither seemed bothered by the mass of bugs buzzing around their faces. It couldn't be Esther. All she could do was sense people, and Gregor was an Inculcator like Alison. Nothing fly related there.

But even as I ruled Gregor out as the source of the swarm, something clicked in my head.

"It's him!" I pointed across the room. Alison needed physical touch to use her abilities, but maybe Gregor didn't. "He's an Inculcator. It's not real!"

Naomi glanced around for help, but there was no one else.

"Just go!" I insisted, hoping I was right. "I'll be fine."

"Don't go anywhere!" she warned, as if I might wander off, and broke into a dead sprint down the exhibit. Gregor braced for her attack, but watching her lunge at him, one thing was clear. Naomi had been going easy on me all month.

Gregor grabbed her by the wrist, but in a flurry of limbs, she broke his grip and flipped him onto his back. As Naomi knocked the air out of him, the flies dissolved.

With the bugs gone, I could see Amanda and Winnie clearly now. Amanda's hair was singed short, and her shoulders heaved. Dad tried to hold her back as she threw a column of fire, not at Winnie, but at one of the few statues that remained standing.

The heat cracked the stone, and the statue disintegrated. Winnie tripped over her cloak as she tried to stumble away and fell on the tile as chunks of rock rained down over her.

Dad abandoned Amanda to throw himself at Winnie, landing on top of her as the rubble crashed to the ground.

"Dad!" My shriek cut through the havoc. I struggled to my feet, slipping in my own blood, and tried to run to help him. How could he put himself in danger like that? And for *Winnie*?

Arms wrapped around my middle, and I screamed in protest. I had to help him, but the room was getting darker around the edges of my vision.

"Sammy, stop." Wes spun me around to face him. He held me close and pulled his helmet off with his free hand. Dust stained his face, and his hair stuck out in odd directions. The way he frowned, I couldn't tell if he was mad at me or felt sorry for me.

"Put that back on," I mumbled. The museum floor was rolling beneath me, but no one else seemed to notice. "My dad—"

Wes's eyes widened as he took in the sight of the gash along my neck.

"Alpha!" he yelled. "She's hurt! We've gotta go!"

Fleming paused his fight with Adrestus to look back at us.

"Get that helmet back on!" he shouted. "Everyone else, retreat!"

Wesley jammed the helmet back on his head and scooped me up in his arms. I pointed my knife towards the pile of rubble where Dad had been.

"I need my dad!"

But Wesley didn't listen. He carried me back towards the blocked exhibit entrance while Amanda took up the fight against Mira. Mira had lost her hold on Andersen, and he fell back to join us with Naomi close behind him. Across the room, Esther tended to Gregor where Naomi had left him incapacitated on the floor.

Fleming backed up towards us, and Adrestus followed with strong, self-assured strides.

"She won't make it past the front door. Only I have the power to save her."

The sound of Adrestus's voice snapped my attention away from my dad.

"It's Cunningham," I spat between breaths. "Adrestus. And he's thousands of years old."

"Thank you, Sammy," Fleming said softly, keeping his eyes on the curator. "Eight, get this debris out of the way."

Stone scraped against stone as Andersen sifted through the rubble.

"Here to make up for your brother's sins?" Adrestus taunted Fleming. "It's too bad, even with his flaws, you'll never reach his level of stardom."

"I'm just here for my student," Fleming said evenly.

"My dad—" I mumbled. We couldn't leave without him.

"I've always been surprised you've sided with traitors," Adrestus continued. "After what happened to Paul and what happened at his funeral. It's not too late, though. I could even Bless you, if you like."

Even in my fading vision, I could see Fleming's back tense. Adrestus had stopped so that he stood over the sword he'd earlier discarded on the floor.

"Almost clear!" Andersen grunted behind me. Fleming let his guard down for a half second to glance back at Andersen's progress. As he did, Adrestus flicked the sword into the air with the toe of his boot, catching the handle.

I rolled out of Wesley's arms, brandishing the knife Adrestus had used to cut me open.

He was quick with the sword, but I was quicker. Fleming didn't even have time to register that he was about to be run through. It wasn't Alison's skills that took over as I twirled the blade in my fingers and spun it through the air.

It was Eydis.

The knife slid through the slit of Adrestus's helmet, lodging itself so the handle stuck out of the eye hole. The sword fell from his hands, clanging against the ground as Mira screamed. Adrestus turned to look at me, stumbled forward, and collapsed.

My knees buckled as my body finally gave out, and the last thing I felt were the arms that rushed to catch me.

40

Waiting to Hear

Consciousness kaleidoscoped around me. Screaming and explosions interspersed the darkness that threatened to swallow me. Just when I thought the darkness had me in its jaws for good, my eyes fluttered open. I could see street lights streaking past the windows from where I was stretched across the backseat of a car.

"We've got you," Wes said, but I couldn't see him. "Try to stay still, okay?"

"Is she awake?"

"Barely."

Seconds, or maybe an eternity, later, bright lights blurred overhead, and a gurney jostled underneath me.

"What the hell happened?" Everly demanded.

Something heavy was wrapped around my neck. I tried to lift my hand to feel for it, but someone held me down. My hair was matted to the side of my face with blood. The darkness began pulling at the edges of my mind again.

It's okay, I thought dreamily. *I can't die.*

The darkness took over, and as it did, I thought I heard someone shouting my name.

I thought the nothingness I had felt when Adrestus had snapped my neck would return, but it didn't. I could still feel where the blade had pierced my shoulder and scraped against my collarbone. Black began to fade and give way to heavy smoke that clogged my lungs.

I was back in the burning village I'd dreamt about the last time I'd died. It was hard to see and breathe, but I struggled forward. A shriek rose from my throat when I saw them lying in a row. I fell to the dirt and crawled towards the closest body. They'd been killed before the fire had been set. How else could they be lying here so neatly?

I reached out and brushed the matted hair from Erika's face. She was so little. Tears dripped off my chin, splashing onto her cheeks.

Large hands grabbed my shoulders, and I screamed in protest, but they pulled me into a warm embrace and wrapped around me.

"Vidar," I sobbed. They hadn't all died. I still had Vidar.

"We can't stay here," he said, drawing me away from our family. "Please, we need to go."

Relief that he was alive ran with the horror of seeing our family lying in a row on the ground.

"Who—"

"You already know."

I wanted to scream again. Despair threatened to suffocate me. My steps faltered and Vidar pulled at my arm.

"Come on," he said. "We need to keep going. It isn't safe here."

But I didn't deserve to be safe. I didn't deserve to be alive, not when it was my fault my family was dead.

"Eydis, please," Vidar begged. When I didn't move, he picked me up in his arms. As he carried me away from the burning wreckage that had been our home, I screwed my eyes shut against the acrid smoke. I would let Vidar save me now, but I knew what I needed to do.

I was going to kill Adrestus. I was going to kill my best friend.

Something warm and wet lapped at my neck and face. I opened my eyes to the familiar site of the Sickbay ceiling tiles. Everything hurt. My arm, my shoulder, my face, my side, but everything dwarfed in comparison to the ache in my stomach. It growled loudly.

"You're awake?" The wet cloth stopped rubbing my neck as Wesley looked down at me. The relief that spread across his face quickly clouded with anger, and he dropped the washrag he'd been holding to my face on me. "What the hell, Sammy!?"

"Watch it!" I rasped, flicking the rag back at him. A tube stuck out of my arm. If Fleming had agreed to let Everly give me Serum, I must've been in pretty bad shape.

"What were you thinking?" Wesley demanded. "I get that Andersen pissed you off, but sneaking out on your own? And for what?"

"Amanda had texted me," I mumbled. "I wanted to show you, but—"

"But what? You decided you'd rather take care of it yourself?"

I hated how Wesley was looking at me, but I knew I deserved it.

"I didn't know it was a trap." My stomach growled loudly again. Unlike last time I'd woken up in the Sickbay, Wesley didn't have any burgers hidden nearby.

"I told you, I didn't want to watch you die anymore."

"I didn't die!" I said.

"You don't know that!"

"Yes," I insisted. "I do."

Concussed and bleeding out, I'd still been certain I couldn't die. Now that I was awake, I remembered Adrestus pulling the Lapis from my shoulder. He'd said that had been the source of my apparent immortality. With it gone, I was vulnerable again.

We stared each other down for a moment until Wesley looked back at my neck and raised the washrag to it.

"Your wound finally healed enough for me to clean the area around it," he explained. "Everly only let me in here about ten minutes ago."

The warm cloth felt good against my skin, and I settled into the pillows, letting Wesley wash away the dried blood that caked my hair to my neck.

"Where are the others?"

"Naomi's sleeping in the call room. Fleming's been in a meeting with the Council for the last hour, and I think Everly's got Andersen cleaning locker room toilets." A small smile crept across Wes's face in spite of himself. "Fleming really chewed him out."

"The Council's meeting right now?" I struggled to push myself up, but Wes stopped me.

"They'll come to you, I'm sure," he said. "Just hold still, alright?"

"But I need to tell them—"

I cut myself off. Tell them what? That I was an immortal Viking girl, and Adrestus was an Ancient warrior hell-bent on revenge, and who knew what else? I squeezed my eyes shut. Thoughts of Adrestus and Eydis made my head hurt.

"I'm sorry I ran out on you," I said, opening my eyes. "Andersen said some things and...I don't know. I just got mad."

"He told you about the mission?" Wes asked flatly.

"So he wasn't lying?"

"I'm sorry."

I looked away to stare at the ceiling again. I knew I didn't have much room to be mad at the moment, but it still stung to know Wesley had only taken me to the dance because he'd been told to.

"It's fine," I lied. "When did you realize I'd left?"

"We figured it out pretty quick. Andersen was a bit too pleased with himself considering Jamie had just broken up with him."

"She did?"

"Right before Homecoming royalty was announced," Wes explained, pausing to rinse the rag in a tub of warm water. I turned to watch him wring it out, turning the water pink with my blood. "Anyway, we found Fleming at the dance, and he dragged Andersen down to his office to interrogate him."

I felt awful thinking about Naomi and Wes looking for me. They'd deserved to enjoy the dance like anyone else.

"Fleming put out an alert, but most of the team was at the dance and not checking their phones. Even with help from the University team, we only had enough to make two squads. Fleming almost never suits up, by the way. It's funny, he kinda reminded me of Paragon in his armor." Wesley picked up a silver chain from the bedside table. It was stained red. "And then I heard this stupid whistle."

"Wesley," I said quietly. "Where's my dad?"

His expression darkened, and he concentrated on untangling a mass of hair and blood.

"I'm sorry. We couldn't get to him. We had to leave Amanda, too."

I shut my eyes and blocked out the room. I bit my tongue to hold back the sob that had jumped into my throat. All that work and I hadn't even managed to save Dad.

No, not Dad. Vidar.

"He's alive, though. I could hear him trying to dig himself and that masked creep out of the rubble." Wesley said quickly. "Why he'd try to help him is beyond me."

I clenched a handful of linen in each hand and opened my eyes. Rage replaced heartache.

"Because it was Winnie."

Wesley dropped the rag.

"Wait, but—" Wesley bowed his head. "That guy in the mask, the one from before, he wasn't—"

"I thought it was Andersen at first. I kinda wish she had been. Then her mask fell off, and she kicked me in the face."

Wesley was silent for a moment.

"I'm sorry," he finally said.

"What for?"

He shrugged and picked up a clean rag.

"I just am."

I flinched as the rag ran over a sensitive spot. Wesley mumbled another apology.

"So what happened?" he asked. "What did Adrestus want?"

I shook my head.

"You killed him."

"No. I didn't."

He raised an eyebrow at me, but I didn't elaborate. Adrestus had the Lapis. Even if I'd put the knife through his skull, he'd be back.

I didn't want to think about the museum, or Adrestus, or the Lapis, or Vidar, or Eydis.

"Fleming is coming," Wesley said, looking towards the door. "Do you want me to stay?"

"I'll be alright." I would have to tell Fleming everything, but I wasn't ready for my friends to know about Eydis just yet.

Wesley tried to smile and picked up the tub of bloody water.

"I'm glad you're okay," he said, pushing the door to the back open with his shoulder. "You're an idiot, though."

"I know."

Facing Fleming was almost as difficult as facing Adrestus. Disappointment was etched across his face when he came in, and it remained there as I recounted the night's events. Even when I told him Winnie had been under Dion's mask, the only sign that he'd registered the news was the way he closed his eyes for a moment before telling me to continue.

He'd stood up for me, vouched for me over and over, and I had run away and gambled my life.

I'd already warned them all that Cunningham was Adrestus, but I still had to explain Vidar and Eydis and the Lapis. I hoped he didn't tell the council. I wasn't ready to be the thousand year old girl.

I thought he might tell me I was crazy. I could barely believe it all myself, but he didn't interrupt.

"We're going to keep you here overnight," Fleming said when I was done rehashing the night. He stood up and scanned over the notes he'd been taking the entire time. He had bags under his eyes. "I have another meeting with the Council. I'll let you know what they say."

"Please don't tell them everything," I begged. "I don't— I'm not—"

"One of them is already calling for your expulsion," Fleming said. "If I tell them everything, you have a better chance of staying here."

If I was expelled, where did I even have left to go? But on the other hand, if they found out who I was, they might send me away regardless. I was a living historical artifact and was, until recently, immortal. I could end up in a lab.

Fleming frowned and sighed, seemingly reading my mind.

"I know. I'll see what I can do. You're still in my custody, after all."

He made his way to the door, but I stopped him.

"What did Adrestus mean about Paragon?" I asked. "He said something about atoning for his sins."

Fleming studied me but shrugged.

"I suppose he meant that even the best of us have our shortcomings. Try to get some rest. I'll see you in class tomorrow if you aren't expelled."

I couldn't tell if he was joking or not, but I thought it best not to ask.

Everly wouldn't let Wes back in to see me and barred Naomi from visiting as well, insisting I needed the rest. I suspected it was his way of punishing me for running off. I figured they were keeping me in the Sickbay for the day to make sure I didn't go back for Dad.

Not Dad. Vidar. His name was Vidar.

I threw my arm over my face to block out the ceiling lights that filtered through my eyelids. My real dad was dead and had been for a thousand years. The man I knew as my father was actually my brother, Vidar. I was Eydis.

But the revelations of my past life grated against the fake memories in my head. Dad had taught me to ride a bike. Vidar, meanwhile, was the much younger man who'd carried me away from my burning home in my dreams. He felt fake while the fake memories felt real.

The door creaked open, and I peeked out from under my arm, hoping Everly had let Wesley or Naomi in. I scowled when I saw Andersen pushing a mop bucket instead.

He glowered when he saw me.

"Calm down," he said. "I'm just looking for Everly. No need to look so sour."

"I'm not sour." I gave him my best deadpan glare.

"It's not my fault, you know," he insisted. "Everyone's blaming me, but all I did was tell you the truth. They're the ones that tricked you."

It wasn't like Andersen to not take credit for his handiwork. I grabbed a granola bar from the stack that Everly had left on my bedside table and ripped it open.

"It's fine." It felt weird seeing Andersen, knowing he'd been the one to make me mad enough to run off but had then been part of the team to rescue me, even if it was only because Fleming had made him.

"And you're the one who dipped out," Andersen argued. "I'm in trouble, but it's not like I made you go try to get yourself killed."

"I said it's fine."

"Could you tell that to Fleming? I swear I've had to clean everything twice today."

I noticed the deep shadows on Andersen's face for the first time. I wondered if Fleming had even given him the chance to sleep.

"Besides," he spat, wheeling the mop bucket towards Everly's office, "I helped save you. You'd think that'd be enough. You're welcome, by the way."

He'd also killed me once, too. I bit my tongue to keep from retorting. He wasn't worth it. Besides, I could tell he was already on edge.

"Ask Everly if he has these in peanut-butter flavor when you're in there." I waved my granola bar at him. "I'm getting tired of the plain ones."

He struck a face and pushed his way into the back hall. I smiled, though I doubted I was going to get any peanut-butter granola bars.

I'd spent the whole day in and out of sleep, so the night was long and lonely, giving me plenty of time in the dark to worry about class the next day. Fleming hadn't stopped by after his second Council meeting. I didn't know if that was good or bad.

However, by the time the wall clock read six AM, Everly was back to officially check me out of the Sickbay. He didn't mention any expulsions, and I took it to mean I was safe, at least for the day.

I was sore everywhere, but it felt good to stand under the hot water of the locker room shower. I watched the last bit of blood wash away from my hair and slip down the drain. I sighed and closed my eyes, wishing I could disappear in the steam.

After my shower, I stared at my reflection in the mirror. I pulled at the collar of the sweatshirt to look at the angry, jagged scar. It looked as if the Serum didn't know how to fuse the skin back together.

I could still see the bike crash in my head. I felt the front wheel catch. I could see the handlebars pass beneath me as I soared over them. None of it was real.

"Samantha?"

I startled at the sound of Heather's voice.

"What are you doing down here?" The smile fell from her lips when she saw my face. "Holy crap, what happened?"

I tried to smile through the bruises.

"It's nothing."

"Is this what the alert was about the other night? Does this mean you're back on the team?"

"I don't think so," I laughed sadly. "I think I'm lucky to even still be a student here."

"Too bad. I miss having you down here. Come here, people will ask questions if you go to class looking fresh from a brawl." She pulled a make-up bag from her backpack and held her foundation up to my face. "You're a little paler than me, but it'll look better than purple."

"Has Fleming said anything?" I asked as Heather began to rub the make-up over my face. "About the other night?"

She frowned and shook her head.

"No, everyone who missed the alert has been kept in the dark. He's called a team meeting after school today, though."

My stomach twisted. How much would he tell them?

"That should do it." Heather zipped her bag shut. "Try not to rub it off."

I glanced in the mirror. It was much easier to look at my face now.

"Not bad." I grinned. "Thanks."

I shouldered my things and breathed a sigh of relief. Heather could've interrogated me on what had happened, but instead she fixed my face and let me on my way. It was too bad I saw less of her now that I wasn't on the team anymore.

"Sammy!" Naomi wrapped her arms around me when I came out of the locker room. "I tried to text you to see if you wanted to get breakfast, but you didn't answer."

"Yeah, my phone ended up in the museum fountain."

A group of upperclassmen passed on their way out of the gym, and Marcus did a double-take when he saw me.

"We should probably get going," Naomi muttered. "People are about to start asking questions."

She led the way out of the atrium and up the stairs to the main floor. She moved slowly for me . My injuries were mostly healed, but I was still stiff and sore, discovering aching muscles that I hadn't even known existed before this.

The cafeteria was busy, and everyone we passed chattered excitedly about homecoming.

"It was two days ago," I mumbled to Naomi as we passed the girl who'd been crowned Junior Class Queen. Her tiara sat on top of her curled hair. "You'd think there'd be something new to talk about."

"You mean like your roommate's sister?" Someone jeered behind us.

Jamie stood with Madison, both grinning maliciously. Jamie twisted a morning paper in her hands. She unfurled it with a whip and read from the front page.

"'New Delos University student Amanda Hendricks wanted in connection with arson and attempted murder'. Yikes. Maybe it's a good thing Winnie disappeared. It was only a matter of time before she lit one of us on fire."

Naomi put a hand on my shoulder and tried to draw me away.

"Go cry to your dad about it," she sneered. Jamie snickered.

"Maybe I will." She scanned over the article again. "It says right here she's a known Apex. Just further proof that they need to be muzzled."

"What?" I snatched the paper from Jamie's claws and searched the page. "They can't say that, can they?"

"If an Apex commits a crime, like, say, trying to murder the curator of the city's museum, they forfeit their rights to anonymity," she said smugly.

I ignored her and continued to devour the newspaper page. The knot in my stomach loosened. It didn't mention me. I caught Cunningham's name. He was alive. Adrestus was alive.

The Lapis had worked. I knew it would, but it still felt like a punch in the stomach to know he was still out there.

"You can keep that," Jamie said. "I don't really need newspapers. I get my news straight from the City Council."

"No one cares about your dad." Naomi extracted the newspaper from my hands and threw it at Jamie. "Go bother someone else."

I realized I was shaking as we walked away.

"Arson?" I hissed. "Since when is self-defense arson?"

"I know," Naomi whispered, "but we shouldn't talk about it here."

"And attempted murder!" I said, ignoring her warning. "I was the one who killed him!"

Naomi looked around nervously, but no one was paying us any attention.

"I know, it's not fair. But listen, I've got a theory about Schrader—"

"You think he's involved?" I snorted. "His disembodied voice chased me through the museum, so that's probably a good lead."

Naomi's brow wrinkled as she piled yogurt and fruit onto her plate.

"So it makes sense the paper is printing garbage. He owns them."

"Then why not use the paper to turn on me?" I asked. "He could easily print something about how I was an accomplice and boom. I'm arrested, and Adrestus has me in his clutches again."

Naomi shook her head.

"Maybe he doesn't need you anymore?"

I knew that wasn't true. Adrestus hated me. He wanted me to die for each day I'd made him die a little more or whatever melodramatic nonsense he'd been spouting. I wondered what Eydis had meant to him back when she was still me. I couldn't shake the feeling we had been close. The cafeteria suddenly felt much colder.

"I hate to change the subject," Naomi said nervously, "and you can say no, but Jamie and I haven't been getting along lately, and I heard about Winnie."

My stomach re-knotted itself at Winnie's name. I didn't want to think about her ever again.

"And?"

Naomi shifted uncomfortably as she took her seat.

"It's just...you don't have a roommate anymore, and I think mine wants to kill me. I thought maybe...I don't know...you already know about the team, too, so I wouldn't have to make excuses for being out at weird times, and I figured we could talk to Renee but..."

She trailed off and prodded awkwardly at her yogurt. I grinned, all thoughts of Adrestus and Winnie falling to the wayside.

"You want to be roommates?"

Naomi's cheeks reddened, and she cleared her throat.

"Only if you want to."

"Yes! That would be perfect!" However, my happiness evaporated when I remembered I might be kicked out. "If I'm not expelled, I mean."

Naomi grinned in relief and shrugged.

"I'm sure you're fine. Besides, if you are expelled, I'll ask for your room, anyway," she joked. "I might feel bad at first, but anything is better than living with Jamie."

The closer we got to History class, the more knotted my stomach became. I didn't want to see Fleming or Wesley or Andersen or anyone. I'd have to face them eventually, though. I wiped my sweaty palms off on my jeans as we walked in.

Anthony waved at Naomi and me from the front row. Wes's normal seat was empty.

"Hey, Samantha," he said in a low voice. "I heard about Saturday. I hope you're okay."

My cheeks warmed, but I shrugged casually. I wondered how much Wes had told him.

"I'm okay. Where's Wesley?"

"He's not feeling well." Anthony frowned. "You guys can sit with me today if you want."

I would have preferred to hide from Fleming in the back of the class, but I took the seat next to Anthony. Naomi found room on my other side since Jamie probably wouldn't welcome her to sit in her usual spot. I hoped Wes was okay. I couldn't help but to feel like it was my fault he was absent.

Fleming's gaze flicked over me when he entered the classroom, but he otherwise ignored me. I told myself if I had been expelled, he'd say something before class started. This had to be a good sign.

However, his mouth was drawn in a firm frown, and after rifling through his bag for a moment, he crossed over to my desk and set a hall pass face down in front of me.

"You're excused from P.E. today. You'll go to Dr. Weaver's office instead."

I stared at the backside of the slip as he walked back to his desk, my hands gripping the edge of mine.

"He doesn't feel that upset," Naomi whispered. "I'm sure she just has questions for you."

"Yeah, like 'what's the earliest you can be moved out of your dorm?'"

It was impossible to pay attention in my next classes. I tried to distract myself by taking notes on the lessons, but by the time the bell would ring, I'd look back and not remember writing any of it.

I could hardly eat at lunch, my stomach was so upset. Naomi pushed a piece of toast my way.

"You should eat something. I saw how much Serum Everly had to pump into you the other night. I'm surprised you're not still hungry from it all."

"I had a lot of granola bars." I shrugged, but took the toast anyway. I nibbled on the crust, wondering if this would be my last meal at New Delos Prep.

If I was expelled, where would I go? Would Fleming still be considered my guardian? Did he even have a house for me to live in or did he just sleep at his office desk?

The bell rang to signal the end of lunch, and I scowled at my toast.

"Eat it on the way," Naomi instructed. "I'll find you later for dinner, okay?"

"Yeah, sure," I mumbled.

My legs had never felt heavier than they did on my way up the stairs to Dr. Weaver's third floor office. Would the entire Council be there to show me out? I couldn't help but to feel jealous of the kids that crowded the halls on their way to class. I'd much rather be headed wherever they were than where I was.

I knocked on Dr. Weaver's door, bracing myself for whatever news was waiting for me inside.

"Come on in, Samantha," Fleming's voice replied.

I sighed. At least Fleming was here. He'd had my back in the past. Hopefully I hadn't lost that.

"Miss Havardson," Dr. Weaver said without looking away from her computer screen. "Take a seat."

Fleming stood in front of the window behind Dr. Weaver's desk. He did his best to smile at me as I lowered myself in the chair. I waited while Dr. Weaver finished typing and then spun to face me. I gulped.

"I'm glad to see you looking well," she said curtly. She kept talking before I could get the words "Thank you" off my lips. "We need to discuss our plan going forward."

I sank back into the seat.

"Am I expelled?" I thought I saw the ghost of a smile flicker across her face.

"No, you're still a student here."

I sank even further into my chair as I went weak with relief.

"The vote was five to one," Fleming said. "The representative from Schrader Industries was less than thrilled, but, ultimately, he was outnumbered."

I remembered the man named Trev, who always seemed to have a massive cup of coffee on hand.

"Of course he wants me gone!" I exclaimed. "I accused his boss of being behind everything!"

Fleming looked at Dr. Weaver uncomfortably.

"Although, now we know that he isn't," Weaver said. "You named Warren Cunningham as Adrestus."

"But Schrader was there," I insisted. "I could hear him—"

"But you couldn't see him."

"He was there! He's got to be some sort of Apex."

Fleming and Weaver exchanged looks again.

"Adrian Schrader was on the mainland at a well-attended and televised banquet. He couldn't have been at the museum," Dr. Weaver explained. "And we know he's not an Apex. His whole family has submitted to the genetic test. None of them have ever tested positive for either Epsilon gene."

"No," I said, "he was there. It was his voice."

"Samantha, Everly said you were pretty concussed when we brought you in," Fleming said gingerly. "He had to use up the last of his specialty Serum to heal you."

"Thanks for that, by the way," Dr. Weaver interjected wryly. "I'm not looking forward to donating spinal fluid again."

"Winnie gave me that concussion *after* I heard Schrader," I argued.

"We have three hundred eye witnesses that put him off the island." Fleming shrugged. "That said, I promise we'll continue to look into him. The circumstances are suspicious at the very least."

I scowled but dropped it. As soon as their guards were down, I'd have to pick the investigation back up myself. I'd be more careful this time. I'd save Dad and Amanda and prove Schrader was involved.

"Moving on," Dr. Weaver clipped, folding her hands in front of her. "We need to figure out what we are going to do with you."

"I thought I wasn't expelled!"

"You're not, but your mother is in hiding, and your father is prisoner to a man who wants you dead," Dr. Weaver summarized. "And Mr. Fleming has told me an interesting story about you not being their daughter in the first place."

I glared at Fleming, and he turned red.

"You told the Council!" I accused him.

"Miss Havardson, he told *me*," Dr. Weaver said. She leaned in over the desk, and her voice dropped. "And I agreed that we shouldn't tell the Council. The others might see you as a liability, but Mr. Fleming and I see you for what you are."

"And what's that?" I scowled. A freak? A relic? A faker?

Dr. Weaver's face softened.

"A child, even if you are a thousand years old." She pulled her glasses off and began to polish the lenses on the sleeve of her blazer. "I know a few of my colleagues might think it best to hand you over to Adrestus, but I made a promise to protect all of my students, and that includes you."

I looked down at my hands, unsure of how to respond.

"Thank you," I finally said.

"That said," Dr. Weaver continued, "your situation is unique. There can be no more running off on your own, but if we're being honest, we both believe that you will."

"So what?" I blanched. "I'm gonna have to be babysat every second of the day?"

Dr. Weaver smiled again and leaned back in her chair.

"We had something else in mind," she said coyly. "Alex?"

Fleming took a deep breath and smiled.

"Samantha, would you like to join the Apex Team?"

41

Blessing Bestowed

I stared at them, waiting for either of them to yell "Gotcha!" However, neither of them did. They stared at me expectantly.

"I—but I failed," I said simply. "I didn't make the cut."

"The student who's done more for the team than anyone's done in years fell in the last second to our strongest student." Dr. Weaver suppressed a laugh. "You failed the Final Trial, but anyone who says you don't belong on the team would be lying to themselves."

I struggled to make sense of what they were offering.

"I got kicked out. Why would I want to come back?"

"Because it's the best chance you have at finding your father," Dr. Weaver said. "Plus, it's our best chance at figuring out what Adrestus wants and how to stop him. You've known him longer than anyone, even if you don't remember it."

I picked at my fingernails, mulling the offer over in my head.

"It's not fair, though," I said. "Why would I get special treatment when there are kids every year who don't make the team?"

"You're right, which is why we'll be extending this offer to all current students who have attempted the trials and failed. You'll be considered full team members but will be required to partake in additional training."

"The Council agreed to this?"

Dr. Weaver crossed her arms and looked down her nose at me.

"The Council doesn't get to decide how Mr. Fleming manages his team. He only needs my approval, which I've given him wholeheartedly." She glanced at her watch. "Speaking of, I'm meeting Allen downstairs in five. Take a few days to rest, but we expect you at practice after school on Wednesday."

I sat dumbfounded in my seat as Dr. Weaver rounded her desk. She reminded Fleming to lock the office door when we left, and then she was gone.

Fleming took one of the spare seats near her bookshelves. I stared at Dr. Weaver's nameplate.

"I thought you'd be happier," Fleming said. I shrugged.

"I am happy." I felt hollow as I said it. All that work, just to be crushed and disappointed. And now, I got to simply walk onto the team? "I–I didn't earn it."

Fleming surprised me by laughing.

"Didn't you hear Dr. Weaver?" he said. "No one's done more to earn a spot on the team than you."

"It doesn't feel that way!" I insisted. "I lost fair and square. How's that going to look to everyone else? I won't be a real team member to them."

Fleming ran his hands through his hair. He stared at the ceiling for a moment before responding.

"Honestly, anyone who isn't okay with it wouldn't have been okay with you making it on the team the traditional way," he said. "No matter what, it'll be something. To them, you're just a Beta. You can do everything right, and they'll still say you were wrong, just because you aren't like them. So who cares if you do something the wrong way? It's all the same to them."

Andersen came to mind, as did Skyler. They'd accidentally killed me when I'd tried joining the team the normal way. Who knew what they would do if Fleming allowed me to walk back in.

"But I'll also say this," Fleming said, looking away from the ceiling and locking eyes with me. "Most of those kids respect you and miss you. They know what you're capable of, and they trust you to have their backs."

I thought of Heather, eagerly asking if Fleming had let me back on the team. This morning, that thought had been ridiculous, but here he was, insisting I rejoin. Naomi would be happy, too.

But what would Wes think? The decision wasn't his to make, of course, and while I hadn't enjoyed the rough patch in our friendship, I hated to think all that strain was for nothing. But he'd still come after me when I left him at the dance. He'd found me, and even when he was mad, he'd cleaned the blood from my face and neck.

"Wednesday?" I asked.

"I expect to see you there." A smile spread over Fleming's face. "I know she's not your real mother, but I see a lot of Alison in you. Don't worry about the others. You're going to do great."

A strange sense of defeat settled over me over the next day. I'd gotten what I wanted, but it felt wrong. Fleming told the team what had happened at the museum but left out all the parts I'd told him to. Justin found me in the hall between classes on Tuesday and pulled me into a bear hug. Isabelle somehow procured an artisanal cupcake and had it delivered to my Sixth Period. It felt weird to receive praise for something I knew had been stupid.

None of them indicated that they knew I'd be back on Wednesday. I wondered if their feelings would change when they found out.

After class on Tuesday I went back to the dorm to pack up Winnie's things. Naomi had been cleared to move in, but with Roy and Val Hendricks taking care of Alison somewhere on the mainland and Amanda an apparent wanted criminal, it fell to me to clean up Winnie's side of the room.

Renee brought me boxes and offered to help, but I sent her away. Winnie's absence felt like my fault, too. I knew I wouldn't have been able to save her. She was following Adrestus willingly, after all, but I'd been so dead set on rescuing her.

As I stacked her textbooks in a box, I remembered her in the museum, bitter about how her only friend had been a lie. I pressed my fingertips into the hardcover of her math textbook. I'd been her only friend. I should've paid more attention. I could have helped her before it was too late.

Even if our earlier memories of each other weren't real, she had been my only friend, too, for a few days. I'd let her down. I set the textbook down in the box and stretched. Each item of hers that I moved into boxes seemed to unearth layers of bitterness and regret. I'd barely made a dent in her things, but I already needed a break.

It looked like it might start raining, but I'd rather take my chances with a walk in the rain than continue packing Winnie's things. Dark gray clouds rolled towards the mainland overhead as I stared out at the slate-colored water. I had found a bench along the campus waterfront. It was cold enough that no one would bother me here, so I could turn over the events from the last few days in my head in peace.

However, my solitude was short-lived.

"Hey."

I pulled my jacket around me tighter and stayed facing forward.

"I thought you were sick," I said as Wes took the seat next to me. He'd missed class again that day.

"I'm feeling a little better," he said. "What about you?"

I drew the heels of my feet up to the edge of the bench and hugged my knees, watching white caps form in the distance.

"Yeah, I've been okay." I turned my head to look at him and laid my cheek on my knees. "Anthony gave me your seat in First Period, though. You'll have to find a new place to sit."

Wes gave me a crooked smile and slid his hands into the front pocket of his hoodie.

"That's alright. Maybe I'll just take Andersen's spot."

"He'll have a fit if you do."

"That might be fun."

The smile fell from his face, and his throat contracted as he swallowed.

"I heard Fleming is letting you back on the team."

"Apparently."

"Are you going to? Join, I mean."

I sighed.

"I need to find my dad."

Wesley nodded, as if he'd known I would say that.

"Are you okay?" I asked. Wesley forced a smile.

"I think so. I-I'm sorry about everything I said before. I never should have quit on you. I panicked and was scared and—" He cleared his throat. "Just know I'm going to give you everything in practice. I can make sure you're ready for whatever that Adrestus creep throws at you next."

I gave in to a reluctant smile.

"Watch it, I still have my dog whistle."

Wesley glared.

"That's cheating. Hand-to-hand only."

"I went easy on you in the trial. I'll beat you every time. Guaranteed."

He chuckled, but the laughter died from his eyes, and he looked serious again.

"I just wanted to say that I'm sorry."

I snorted, and he scowled.

"I'm serious," he said. "I lied to you. I should've told you that Fleming made me ask you to the dance, or I should've let someone else do it."

I grimaced and looked back at the gray water. I didn't want to talk about Homecoming.

"I'm sorry, too. I didn't mean to be a bother, and I know you would've rather have gone with Remi."

"Remi?" Wes struck a face. "Why would I want to go to Homecoming with Remi?"

Despite the cool wind, I felt my face grow hot.

"Because you like her!" I said quickly. "You guys used to date, didn't you? And you've been hanging out with her more lately."

"That doesn't mean I like her." He groaned and ran a hand over his face. "The first time Remi and I broke up was when she didn't make the team last year. After that, it was pretty on and off, but it became clear that we didn't work together."

"But then you started reconsidering that?" I asked. I remembered the night I ran into them eating froyo together.

"No, I wanted to know if I could still be her friend," he mumbled. "I thought maybe it wasn't us that didn't work, but the fact that I was on the team, and she wasn't. And with your trials coming up..."

I looked back at him and was shocked to see him blushing furiously.

"You wanted to know if you and I would still work if I didn't make the team?" I asked, wrinkling my nose.

"Right," he said but quickly cleared his throat. "Like as friends, obviously."

"Obviously." I snorted. "That's not very fair to Remi, though. She deserves better than to be your friendship guinea pig."

Wes leaned over and put his elbows on his knees.

"I know," he sighed. "But she does matter to me. She's cool."

"Right, and you would've had fun at the dance with her. So, I'm sorry that Fleming put you up to ask me."

"He didn't put me up to ask you," Wesley said. "He wanted someone to hang out with you at the dance after I beat you in the trials, and I figured since I'd been trying to ask you for weeks, I might as well go for it."

I choked on my spit.

"What do you mean you were trying to ask me for weeks?" I exclaimed. Wes turned away so I couldn't see his face.

"It wasn't easy, alright? Either you were yelling at me, or Naomi would show up, or your dad was kidnapped!"

"You'd wanted to talk to me after the Industry Fair," I remembered. "Were you...?"

"Yeah." He shrugged. "But then, you know..."

The first few raindrops landed on the path in front of us, dotting the pavement with sparse, dark spots.

"Do you want to go inside?" Wes asked. I shook my head, resting my chin on my knees. I could feel the confession building inside of me.

"I, um, I figured out the flash drive."

I felt the bench shift as he turned to look at me. I shut my eyes.

"And?"

I squeezed my knees tighter.

"And I was right." My throat tightened, making it hard to say the words. "Alison invented me."

"How do you know?"

"Adrestus told me, and so did my dad, at the museum. He's not my dad, though. He's my brother, apparently."

Wes was quiet. Maybe I shouldn't have said anything. It was unfair to put this on my friends, but the pain of the last few days' revelation was threatening to rip me open from the inside.

"Did they say who you were?" he asked slowly. I stretched my legs out, setting my feet back on the ground.

"Remember those statues Cunningham showed us on the field trip?" I said, hyper-aware of how ridiculous this was going to sound. "Turns out he's the actual Adrestus, and I'm the Icelandic girl who tried to kill him a thousand years ago."

Wesley laughed awkwardly.

"You can't be serious."

He was going to think I'd lost it. I wouldn't blame him if he did. Embarrassment mingled with the pain in my head.

"My real name is Eydis, and I stole a magic stone or something from him that kept me alive but in a coma for a thousand years until my brother could find a way to wake me up."

Wesley didn't say anything, but I couldn't let the silence sit between us.

"He took it back, though," I said, rubbing the scar that the Serum had haphazardly fused back together. "So, bad news, I can probably die again."

I dropped my hands into my lap and stared at them. I didn't want to look at Wesley. I couldn't look at Wesley. But I could feel him staring at me.

"It's kind of funny, you know," he said. I turned my head just barely enough to see him. He had a stupid grin on his face.

"What?"

"It's just, you've spent all semester trying to convince everyone that you could do anything we could do even though you weren't...you know... but now, it's like, you were immortal the whole time and are some sort of ancient warrior."

"I'm not ancient!" The word felt surprisingly offensive.

Wesley threw his head back and laughed.

"No, not ancient, just a thousand years old!" He tried to put a comforting hand on my back, but I shrugged it off.

"I don't feel a thousand years old," I whispered. I appreciated Wesley trying to cheer me up, but it was hard to shake the heartache that had been eating away at me. "I don't even remember any of it."

As I said it, I could see the burning village in my head and my blood running out in the cold stream. Out of everything to remember from my past life, why did it have to be something so horrible? What if it had all been like that?

"That's okay," Wesley said. I could tell he was searching for the right words to say, but what can you say to someone who's just discovered everything she knows is a lie? "You still remember how to fight, apparently! Remember at the museum, with the sword? That had to have been the Eydis part of you."

"But I'm not Eydis," I asserted. "And apparently I'm not Samantha, either. My whole life is a made-up story. I'm not even a real person."

I buried my head in my hands as the reality of my words washed over me. I wasn't real. I was just the shell of a person programmed with false memories.

I wasn't Samantha, but that was the only life I knew.

Wesley wrapped his arms around my shoulders and pulled me in. I let him and buried my face in the cotton of his hoodie as he ran a hand through my hair.

"I know you're real," he murmured in my ear. I couldn't stop the tears that seeped into his sweatshirt. "Everything I know about you is real. You're real stubborn, for one. And you can be a real pain in my ass, but you're real brave, too. And real smart and real kind and—"

He cut himself off and continued to stroke my hair in silence for another moment.

"You're just really, really great," he finally said. "And you're really, really real."

I stood outside the training gym, dressed in my exercise gear and wrist guards. By now, the team knew I was back. I'd received a few icy glares in the hall earlier that day. Andersen, who had already gotten back together with Jamie, was particularly vindictive. The metal clips of my school binder bent out of shape and wouldn't stay clasped together so the inside of my backpack was an explosion of loose papers. Later, I had caught my shoelaces tying themselves together under the table in math class.

I was more nervous now than I had been on my first day in the training gym.

"It's okay to take it easy on your first day back," Naomi said next to me. "You don't need to prove anything to anyone."

A hand slid into mine and squeezed my fingers. I turned to Wes and smiled.

"And you're not alone," he pointed out. "Remi and Erik are already in there."

Naomi glanced at her watch

"I've gotta go. I forgot the captains are meeting beforehand."

"Why are you meeting with the captains?" I asked. She smiled coyly and raised an eyebrow. "You're not..."

"Heather nominated me after the trials, and Fleming put it to a vote."

"Even Andersen voted for her," Wes beamed. "We've been wanting to tell you, but you know. Team secrets."

I grinned at Naomi.

"That's amazing. No one deserves it more than you."

She blushed and began heading back down the hall to the atrium.

"You guys go ahead and get started! You're gonna do great today, Sam."

I looked at Wes, and he squeezed my fingers one last time before letting go of my hand.

"You ready, Scourge Queen?"

I snorted and pushed the door open.

"Just try not to feel too bad when I beat you."

Andersen glared at us from across the gym. A few upperclassmen huddled around Carmen glanced over and turned away as we walked in. Freddie looked like he might wave, but Skyler shot him a look, so he pretended to be messing with his hair.

However, Heather and Everest hurried over and clapped me so hard on the back, I almost fell over.

"I knew it!" Heather exclaimed. "Didn't I say Monday morning? Fleming had to let you come back!"

Remi waved from the corner where she and an upperclassman named Erik were reviewing basics with Mike and Desirae. She smiled meekly at Wes, and he waved back at her. They were the only two Apex who'd taken Fleming up on the offer to join the team.

"Samantha, I expected you to be hard at work already." Fleming came in behind us, flanked by Naomi and the other captains. Naomi tried to smile, but a strange look passed over her face. "You're a few weeks behind everyone else, now get to work."

Wes led the way to an empty spot on the floor and squared up.

"I hope you aren't rusty."

I took my stance opposite him, feeling every pair of eyes trained on us. I nodded to Wes, letting him know I was ready.

He swept my legs out from under me, and the mat greeted me with a familiar slap as I fell hard on my side.

Andersen's derisive laugh filled the gym, but when I looked up, Wes was offering me a hand. I clasped it, and he helped me to my feet.

I reset my stance and shook my ponytail out of my face. I couldn't help but grin despite my smarting shoulder and pride. It felt good to be back.

"Okay, then," I smirked. "Again."

Wesley grinned back at me and mirrored my stance. I steeled myself for his attack, but his smile slid from his face, and he cocked his head to one side.

"Something's wrong," Naomi gasped. I turned to watch her double over, like she had during the Night Games. Fleming and Marcus tried to steady her, but, just then, the gym door burst open.

A torrent of hot, whistling air slammed into my chest, knocking me back into Wesley, who barely managed to stay standing as the cyclone ripped through the room. Wesley held me steady, and I looked into the wind to see Isabelle stagger through the door.

Long, dark hair whipped around her face. Her arms shook, and her teeth gritted from the strain of supporting the hunched figure next to her, who kept his face buried in his hands.

"Isabelle! Stop this!" Fleming shouted over the roaring wind that continued to tear through the room, knocking kids over and upturning equipment.

"It's not me!"

She kept her arms around the boy next to her as he slowly raised his face from his hands to look at the destruction that had overtaken the gym. Panicked tears streaked Anthony's face. Wesley's arms tightened around me.

"Please," Anthony choked, barely audible over the whistling in my ears. "Help me. I can't make it stop!"

Justin fought his way through the gale from where he'd been standing with Fleming and the captains. The wind stopped as soon as he grabbed Anthony's hand and forced him into a stasis.

Fleming was already barking orders, but Wesley turned away, probably so he wouldn't have to look at his friend frozen in a state of horror.

"It doesn't make sense." His voice was far away, and he stared vacantly at the far wall. "Anthony's not an Apex."

Everly ran in, ready with sedatives. Anthony went limp, and I gulped as the pit in my stomach set my hands shaking. I could see Cunningham's face twisting in my mind, spitting at me, *you could've been Blessed!*

"This is Adrestus." I reached for Wesley's hand, trying to stay my quaking fingers against his, but his hand shook, too. "I think...I think he Blessed Anthony."

The whole gym was silent as Marcus and Justin lifted Anthony and carried him towards the Sickbay. I wrapped my free arm around myself to keep from shivering. Our fight with Adrestus had only just begun.

Acknowledgements

First and foremost, thank you to my mom, who taught me to read and write in the first place, and to my dad, for teaching me there is nothing wrong with girls liking superheroes.

Thank you to my test readers, who diligently sniffed out each typo (I hope), and became Samantha's first fans. Each of you contributed, even if you only read the first chapter (Julia).

Melissa, thank you for reading, re-reading, and reading again Sammy's story. You probably know it better than I do at this point, which is fitting since I'm not sure it would have ever been finished without your constant, unwavering support and encouragement.

Finally, thank you, Connor, for giving me the courage to write, for loving me even when all I wanted to do was edit, and for patiently waiting to read it when it took longer to write than anticipated. You've stood with me every step of the way and have been the best, most loving husband I ever could've hoped for.

SAMANTHA WILL RETURN

IN

THE APEX CYCLE
BOOK 2

WESLEY

Like it had freshman year, the Welcome Back festival on the pier sounded like a good idea, but, also like the year before, Wesley immediately regretted his decision to go. After a summer in his mother's quiet apartment outside of the city, the smells, lights, and sounds of the festival rocked every one of Wesley's super-senses.

He leaned against a wood railing behind the ferris wheel with his hands pressed against his ears and his eyes screwed shut. His roommate Anthony had gone to find lunch, but thanks to an oncoming migraine, Wesley wasn't feeling hungry.

"You good?" Anthony's voice was garbled, and Wesley lowered his hands from his ears and opened his eyes, readjusting his glasses. Anthony joined him at the railing, wafting the smell of his lunch over Wesley.

"You smell like squid."

"I smell delicious, thank you." Anthony grinned. "I had calamari from one of the food trucks. You should go try some."

Wesley wrinkled his nose.

"Nah, I'm getting a pretty good serving of it right now actually."

"Hey, I met the new girl!"

"The one who puked on Jamie's shoes?" Wesley looked around as if Winnie Hendricks's new roommate might also be lurking behind the ferris wheel. "How long you think she'll last?"

Anthony laughed, and Wesley caught a fresh wave of fried-squid smell. He turned to lean his back against the railing and pointed across the pier at a miserable looking girl in a zip-up hoodie following Winnie from booth to booth.

"She looks ready to leave the island, honestly."

Wesley looked through the throng of students, tuning out the snippets of conversation that bloomed from all angles. Someone nearby won a carnival game, causing a series of bells and whistles to go off. Wesley winced at the sound.

"Are you sure you're okay?" Anthony peered at him, and Wesley forced a smile. "We can go back to campus, if you like."

"No, I'm fine!" Wesley lied. "Let's go play some games."

"So you can win them all?" Anthony snorted, but led the way to the row of booths boasting carnival games. "You just want to hang around in case something happens."

Wesley's face turned warm, and he tightened his grip on his backpack.

"No, I'm here for fun, not work."

"Oh, we're pretending your uniform isn't in that bag?"

Anthony may not have been an Apex, but he was still perceptive in ways that caught Wesley off guard. He scowled.

"There's been scuffles all over the city the last few weeks. Who's to say there won't be one here next?"

"And who's to say you shouldn't try to enjoy yourself, and let the adults in charge worry about that sort of thing? Just relax." Anthony rolled his eyes, stepping up to a ring toss.

"I relaxed all summer."

"I met your mom, and she's not relaxing."

Wesley tightened his backpack straps again, watching Anthony bounce his metal ring off the lip of a cone.

"You know what I think?" Anthony continued. His second ring missed, too. "You're bored. You want something fun to happen."

"Scuffles aren't fun, Anthony." Wesley bit his lip. "I just get nervous thinking about not being prepared."

The third ring missed, too, and Anthony clicked his tongue in irritation. He held up his fourth and final ring to Wesley.

"You do it. I swear it's rigged."

Wesley stepped up to take Anthony's place. Not too hard, he told himself. Just a flick of the fingers is enough. He'd broken enough windows to know how to not throw things.

The ring floated to the cone, and then, just when he was sure he'd landed it, it bounced off the lip. Howling laughter echoed across the pier, and Wesley turned to see Jamie Ratcliffe and her friends guffawing at his expense. Jamie's boyfriend, Andersen, sneered, and shoved his hands into his hoodie pocket. Of course. That was why they hadn't been able to land any rings. Andersen was messing with them.

Anger boiled inside Wesley, but one of Jamie's friends shook her head. Naomi's lips pressed together in a silent warning, signaling to Wesley it wasn't worth it. But how good would it feel to tell Jamie all about her boyfriend's secret Apex powers?

"Nice shoes, Jamie." Anthony grinned. "Are they new?"

Jamie flushed and pushed the sleeves of her cardigan up as if getting ready to fight, but Naomi cut in.

"Come on," she murmured. "They're not worth our attention."

Jamie deflated and stomped away. Her friends followed, but Naomi looked back at Anthony and Wesley to give them one last apologetic frown.

"Why does she even hang out with those losers?" Anthony groaned.

"Jamie's her roommate. If anyone can control her, it's Naomi." But Wesley didn't like it, either. In training and PE, Naomi was his best friend while to the rest of the school, she was part of Jamie's elite posse, and Wesley wasn't worth the time of day.

Wesley let Anthony lead the way for the rest of the afternoon but kept an eye out for Jamie, Andersen, and their friends and made sure to give them plenty of space. A dull ache thrummed behind his eyes.

Anthony was playing another carnival game when Wesley tried to close his eyes again, trying to ward off the oncoming migraine. A distant beat caught his ear, and he focused on it. It was too far away to make out clearly, but concentrating on the rhythm helped dull the roaring pain in his head.

Somewhere, a security guard's radio crackled.

"...protest headed towards the pier..."

Wesley's eyes snapped open, and Anthony cheered as he won whatever game he was focused on.

"Did you see that?" he guffawed.

"You need to get out of here." Wesley stood on tip-toes, trying to see over students and booths towards the entrance gate. That distant rhythm he'd found comfort in just a moment ago was getting louder. Angrier. Words began to take form.

"No more Apex, no more fear!" A voice led the chant over a bullhorn.

"What's wrong?" Anthony furrowed his brow at Wesley.

Wesley whipped around, looking at the students, wondering if there was a way to get them all out. It was probably fine. It was just a protest. Sure, it was a protest against him and anyone like him, but they wouldn't actually come near the festival, would they?

Screams and shouts mingled with the sounds of the protests, and Anthony's face went slack. He could hear it, too, now. The students around them turned quiet, all listening. Somewhere in the distance, Wesley heard the unmistakable sound of a fist hitting a face. A fight had broken out. A surge of people stormed the pier, chanting and smashing booths.

"Go!" Wesley shouted, pulling his backpack off his shoulders. "Get back to school! I'm right behind you!"

"What are you going to do?" Anthony demanded, fighting against the tide of frightened students to stay at Wesley's side.

"Someone might need help!"

"You need to get somewhere safe, too! You aren't invincible, Wesley!"

Wesley stopped. His roommate had a point, but there was no one on duty, and what if someone got hurt when Wesley could've helped?

He pulled his glasses off, and his vision sharpened, throwing every line of Anthony's frown into deep detail.

"Take these for me." He pushed them into Anthony's hands.

Wesley forged ahead and was relieved to hear Anthony retreating with the crowd of students. He found a spot behind a booth that smelled like kettle corn and tore his backpack open, revealing the glinting gray helmet inside. He brushed his fingers over the number "7", painted onto his shoulder armor. Summer had been long, and he'd missed wearing his Apex uniform.

He made quick work changing and pushed his shirt and jeans into the backpack and tucked it behind a counter. He'd have to come back for it later, but for now, the crowd was growing louder, reminding him that he had more pressing business.

Wesley pulled his helmet on and relaxed as the visor lit up, but a violent bang from the protestors made him tense back up.

"There better be a good reason I just saw your helmet go online."

Wesley winced at Fleming's low growl in his earpiece.

"Is an angry mob a good reason?"

"No, no it is not. Where are you?"

"The Welcome Back Festival?"

"Why do you have your uniform with you at the festival?"

Crap. This was at least going to earn Wesley extra laps around the field. Worst case scenario, he might even get benched. He skirted behind a row of portable restrooms. Kids screamed and protesters chanted. It was too much. Too loud. His head felt like it might split in two. Maybe it already had, and the helmet was all that was holding him together.

"I brought it just in case."

"It's a festival!" Fleming squawked. "What were you thinking would happen?"

"I was right, wasn't I?"

A bullhorn cut through the noise, emitting a sharp, high pitched squeal. Wesley clamped his hands over the outside of his helmet, but it was no use. Police sirens made the pain behind his eyes spread until it was pressing against the confines of his skull.

"Wesley?" Fleming's voice was sharp, less angry now and more concerned. "Talk to me."

"It's Seven," Wesley scowled.

"Fine. Talk to me, Seven."

His knees buckled, and he fell to the wooden planks behind a row of booths. Too loud. Too much. Too many people. And he could hear them coming towards him.

He slipped into the nearest booth and ducked behind the counter before anyone saw him, but someone shouted from where he'd just been.

"Did you see that? I swear it was one of them!"

Footsteps pounded against the pier, and Wesley saw a gap in the stall, leading into the next one. Great. He'd crawl along through the train of booths until he was at the exit.

"Tell me you're getting out of there." Fleming was still in Wesley's earpiece.

"Working on it." He passed into the next stall, and then the next.

And then, a dead end. He met solid wall. That was fine. There had to be another way—

The bullhorn squealed again, louder this time, accompanied by renewed chants, and the sound was like hot iron in Wesley's head. He grunted in pain and clawed his way under the booth table where he curled in on himself. Maybe he could stay here until everyone left?

"What's wrong? What's happening?" Fleming demanded. "Do I need to send Justin or—"

"I'm fine! I'm safe. I'm under a table. No one can see me here. I'll wait for things to calm down and—" Wesley cut off at the sound of a scuffle overhead.

"Leave me alone!" a girl's voice shouted. The table skirt fluttered, and a body rolled into Wesley.

"Hey, watch it!"

The girl froze. The ba-bump of her heartbeat cut through the noise, and Wesley listened to it quicken in her chest at the sight of him.

"Seven, what's going on?" Fleming barked in Wesley's ear.

"What are you doing?" Wesley ignored Fleming, instead directing his question to the girl. She hunched over in the dark, the tips of her brown-blonde hair brushing the boardwalk planks, but Wesley recognized the girl Anthony had pointed out as Winnie's new roommate.

"Me? What are you doing? Shouldn't you be out there?" She jerked a thumb over her shoulder. "You know, restoring peace or whatever?"

"Are you compromised?" Fleming growled. "Get out of there! Wesley, if I have to deal with one more phone call from your mother—"

Wesley tapped a button on the side of his helmet, cutting his sound off. Fleming's lecture continued to scroll as text along the bottom of his screen, but he ignored it, instead looking at the girl. Her feet stuck out from under the table, and he reached forward, helping her under.

"Yeah, that's what I should be doing!" The pain from the noise outside threatened to lay him out, but he forced his way through it. "But I didn't realize how quickly they were moving, and if I went out now…"

"They'd tear you apart." She nodded sagely, taking the fact she'd found an Apex in pretty good stride all things considered. "But you're an Apex, aren't you? You can't take them?"

She was definitely new, then. Had she not seen the angry mob?

"And give them more reason to hate us? Besides, the paperwork alone would be a nightmare."

She smirked and peeked under the table skirt. Wesley tried to remember if Anthony had mentioned her name, but he drew a blank.

"It looks like we might be stuck here for a while." She turned back to Wesley, frowning. "There's no way we're getting past that crowd."

Even with her sitting so close to him and his super hearing, it was hard to hear anything over the crowd's chanting of "We want Epsilon Epsi-gone!" The sound of splintering wood cut through the noise. The crowd was getting more aggressive.

"They've started tearing apart booths farther down the pier," he explained. "It's only a matter of time before they flatten this one."

As if on cue, the table overhead shuddered and bumped as the crowd knocked against it, and Wesley tensed, ready to jump on the girl and stave off whatever wave of people was waiting to come crashing down on them, but the shaking passed, and the girl sighed in relief.

"Why don't you just take off your uniform?" she asked, pressing her hands over her eyes. "I can't get through all those people, but maybe you can? Without your uniform, no one will know you're an Apex, and maybe you could help clear us a path to the exit?"

A warning from Fleming scrolled across the bottom of Wesley's screen, but it wasn't needed. Wesley felt the heat rise in his face as he thought back to his discarded backpack with his street clothes.

"That's a no-go. I, uh, I don't have anything on under this." Thank god the helmet's voice modulator hid the embarrassed crack in his voice. "And if I took off my helmet, you'd see my face, and that'd be paperwork for both of us, maybe even a memory alteration—"

"Fine, I get it."

Wesley hoped this girl didn't show up in any of his classes. He'd never be able to talk to her without blushing now.

But they were running out of time, and his brain didn't have time to be embarrassed. He tried to think of a way out. He looked at his gloved hands.

"I could probably punch a hole in the pier, and then we could drop and swim away?"

She stared back at him blankly while Fleming flipped out on his screen, threatening Call Duty and bathroom cleaning if Wesley went through with that plan.

"I'm sorry," the girl deadpanned. "Punch a hole in the pier?"

"It might take a couple goes, but—"

She pulled her jacket off and threw it at him.

"Hey!" Wesley wrestled the jacket off his visor. "It's a good idea!"

"It's ridiculous. Put that on over your uniform, and we'll do my plan."

He maneuvered in the tight space, trying to get the zip-up on over his uniform, but it didn't do anything to cover his helmet.

"Try the hood," the girl said, and Wesley obliged, feeling the fabric straining to fit. "Can't you carry it? Look, it's dark under here, and I promise not to look at your face. Just keep the hood up, and no one will look twice at you."

Wesley hesitated. It was dangerous. He looked at Fleming's text.

If she sees your face, you're on probation.

A loud bang accompanied renewed cries from the crowd outside.

"Now or never," the girl prompted.

"Fine." This was a bad idea. "Look away. And don't tell anyone I did this."

He made sure she wasn't looking and then slipped the helmet off over his head. He turned away from the girl as he pulled the hood up, tugging on it to pull it as low over his face as he could.

"You're good." He didn't look back to see if she'd opened her eyes, instead lifting the side of the table skirt that led into the empty booth.

"Stay close." He tried to speak low in an effort to disguise his voice, but he sounded ridiculous. "If you lose me, I might not be able to help you."

The girl crept to the back door and tried the handle, but the vendor had locked up. Wesley could probably bust it open, but he didn't want to draw attention to his power in case anyone saw.

"Over the table, then," the girl said, turning back. Wesley bowed his head before she could catch a glimpse of his face, but he extended a hand towards her.

"Keep up, and hold on."

He took her hand in his, her fingers tightening in a way that told Wesley he had her trust. He hoped he could live up to it. He slid across the table, pulling her after him to chants of "Schrader is a Traitor!"

The pier had filled with protesters, and Wesley's heart sank. He knew there'd always be those who hated Apex, but he'd never imagined there were enough in the city to fill the entire pier.

Those nearest to the booth cried out in shock as Wesley bowled into them, pulling the girl after him. He passed his helmet back to her, careful to keep his face down and threw his free arm up to force a pathway through the crowd.

Gentle, he told himself as he shoved people to the side. Don't hurt anyone.

The girl followed so close that she stepped on the back of Wesley's boots more than once and mumbled breathless apologies as she struggled to keep up. Through it all, she kept her hand firmly in his until, as Wesley continued forward, he found resistance when he tried to pull her after him. She cried out, and her hand slipped from his. Wesley twisted around.

She clutched Wesley's helmet against her chest as an angry man towered over her, holding her by the elbow. To Wesley's shock, she smacked the man in the nose, and his eyes bulged in rage. He lunged at her.

"You filthy, little Apex!"

Wesley leaped between them, pulling the girl back.

Gentle, he reminded himself again, as he pressed one hand against the man's sternum and forced him backwards, hard enough so the man and the three people behind him fell but not so hard that he broke any ribs. The girl's smack to his nose probably left more lasting damage.

Wesley had a half-second of stunned shock from the onlookers to get moving again. He threw an arm over the girl, holding her close, trying to ignore how she smelled like fried dough and powdered sugar. The shrieks of the crowd and the glare of the sun and the blaring of the bullhorn beat against Wesley, threatening to overwhelm him, and he clung to the girl, not just in a bid to keep her safe, but because he knew if he let go, he'd get lost in the noise.

He needed to put his helmet back on. As annoying as Fleming was, Wesley needed a sound to focus on and to cling to. But his arms were around the girl, and he didn't dare let go.

And then...

Ba-bump. Ba-bump.

A new rhythm. A new sound to cling to. A heartbeat. It hammered in the girl's chest. She was terrified, and her heart raced, but Wesley zeroed in on the sound, drowning everything else out, letting the steady rhythm carry him through the crowd.

And then there was the exit gate and a police officer ushering them out, along with the last few students struggling to escape.

Wesley let his arms fall from the girl, and they ran, not stopping until they had put a couple blocks between them and the pier. They ducked into a small alley between two shops, and the girl collapsed against the brick wall, gasping for air, her heart still pounding.

"Helmet?" Wesley asked. He tugged on the lip of the hood, drawing it down over his face the best he could. The girl averted her gaze and tossed the helmet to him. Wesley spun his back towards her as he pulled it back over his head. "Thanks. I probably would've been stuck under that table without your jacket."

"Unless you, what was it? Punched a hole in the pier and swam away."

"Property damage is paperwork." He couldn't help but smile. They'd made it, and the alley was quiet. The pain in his head lifted, turning him giddy with relief.

"Right. And you hate paperwork."

Wesley could see her better out here. Her skin had a sickly pallor to it, and a long scar tracked the length of her neck to hook around her collarbone, but her eyes were bright and inquisitive, glittering gray in the shadowy alleyway. His cheeks turned warm, and he was thankful for the visor covering most of his face.

He lifted finger guns in her direction.

"Exactly."

"Oh, good, you made it," Fleming growled in the helmet earpiece. "There's a shuttle taking students back to campus. Get her on it, and then I expect you in my office."

Wesley gulped. He could hear the rattle of the campus shuttle and the buzz of anxious students a few blocks off, and nodded in that direction.

"I can hear the campus shuttle a few blocks that way. It's still picking up stragglers if you want to grab it."

"What about you?" Her gray eyes narrowed.

"What about me?"

"How are you getting back to campus?"

Crap.

"Wesley, I swear if she knows you're a student—"

"I don't know what you mean." It was a weak cover. Wesley knew it. The girl knew it. Fleming probably knew it.

"You're a student, aren't you? You can't be that much older than me."

"My office, Wesley. Now," Fleming growled.

"Still don't know what you mean." Wesley shrugged. A fire escape hung overhead, and he leaped upwards and hoisted himself over the railing. He caught a glimpse of the girl's face and felt a thrill of satisfaction at seeing her shock. "Besides, I've got my own way home."

Metal rang out underfoot as he climbed up to the roof. The girl watched him the whole way up, and at the top, he paused to look down at her. It was much fainter from up here, but he could still hear it— the gentle ba-bump of her heart beating in her chest.

"Thanks again! Now hurry! The shuttle won't wait forever!"

And with Fleming still lecturing him in his ear, Wesley spun around and sprinted across the rooftop towards campus.

CHARACTER GLOSSARY

THE STUDENTS OF NEW DELOS PREP

Samantha Havardson: The main character. She is not an Apex, but someone is trying to kidnap her.

Winnie Hendricks: Samantha's roommate with a passion for investigating the Apex that run loose in the city. She is not an Apex.

Jamie Ratcliffe: A classmate of Sammy's who is dating Andersen. Like her father, John Ratcliffe, she hates nothing more than Apex and lets everyone know.

Naomi Bradford: Jamie's roommate and close friend. She's not as volatile as Jamie.

Madison: Jamie's best friend. Like Jamie, she has no powers and is happy to go along with her friend's many Anti-Apex tirades.

Anthony Schultz: Sammy's first friend outside of Winnie. He is not an Apex, but his grandma was once on the island's most famous heroes.

Wesley Isaacs: Sammy's assigned project partner for the New Delos Industry project. His roommate, Anthony, is one of Sammy's first friends.

Andersen Lewis: Jamie's boyfriend who has it out for Sammy after she vomits on his girlfriend's shoes and steals his favorite seat in class.

Remi Whitlock: Wesley's ex-girlfriend with computer-interfacing Apex powers. She failed the trials to make the team her freshman year.

Heather Hisakawa: Apex teammate and powerhouse who can control and travel through darkness. She is known for always wearing a bow in her hair.

Skyler Cripps: Apex teammate and best friend of Andersen. He doesn't believe Samantha should be allowed on the team.

Everest Archer: A dark haired and reserved Apex teammate with the power to change his body density.

Freddie Williams: Apex teammate with the power to create and disperse fog. He has fluffy, hay-colored hair and freckles.

Olivia Orwell-Chase: Apex teammate with the ability to turn herself and those she touches invisible.

Bethany Valente: A non-Apex classmate of Sammy.

Jessa Davidson: A freshman on Apex Team with the ability to alter gravity's effects.

Christopher Prescott: A freshman on Apex Team with amphibious abilities, including webbed fingers.

Justin Pomeroy: A senior with the ability to lock those he touches in a stasis. He's one of four team captains on Apex Team.

Marcus McDougall: A senior with the ability to see heat signatures. He's one of four team captains on Apex Team

Jen Reeves: A junior and one of four team captains on Apex Team.

Isabelle Abarca: Junior on Apex Team and Anthony's cousin. Unlike her cousin, she has inherited their family's wind powers.

Desirae Sheffield: Twin to fellow junior Mike. They share a telepathic link.

Mike Sheffield: Twin to fellow junior Desirae. They share a telepathic link.

Harvey Hernandez: A junior on Apex Team.

Carmen Hawkins: A junior on Apex Team. Her abilities allow her to anticipate several seconds into the future, making her a difficult opponent.

Jeanie Little: A junior on Apex Team who can turn invisible in rain or fog.

Faculty

Everly Jacobi: School nurse who doubles as the Team's doctor. His powers that allow him to assess physical wellness and injuries serve him well when caring for injured team members.

Alexander Fleming: History teacher and Apex Team coach. He was friends with Samantha's mother in his youth.

Dr. Penelope Weaver: The principal of New Delos Prep and the head council member of the Apex Team Council. Her healing ability allows her to donate blood plasma to the team to be used in treating injuries.

Vanessa Reiner: Team Combat Specialist and Apex PE teacher. Her Apex abilities allow her to perfectly replicate hand-to-hand combat techniques.

Mrs. Young: Sammy's math teacher.

Families and Parents

Vic Havardson: Sammy's father. He doesn't trust Apex, but he's moving his family to New Delos anyways as he's been hired as a professor at the university.

Alison Taylor-Havardson: Sammy's mother, who keeps her family's secrets close to her chest.

Avery Havardson: Samantha's brother. He's bright and curious and in love with all things Apex.

Roy Hendricks: Winnie and Amanda's father. He's unpleasant.

Valerie Hendricks: Mother to Winnie and Amanda. She's more pleasant than her husband.

Amanda Hendricks: College sophomore and older sister to Winnie, Sammy's roommate.

Warren Cunningham: The quirky museum curator at the New Delos Museum. His favorite exhibit is the Hall of Heroes.

Dr. Diane Parker: The head of the University Apex Team.

Trev Baker: Apex Council Representative from Schrader Industries and coffee enthusiast.

Mickey: Is it his first name or his last name? Sammy isn't sure. He's the city council representative on the Apex Team Council and has telepathic abilities.

Officer Allen: The New Delos Police representative on the Apex Team Council.

Adrian Schrader: Head of Schrader Industries and host of the New Delos Industry Project. His family built the island fifty years ago.

The Villains

Adrestus: A mysterious man in a Spartan helmet who has been kidnapping children across the island.

Mira Aimes: Adrestus's right-hand woman with the power to take control over the motor function of anyone she touches.

Gregor: One of Adrestus's followers with powers that allow him to manipulate memories and create illusions.

Hackjob: Another follower of Adrestus. His raw strength and durability make him a difficult opponent.

Miles: A follower of Adrestus with the power to make force fields.

Esther: A follower of Adrestus who has the ability to sense the presence and location of others.

Dion: A masked follower of Adrestus and accomplished fighter.